GENOME

A.G. RIDDLE spent ten years starting and running internet companies before retiring to focus on his true passion: writing fiction. He lives in North Carolina. Visit www.agriddle.com

THE EXTINCTION FILES

GENOME

A.G.
RIDDLE

HEAD
of ZEUS

First published in the US in 2017 by Riddle Inc.

First published in the UK in 2018 by Head of Zeus Ltd

Copyright © A.G. Riddle, 2017

9 7 5 3 1 2 4 6 8

A catalogue record for this book is available from
the British Library.

ISBN (TPBO): 9781788541312

Typeset by Adrian McLaughlin

Printed and bound in Great Britain by
CPI Group (UK) Ltd, Croydon CRO 4YY

Head of Zeus Ltd
First Floor East
5–8 Hardwick Street
London ECIR 4RG

WWW.HEADOFZEUS.COM

This novel is dedicated to a group of heroes we rarely hear about. After hurricanes and other natural disasters, they are among the first to arrive and the last to leave. Around the world, they operate in war-torn regions, though they carry no weapons to protect themselves. Right now, these individuals are putting their lives at risk to protect us from threats that pose a danger to every human, in every nation on Earth.

They live among us; they are our neighbors and our friends and our family members. They are the men and women working in public health in the US and abroad. Researching their exploits was a source of great inspiration while writing this novel. They are the true heroes of a story like *Genome*.

GENOME

PROLOGUE

July 17, 1941

ADELINE'S FAMILY LEFT Berlin in the middle of the night. Her father told her they were going on a vacation, but she knew something was wrong. Her parents were too nervous. Her mother had packed too much—and the wrong things: sentimental items and documents from the safe.

For two days and three nights, they lived on the train. They took their meals in the dining car. Her parents played cards in the afternoon. Her father read her favorite book aloud—*Alice in Wonderland*. The train cars were crowded, mostly with troops and business people, but also a few families. The adults looked as nervous as Adeline's parents.

The train was searched periodically. Stone-faced soldiers demanded their papers. Adeline's mother always held her breath, but her father's expression was a mirror of the soldiers'.

The Nazi flag hung from the roof of every train station in France, and soldiers crowded the platforms. The searches grew more frequent, the interrogations longer.

At the Spanish border, Adeline was surprised when her father presented a paper to the soldiers and said, "I am conducting research for the betterment of the Reich."

The SS officer scanned the paper, then eyed Adeline and her mother. "And why have you brought your wife and child?"

"My wife assists me, and my daughter is only five."

"I asked why she is here, not her age."

"She is *here* out of necessity. She simply could not remain in Berlin alone, and we were unable to find anyone for her to stay with."

The soldier looked unconvinced.

Adeline's father sighed. "*Obersturmführer*, if you would like to take my daughter back to Berlin and babysit her for a month until I return, I invite you to do so. It will aid my research greatly."

Adeline felt her eyes welling with tears. She turned away so no one could see.

The soldier grunted, and loud clicks followed. The passes being stamped, Adeline assumed.

Her mother relaxed when the train started again. Her father moved over beside Adeline and pulled her into a hug. With his lips brushing her ear, he whispered, "That was just a story to make the mean man go away. You're the whole reason for our trip, my dear. You'll see."

He tried to distract her by reading *Grimm's Fairy Tales*, *Snow White*, and *Cinderella*.

The train was searched less frequently in Spain. Finally, they disembarked in the small town of Santillana del Mar, just miles from Spain's northern coast. In the town square, they met up with a dozen men her father said would be helping with his research. Together, they drove out of town, through the countryside, and made camp at the mouth of a cave.

Adeline's father said it was the Cave of Altamira, and that it was a very important place—a place where messages had been left for them. He and the men spent every spare minute in the cave, only exiting to eat, sleep, and use the restroom.

They had been camping for a week when Adeline's father woke her one morning, just before dawn. Her mother lay beside her, still asleep in the tent the three of them shared.

"Be quiet, my love," he whispered.

He led her through the camp, where two men were warming coffee by the fire. He held a battery-powered lantern to light their way.

At the entrance to the cave, he paused and raised his eyebrows. "Ready?"

Adeline nodded, excited.

The cave wasn't what she expected. One second the passage was wide and tall, the next it was cramped, requiring her father to stoop, and occasionally to crawl. It twisted and turned and branched at random, as if they were in the roots of a giant tree. But her father seemed to know just which way to go, as if he had a map in his head. Adeline felt like Alice after she had gone down the rabbit hole. She was big, and the world around her had grown small and cramped.

Her father stopped and shined the lamp on a wall. Adeline gasped. Red handprints covered it. Some were merely the silhouette of the hand, as if the artist had spray-painted the wall while holding her hand against it.

"It's a message," her father whispered. "They're saying to us, 'We were here. And we think the way you do. You are in the right place.'"

Adeline held her hand out to touch the wall, but her father caught her. "You mustn't touch. The art is too fragile. Come, there's more."

A few minutes later, her father stopped and squatted down, his face next to hers. "Look up."

He pointed the electric lamp at the ceiling, revealing a mural of a herd of dark red animals, the size of cows but with dark fur on their backs and legs.

Adeline was speechless. She felt herself wandering, taking in the vast tableau that seemed to have no end. The animals were detailed. The rolling contours of the cave ceiling made some look three-dimensional. Her father stepped back and swept the beam across the ceiling, casting some of the animals in shadow, making the herd look as if it was moving.

"What are they?" Adeline asked.

"Steppe bison."

Adeline had never heard of the animal.

"They are all dead now," her father said. "They have been for a long time. Do you know what it means when every member of a species is dead?"

Adeline shook her head.

"They are *extinct*. This is another message. Can you guess it?"

Adeline thought for a moment. "They hunted bison?"

"Yes. But more. It tells us when. They hunted them a very, very long time ago. They *lived* a very long time ago. Taken together, the artists are telling us: 'We were here. We think the way you do. And we lived a very, *very* long time ago.'"

He led her deeper into the cave, to a painting on the wall. It was a doe, standing alone, regal. "Beautiful, isn't it?" he whispered.

She nodded.

"Not half as beautiful as you."

A few feet away, they stopped at a small alcove where several holes had been dug. Metal containers were stacked up.

He opened one, revealing long bones, of legs, Adeline thought. Another held part of a skull.

"These are the artists?" she asked.

"Perhaps. Or someone like them. But these bones are much more. They are part of a larger message, sent across time, waiting for us to find, to study, and understand when we're ready."

Adeline bunched up her eyebrows.

Her father seemed to read her confusion. "These bones are like Hansel and Gretel's bread crumbs."

Adeline knew the story well. During a great famine, Hansel and Gretel's parents were afraid of starving. They were so scared that they led their only two children into the woods and left them there, ridding themselves of two mouths to feed. But Hansel and Gretel dropped bread crumbs along the way, marking the path back home. To the children's horror, they discover that wolves had eaten the bread crumbs, stranding them in the dangerous wilderness.

Adeline considered the story, but she couldn't figure out what it had to do with the bones. "Bread crumbs to what, Papa?"

"The truth. Someday, we will find all the bones like these. They will mark a path, just like Hansel and Gretel's bread crumbs, and we will finally know *how* we became what we are... and *what* we are destined to become."

He squatted down to look her in the eye. "The bones are pieces of a puzzle, left for us to find someday—when we are ready to put them together, when our technology can unravel the mystery. It will be the greatest discovery of all time. We only need to find the pieces. Would you like to help me search for them?"

Adeline nodded.

"Someday we will. But right now, the world is like the woods in Hansel and Gretel. Dangerous. You've seen the wolves."

She knitted her eyebrows.

He smiled. "The mean man on the train." He tucked her hair behind her ear. "But they will never harm you. When your mother wakes, she will take you to a city on the sea, and you'll sail away, to another city on the sea, in a faraway place that your mother knows well."

He gripped her shoulders. "You'll return when it's safe."

"And you're coming with us."

He said nothing.

She shook her head.

He gripped her tighter. "I can't."

"Why, Papa?"

"They want my work. They would chase me to the end of the Earth for it. I'll go back to Berlin, and hide what I've found. And wait. You and your mother will return when the world is out of the woods. And we'll go off and find the rest of the bread crumbs. Together."

CHAPTER 1

THE SHOUTS WOKE Dr. Peyton Shaw. She reached down and tucked the heavy wool blanket into her sides, trying to get warmer. A space heater buzzed a few feet away, struggling against the cold. The small office was still frigid.

Beyond the closed door, the shouts turned to excited conversation. Peyton caught only phrases.

"No genomic match."

"Definitely not a Neanderthal."

"... a new human species."

The office's only window was a wide piece of plate glass that looked out on the ship's cargo hold. The cavernous space had been converted into a research lab for the mission, and it was always teeming with activity. The glow of fluorescent lamps seeped into the office, casting it in a pale light, like the streets of London on a foggy night. Peyton wanted to go out and see what the commotion was about, but she was still exhausted from the last dive to the wreck of the *Beagle*. So she lay in bed and listened, her eyes drifting to the walls covered with photographs of bones and dead bodies. It looked like a crime scene investigation was under way.

Peyton was used to investigations and uncomfortable quarters. She had spent her life investigating outbreaks in hot zones around the world. The biggest challenge of her career had come last month, when the X1 pandemic had ravaged the world. Billions were infected. Thirty million had died, including many of Peyton's colleagues at the Centers for Disease Control and students in her Epidemic Intelligence Service program. The losses had been hard, especially once she learned the truth about the deadly event.

In the course of tracing the pandemic, Peyton had learned that the outbreak was an act of bioterrorism. Yuri Pachenko and his organization, the Citium, had unleashed the pathogen on the world for one reason: to offer a cure. But the cure was more than it seemed. It stopped the pathogen, but it also contained a nano-technology called Rapture.

Little was known about Rapture, other than that it was part of a larger device called the Looking Glass. When combined with two other technologies, Rook and Rendition, Rapture and the Looking Glass would give Yuri control of every person on Earth.

Already struggling in the wake of the millions of deaths caused by the pandemic, governments around the world were now desperate to prevent the completion of the Looking Glass. They were searching the world for the Citium, but they had very few leads to go on, and that search had been fruitless so far.

Lin Shaw, Peyton's mother, had offered another solution. She insisted that the only hope of stopping Yuri lay in the research from a competing Citium project. That research was aboard the *Beagle*, a Citium submarine that Yuri had sunk thirty years ago. Lin had served on the *Beagle* and was more knowledgeable about the vessel than anyone alive. She believed the data and samples aboard the submarine would reveal a code buried in the human genome, and a revelation that would rewrite human history.

Many remained skeptical of Lin's claims, and for good reason: until recently, she had been a member of the Citium. She had also been cryptic and unwilling to share what she knew. But her promise was good enough for Peyton. If there was even a chance that the research on the *Beagle* would stop Yuri and the Looking Glass, Peyton would go to the ends of the Earth to find it. In a way, she had.

Two weeks ago, in Alaska, she, along with her mother, had boarded a Russian icebreaker, the *Arktika*, and sailed north toward the Arctic Circle. Four days into the voyage, everyone gathered on the deck to watch the sun slip past the horizon for the last time. They worked in darkness after that, the sun never rising. It was as if they were a ship out of time, in another dimension, where the laws of the planet didn't apply. The only natural light came from the aurora borealis, which made the place feel even more alien. Its phosphorescent green, blue, and orange streaks reminded Peyton of the first time she saw them—a mere three weeks ago, on the Shetland Islands. She had reunited with her father there. And spent time with Desmond after thirteen years. That seemed like a different lifetime now. A dream. And a good one.

For the researchers on the *Arktika*, this mission was about stopping the Citium and making a scientific discovery of historic proportions. For Peyton, it was about that as well—but also much more. Yuri and the Citium had taken both her father and Desmond from her. Her father they had killed; Desmond they had captured. The *Beagle* was the key to stopping the Citium, but she hoped it would lead her back to Desmond. Her mother had promised her that it would.

Peyton rolled onto her side and looked up at the longest wall of the office, half of which was covered with a map of the sub. Sections they had explored were highlighted, yet although they had been making dives from the *Arktika* to the *Beagle* for ten days now, and cataloguing everything they found, they'd still explored less than half of the massive nuclear submarine.

Below the map was the decrepit coffee machine. Peyton desperately wanted a cup, but she didn't dare turn the noisy thing on. Her mother lay only a few feet away, on the other small bed in the office, sleeping soundly. Lin had slept very little of late—and she had barely allowed anyone else to, either.

Peyton threw the blanket off and pulled a thick sweater on. She slipped into her pants and placed a small glass heart in her pocket. The item was the only personal effect she had brought with her from Atlanta. It was all she had left of Desmond. She carried it with her to remind her why she was here—and to keep going, no matter what.

Quietly, she opened the door and stepped out into the ship's cargo hold, squinting momentarily at the bright lights. A bank of computer stations lay just beyond the office, with a dozen technicians peering at large screens, typing, sipping coffee, and occasionally leaning back in their task chairs. Five research scientists hovered over them, pointing at the images and text displayed.

"Could have diverged before AMH."

"Or an isolated population—i.e., *floresiensis*."

"We could call it *Homo beagalis*—"

"We're not naming anything yet, ladies and gentlemen. It's specimen 1644—that's what the researchers on the *Beagle* labeled it, and that's its name for now."

Peyton recognized the last voice: Dr. Nigel Greene. He was an evolutionary biologist leading the team analyzing the samples brought up from the *Beagle*.

At the sound of Peyton's footfalls on the metal floor, he turned and, seeing her, immediately smiled.

"Sounds like you all won the Super Bowl," she said.

The British scientist cocked his head. "What's that?"

"Nothing." She nodded toward the screens. "Found something?"

He raised his eyebrows. "Indeed."

Nigel made a show of telling the other scientists and techs to "carry on," then lightly touched Peyton's back, corralling her to an empty computer workstation. He spoke in a hushed tone, as if what he was about to say was a closely held secret.

"We just received the first data set back from Rubicon. The samples from specimen group one are all from extinct species— as your mother predicted." He leaned over and worked the computer, pulling up an image of a long bone lying in a metal case. "We suspected specimen 1642 was a femur bone from a canid species. We were right."

An image appeared of what looked like a large wolf.

"It's from a dire wolf. They inhabited North America from roughly 125,000 years ago until their extinction 10,000 years ago. Some of the best fossils have been found outside Los Angeles, at the La Brea Tar Pits." Nigel studied the artist's rendering.

4

"They were magnificent creatures. Imagine a wolf weighing roughly 150 pounds with a massive head and jaws. They died out with the Pleistocene megafauna, near the end of the last glaciation. Or so we thought."

He brought up a graph that Peyton recognized as a carbon-dating test.

"The specimen recovered from the *Beagle* is roughly 9,500 years old," he said. "Which means it came from an animal that walked the Earth 800 years after the youngest known dire wolf. That species' timeline just got rewritten."

Nigel worked the mouse. "That's not all."

An image of four rib bones appeared.

"Any guesses?"

Peyton exhaled. She really, really wanted that coffee.

She had requested that Nigel and his team keep her in the loop on what they found. It was outside her area of expertise, but it was in her nature to throw herself into her work, and she had always been naturally curious, especially when it came to questions of science. And deep down, she held out hope that knowing what was down there would increase her chances of stopping Yuri—and getting Desmond back. Now she sensed that Nigel had another motive for describing what he had found, though she had no idea what that was.

"I'm guessing they're the bones of an extinct species."

"Ha. Yes, but which—"

"Nigel, I have no clue."

"Really?"

"I'm an epidemiologist. My expertise is keeping us from going extinct."

Her rebuff did nothing to dampen his enthusiasm. "Right you are. Well, anyway. The fossils are from an American lion."

Peyton had never heard of that species either. She again wondered what he was working up to.

An artist's rendering appeared on the screen. It looked to Peyton exactly like an African lion, only much larger.

Nigel spoke in a professional tone, as if he were narrating

a *National Geographic* special just for Peyton. "The American lions emerged about 340,000 years ago. We think they diverged from the Eurasian cave lion at some point and made their way across the Bering Strait to North America, where they diverged further. They were giants. They're still one of the largest types of cats to have ever existed—roughly 25 percent larger than modern African lions."

He minimized the screen and turned to Peyton. "Like the dire wolf and many other large mammals, they became extinct at the end of the Pleistocene. The youngest fossil dates to 11,355 before present. Or so we thought. *These* bones are far younger—around 9,500 years old, like the dire wolf. We're assuming they were recovered from the same site, possibly the La Brea Tar Pits, which is the most abundant source of American lion fossils."

He paused. "Taken together, the fossils imply an interest in the Quaternary extinction event."

Peyton squinted—she wasn't following.

"Ah, that's the extinction of mostly large animals around the time the last ice age ended. It's perhaps one of the greatest scientific mysteries—well, at least for an evolutionary biologist like myself." Nigel held his hands out. "Imagine the world roughly 12,000 years ago—it was a land of giants. Mastodons. Saber-toothed cats. Giant condors. Ground sloths. Saber-toothed salmon. At the same time humans were founding the city of Jericho, massive beasts walked the Earth, dotted the skies, and swam in the oceans. Some had been around a lot longer than us—tens of millions of years. Then, in the blink of an eye—in evolutionary timescales—they were gone."

Nigel paused dramatically.

"For years, researchers have desperately tried to figure out why. Is that what they were studying on board the *Beagle*? Did they find the source of the Quaternary extinction event?"

Peyton shifted uncomfortably. "Hard to say, Nigel."

"Because you don't know?"

For the most part, Lin had kept the research team in the dark. She had told Peyton a bit more, but not much more. Only that the scientists on the *Beagle* had been testing what they called a "second theory of evolution"—a revolutionary hypothesis that would radically change our understanding of what it means to be human, a discovery as fundamental as gravity. For whatever reason, Lin hadn't shared that information with Nigel or the other researchers.

Peyton realized then why Nigel was walking her through it. He wanted to know what Lin had told her. He was hoping to learn exactly what the *Beagle* researchers were studying. That put her in an impossible position. She needed to speak with her mother.

"Is that all, Nigel?"

The pudgy biologist grew animated again. He turned back to the computer and brought up a photo of a small human skull. "Saved the best for last. We were able to extract a DNA sample from a tooth. It's human, but the genome isn't a match for ours."

"Everyone has a different genome."

"True enough, but each species—and subspecies—has a different... template, if you will. Our genome is 98.8 percent identical to chimpanzees. Every person and chimp has different values in their sequence, but the framework is the same: twenty-three chromosomes. Neanderthals are also similar to us: their genome is a 99.5 percent match to our own."

Nigel pointed to the picture of the skull. "And this mystery human is even *more* closely related to us. A 99.6 percent match. That's extraordinary. A genome we've never seen before. And this person died around 9,000 years ago. They are perhaps our closest extant ancestor—or cousin. We don't know if they diverged from the human family tree before we evolved or after."

He studied the picture. "We're assuming it was recovered near or at the same site as the lion and wolf, but that's just guesswork." He glanced toward the office Peyton shared with her mother. "It would be extremely helpful to know what you all have found in the offices—any notes associated with the bones. Maps of where they were found..."

"It's not my call, Nigel."

"Perhaps, but she listens to you. Those bones have been down there since the *Beagle* sank thirty years ago. Who knows when they were recovered. And what else they found. We need context to figure out what we're dealing with here."

Peyton shook her head.

"Please, Peyton. This is vitally important. I'm not sure you appreciate the gravity of this discovery. We're literally rewriting history here."

A sharp voice startled Peyton. "We're not rewriting history."

Lin Shaw stood only feet from them. She looked haggard, but her voice betrayed none of her weariness. She walked closer, glanced at the image of the skull, then looked away, as if she found it unremarkable. She focused on Nigel. "History is history, Doctor Greene. It's only forgotten and rediscovered. In our case, we're merely recovering what the brave crew of the *Beagle* rediscovered."

"And what exactly is that?"

"You'll know when we have all the pieces. And it's time we recovered more of those pieces. Have the Russians prepare to launch the submersible."

Nigel glanced at his watch. "It's only been six hours since the last dive."

"Your point?"

"The crew is exhausted—"

"*I'll* see to crew morale. Get it done, Doctor Greene."

His gaze drifted to the floor as he nodded. "Yes, ma'am."

To Peyton, she said, "Coffee?"

☣

Inside the office, Lin turned the old coffeemaker on.

"He's asking questions, Mom."

Lin ran a finger down the length of the map of the *Beagle*, as if mentally walking through the wrecked submarine, trying to decide which compartment to explore next.

"What are you going to tell them?"

"Nothing," Lin whispered, still staring at the map.

"They want to know exactly what's down there. What these experiments were about. And frankly, so do I." Peyton glanced out the window to make sure no one was lurking near the office. "This... code in the human genome—what is it? What does it do? How will it stop the Citium?"

Lin didn't make eye contact. "Do you trust me?"

"Yes." Peyton paused. "But obviously there's somebody out there you *don't* trust."

"You're wrong."

"About what?"

"There isn't somebody out there I don't trust. There's nobody out there I *do* trust. The only person I trust is standing in this room."

CHAPTER 2

DESMOND HATED THE prison, but he had to admit that it was effective. His cell was an outdoor pen surrounded by a tall electric fence. The interior was hard, dusty earth with a few patches of grass. A second electric fence lay ten feet beyond the first. Guards marched by every two hours, and cameras atop poles watched him in the minutes in between. Large canopies, printed with island foliage, towered above, providing some relief from the South Pacific sun, but more importantly, they hid Desmond from the satellites he knew were searching for him and the Citium.

At the center of the pen, Desmond stretched out on a cot, trying not to think about Peyton. Trying and failing. There was too much left unsaid between them. But it was more than that. He was worried about her. He would have traded the possibility of never talking with her again just to know that she was okay, that she had survived the carnage on the Isle of Citium. Desmond had sacrificed himself that morning—allowed himself to be captured in hopes that Avery might complete their mission—distributing a cure to the Citium's pandemic. He wondered if Avery had succeeded, if the billions infected had been saved. Or if the world had collapsed. Or both.

Desmond's brother, Conner McClain, visited at sunset each day. He sat on a folding chair inside the outer fence. Some days he talked, others he would read, and occasionally he sat in silence. Desmond never responded. He simply stared out at the beach below.

As the blue horizon once again swallowed the sun, Desmond wondered what they were waiting for.

☣

A mile away, Conner walked to the silver double doors and slid his hand into the palm reader in the wall. When the device beeped, he leaned closer and stared into the retinal scanner.

The doors opened, revealing a small room with brushed metal walls. Another set of closed metal doors lay ahead. Conner waited while the scanners embedded in the ceiling and walls checked him for any weapons, explosives, and unidentified devices.

Finally, the double doors parted, revealing a long room with illuminated tiles on the floor and ceiling, providing an even, white glow. Rows of servers and monitoring equipment spread out before him, and lights blinked—red, green, yellow, and blue, like an orchestra playing with no sound. Several technicians milled about, checking the equipment and slipping into the enclosed cages to fix any problems, their faces obscured by the wire mesh, like penitents in confessionals.

To Conner, the analogy was fitting. This place was a sanctuary. A place of reverence, of rebirth. A fresh start for him and the entire human race.

He walked past the servers to the glass wall on the opposite side. The chamber beyond was vast and dark, a grotto with gunmetal gray walls and a thin white cloud at the bottom, floating above a sea of liquid. A hundred black towers rose through the cloud, like skyscrapers with no windows, a model of a city of the future.

Conner admired his creation. Soon Rook would come online, and he would be free.

☣

Outside, Conner marched along a dirt path. Camouflaged canopies hung overhead, blocking some of the sun's oppressive heat, but also serving a far more important purpose: hiding the Citium base. US, Australian, Russian, and Japanese ships and their drones were scouring the South Pacific, trying to find Yuri and Conner. They were getting closer.

The path ended at an open space hidden under even larger canopies. A ten-foot-tall chain-link fence surrounded a central pen, and inside, Desmond lay on a cot, staring at the canopy above.

Conner opened the outer gate. As usual, his brother didn't stir.

Since Conner had brought him here two weeks ago, Desmond hadn't said a word. Hadn't requested food, or shelter from the elements.

Yesterday they had interrogated him—against Conner's wishes. It was a desperate act that had pained Conner to watch. But they'd had to. Time was running out—and too much was at stake.

Under the influence of the chemical agent, Desmond had revealed that he hadn't recovered the memory of what he'd done with Rendition. He had hidden the information somewhere else—for a time when he was ready to use it.

Conner desperately wanted to reach his brother and bring him back into the Citium. Their cause depended on it. But it was more than that. Desmond was his only true human connection; Conner felt alone without him. Mentally, he felt like he did before Desmond found him in Australia: hopeless and isolated.

Desmond had been in the same place before they reunited. His only solace in those days was books. They had helped him escape his childhood. And one of his favorite books was *Treasure Island* by Robert Louis Stevenson.

Conner opened another of Stevenson's classics—*The Strange Case of Dr Jekyll and Mr Hyde*—and began to read.

☣

When the sun had set and the moonlight was too dim to read by, Conner got up, locked the gate behind him, and trudged back down the path. As usual, Desmond hadn't said a word, hadn't moved or even acknowledged his brother's presence. That hurt most of all.

Inside the camouflaged building, Conner made his way to the

programmers' team room. As always, it was a pigsty. The trash bin overflowed with crushed cans of energy drinks and microwave wrappers. Server towers with their side panels removed lay on a long table, their silicon guts spilling out. Balled-up papers dotted the floor like golf balls at a driving range.

Conner knew what one of those papers was. The first time he had entered the room, he had seen his own face printed on a sheet tacked to the wall. The scars that covered his forehead, left cheek, and chin were partially covered with Borg implants. The words RESISTANCE IS FUTILE were printed below the image. He wasn't sure if they referred to his management style or his plan for humanity, and he didn't care. He had been ridiculed his entire life. He was used to it.

But soon it would end. The poster that mocked him confirmed that the programmers knew the strength of his resolve.

Them taking it down confirmed that they were scared of him.

The lead developer saw Conner's reflection in the plate glass window. He ripped his headphones off, spun his office chair around, and stood. The man's name was Byron, and he was tall and gangly, with pasty white skin.

"Where are we?" Conner demanded.

"On which one?" Byron asked.

"Desmond Hughes. The Labyrinth."

The programmer swallowed. "It's impossible."

"Your job is to do the impossible," Conner snapped.

"Look, this is like a black box inside a black box."

"Meaning?"

"Meaning it's like—"

"I don't care what it's *like*. Be specific. What's the problem?"

"The problem is that we have no idea how the Labyrinth Reality app works."

"So do whatever you do—reverse engineer it. De-obfuscate it."

"We did that. Five days ago. That's not the issue."

"What is?"

"Location awareness."

"I don't follow."

Byron rubbed the bridge of his nose, as if dreading having to explain. "The app sends a code to the implant in Hughes's brain that unlocks his memories, but it only does it at certain locations. At first we assumed it was using the phone's built-in location programming interface, but now we know it's double-checking with an external server. It's probably using cell towers, or more likely a private satellite to verify—"

"So hack that server. Hack the satellite. Make it happen."

"It's not that simple. The server returns a code to the implant inside his brain—that's the second black box. The code is encrypted with a proprietary algorithm. We don't even have a place to start. It's like a checksum to make sure the request is valid. Sending a malformed code could have unexpected consequences."

"Such as?"

"Who knows?"

"Guess."

Byron exhaled. "Best case, the checksum fails, the system realizes it's being hacked, and it completely shuts down. We'd have no chance to enable him to *ever* recover his memories."

"Worst case?"

"Brain damage. The faulty code scrambles the memories or releases the wrong amount of trigger. He could end up a vegetable, or dead."

Conner closed his eyes. "Where does that leave us?"

"Same place we were on the *Kentaro Maru* cargo ship."

"Let him go again? Be serious. We barely recovered him last time."

"True, but this time one thing is different." Byron held up the phone and opened the Labyrinth Reality app. "On the ship we didn't have a location."

A dialog appeared on the screen.

1 Entrance Located.

Byron tapped it, and GPS coordinates appeared. Conner committed them to memory.

"We don't have to let him go," the programmer said. "We just have to take him here."

Conner didn't like it, but it *was* a solution. At the moment, their only solution.

"All right. I'll take care of Hughes. Where are we with rebuilding the Rapture Control software?"

"*That* we've made some progress on."

"How much?"

"Hard to know. We're maybe... 15 percent done."

Conner shook his head. "You have to work faster."

"We can't—"

"You will. Time is running out. Those ships out there looking for us will find us within a week. At that point, they'll attack this island just like they did the Isle. They'll kill most of us. The rest will be imprisoned for life, or executed." Conner paused, letting the words sink in. "Rapture Control is our only chance of survival."

Byron nodded. "We'll get it done, sir."

Conner stared at him a moment, then turned and walked out.

He went straight to the situation room. A large screen covered the back wall, displaying satellite photography and real-time stats. Rows of desks ran the length of the room, and almost every station was occupied. It was crunch time, and all hands were on deck.

Conner stopped at the watch commander's desk. The red-haired woman, Melissa Whitmeyer, was the best operations technician they had left.

Conner scribbled the GPS coordinates on a sheet of paper on her desk. "I need to know where this is."

Whitmeyer glanced at the numbers and pulled up a map. The location was near San Francisco, and on a road that ran from the coast to the mountains. Conner knew it before she called out the name: Sand Hill Road. For a few months in the year 2000, during the dot-com bubble, office rents along that lonely stretch in the rolling hills of California were the highest in the world. Rent rates crashed along with the stock market soon after. The glowing dot was the building where Desmond's firm, Icarus Capital, had operated. Getting there might be a problem.

"What's the American security situation?"

"Airspace and coastlines are locked down. They're very worried about a conventional invasion given their degraded military status."

"Land borders?"

"Little more porous. Lots of troops massed on the Mexican border in Texas, Arizona, and New Mexico."

"What about California?"

"They've reinforced the checkpoints at the major roads, but that's about it."

"Situation in Mexico?"

"Civil war."

"Who?"

"Cartels and organized crime versus the new Mexican government. Cartels are winning. They see it as their opportunity to turn the country into a legitimized narco state."

"Okay. Get one of the planes ready. I need a tactical team prepped for departure in thirty minutes. Seven members. I want the best."

Conner told her the rest of his plan, and she began searching the map, looking for a suitable location.

Conner briefed Yuri in his office. The Russian sat impassively, as if Conner was relating the weather forecast. Conner wondered if living through the Nazi assault on Stalingrad as a child had permanently altered the man. Or maybe Yuri already knew what was going on… or had expected it. Sometimes his gray eyes and placid stare unnerved even Conner.

Yuri's voice was just above a whisper. "Your brother is sublimely clever, Conner. He may have planned for this contingency. Taking him to the locations where he's hidden his memories could be the next phase of *his* plan, which we still don't understand."

"We have no choice. I'll handle him."

"And if he won't turn over Rendition?"

"He will."

Yuri looked away. "He betrayed us once. He will again if given the opportunity. Remember what's at stake. And that no matter what happens, we can repair him with the Looking Glass."

"He's not the only one who betrayed us. Lin Shaw conspired with the Americans during the assault. She ordered our troops to surrender."

"It seems she's been playing a larger game."

"What kind of game?"

"Lin is the last surviving member of the original Citium cell. True believers, committed to finding the ultimate truth. The purpose of the human race. I think we can assume that all these years she's been secretly working on her own Looking Glass project."

That could be a problem. "So why hasn't she completed it?"

"I see several possibilities. We had her son. And I threatened her daughters. But I think the most likely reason is that she lacked the requisite research."

"The *Beagle*," Conner whispered.

"Yes. Fifteen days ago, teams began bringing artifacts and notes to the surface."

"What have they found?"

"I don't know. If it's the piece Lin needs to complete her Looking Glass, she apparently hasn't used it yet."

"What does that mean for us?"

"I don't know exactly. We can assume her work might be a problem—if she completes it. But she never will. I'm seeing to that."

CHAPTER 3

IN THE OFFICE off the ship's cargo hold, a handheld radio crackled to life. The sound of wind and static overpowered Dr. Nigel Greene's voice. On his second attempt, Peyton was able to make out the words.

"Doctor Shaw, come in."

Lin stood from her narrow bed and snatched the radio. "Shaw here."

"Ma'am, you're needed on deck."

Lin shot Peyton a knowing glance.

"On my way."

Both women downed their coffee and zipped up their cold weather coveralls. Outside the office, the biology team was still crowded around the bank of computers, reviewing the data set from Rubicon. Just beyond them lay two rows of cubicles with a wide corridor between them. The cubicles were wrapped in milky sheet plastic, and inside, archaeologists leaned over metal tables that held bones recovered from the *Beagle*. Their high-pitched drills played the anthem of their painstaking work.

The biology team was constantly frustrated with the archaeologists' pace. They wanted the samples extracted and sequenced quickly, whereas the archaeologists insisted that preserving the integrity of the specimens was the highest priority. Lin had struck a balance between the groups, a fragile detente, but the truce didn't stop the biologists from name-calling. The archaeologists were referred to as the polar bears—or simply "da bears." The archaeology labs were the "polar bear cages," arguments with them were "bear attacks," and delivering bone samples was "feeding the bears."

Peyton couldn't get the bear analogy out of her mind as she walked down the aisle, watching the white-clad figures lumbering around the cubicles, peering down to inspect the bones, then drilling deeper.

Outside the hold, she and Lin climbed the ladders between the decks in silence. At the top, Lin spun the hatch's wheel and charged outside. Peyton gritted her teeth as the blast of Arctic air hit her.

The deck of the Russian icebreaker was crowded with sailors. The research personnel needed to launch the submersible stood behind them, at the rear of the vessel. The researchers called the shots on what to do, but the Russian Navy was in charge of how to do it. Like the biologists and archaeologists, there was always friction between the two groups.

This morning was no different. The ship's executive officer, Captain Second Rank Alexei Vasiliev, was shouting at the researchers gathered around the submersible, and his own crewmembers were crowded behind him, like a street gang showing their numbers.

Lin's lithe form cut a sharp contrast with the burly Russian sailors as she pushed through the crowd, looking like a child wading through a lynch mob. Peyton followed on her heels, sticking close to her mother for fear that the hole she created would close and leave her trapped in the mob.

Vasiliev stopped shouting when he saw them.

Lin's voice was as crisp as the frigid air around them. "Captain, can your crew support our dive schedule or not?"

Vasiliev threw up his hands and continued shouting. His words came out in puffs of white steam, reminding Peyton of a massive engine revving up, growing louder, more and more exhaust spewing out.

Lin turned to the research team. "Doctor Greene, inform the Alliance that the crew of the *Arktika* is unable to support our dive schedule, and thus we cannot complete our mission with the urgency they require."

Nigel nodded and broke from the pack, but Vasiliev stopped him with a meaty outstretched hand. He turned to one of his own men and grumbled in Russian. The Russian officer said something to Nigel before striding off the deck.

When he was gone, Nigel said to Lin, "They'll be ready in fifteen minutes."

"Good."

Peyton watched as the entire deck plunged into frenzied activity, the researchers and Russian naval personnel rushing, bumping into each other, and arguing.

Nigel stepped closer to Lin, his voice low, British accent thick. "Doctor Shaw, I must again press my request that you remain on the ship."

"No." Lin looked away, focusing on the preparations.

"You're irreplaceable." Nigel waited, then exhaled. "The risk is unnecessary."

"No one knows the *Beagle* the way I do."

"Perhaps. But we've mapped the vessel extensively. Our recovery personnel are trained—"

"Your objection is noted, Doctor Greene. I've made my decision."

Nigel glanced at Peyton, who shrugged, silently saying, *I've tried too.*

Peyton had begun to wonder if there was something in the wreckage her mother didn't want anyone else to find. She couldn't shake the sense that her mother was hiding something—and Peyton didn't want to miss it. For that reason, she had insisted on accompanying her mother on each dive. If there was something going on that would help save lives—or help her find Desmond— she wanted to know about it.

She also wondered if Nigel suspected something. If he did, he didn't let on. He merely nodded and stepped away, leaving Peyton and Lin standing silently in the midst of the chaos, like statues amid a Mardi Gras procession.

Up here on the deck, Peyton got a better appreciation of the massive Russian ship's size. At roughly a hundred feet wide and almost two football fields long, the *Arktika* was the world's largest icebreaker. Its two nuclear reactors allowed it to cut through ice thirteen feet deep, also a world's best. Its decks were painted a shade of green that reminded Peyton of a miniature golf course, and its exterior walls and hatches were a faded red. Perhaps the designers had thought that the red and green color scheme would stand out against the Arctic ice, but to Peyton, it was a reminder of Christmas, which was less than a week away. And she couldn't think about Christmas without thinking about Desmond—about the night they spent at Half Moon Bay, and the moment he opened the box with the heart of glass. Unconsciously, her fingers touched the object in her pants.

She walked away from her mother, to the edge of the ship's deck. The sheet of ice floating on the Arctic Ocean stretched into the darkness in every direction, seemingly with no end. The ship's floodlights formed a bubble of illumination around the ship, making Peyton feel as though she were standing on the deck of a toy ship at the center of a snow globe, the world beyond shrouded.

From the ship's rail, Peyton could see the US Navy helicopter perched on the helo pad above. Twice her mother had asked her if she wanted to board the helo and leave the expedition. Twice, Peyton had declined. She wasn't leaving without answers.

Footsteps echoed on the deck behind her. Lin's voice was quiet, less commanding now. "It's time, Peyton."

Minutes later, they were diving toward the wrecked submarine.

☣

At the same time that Peyton and Lin's research submersible was docking with the shipwrecked submarine on the ocean floor, a second submersible was moving closer to the Russian icebreaker *Arktika*. It carried a five-man team, all specially trained for the type of mission they were undertaking.

Instead of surfacing at the *Arktika*'s launch platform, the submersible slowly moved along the ship's hull. It was searching for a break in the ice—one that was the right size, and hard to see from the aft and fore decks.

The submersible cut its forward thrust, reversed, and drifted toward the surface, stopping when it met the ice. A white tube extended vertically, rising above the water within feet of the hull. A pump at its base drained the water from the tube, the hatch at the top of the tube opened, and Lieutenant Stockton, the mission's second in command, climbed the ladder inside.

At the top, he placed the rover against *Arktika*'s hull. He drew out a control device and activated the rover's magnet. It clung to the Russian icebreaker and began climbing, its rubber tracks silent.

When the rover reached the deck, it extended two small arms and clamped against the metal lip. A finger-sized antenna with a glass tip rose, stopping just as it cleared the deck's metal lip.

On the submersible, Captain Furst, the mission commander, glanced at his watch, mentally marking the time.

Stockton climbed back down, and the tube retracted. For the next twenty minutes, the five men inside the submersible sat in silence, watching the video footage for patrols and other details that would increase their mission's chance of success.

Stockton turned to Furst and tapped his Luminox timepiece.

Furst nodded.

Stockton and a second man strapped on their body armor, then donned Russian naval uniforms. A high-tensile cable extended from the rover. The white tube once again rose from the submersible, the water drained, and the hatch opened. It took the two specialists less than a minute to scale *Arktika*'s hull.

Then they were standing on the deck, blending in with the other 140 crewmembers, ready to complete their mission: to sink the *Arktika* and capture or kill Lin and Peyton Shaw.

CHAPTER 4

AT MIDNIGHT, CONNER exited the building and set out along the island path. Moonlight lit his way. Three camo-clad mercenaries followed behind him. Insects chanted out of sync, like an orchestra scoring their march.

At the holding pen, he stopped outside the fences. Desmond lay on the cot, eyes closed, his breathing shallow. Quietly, Conner opened the outer gate. He reached in his pocket, drew out the syringe, and removed the rubber cap. Speed was key.

He opened the inner gate and rushed toward his brother.

To Conner's shock, Desmond rolled off the cot, crouched low, and barreled forward. His shoulder connected just above Conner's knees. He threw Conner over his back and came up swinging. His first haymaker hit the lead soldier in the face. The man flew back toward the fence, which buzzed as he convulsed.

The other two mercenaries dove for Desmond and wrestled him to the ground. They covered him like football players piling on a fumble. Desmond rolled, trying to throw them off, but Conner was on his feet, the syringe in his hand. He forced his brother's head into the dirt and jabbed the needle into his neck.

I'm sorry, Des. You left me no choice.

☣

The two mercenaries who had subdued Desmond carried him down the ridge, using the cot as a stretcher. Conner left the unconscious soldier behind and replaced him with another. More mercenaries waited by the jet in the camouflaged hangar. The team leader, Major Goins, informed Conner that the cargo was loaded and that they were prepped for departure.

The runway was a grass path that curved slightly. The jet bumped along as it gained speed, then lifted off.

Conner settled into the seat next to Desmond, who was sedated and intubated. The final member of Conner's team, an anesthesiologist named Dr. Simon Park, sat in the seat on the other side of Desmond, monitoring his vitals. The physician had protested at length about the plan and had brought along enough equipment and medical supplies to stock a small hospital. He wore a constant look of worry.

Conner counted this as a good sign. People who didn't care made more mistakes. That was why he had made sure Park knew that Desmond's fate would be his own if anything happened.

☣

Six hours later, Conner stood in the cockpit, peering out the jet's windshield at the rising sun over the mountains of the Mexican state of Baja California. Soon the ridges turned to desert, then the desert met the sea. The Mexican town of San Felipe looked tiny next to the mountains and the Gulf of California.

A few miles inland lay a single-runway airport. Their satellite footage of the potential landing strip was a week old, but the first flyover confirmed that the regional airport was still deserted. Or looked to be.

The plane kicked up a large dust cloud as it landed. Conner and his team waited inside while the dust wandered down the runway, flowing over the white plane like a sandstorm. The soldiers unloaded two dirt bikes first, and four of the mercenaries set off, kicking up new, milky-tan dust clouds as they rode into the sun, toward town.

Dr. Park injected something into Desmond's IV.

"How is he?" Conner asked.

"Stable." Park didn't look up. He was a man of few words. Conner liked that.

As planned, the soldiers returned with four stolen vans, all windowless and slightly beat-up.

They loaded most of the rest of the cargo into the back of one vehicle, which already held the bikes. They placed the medical equipment and Desmond in a second van that carried Dr. Park, Conner, and his three best men. The remaining two vans were filled with troops and other cargo, including large containers of gasoline. Each van carried food, water, and ammo—just in case they got separated.

They locked the plane, threw a tan tarp over it, then drove north, through San Felipe. The tourist town showed no signs of habitation. Conner wondered if the residents had died or sought refuge in the shelter of a larger city.

There was no way to know how long the drive would take. Under normal circumstances, twelve hours was a good estimate— but that assumed the roads were passable. Also, they wouldn't be taking the most direct route, choosing instead to travel back roads and avoid major cities. It would probably take twice as long, but it would allow them to avoid bandits and government checkpoints—both of which could end their mission.

Near the US-Mexican border, they turned the vans off the road and drove through the desert. They crossed the unmarked international border somewhere between Mexicali and Tijuana. The region might as well have been the Sahara—there were no people, or life of any kind save for a few cacti and shrubs. The vans barreled north, four wide, so that the dust trails didn't blind the van behind.

They got back onto pavement at California Highway 98 and drove west, looking for abandoned cars. They found none, just a long flat stretch of blacktop highway baking in the midday sun.

They pulled off the highway at the small community of Coyote Wells, which was no more than a truck stop. But it had what they needed: California license plates. The vehicle descriptions wouldn't match the vans if run through a DMV database, but the tags would do until they found ones from vehicles of a closer match.

They traveled east, driving away from the coast, where there would be more people—and troops. Desert turned to green, irrigated farmlands. Turning north shortly after that, they drove past Salton Sea, Joshua Tree National Park, and Yucca Valley.

The van with the most soldiers drove a few miles ahead now, serving as a scout, looking for checkpoints or trouble. They found neither, only a few fallen trees and a rock slide, both of which they dealt with.

And with each passing hour, Conner started to relax.

A mile outside Barstow, California, they found tags on vans that were near matches to the makes and models they drove. Near Mariposa they cut toward the sea. Conner didn't want to take a major interstate into the bay area, so they took the scenic roads that wound through the many parks, preserves, and national forests that stretched between San Jose and Santa Cruz.

Somewhere along the way, hours after the sun went down, Conner drifted off to sleep. The soft, rhythmic beeping of his brother's heartbeat monitor was the last thing he heard.

☣

A hand gripped his shoulder. Conner reached for the gun in his holster, then opened his eyes. Major Goins' face was lit by the van's dome light.

"Report," Conner snapped.

"Scout van is on Portola Road. It just turned into Sand Hill."

"Pull over." Conner sat up. "Have the scout van wait."

He activated the sat phone and dialed Yuri.

"Status?" the Russian said.

"We're in position."

"Resistance?"

"None."

"Good. We'll begin our attack. I hope it will give you some cover."

"Copy."

"Don't forget why you're out there, Conner."

Conner glanced at his brother, lying in a coma just feet away. "I won't."

☣

Yuri disconnected the call and strode to the situation room. To the head of watch, he said, "Pearl Harbor?"

"We're ready, sir."

"Commence."

The large screen at the end of the room displayed a world map covered in green dots. Slowly, the green dots turned to red—an indication of routers shutting down. The Citium had hacked the devices' firmware years ago, embedding the Trojan Horse, all in preparation for this moment. Now the devices were nothing more than bricks of plastic, silicon, and metal—until the Citium chose to reactivate them.

Satellites that transmitted data traffic across the internet also went dark. The only satellites left functioning were the Citium's, along with a few others owned by private companies.

The world had come to rely on the internet.

And now it was gone.

☣

Conner waited until a message appeared on his laptop:

Global Internet Disabled

He switched to the video feed from the scout van and activated his radio.

"Proceed."

The vehicle pulled back onto the road, moving just under the speed limit. The driver wore civilian clothes, as did the others in the van, but Conner knew they would raise concern at any checkpoint. Their buzz cuts, rugged, chiseled faces, and hard eyes marked them as anything but civilians.

The road was deserted. Desmond's office building—and the location of the memory—was just beyond the Sand Hill Road exit on Interstate 280. There was no movement—cars, pedestrians, or otherwise.

"Take us in," Conner said. "And have the vans spread out." Four vans together in a parking lot, belching white smoke into the December morning, would draw attention. Still, he wanted them close enough to help if trouble arose. "Have all units stay within visual range though."

When his van pulled into the office building's parking lot, Conner drew the cell phone from his pocket and opened the Labyrinth Reality app.

To the doctor, he said, "Do we need to be in Des's office for this to work?"

"I don't know, but I'd like to move him as little as possible."

"Fine. We'll try it here."

The app asked Conner how he would like to enter the Labyrinth: as the Minotaur or the hero. Conner smirked. He was the hero of the great game playing out around the world, but to the uninformed he was the Minotaur—a monster with the body of a man and the head of a bull. With his mangled face, he certainly looked the part.

Still, he clicked "hero" because he knew that's what his misguided older brother considered himself to be. He would have programmed it that way, as a reminder to himself after he had lost his memories. Did Desmond put the prompt in the application to help renew his own faith in his cause? There was so much Conner still didn't understand about his older brother.

Another dialog appeared:

Searching for Entrance…

A few seconds later, it read:

1 Entrance Located.

Conner tapped the screen again, and a progress bar appeared with the word *Downloading...* below it.

Ten minutes later, the phone buzzed.

Download Complete

At the same moment, Desmond arched his back and held the pose as if the makeshift hospital bed were on fire. Then he collapsed back to the stretcher and shook. The heartbeat monitor changed from a steady beat to a pounding alarm. Desmond strained against the padded hand restraints tied to the bedside rails.

"What's happening?" Conner asked.

Dr. Park ignored Conner. He pulled one of Desmond's eyelids open and ran a penlight across it.

Conner grabbed the doctor's shoulder. "Hey."

Park threw his hand off. "I don't know."

Conner felt suddenly helpless. *He's dying. And I killed him.*

CHAPTER 5

PEYTON FOLLOWED HER mother and two Navy SEALs through the sunken submarine, careful not to tear her suit. They had tested the air for toxins and found none, but Lin Shaw had reminded them that strange experiments had been conducted on the *Beagle*, and with every lab and office they opened, there was a risk of toxic exposure. The suits stayed on.

As the CDC's leading field epidemiologist, Peyton was used to operating in a suit—a biohazard suit. The hot zones she operated in were mostly near the equator: the Caribbean, Africa, and Southeast Asia. The *Beagle* was the opposite, a frozen tomb, and around every turn lay a new mystery: a laboratory with an experiment, an office with notes, scenes of the aftermath of the explosion that had sunk the sub thirty years ago.

During their first dive, the team had placed tiny LEDs in the passageways. They now glowed up from the floor, illuminating the glittering ice crystals on the walls. Peyton's helmet lights pushed away the rest of the darkness. Floating dust motes rushed past as she walked, as if she were flying through the dark of space and stars were passing by.

This section of corridor had bunks on the left and right. About half of them were occupied by bodies, well preserved by the cold. Some of the *Beagle*'s crew had died with a book on their chest, while others embraced a lover or friend. For Peyton, it was strangely like seeing a village during an outbreak—a tableau of the final hours of people in a hopeless situation.

Walking through the sub and seeing the dead researchers always reminded her of the pandemic, and the people she had lost from her own team. It was a reminder of what Yuri was capable of. For Yuri, the pandemic had been simply a means to an end: distributing Rapture. The microscopic robots were preprogramed to neutralize the pathogen, but they remained in the bloodstream indefinitely, awaiting further instructions. With the right software, the Citium could instruct those nanites to alter their hosts at the genetic level.

Peyton had Rapture nanites in her bloodstream. So did Lin. They were safe for now, only because Peyton's brother had deleted the Rapture Control program. But Peyton assumed that Yuri and Conner were working feverishly to rebuild the software. Her mother was right about one thing: time was running out. With each passing hour, she felt more aware of the tiny invaders inside her, like a poison flowing through her bloodstream, slowly diffusing, waiting to paralyze her body and mind, to take her freedom from her.

Up ahead, the two SEALs stopped, unpacked their gear, and turned on their specialized plasma torch. It glowed blue, and sparks of orange flew off as they brought it to the sealed door.

While they worked on opening a new area, Lin and Peyton ducked into the open office she and Peyton had started searching during the last dive. Without a word, Lin pulled open a drawer of a filing cabinet. Peyton held the camera up, ready to photograph the front and back of every document that came out.

☣

On the *Arktika*, the two members of the Citium tactical team made their way below decks, to a compartment adjacent to the reactor room. One man stood in the passageway, casually keeping watch, while the other attached explosives to the bulkhead.

They then moved to the second location: a bulkhead adjoining the hull on the side of the ship opposite their submersible. They moved down the passageway, listening for footsteps ahead of and behind them. Periodically they would reach into their backpacks, pull out explosives, and affix them to the bulkhead, spreading out the charges to ensure the holes ripped in the hull were in different compartments. Sinking the *Arktika* was a simple matter of getting enough water inside.

When all the charges were placed, the team leader tapped his open comm line three times. They were ready to proceed.

☣

Peyton's mother froze when she saw the page. "Switch the camera off."

"Why?"

Lin turned to face her daughter, her helmet lamps temporarily blinding Peyton. She held up four fingers.

Peyton switched to channel four on the comm.

"We're not cataloging this one," Lin said.

"Why not?"

"It's important."

"Even more reason to catalog it."

Lin paused. "Trust me, Peyton. I'm trusting you."

Peyton opened her mouth to respond, but stopped. She realized how much her mother's words meant to her. She desperately wanted her mother to trust her and more than that, she wanted to trust her mother. As if in a trance, she powered off the camera and let it fall to her side. She held out her hand, and her mother transferred the page gently, as if it was a sacred document.

Peyton was surprised when she saw it. She had expected a written document, but this was a color photograph. It depicted a cave painting of steppe bison, shown in rich tones of red and brown.

"You said this was important. Why?"

"It's a picture from the Cave of Altamira."

Peyton had never heard of it. "How's it connected to the Citium?"

"Turn it over, dear."

On the back, someone had handwritten two lines of text:

Do fidem me nullum librum
A Liddell

"The first line is Latin. What does it mean?"

"It's the beginning of an oath. An ancient one. A solemn vow to protect knowledge."

Peyton waited, expecting her mother to elaborate, but she didn't.

"A Liddell. Sounds like a name. Maybe that's who wrote it."

"It's not."

Peyton stared at her mother. "You know who wrote this?"

Lin nodded. "Doctor Paul Kraus."

"You know his handwriting?" Peyton instantly realized why. "Because you worked with him when you served on the *Beagle* fifty years ago."

"Yes."

Peyton looked at the page again. "That's what this has been about: finding this. He left this for you, didn't he?"

"In case something happened."

"Like Yuri's betrayal."

"There were always factions within the Citium. Research was stolen. People played politics, tried to divert funds from competing projects. And Kraus was used to hiding his research. He was a German scientist forced to work for the Nazis during World War Two. He emigrated to the US as part of Operation Paperclip."

"I've never heard of it."

"Paperclip was a post-war program that brought German intellectuals to the West. It had a huge impact on the course of history. A lot of American innovations in the fifties and sixties were a continuation of Nazi-funded research. The Saturn V rockets that carried the Apollo spacecraft to the moon? Just larger versions of the V2 rockets the Nazis fired at London in 1945. Same scientist designed both: Wernher von Braun."

"What was Kraus researching?"

"Human origins. A second theory of evolution."

"That's why the Citium recruited him."

Lin nodded. "They thought his research would reveal the true purpose of the human race—our future, what they called our ultimate destiny. Kraus spent his life looking for human ancestors—hominid species that went extinct before us. He believed they were the key to finding the code hidden in the human genome."

"What kind of code?"

"There are multiple theories about what the code is—or does."

"What's your theory?"

Lin glanced away, her helmet lights following her gaze. "I'll know soon."

Realization hit Peyton then. "You're going to finish his research."

Lin said nothing.

"That's why you took DNA samples. During the pandemic, in the cordons, governments around the world took samples and provided it to Rook Quantum Sciences. That was part of your research, wasn't it? You wanted the genomic data to combine with Kraus's research, which you hoped to find down here."

"Yes. As I said before, I had hoped the data would complete Kraus's work, but I was never told *how* it would be collected. If I had known Yuri was planning a pandemic..."

Peyton held up a hand. "I believe you, Mom. Wait—you said you *hoped* the data would complete Kraus's work. It didn't?"

"It's incomplete."

"How?"

"The key to understanding the code isn't sample size. It's sample diversity. We need to know how the human genome changed over time. There's a pattern to the changes, like a mathematical equation. If we can gather enough data, we can see how the data is produced."

"And what comes next."

A smile curled at Lin's lips, as if she were proud of Peyton for putting it together.

"Is that what the code is? An algorithm for advancing evolution?"

"It could be used that way, but we believe it has another purpose."

"Which is?"

Lin was silent for a moment. "Trust me, Peyton."

"You keep asking me to trust you, but you won't tell me what's going on. You're not trusting *me*. That's not fair."

"There are forces here that you don't appreciate."

"Because you're keeping me in the dark."

"No, because every question leads to another question. Eventually, they'll lead to answers you don't have the scientific or historical background to understand."

"Then I'll get a library card."

"Don't be flippant, Peyton. It's rude."

"You're lecturing me on etiquette while condescendingly telling me I'm not smart enough to understand what's going on?"

"I never said you weren't smart enough, and I never meant to condescend. I apologize if you interpreted it that way. It wasn't my intention."

"What *is* your intention?"

"To save time. Darling, you don't lack the intelligence to understand what's going on, but you do lack the knowledge. Imparting that knowledge would take time—which is a commodity we don't have. Some of this research has been going on for two thousand years. Most of it isn't available at a library or university or anywhere else. Some is buried down here, and some is hidden somewhere else, waiting for us to find it. And the rest, frankly, is only in my head."

Peyton looked away. "At least tell me *why* you're doing this— what your goal is."

"You know that. To stop Yuri. To stop the Citium."

"But how? How does this code in the human genome do that?"

Lin exhaled.

"Give me the simple version."

"We believe the code is the key to creating a device. One that will render Yuri and Conner's Looking Glass harmless. And unravel the greatest mystery of all time."

Peyton stared wide-eyed. "This is you versus Yuri, for control of the Looking Glass. He wants it because of the power it would give him. You want it for the sake of science. You don't want to destroy the Looking Glass. You want to control it."

Her mind flashed to thirty years ago, leaving London in the dead of night, traveling to America, living in hotels, her mother hiding in the bathroom, the phone cord stretched from the nightstand, whispered conversations, demanding to know what had happened to the *Beagle*. "Thirty years ago, you were distraught when the *Beagle* sank. It was because you needed the research for your own Looking Glass experiment."

"Yes."

"What does it do—your Looking Glass device?"

"We call it the Rabbit Hole. It's nothing like Yuri's Looking Glass—in operation or effect—"

"Mom. Just tell me what it does."

"This really is all I *can* tell you, darling. I'm sorry."

The beam of a helmet light poured into the room. Peyton turned to see a figure stepping through the doorway toward them.

CHAPTER 6

IN THE MEMORY, Desmond sat in his office, staring out the window at Sand Hill Road, watching cyclists pass, dressed in expensive gear, pedaling hard as the drizzling rain began. It was the fall of 2003, and the dot-com crash was still fresh in investors' minds. Funding was scarce. Venture capitalists asked tougher questions—and more of them. Drive-by investing, as it was called, had gone the way of the dinosaur. Those left were the cautious, methodical investors like Desmond. He did his research. And he never gave up on the causes he believed in.

A knock on the glass door drew his attention.

Yuri Pachenko stood impassively, his expression blank as usual. Without a word, he turned and walked out of the office.

Desmond grabbed his raincoat and followed.

They drove north on Interstate 280, both sitting in silence, watching the green rolling hills turn to strip malls, office buildings, and apartment complexes. The rain picked up as they got closer to San Francisco. The city was like a virus spreading south from the Golden Gate Bridge, transforming any housing that was even remotely dated into something shiny and new. And more expensive. Housing was increasingly out of reach for many who worked in the city.

Yuri took the exit for Highway 1, and they drove past block after block of homes packed into every square inch of space. Garages took up ground floors, with living areas stacked two and three levels above, mini skyscrapers standing shoulder to shoulder at the edge of the street.

Campaign signs for Gavin Newsom hung in more than half the windows, and stickers adorned the bumpers of most cars. There were even more signs for the gubernatorial recall, some in support of Governor Gray Davis, others for one of the replacement candidates, mostly Democratic candidate Cruz Bustamante. A banner hanging from the awning at a Flyers gas station simply read *Hasta La Vista Baby*—indicating support of Arnold Schwarzenegger. The signs reminded Desmond of their *Terminator* jokes at SciNet, and his initial encounter with the Citium and their front company, Rapture Therapeutics.

The Golden Gate Bridge spread out in the distance, its two red towers standing proud as the sun set over the Pacific. Fog was drifting in from the sea, creeping toward the bridge like an avalanche in slow motion.

Yuri took the winding road through Golden Gate Park into the Presidio. But instead of continuing toward the bridge, he exited onto 101 South, into the marina district. Alcatraz Island loomed in the bay. A ferry carrying tourists was departing, another arriving.

When he turned onto Lombard Street, Yuri finally spoke.

"The world is not as it seems, Desmond." He stared through the windshield, and Desmond thought the older man was going to elaborate, but he simply drove on in silence.

At Russian Hill, Yuri turned left toward Fisherman's Wharf. Ghirardelli Square was packed with tourists out for the night, shopping and heading to dinner, consulting maps, and huddling under umbrellas and racing for cover as the drizzling rain turned into a downpour.

Yuri nodded toward the crowd. "Do you know the difference between us and them?"

The car came to a stop. The pitter-patter of rain grew louder by the second, making Yuri's soft voice seem almost far away. "We are awake. We sense the truth: that something is deeply wrong with the world."

Yuri pulled back into the street, driving slowly by the crowds.

They passed the Argonaut Hotel, the Cannery Shopping Center, and Anchorage Square. He parked again outside Pier 39, the tourist hot spot where the bars, restaurants, and stores were packed.

"Deep down, they know it too. The feeling ebbs and flows. Some events cover it up for a time: you fall in love, you get a new job, you win the game. You think that's all you needed, that the feeling will go away, but it doesn't. It returns, again and again. Our species has become exceedingly adept at covering up the feeling. We work ourselves to death. We buy things. We go to parties and ball games. We laugh, shout, and cheer—and worse, we fight, and argue, and say things we don't mean. Alcohol and drugs quiet the most acute episodes. But we are constantly keeping the beast at bay. Underneath it all, our subconscious is crying out for help. For a solution—a cure for the root problem. We're all suffering from the same thing."

"Which is?"

"We've been told that it's simply the human condition." Yuri turned to face Desmond. "But that's not true. Our problem is really very simple: the world is not as it seems."

"Then what is it?"

"Science gives you one answer. Religious texts offer countless others. But the human population is slowly tiring of those answers. They are starting not to believe. They are awakening—and that awakening will soon tear the world apart. It will be a catastrophe with no equal." Yuri paused to take a slow, deep breath. "But we can stop it, Desmond. We offer an answer to the question that has haunted us forever. *And* a solution. Our fix isn't quick. It won't be easy to build. Those of us in our… group—"

"The Citium."

"Yes. We've been trying to solve this problem for a long time."

Desmond's heart beat faster. "What's your solution?"

"When you're ready."

If Desmond's life had taught him anything, it was that nothing was truly free. There was always a catch. He was sitting in that car because Yuri wanted him there—because Yuri wanted something from him.

"Why me? What do you want from me?"

A hint of a smile crossed Yuri's lips. "Two reasons. First, as I said, you're awake. If one of those people out there were sitting in this car, and I said what I just said, they would have laughed and walked away. But you know what I'm telling you is true. The world is not as it seems."

"And the second reason?"

"Is one you've likely already guessed."

"You need me."

"That's right."

"Why?"

"Your skills. I think you are uniquely qualified to construct one of the components of our solution."

"The Looking Glass."

"Yes."

"What is it?"

"All in good time. There's still a lot you need to learn."

"Such as?"

"If you want to join the Citium, you must first see the human race as it truly is. You must confront the truths we bury." Yuri paused again. "This is not a part-time job or a hobby, Desmond. You must commit fully. And once you do, there's no turning back. Do you understand?"

Desmond's mind flashed to the bushfires in Australia, to the day he rushed into the fire that burned his family home and killed his family. And he thought of the day he learned that his uncle was dead, the day Dale Epply came to rob him. On both days, he had decided to act. He had chosen to wade into the fire in Australia. He had turned and fought Dale, killed him to save himself. Both decisions, both actions, marked points of no return.

He knew that this moment was like that, too. And once again, he had no hesitation. He knew what he had to do.

"I'll give you some time to think about it."

"I don't need any time."

Yuri pulled away from the curb. He took the Embarcadero out of Fisherman's Wharf. The hotels, restaurants, and shops were replaced by skyscrapers and parking decks as they moved toward the financial district and the Bay Bridge.

Yuri parked the car in a deck under a tall, steel-and-glass building that Desmond found unremarkable. It had a CVS and a Banana Republic clothing store on the ground floor and two empty retail spaces. They got out of the car, and Desmond scanned the directory outside the elevator. Rapture Therapeutics was on the fourteenth floor.

To his surprise, Yuri inserted a key card in the slot and hit the button for the twenty-fifth floor.

The elevator opened onto a marble-floored lobby with wooden double doors. Yuri placed his hand on a palm reader by the doors, and they swung open.

A slender woman in a black business suit sat behind a raised reception desk. There was no logo on the wall or descriptor of any kind. She smiled at Yuri. "Good evening, sir."

"Good evening, Jennifer. I'd like you to meet Desmond Hughes."

She rose and shook his hand.

"Desmond will be staying with us for a while."

"Welcome."

"Thanks," Desmond said, looking around, still not sure what this place was.

Yuri led him down a hall that ended in a tiny lobby with four doors. Yuri drew another card from his pocket, swiped it across a pad by one of the doors, and pushed it open.

Inside was an apartment with modern furnishings. The living room had a breathtaking view of the bay. There was a single bedroom, a study, and a well-appointed kitchen.

"This is home now."

Desmond nodded absently. "Is this..."

"A hotel of sorts. The top three floors are condos. We own them all."

Desmond tried to put the pieces together. "I'll be working at Rapture?"

"No."

Yuri led Desmond out of the apartment, back down the hall,

and past the reception desk. With both hands he slid open a set of pocket doors, revealing the most impressive room Desmond had ever seen.

Desmond wandered inside, staring, unable to speak. Behind him, he heard the doors close.

"I thought you'd like this."

The library was three stories tall, with a spiral staircase in the corner that led to a horseshoe-shaped balcony on two levels. At the opposite end, a three-story wall of glass provided a view of the bay. The last rays of sunlight were clinging to Alcatraz and the Golden Gate Bridge like seaweed being pulled out with the tide. Long reading tables with glowing lamps sat empty.

"It starts here," Yuri said softly.

"What?"

"Your education." Yuri walked to the window. "Your real education."

"How?"

"With a question." Yuri faced him. "I will ask you three questions. Each will reveal another layer of truth."

"The truth about what?"

"The human race. You must understand the problem before we solve it. The answers are in this room."

Desmond scanned the shelves. Science and history books. Biographies. And tomes with no markings at all. In the corner, he spotted a computer on a podium. A digital catalog?

He smirked. "So once I read all these books, I'll know?"

Ignoring his levity, Yuri replied seriously. "It wouldn't help."

"Why not?"

"You don't know what you're looking for."

"What am I looking for?"

"The answer to a very strange mystery." Yuri walked to a world map and pointed to Africa. "Six million years ago, an ape was born in Africa. We know one thing for certain about her: she had more than one child. Every human is descended from one of those children. And every chimpanzee is descended from another one of her children. Incredible, isn't it? Our last common ancestor with chimps lived six million years ago, yet our genomes are 98.8 percent the same. After millions of years, only 1.2 percent of the genome has diverged. It tells you what an incredible difference just a small number of genes can make."

He studied the map. "The story gets stranger from there. Two and a half million years ago, the first humans appeared—the first members of the genus *Homo*. Also in Africa. They hung around for about half a million years, then began exploring. Eurasia first, then Europe and Asia.

"Neanderthals evolved half a million years ago—in Europe we believe. They eventually migrated to Asia, where they lived beside *Homo erectus* for hundreds of thousands of years, perhaps even using similar stone tools to hunt the same game.

"Our particular human species evolved two hundred thousand years ago—again in Africa. Think about it: at the time, there are other human species all over Europe and Asia. These other early humans have survived for two million years. *We* are the upstart. At first, we seem unremarkable. The order of the world continues.

"Where things begin to get interesting is about seventy thousand years ago. We change—we develop some sort of advantage. A small band of humans treks out of Africa—and proceeds to take over this planet like no species ever has before. Every other human species dies out. The megafauna fall. We remake the world. But perhaps the most extraordinary event happens forty-five thousand years ago—in your homeland."

"Australia."

"Yes. Before then, no human species had ever set foot on the continent of Australia. And for good reason. It was isolated, separated from all other landmasses by a minimum of sixty miles of open sea—and that's if you had a map, and knew which islands to hop to and which direction to take."

Yuri pointed to a small island in the Solomon Sea, on the eastern edge of Papua New Guinea. "Buka Island. Separated by over a hundred and twenty miles of open sea. Human remains have been found there that are thirty thousand years old. Think about that: a group of humans, thirty to forty thousand years ago, with the ability to make boats and navigate over vast distances of open sea. At that time, it would have been the most advanced invention in history; they would have been on the cutting edge. It would have been like a country landing on the moon in the 1700s—while the rest of the world was exploring in wooden boats."

Desmond studied the map. "So what's the mystery?"

"The mystery," Yuri said, "is what happened to them."

Desmond waited.

"Forty-five thousand years ago, they were on the leading edge of the human species. Light years ahead. Yet when the Dutch arrived in Australia in 1606, their descendants were primitives, hunter-gatherers. They hadn't even invented agriculture, or writing.

"Your first question, Desmond, is: What happened to them?"

☣

In the van off Sand Hill Road, Conner sat watching the heart rate monitor. The rhythm had stabilized in the last few minutes.

"What was that?"

Dr. Park looked up from his laptop. "I assume we just saw his physiological reaction to regaining a memory."

"So he has the memory now?"

Park held up his hands. "I don't know."

"Why not?"

"Well, because I've never done this, for one. I'm monitoring his brain waves. He's definitely in REM."

"REM?"

"Rapid Eye Movement. It's a sleep stage where we see alpha and beta brain wave patterns and desynchronous waves—"

"I'm not here for a brain wave lecture. Tell me what's going on with him."

"REM is a unique sleep stage. The body is effectively paralyzed. It's the stage where we have vivid, story-like dreams. The only dreams we remember occur during this period."

"So you think the memory is literally playing out like a dream he's going to remember?"

"That's my assumption. It seems logical. The implant could simulate dreaming—it would be a good way for the brain to regain the memory. It already understands that process."

"So you'll know when the memory ends?"

"Conceivably. If we see a change in brain waves, I think it's safe to assume the memory has unspooled."

"Good. Let me know when the credits roll, Doctor."

Conner would have to drug his brother and interrogate him later—discover what he learned. Hopefully the key to finding Rendition was in this memory.

Through the window, he watched two armored troop carriers barrel down Sand Hill Road, east toward Stanford and Palo Alto. A minute later, three Humvees led a convoy of medium tactical vehicles loaded with troops, who peered out the back, past the canvas flaps, their automatic rifles in their laps.

The collapse of the internet was doing exactly what Conner needed: causing chaos. That would buy him some time.

CHAPTER 7

PEYTON SQUINTED AT the bright helmet light and held up a hand to block the beam.

The SEAL stepped into the cramped office, toward Peyton and her mother. His mouth was moving, but no sound broadcasted over the comm line.

Lin raised a hand to her helmet, changed channels, and began speaking.

Peyton also switched back to channel one.

"... just got through," the technician said.

"Good." Lin's voice was emotionless.

"Should we proceed to the next office?"

"Negative. Seal the office you just opened per SOPs and prepare for departure. We're done here for now."

The SEAL stepped out of the office and disappeared back down the passageway.

Lin turned her helmet, stared at Peyton, and held up four gloved fingers. Peyton switched channels again.

"Can we proceed?"

Peyton studied her mother's slightly lined face. "What does it do? Your Looking Glass. The Rabbit Hole."

"It's very hard to describe—"

"Will it hurt anyone?"

Lin looked pained at the question. "No. It's not like that."

"What *is* it like?"

"It will change our theory of everything."

Like most children, Peyton had grown up taking her mother's word as fact. Usually, Lin Shaw's pronouncements were the final word on matters. Peyton hadn't been a rebellious teenager; she was the quiet one, her nose always in a book or playing alone. She wasn't used to conflict. That's one of the things that drew her to epidemiology. Viruses and bacteria hurt people, but they were microscopic. The fight wasn't large and in your face, but it mattered. A lot.

Yet, here and now, she felt that she had to press her mother. She needed to know that what they were doing mattered—and that it would do what her mother promised. "Will it stop Yuri and the Citium?"

"If I'm right, it will neutralize him."

"And will it help me find Desmond?"

"No. But *I* will. I promise you that, Peyton. I know what he means to you. I know what it's like to lose the love of your life to circumstances you can't control."

The reference to Peyton's father brought a pang of sadness. Her mother didn't waver though.

"You and I will finish this. Together."

In the submersible, Peyton watched the depth reading count down to zero. The specially built vessel had no windows, but a flat panel computer screen showed the view from six cameras: one mounted above, one below, and one on each of its four sides. Peyton watched the thick sheet of ice approach, then pass by. The vessel shook as it crested the water line.

Peyton unlatched her helmet the moment her boots hit the deck. A thick white cloud spread out, a mixture of cigarette smoke and the Russian sailors' hot breath in the Arctic air. The voices of the sailors and research team were a chaotic cacophony, seemingly with no source. Floodlights shone down from the deck above, like four moons beyond the cloud cover on an alien world.

Through the din, Peyton could make out some of the arguments—discussion about whether they should leave. Something was very wrong.

Lin walked over to the US Navy sailor who was operating the controls that tethered the submersible to the *Arktika*. "What's the problem, Chief?"

"Internet's down, ma'am."

"A problem on our end?"

"Negative, ma'am."

"Elaborate."

The man turned from the controls. "Sat link went down fifteen minutes ago."

"Ours or theirs?" Lin jerked her head toward the Russians.

"Both."

Lin's eyes darted back and forth, as if speed-reading.

"The links are good, there's just no response on the other end. JTF-GNO. Rubicon. They're dark—"

Lin spun and shouted across the deck.

"Vasiliev!"

The burly Russian officer emerged from the cloud, anger on his face.

"Sound the alarm!" Lin yelled.

He stared, confused.

"Do it! Now, Vasiliev! We're under attack."

His expression softened as if he were putting the pieces together. He unclipped the handheld radio from his belt and brought it to his face, but he never got a word out.

The deck shuddered as the bomb went off. The floodlights went out, and dim yellow emergency lights flickered on, only to wink out when a second explosion rocked the ship. This one lasted longer, like thunder rolling through the massive structure.

The deck seemed to churn with bodies as everyone sprang into motion. The sailors raced toward their muster stations. Their shouting echoed off the metal decks. Peyton thought she heard muffled rifle reports, thumping, rhythmic in the darkness. A gust of air blew the white cloud of cigarette smoke and steam away, like dust blowing in the wind, and with the misty curtain gone, Peyton realized that everyone had stopped moving. They were staring at the helicopter on the deck above. Its rotors were spinning up. The sailors screamed obscenities, knowing their best chance of escape was slipping away.

Lin's voice sounded, barely audible in the shouts: "Get back!"

The helo exploded in flames and shrapnel. The blast blew Peyton off her feet. Two men landed on top of her. Their weight and the impact with the deck would have crushed her if not for the thick suit. Her ears rang, and blood trickled down her face. She realized it wasn't her own blood, but was dripping from above—from one of the sailors who'd landed on top of her. She looked up, and saw a piece of metal lodged in his face.

She reached up and pushed against the man on the top. He shifted and slid off. She arched her back, trying to move the other man, but he was too heavy. She rocked back and forth on her elbows, and finally managed to turn and crawl out from under him.

She checked his pulse. Nothing. He was dead.

The deck was a horror scene. Bodies lay in stacks at awkward angles, like a box of matches that had been emptied haphazardly. A fire crackled in the helicopter's charred wreckage, sending puffs of black smoke down to the lower deck. A few sailors had started to move, like zombies rising from a mass grave, their movements lit only by the green and purple streaks of the aurora borealis.

Their mouths moved, but Peyton couldn't hear the words—all was silence. No—a dull ringing. Peyton shook her head and crawled to the closest sailor. Dead.

But the next one was alive.

She called to a man nearby, who had just gotten to his feet. But she couldn't hear her own voice, and if *he* could hear her, he ignored her. He ran to a lifeboat and began untying it.

Peyton tried to focus. The research team. Below decks. In the dark. She had to warn them, help them get out. And save the data.

What else?

Her mother.

Lin Shaw lay ten feet away. Not moving.

Peyton stumbled across the deck, wincing as her feet dug into the bodies. Only a few squirmed at her touch.

She took her mother's face in her hands, then slid two fingers down to her carotid artery and pressed, waited, dreading...

She felt a pulse.

Lin's eyes stayed closed, but her breathing was slowly accelerating. She was coming to. But Peyton couldn't wait. Her mom was okay, and that was good enough for now.

Peyton spun and searched the deck for her helmet. It was still near the submersible where she had taken it off. She pulled it on and activated the lights.

She moved to the closest hatch, still taking careful steps. Inside, she found a ladder and descended.

The passageways were dark, lit only by her helmet lights. They reminded her of the *Beagle*, except without the ice crystals and dust motes flying by. She wondered if a watery grave on the ocean floor would be the *Arktika*'s fate. Or were the attackers only trying to retrieve the data and artifacts?

Gradually, her hearing returned. Voices and footsteps echoed all around her. She had to stop in the passageways several times to allow Russian sailors to pass. Soon the corridors were swarming with people. Peyton felt like a pinball in a machine, tossed about with no control.

She was almost to the cargo hold when a hand gripped her shoulder, pulled her back, and pinned her to the wall.

Another set of helmet lights shone into her eyes.

Her mother's.

Her visor was up, and she was panting, desperately trying to catch her breath. Peyton raised her own helmet visor so she could hear her mother's voice.

"We have to..." Lin leaned forward and put her hands on her knees. "Get off the ship."

"Mom, the researchers, the data—"

"No time, Peyton. They'll sink her."

"Who?"

"Yuri."

"He's here?"

Lin shook her head. She was finally getting her breath back. "His men. I know it."

Two beams of light rounded the corner, then stopped moving. A man's voice called into the passageway. "Doctor Shaw."

Both women turned.

A small smile crossed the man's lips. "*Doctors* Shaw, I should say."

The men were dressed in US Navy working uniforms. Peyton recognized the desert digital pattern—it was restricted to SEALs and other sailors assigned to Naval Special Warfare units. The two men also wore headlamps, body armor, and cold weather gear. Automatic rifles hung from their shoulders.

"Lieutenant Stockton, ma'am," the first man said. He nodded to his companion. "Chief Petty Officer Bromitt and I have orders to get you off this ship."

Lin eyed the man carefully, but didn't respond. Peyton sensed her hesitation.

"Afraid we don't have much time, Doctor Shaw. If you and your daughter will follow us…"

To Peyton's surprise, Lin fell in behind the petty officer. Not knowing what else to do, Peyton followed.

With each step, the passageways started to fill. Russian sailors rushed by with flashlights. Members of the biology team strained to see by the light of their cell phones. Archaeologists in white suits lumbered through the cramped corridors, some holding up LED bars and penlights.

Lin's voice was barely audible over the pounding footfalls. "Where are we going, Lieutenant?"

"Emergency evac, ma'am. Can't say."

"Whose orders?"

"CENTCOM direct, ma'am. Standing emergency orders for the deployment. You two are high value."

At a ladder, Bromitt began climbing. Lin and Peyton followed, and Stockton brought up the rear. They didn't stop until they reached the main deck. They stepped out of a hatch near the middle of the ship, on the opposite side from the submersible launch area. Around the deck, Russian sailors were untying lifeboats and placing their fallen comrades inside. An officer with a bullhorn was directing them in Russian.

Stockton gestured toward a rope that hung from the outer rail. "Up and over, ladies."

Peyton peered over the rail. In a pocket carved out of the ice, roughly fifty feet below, sat a submersible slightly larger than the one tethered to the *Arktika*'s launch bay.

"Where are you operating from, Lieutenant?"

"Another icebreaker, ma'am. Close by. Now we really need to move."

The ship jolted, like something had broken free below. A bulkhead maybe?

Peyton watched the water line. It was creeping up the hull. The massive icebreaker was sinking into the Arctic.

Stockton stepped closer to Lin. "I really must insist, Doctor."

Lin motioned to the rope. "Fine. Have the chief descend first to test the line."

Stockton shook his head. "Ladies first."

"No, Lieutenant. The chief goes. When he's halfway, I'll go, Peyton will follow, and you will bring up the rear, just as we exited." She stared at him a moment. "Or you can throw me off."

Stockton smiled and nodded to the chief, who cartwheeled his legs over the rail, gripped the rope, and began rappelling down.

As Lin stepped over to the rail, she slipped her hand inside her suit pocket. Then she jerked toward the lieutenant with incredible speed. Her blow struck his lower abdomen, right under his body armor. Rapid electrical pops went off—the clack-clack-clack of a stun gun. Stockton convulsed and collapsed to the deck, his face hitting hard as he screamed out.

Lin drew a combat knife from the sheath on Stockton's calf and slammed it into the rope. It didn't slice through, but a vibration went through the line, making a sound like a violin holding a note.

Bromitt was thirty feet down. He instantly started climbing back up.

Peyton turned to run, but the drone of the knife being drawn across the rope continued. Her mother had flipped the weapon around and was sawing the rope with the serrated edge.

"Mom!"

Lin didn't look up.

Bromitt was climbing fast, breathing hard, putting hand over hand. He was twenty feet away.

Strands of rope frayed. It would never break in time.

Overhead, signal flares went up—the Russian crew desperately calling for help.

Bromitt began running side to side, like a human pendulum swinging back and forth, trying to gain enough speed to reach the rail. He got closer with each run. He would grasp it on the next go.

"Mom!"

Lin shot Peyton a quick glance, spun the knife again, and hacked hard at the rope. It finally snapped, sending Bromitt plummeting to the ice below. He landed right where the massive twelve-foot thick sheet met the water, his bones cracking on contact. He cried out, flailed, then reached back and tried to gain purchase on the sloped ice. He was sliding down, toward the water.

Thirty feet away, the hatch on the submersible burst open. A man's head popped out, and he spotted Bromitt. He watched with an expression of horror as his comrade slipped into the freezing water, barely able to move his broken bones, his last words only grunts and gurgles as the Arctic water flowed into his mouth.

The soldier in the submersible turned his gaze upward, hatred in his eyes. He drew his sidearm and fired. His first shot hit the rail beneath Lin, missing by only an inch.

She reeled back and yelled, "Intruders!"

Sailors from the aft deck poured onto the narrow gangway. They fired on the submersible, their bullets ricocheting off the hull as the man ducked down.

Stockton groaned, reached out a trembling hand, and grabbed the metal cord railing. His partially paralyzed limbs shook as he pulled himself toward the edge.

Lin lunged for him, but not fast enough; he slipped over the lip of the deck, face-first, sliding down the hull as if it were a giant water slide. He screamed as he hit the icy water.

Another figure popped up from the submersible, spraying automatic gunfire at the gangway. More Russians poured onto the deck and began firing. The submersible was in the crossfire now, with shots coming from both the foredeck and aft deck.

Lin grabbed Peyton and pulled her toward the ship's hatch. "Run."

"Mom."

"*Move*, Peyton. Or we're dead."

Lin slammed the door shut behind them and turned the wheel to lock it. The two women snaked through the passageway, their way lit only by their helmet lamps.

They emerged onto the aft deck, which was still littered with bodies and debris from the helicopter's explosion. A throng of people had crowded around the launch platform—biologists in Arctic weather gear and archaeologists still in their white clean suits, shouting and waving their hands. Peyton realized then what her mother apparently had already realized: there were only two ways off the sinking ship—the lifeboats and the submersible. The lifeboats could be offloaded to the ice, but the survivors would be left to brave the elements in tents and cold weather gear. If help didn't arrive soon, that would be a death sentence. She wasn't sure the submersible was much better, but clearly her mother had opted for it.

Lin made a wedge with her hands and charged into the crowd.

At the launch controls, six SEALs were holding the mob back at gunpoint. But they waved Peyton and Lin forward, made an opening for them, and closed ranks the moment they passed. Nigel Greene stood behind them, clutching a messenger bag to his chest, his pudgy stomach protruding below.

"Lieutenant," Lin said to a tall SEAL with two silver bars on his lapel.

"Ma'am," he replied, not looking back. "Thought you might favor the submersible."

"Assignments?" she said flatly.

"Adams and Rodriguez will accompany you, ma'am. They know the *Beagle* the best. We'll cover your exit."

Why do they need to know it the best, Peyton thought? And then she answered her own question: in case the wrecked sub was boarded by the men in the other submersible. In case they were pursued—and had to fight in the *Beagle*.

"You and your men will be remembered for you act of bravery here today, Lieutenant," Lin said. "You have my word." She turned to Nigel. "Doctor Greene, if you please."

The biologist shuffled quickly to the submersible. As he boarded, the crowd surged forward, screaming at the sight of what might be their only chance of survival slipping away. The SEALs fired into the air, quieting the mob and forcing everyone back.

Peyton stared at the faces in the crowd, the looks of hopelessness and fear. They were expressions she knew well—had seen countless times during outbreaks around the world, in huts and ramshackle tenements and field hospitals. But this was different. As an epidemiologist, she had done everything she could to help the dying. She had even risked her life. Pandemics pit humanity against the forces of nature—every person was in it together, fighting to survive—and that was a fight she could get behind. But this... this was choosing her life over theirs, sentencing them to death. Her against them. It felt wrong to her.

She stopped. Watched the others board.

"Peyton." Her mother's voice was like a whip, but her eyes betrayed no emotion. "We have to go, Peyton. People are counting on you." She stepped closer. "To survive."

In her mind's eye, Peyton saw Desmond's face. Her brother, Andrew. Her sister, Madison.

As if in a trance, she moved to the submersible, felt herself climb down the ladder. Heard her mother descending after her, then the two Navy SEALs. The hatch closing. The submersible sinking.

A single thought echoed in her mind. *We left them there to die.*

Her mother seemed to understand. She leaned forward and looked Peyton in the eyes. "Listen to me. We didn't create this situation." She motioned to the surface. "They did. Yuri did. They put us in this position. They sank the ship and killed those people. And that is only the beginning. You've seen what they're capable of. We *have* to survive, if for only one reason: to stop them. If we allow our emotions to cloud our judgment, if we make the wrong call, if they capture or kill us, a lot more people are going to suffer."

She paused.

"You have to consider the greater good, Peyton. Do you understand?"

Peyton nodded. "I understand. But I don't like it."

"You shouldn't. You should never be comfortable with what we just did." Without looking at him, Lin said, "Doctor Greene?"

"Ma'am?"

"Report."

He exhaled. "I executed our exigency protocol. I have the latest data dump and maps of the sub."

"Good. Chief Petty Officer Adams."

"Ma'am?"

"We need a plan for defending the *Beagle* against intruders. If I'm right, we'll soon be in a fight for our lives."

CHAPTER 8

CONNER WAS STRETCHED on a cot in the back of the van. Still parked outside the office building off Sand Hill Road, the vehicle had drawn no interest from the X1 troops. He counted that as lucky.

Desmond lay on a hospital bed next to him. The rhythmic beeping of the machine monitoring Desmond's vitals was like a metronome, coaxing Conner to sleep. He resisted.

The reports on the police scanner narrated the Citium's conquest of the world, and the start of a second American civil war. The voices of the National Guard troops and police rang out, the stress and worry in those voices growing by the hour.

Enemy combatants moving up El Camino Real Street. Request backup.

Riot beginning at the Stanford Treatment Shelter.

Fire started at Trader Joe's at the corner of Embarcadero and Alma. Request fire crews.

Conner was too young to remember the fire that had burned and disfigured him, but the effects had shaped his life. He didn't wish that on anyone. Fear rose in him each time a fire was mentioned on the radio. He felt like running, getting far away, going somewhere safe, where he could never be burned again.

But only one place like that existed: the Looking Glass.

Dr. Park's face was lit by the glowing laptop screen.

"Status, Doctor?"

"He's still experiencing the memory."

"Any idea how much longer? The fighting is moving toward us."

"Yes, I can hear that..."

"Watch your mouth, Doctor, or you'll lose the senses you don't need for this task."

Park swallowed, and when he spoke, his tone was neutral. "I've been monitoring his brain waves. I'm trying to develop an algorithm that would tell us the approximate time remaining on the memory in progress."

That was good. Conner needed to know the second they could move on. He sensed that moment was coming soon.

☣

The tables of the library were stacked high with books. The chandelier glowed, its seven rings lighting all three stories of the vast space. Desmond sat at one of the long tables by the windows, scratching his head at his hairline. A notebook filled with writing lay beside the history book he'd been reading.

The library had a spectacular view of the San Francisco Bay, but Desmond had barely glanced at it. Since coming here, he'd spent every waking second reading and thinking about Yuri's riddle. Why did the indigenous Australians fall behind the rest of the world?

Fifty thousand years ago, they had been arguably the most technically advanced humans on Earth. They crossed vast stretches of open sea on primitive boats, with no map, reaching Australia—a landmass that had never before seen human habitation. And they conquered it. Then their advancement stalled. It was as if they entered a time warp, and the rest of the world progressed without them.

Desmond had spent days reading volumes on evolution and history, and now... now he felt he was close to a working theory.

He rose and paced the library, stretching his legs. Sometimes when he wanted to think, or when he was too tired to think, he walked along the library's stacks. He ascended the spiral staircase to the second floor, made a lap around the horseshoe-shaped balcony, then moved to the third floor.

A row of leather-bound volumes caught his eye. They were labeled *Archives of the Citium Conclaves*. Desmond opened the first book in the set. It contained printed scans of documents that looked old—the paper yellow, the text handwritten in faded letters. The originals were in Latin, and in each case, an English translation was on the opposite page. He brought the tome back down to his table and read it. Then he went up for another, and another.

The records detailed meetings that stretched back over two thousand years. The conclaves were held annually, and were attended by leading thinkers from all over the world. The documents told of debates about the nature of existence and the purpose of the human race, its origins, and its destiny.

The first meeting of the Order of Citium took place in 268 BC on the Greek island of Kition, also known by its Latin name, Citium. The conclave was moderated by the order's founder, Zeno, a leading philosopher at the time. The roll call read like a who's who of the ancient world. Even Archimedes was there, though he was only nineteen at the time.

The central presentation at the first conclave was given by Aristarchus. He proposed that the Earth was not the center of the universe—as was the general consensus at the time. He placed the sun at the center, giving credit as he did to Philolaus, a Greek Pythagorean and pre-Socratic philosopher who had lived a hundred years earlier. Philolaus had proposed that the Earth, sun, and moon rotated around a central fire.

But Aristarchus went further. Not only did he identify the sun as the central fire and the center of the solar system, and assert that the path of Earth's orbit was circular, he was also the first to propose that the stars were very far away from each other and that the universe was much larger than anyone suspected. He even proposed that Earth was spinning on its axis and that it took one day to complete a revolution.

Desmond was surprised. He had always associated the heliocentric theory with Copernicus and then Galileo. But Aristarchus had proved the truth, mathematically, over 1,800 years before

Copernicus. In fact, Copernicus acknowledged Aristarchus in the first draft of his book, but the reference was removed before it was published.

Unfortunately, Aristarchus's own book on the subject was lost. The best-known mention of his work comes from Archimedes. In a letter titled, "The Sand Reckoner," sent to King Gelon, Archimedes stated:

> *Aristarchus has written a book in which he says that the universe is many times bigger than we thought. He says that the stars and the sun don't move, that the earth revolves about the sun, and that the path of the orbit is circular.*

Galileo Galilei, who was born twenty-one years after Copernicus died, restored Aristarchus's place, identifying him as the discoverer of the heliocentric solar system. He referred to Copernicus as the "restorer and confirmer" of the hypothesis. The heliocentric theory would of course go on to land Galileo in trouble with the Roman Inquisition, who placed him under house arrest until his death.

Desmond soon found that Aristarchus's heliocentric presentation set the tone for all future Citium conclaves—and for the organization itself. They were a society open to bold ideas, no matter how radical. They only demanded proof, and open discussion. They held humanity at a distance. They saw themselves as part of a universe that must be studied objectively and understood, not at the center of creation or on a pedestal. And they sought truth above all else.

Desmond pored through the archives, watching the group's thinking progress as the years and then centuries passed. Some theories were thrown out, others disproved over time, but gradually a central, unifying theory emerged: the universe is a single organism, a biochemical machine of some sort, and the human race is a component of that organism—a component with an important role to play. They believed the universe's beginning and ending were linked somehow—that in fact they *had* to be.

And central to this theory was the idea that something *powered* the universe, a process or entity that drove it from its origin to its destiny. They called this force the Invisible Sun.

Desmond read in rapture, his mind opening with each volume.

The tenor of the meetings changed in 1945. Where before they had been consistently reflective and patient, now the members of the Citium began to grow anxious, eager to transition from theory to action. Instead of an annual meeting, they began having quarterly conclaves. They focused more on their experiments, and every priority was now aligned with the construction of the Looking Glass. The urgency to finalize their plan for the mysterious device grew with each meeting. In the 1960s, while the USSR and USA were stockpiling enough nuclear weapons to annihilate the human race many times over, the members of the Citium cried out for action. Their members had given the world the atomic bomb, and they were convinced it would be humanity's end. They desperately wanted to atone.

A group of members launched the *Beagle* from Hong Kong in May of 1965. At every conclave thereafter, members of the *Beagle* expedition returned to reveal their findings. Desmond was shocked at what they found. He felt as though he were sitting in the Library of Alexandria, reading records long forgotten, filled with discoveries that would forever change the world.

And then, in 1986, the records stopped—without explanation.

Yuri visited three times a week, usually in the evening. They played chess by the window overlooking the bay, the headlights of cars driving over the Golden Gate Bridge glittering in the distance like fireflies skimming the water.

"I'd like to read the rest of the Citium conclave archives," Desmond said.

Yuri took one of Desmond's knights with a rook and raised an eyebrow.

"The records after 1986," Desmond clarified.

"There are none."

Desmond leaned back in his chair. "You might be the least talkative person I've ever met." That was saying something, given that Orville Hughes had raised him.

Yuri ran his thumb over the knight he had just taken from Desmond. "I grew up in a place where words could get you killed. Even the wrong look."

Desmond knew Yuri had grown up in Stalingrad and had been only six years old when the Nazis had invaded. Yuri had lived under Stalin in the years after. And Desmond knew what it was like to grow up scared to speak your mind. He had gotten more than a few tongue-lashings—and worse—from Orville.

"Why did they stop keeping records?"

"You have it backwards."

"How so?"

"The meetings stopped."

"Then..."

"You read the minutes. You saw the fear creeping into the members."

"They felt time was running out."

"Yes. And there were competing projects."

"So what happened?"

Yuri set the knight on the table. "Your move."

Desmond advanced a pawn, barely able to focus on the game.

Yuri moved his king, positioning it out of Desmond's reach. "A tragedy occurred. A sort of... force of nature." He paused. "I believe you're familiar with such things."

The massive fire that had taken Desmond's family—why was Yuri bringing that up? Was he trying to distract him? Was the older man hiding something?

Desmond moved his only remaining rook to protect his own king.

Yuri took it with a bishop.

Desmond studied the board. He was going to lose. He didn't care. He wanted to know why the archives had stopped. There was something more to it—he sensed as much.

"Your focus is misplaced."

Desmond glanced at the board, but Yuri pointed at him. "All I can tell you is that in 1986, we were forced to go into hiding. But that will end soon."

"I don't understand."

"The Looking Glass. It will heal all wounds. Even our deepest burns."

Conner listened to the orders from the National Guard units coming over the radio. A curfew had been established—nationwide. Anyone caught out after dark would be taken to the X1 pandemic camps and confined.

He glanced out the window. He guessed that the sun would set in about two hours. The units were taking up positions, gearing up to conduct a grid search just after nightfall. When they did, they would find the vans off Sand Hill Road. Conner and his men would need to be gone by then.

If they weren't, they'd have to fight.

CHAPTER 9

ON THE FLAT screens inside the submersible, Peyton watched the *Beagle* come into view. The wrecked submarine seemed almost embedded into the ocean floor now, as if the Earth were wrapping its fingers around it, trying to pull the wreck down and swallow it whole. Beside her, Nigel shivered, the messenger bag clutched tightly to his chest like a life vest.

"Our first order of business," Lin said, "will be to equip Doctor Greene. There's cold weather gear in a supply room here." A map of the *Beagle* was spread out on the floor, and she pointed to a chamber near the submersible docking port. She turned to the two Navy SEALs sitting at the controls. "Chief Adams, you and Seaman Rodriguez must prepare to repel a boarding party. I defer to you on that matter. What can we do?"

"We have to consider our advantages," Adams said. "First, we know the battlefield. Second, we can choose where in the sub to fight. If they want to capture you, they have to come through us."

"And working against us?" Lin asked.

"Time and surprise."

The submersible banked as Rodriguez maneuvered to the *Beagle*'s docking port.

"They can wait us out," Lin said flatly.

Adams nodded. "Given the choice, you'd rather attack a starving, fatigued enemy. And they can do it at a time of their choosing. We must always be ready. They can rest and plan and choose their moment."

A good analysis, Peyton thought. And deeply concerning.

"But we'll be ready," Adams said. "We can make the *Beagle* an extremely hostile environment for them to operate in."

On the Citium submersible, Commander Furst watched the video feed from the camera they had placed on the ice. He kept hoping to see Stockton's arm reach out of the water, grip the surface, and crawl out. But there was no sign of him. It was as if the water had paralyzed him. Stockton had extensive cold weather training. What had Lin Shaw done to him? The former Citium researcher had killed two of his men—highly trained operatives—in minutes.

Furst had underestimated her. He wouldn't make that mistake again.

The crew had anchored poles in the ice to hold battery-powered lights, which shone like buzzing lamps in an ice parking lot. The sailors were working feverishly, throwing supplies off *Arktika*'s deck, which was less than ten feet above the water line; the ship was sinking fast now. The captain was shouting orders and pointing. A column of men carried a long metal ramp out of the ship, clamped it to the lip of the deck, and let it fall to the ice.

A column of people poured from the ship—dressed in white clean suits and civilian cold weather gear. They carried bundles and crates, some of which had the word SPECIMEN scrawled on the side in white letters.

Furst shook his head. Priorities.

The civilians began unpacking the bundles, laying insulated pads on the ice, and erecting tents. They knew each minute they spent out in the elements would push them closer to death.

A second group began cutting into strips the red tarps that had covered the lifeboats. They placed the pieces on the ice, tacked them down with metal stakes, and spread them out, forming a large X.

Furst smirked. Futile.

The roar of an engine drew his attention. A snowmobile emerged from the aft bay doors, turned on the deck, and slowly powered onto the ramp and down it to the ice.

Furst watched, hoping...but the ice held. Of course it would.

Another snowmobile followed. The drivers were wrapped in layers. Two swollen duffel bags sat on the back of each snow-mobile, with a drone and radio signal booster strapped on top.

Furst smiled ruefully. He had underestimated the Russians. It didn't mean they would survive, but it would force him to expedite his attack. He couldn't wait out the Shaws. Help might arrive.

Lin Shaw had killed Stockton and Bromitt, men who were like brothers to him. She would soon pay for that.

☣

Inside the *Beagle*, Peyton watched her mother pry open the door to the supply closet. The frozen hinges screamed like a trapped animal. Lin took a stack of thick blankets off the shelf and handed them to Peyton, then grabbed the closest suit and a helmet. Both were bulky, and reminded Peyton of the suit Neil Armstrong wore when he walked on the moon—*which was likely only a few years before this one was manufactured*, she thought wryly.

Over the comm channel, Lin said, "It's old, but it'll keep Nigel warm." She checked the suit's heater and oxygen supply, then pushed a button, activating the helmet lights.

Peyton was amazed everything still worked. *I guess they don't make them like they used to.*

Lin squatted down, moved a pair of boots off of a steel box, and lifted the lid, revealing a row of handguns. She tucked two in the pockets of her suit and handed a third to Peyton.

"You know how to use it?"

"I've... had some basic weapons training."

"That's all you need. If you're forced to use it down here, it'll be at close range." Lin looked over at her daughter, her headlamps meeting Peyton's like two lighthouses in the night. "If forced, will you use it?"

She was asking if Peyton could take a life. And Peyton didn't know the answer. Just the thought of it went against the oath she'd taken as a doctor. It went against her very being.

"I'll do my best."

Lin stared at her for a long moment. "Remember, we're not just fighting for *our* lives. We're fighting for others, too."

Peyton felt as though her mother knew exactly which buttons to push. But with each passing hour, Peyton had begun to see a new side of her mother. She'd watched her do things she had thought Lin Shaw utterly incapable of. Like killing those two soldiers aboard the *Arktika*. Those sort of skills and instincts didn't develop overnight. They took years.

Peyton had always felt that her relationship with her mother was split between two periods: before and after that day in 1986 when the *Beagle* sank and she was told that her father was dead. The Lin Shaw before that day had been a nurturing mother, cheerful, doting even. Afterward... she became withdrawn and stoic, hiding a deep sadness. She spent endless hours on her genetics research. She saw to her three children's needs, but she did it with measured distance, as if she was scared to love, to get too close. And perhaps her fears had been well-founded. Her oldest, Andrew, had been taken from her—by Yuri—as a way to control her. She had never married again, or even dated.

Only now did Peyton know the truth: her mother had been waiting all those years, hoping her father would return, that Yuri would be defeated. Half of that hope had come true: three weeks ago, Peyton had found her father, who had been in hiding since the day the *Beagle* sank. But within two days of being found, he was killed by Yuri in the battle on the Isle of Citium.

They had recovered her brother though, and Peyton would forever be grateful for that. He was in Australia now, trying to put his life back together. She didn't know if that would be possible after all he had done—been made to do—but she hoped.

But if Lin Shaw was once driven by hope, Peyton thought, she was no more. Now she was driven by a desire for revenge. Her mother wanted to finish her research, to build a device to counter

Yuri's Looking Glass, but her need for revenge—her driving hatred —was the only thing that could have enabled her to leave those people to die on the ship. The only thing that could give her the will to dispatch those two soldiers without a moment's hesitation.

Peyton motioned to the gun in Lin's pocket. "Do *you* know how to use it?"

"Yes." She stepped out of the supply room. "I learned a lot of things when the Japanese invaded Hong Kong. Things I didn't want to know."

High above the *Beagle*, the Citium submersible was navigating to an indentation in the ice sheet about a mile from the *Arktika*. Furst and his team had made the pocket before the assault, and had used it to broadcast an update to their mother ship, the *Invisible Sun*. A thin layer of ice had formed since then, but the submersible punched through it easily.

When the channel was open once more, Furst said, "*Ice Harvest* calling *Invisible Sun*. Do you copy?"

"We read you, *Ice Harvest*."

"Project report as follows: nest is gone, however two birds were spotted flying south at high speed. Recommend you surveil and tag."

"Copy, *Ice Harvest*."

"Destruction of nest has left some birds on the ice. Also recommend you intervene."

"Copy, *Ice Harvest*."

"Final project update: mother bird and her youngest have flown the nest, believed to be making their way to a previous nest. Going there next in hopes of capturing for further study."

"Understood, *Ice Harvest*. Godspeed."

A hundred and fifty miles north of Alaska, a cruise ship floated in the Arctic Ocean, its engines off. There were no tourists on deck or in the cabins below. The *Invisible Sun* was a Citium vessel, and despite its appearance, it wasn't a cruise ship at all. It was a floating fortress.

In the CIC, a bank of screens showed satellite footage of the ice sheet. The feeds panned across the white desert until it found the snowmobile. Coordinates and speed appeared a second later, updating in real time. A second snowmobile appeared on another screen.

Captain Vasilov watched the feeds, sizing up her adversary. "Fire at will."

On deck, the floor of an outdoor basketball court opened up like a drawbridge, and a platform rose from within it, holding twelve long-range missiles. Two of them launched.

A few seconds later, the screens revealed the result: two hits. Vasilov just hoped the targets hadn't gotten a message off.

One of the satellites began repositioning to surveil the wreckage of the *Arktika*. Prior to now, they had purposefully avoided direct surveillance on the off chance that it would tip off the Alliance about their attack.

An hour later, the video feed showed the location. The massive icebreaker was gone, a pond of blue-green water left in its wake. A large red X was spread out in the ice, with dozens of white tents at one arm, glowing green and purple in the dim light of the aurora borealis. Four lifeboats floated in the still water.

"Captain?" the tactical officer asked.

"Start with two."

Through the windows of the bridge, she saw the missiles take flight. The screens went white as the weapons reached their destination.

☣

Lin climbed into the submersible, dragging the suit behind her. Nigel was shaking violently now.

"Hang on, Doctor Greene. You'll be warm soon."

Peyton unfolded the thick blankets and wrapped them around Nigel. Lin placed the open end of the suit against the electric heater's vent. Nigel stared at it, shivering.

"The suit's been on ice for thirty years," Lin said. "You don't want to get in yet."

Peyton ran her hands up and down Nigel's body, trying to warm him.

A few minutes later, Lin pulled the suit back from the heater and tipped it, letting the water pour out onto the floor. She ran a rolled-up blanket inside, doing her best to dry the legs, arms, and torso area.

When Nigel was suited up, the three of them crawled back into the *Beagle* and set about finishing their part of the preparations. They sealed the bulkhead doors surrounding the docking port, then walked back to the supply closet, where they each took a sack and filled it with duct tape and flashlights. They snaked through the passageways, gathering up the LED lights on the floor and placing them in their sacks. At the rows of bunks, they rolled the corpses toward the wall and peeled off the sheets and blankets. Their plan required everyone they could find.

They closed every door and sealed every hatch they encountered. In the spaces in between, they periodically stopped, squatted low, and stretched a folded piece of duct tape across the corridor— creating false trip lines just above ankle height. The two Navy SEALs had deployed similar measures, except some of theirs were connected to actual explosives. The key was to slow the enemy, to wear away at his vigilance. Make him get sloppy.

In the longer passageways, they hung the blankets and taped them to the ceiling, walls, and floor. Beyond these, they spread out the LEDs and put flashlights in position. Adams had predicted that their adversary would have night-vision goggles. These blankets would create a wall that, when removed, would release a blinding flash of light.

Finally, they met up with Adams and Rodriguez in the labs. The chambers would be their citadel—the arena where they would fight to the end, if forced.

The SEALs merely nodded when they entered.

Meals, Ready-to-Eat sat on a steel-topped table. In the corner sat a stack of guns and magazines—the sum total of the contents of the weapons lockers on the *Beagle*. Adams had insisted that they empty them, depriving their enemy of ammunition.

Over the comm line, Lin said, "What's next, Mister Adams?"

"We've prepared the *Beagle*. Now we prep ourselves. We eat, sleep—in shifts—and stay ready."

Lin said nothing, just moved to the table and took one of the MREs. She raised her visor and began eating.

Peyton did the same. Until the first bite reached her mouth, she didn't realize how hungry she was.

She awoke to the sound of thunder.

The lab was dimly lit. Rodriguez sat with an automatic rifle in his lap, watching the choke point they had created.

There couldn't be thunder down here, Peyton thought. It was from above. The surface. A bomb. Or missile.

Yes. The surface had been attacked. The last survivors of the *Arktika* were dead.

She had no doubt the Citium soldiers would come for them next.

CHAPTER 10

CONNER HATED WAITING, sitting in the van, doing nothing while his brother regained his memories. And when the curfew began, he'd have no choice but to stay put. He needed to stretch his legs. More than that: he needed to *do* something.

"I'm going in," he muttered.

In the front seat, Goins turned back.

"To the office," Conner clarified as he got out of the van. "Des may have hidden something for himself there."

Conner had been to the building many times. He didn't have a key, but Yuri did, and he had sent that key with him. He entered the building, climbed the stairs to the third floor, and pushed open the glass door to Desmond's office. The Icarus Capital logo was emblazoned on the wall in routed aluminum letters. Below it was a directory of companies the firm had invested in, each company name written on a piece of paper slotted behind clear plastic.

RAPTURE THERAPEUTICS, PHAETHON GENETICS,
RENDITION GAMES, CEDAR CREEK ENTERTAINMENT,
ROOK QUANTUM SCIENCES, EXTINCTION PARKS,
LABYRINTH REALITY, CITYFORGE,
CHARTER ANTARCTICA

Conner remembered some of the investments. They were like Desmond's children. He even incubated some right here in his office when they were getting started.

Desmond had expanded the office over the years, taking over adjacent suites and remodeling along the way. The place had been cared for, a source of pride. But now, it looked like a tornado had hit it. A Citium tactical team had searched it from top to bottom when Desmond went rogue, and they had left nothing unturned. The fabric of the office chairs had been cut open, and the foam ripped out; the round legs of the cheap IKEA desks had been unscrewed, searched, and tossed in a pile like gray metal matchsticks; even the tiles in the drop ceiling had been removed, exposing the air conditioning ducts and sprinkler lines. They had been thorough.

What do I know that they didn't?

Conner's eyes drifted back to the directory.

I know where Desmond hid his memories.

Conner walked past the reception desk and pulled out the piece of paper with Labyrinth Reality on it. There was nothing else written on the paper, but in the spot in the directory from which he had pulled it, there was a hole—right through the drywall.

Conner clicked on his flashlight and peered in. A small object was taped to a metal stud. A USB drive. He examined it closely, checking for signs of a tripwire or alarm. Then he took it out, placed it in his pocket, and returned to the van.

☣

After running a thorough virus scan, Conner opened the drive. It contained only one file, titled Conner.mp4.

He thought about deleting it. That's what Yuri would do. He would say, "stay focused."

Conner took the earbuds out of his bag, plugged them into the laptop's headphone jack, and hit play.

Desmond appeared on-screen. He was seated on a private jet, and seemed to be the only passenger. "If you're not Conner," he said, "please give this video to him."

Desmond gazed out the window for a second as if gathering his thoughts. Then he turned back to face the camera. "I just left the *Kentaro Maru*. You should have trusted me. This isn't the way I wanted to do this, but you left me no choice." He stared at Conner through the screen. "I'm doing this for us. And a lot of other people. Trust me. Please, brother. I'm going to need your help before this is over."

The video ended, and Conner ripped his earbuds out. He glanced over at Desmond, lying on the hospital bed, the monitor beeping, the screen showing his brain waves. *What have you done, Des?*

☣

Desmond lost all sense of time. He slept, he ate, and he ran, mostly to clear his mind, but also to get some fresh air. He spent every second in between in the library overlooking San Francisco Bay, reading, taking notes, and thinking about Yuri's riddle. He had answers, and he was anxious to tell Yuri.

The older man arrived around sunset, as he usually did, a placid expression on his face.

"Chess?"

"I'd rather talk," Desmond said.

Yuri sat.

Jennifer, the receptionist, opened the stained-wood double doors and strode across the room, her heels first clicking on the hard-wood floors, then falling silent on the antique rugs. "Coffee?" she asked. "Dinner?"

"No, thank you," Desmond said.

Yuri shook his head.

When the doors closed behind her, Desmond pointed to a stack of books on the table, all volumes of the *Archives of the Citium Conclaves*. "It was in there," he said. "The clues."

Yuri raised his eyebrows.

"Evolution. Survival of the *fittest*. Fittest is a thoroughly mis-understood concept in the theory. Fitness is determined by the environment. It's not about being the biggest or the baddest. It's about being *fit*—the best adapted to the world you find yourself in."

A grin curled at Yuri's lips, as if he and Desmond now shared a secret. "That's right."

"That's what's different about Australia."

"Go on."

"It's isolated. Sure, it took a monumental feat in the ancient world to reach it, but the living was good after. Plenty to eat. Plenty of room to spread out. The continent is getting warm now, but it was a paradise back then."

Yuri made no reaction.

Desmond took a book from the stack. "Here's another example —from one of the *Beagle*'s research expeditions. They found humanoid bones on the Indonesian island of Flores. This species— *Homo floresiensis*—is descended from a completely different branch of the human family tree. Our last shared ancestor lived 1.75 million years ago.

"Like the Australians, they were the innovators of their age. The *Beagle* researchers found stone tools on Flores that are 190,000 years old. And then there's the mystery of how they even got there in the first place. The island of Flores is over six miles from the nearest landmass. These ancient humans must have made rafts or boats almost two hundred thousand years ago. Unless they crossed a land bridge that was wiped out at some subsequent point. Either way, it was adventurous, and would have taken some serious brain power."

"Yes," Yuri said, as if he knew where Desmond was going.

"So this species is isolated on the island of Flores, which is roughly five thousand square miles, about half the size of Massachusetts. There's only so much plant and animal life on the island. And like Darwin observed, they adapt. They evolve to become the fittest humans for this microenvironment. That didn't mean being big or fast, or even strong. On Flores, it meant being *small*. The *Beagle* researchers estimated, based on the bones they found, that these humans were about three and a half feet tall on average."

"And you think that's related to the Australians?"

"It's the same phenomenon. Case studies of evolution in a vacuum—on two islands. Both populations adapted to their environments—environments that didn't require them to innovate. So they reached equilibrium... and stagnated."

"It could be said that Earth is an island. In space."

"That will reach equilibrium," Desmond said. "And stagnate. Then decline. Is that your plan? To leave Earth?"

Yuri paused. "In a sense."

"What does that mean?"

"The universe beyond is dangerous, too."

"Okay..."

"You've done good work, Desmond. But you've only scratched the surface of the truth."

"Then that's depressing, because I've dug through half the volumes in this library."

"Your level of effort isn't your problem."

"All right, I'll bite. What's my problem?"

"You're digging in the wrong place."

"Clearly."

Yuri smiled. It was a sympathetic, almost grandfatherly gesture. "You're here to learn more than facts, Desmond."

The younger man raised his eyebrows.

"Patience. Our road is long and difficult. There are no short-cuts." Yuri gestured at the stack of books that detailed the Citium conclaves. "It took them over two thousand years to discover the full truth. True knowledge is earned, not given."

"Right." Desmond opened his notebook. "So, you were going to give me a map, or a bigger shovel, or something?"

"A question. Humans who looked like us appeared roughly two hundred thousand years ago. For a long time, they were unremarkable. Just another human species, taking root in Africa and struggling to survive. But forty-five thousand years ago, some-thing changed. Not physically—our ancestors still looked like you and me—but they behaved differently. *Thought* differently. We call that event the appearance of "behaviorally modern" humans. This revolution occurred at roughly the same time those intrepid explorers carved their boats, sailed the open sea, and landed on the shores of Australia. It's a very peculiar development."

Desmond nodded. "I agree."

"What happened next is perhaps the greatest mystery of all

time. Around the world, other human species all went extinct in the space of fifteen thousand years. Neanderthals. Denisovans. *Floresiensis*. Some of these human species were very advanced, not unlike us. They made tools, mastered fire. Hunted in groups and cared for their sick and elderly. They were, as you have noted, very fit for their environments. In Europe, the Neanderthals conquered the frigid climate hundreds of thousands of years ago. Our species, *Homo sapiens*, did so again, more recently. We were newcomers, adapted for the warm environment of Africa, with its savannas and open grassland—not the forests, and mountains, and long winters of Europe—yet we prevailed. And expanded. And eventually took over. For the first time since the emergence of the first proto-humans, there was only one human species on Earth. Us."

"That's your second mystery? Understanding why that happened?"

"That's only half of it. At the same time the other human species disappeared, other primates survived. And they survive today. Chimpanzees, gorillas, and bonobos all still walk the Earth. Why? Why did we survive while the others went extinct? Why did the other primates survive as well? *That* is the mystery."

In the van off Sand Hill Road, Conner watched the footage from the drones. The National Guard units were moving closer.

"Units two, three, and four," he said over the radio. "Abandon your vehicles and take up covered positions in the woods."

From the van's front seat, Goins turned to face Conner. "If they look in the vans, they'll see the gear and ordnance."

It was a good point, one Conner hadn't considered. But he would never concede that fact. He glared at the man. "I wasn't finished, Major."

He activated the radio again. "Take all possible measures to cover the van's contents and make sure they're locked."

To Dr. Park, he said, "How long?"

"How long for what?"

"Until the memory finishes, Doctor. Focus."

"I don't—"

"Guess."

He exhaled. "Fifteen minutes? Maybe a little more or less."

"Can we move this van?"

Park's eyes grew wide. Conner knew that expression.

"Speculate, Doctor. If we moved a block away, into a more hidden place, what *might* happen?"

"I have no frame of reference to even speculate."

"Doctor."

"Okay... The memory could stop. Or he could become a vegetable. Or nothing. Maybe it would just keep going. I have no idea."

Goins looked back at Conner, awaiting instructions.

"We stay put," Conner said. "The four of you," he motioned to the mercenaries, "get out and cover the van from the treeline. We'll hide the equipment. The doctor and I will stay with Desmond." He pointed to the beeping monitor. "Can you silence that thing?"

Park punched a button, and the noise ceased.

Ten minutes later, Conner, the doctor, and Desmond lay in the back of the van, covered in thick blankets and empty boxes. They had done their best to make the back of the van look like it was an abandoned shelter.

Conner waited and listened. The minutes dragged by. Finally, he heard the Humvees roar into the parking lot. Doors opened. Boots on the pavement, running. Someone shouting assignments to the troops sweeping the building.

Footfalls, closer, moving toward them. Someone tried the handle to the driver's-side door, found it locked.

Conner gripped his sidearm.

CHAPTER 11

DEEP INSIDE THE *Beagle*, Peyton tried to make herself sleep. Since childhood, she had always dreaded going to sleep. She had often lain awake, obsessing over things, her mind playing out scenarios, rehearsing the future.

She turned over and pulled the thick stack of blankets tight against her. They were cold to the touch. She was still freezing. She, Lin, Nigel, and Seaman Rodriguez lay next to each other on the floor, trying to pool their body heat under the blankets. Their helmets were off, conserving their oxygen.

Chief Adams sat by the entrance, an automatic rifle across his lap. The glow of a video monitor cast the sharp lines of his face in shadow. There was no motion on the four night-vision cameras he'd placed throughout the sub.

An LED bar clicked on right next to Peyton. She saw her mother's face staring at her.

"You need to rest, dear."

"Look who's talking."

"Peyton."

"All right," she muttered.

She closed her eyes, faking sleep like she had done countless times as a child.

"I've seen that routine a time or two."

Peyton opened her eyes.

"What are you thinking about?" Lin asked.

"The attack."

Lin stared at her a moment. "And?"

Peyton hesitated. "Desmond."

"We'll find him."

"You don't know that."

"But I believe it. And you have to believe it. Don't give up hope. It's a very powerful thing, darling."

A silent moment passed.

"If they get Rendition from him, what will they do with him?"

Lin glanced away. "Desmond means a great deal to Conner. He wouldn't harm him."

"Desmond betrayed him."

"Forgiveness is what makes families work."

Peyton knew her mother was actually talking about her brother. "I hope you're right—"

The groaning sound of ripping metal echoed through the sub like a sea creature crying out from above.

Nigel sat up, wild-eyed, breathing fast. "Are they here?"

Rodriguez slipped out from under the blankets and grabbed his rifle.

Adams kept his focus on the monitor.

The sub shuddered.

"Was that a missile?" Nigel asked.

A beating sound thrummed through the vessel, slow at first, then a rush, like a thousand wild horses charging across the sub's hull.

Lin's voice was calm, as if she were merely inquiring about the weather. "Assessment, Mister Adams."

"She's taking on water."

"Source?"

"Unknown. Best guess is the docking port."

It took Peyton a second to put it together. The tearing metal sound was their submersible being pushed away from the *Beagle*, leaving the docking port open, which was letting water flood into the sub. She and her mother had sealed the bulkhead doors around that section, so there was no risk of further flooding, but this meant their only method of reaching the surface was gone. They were now completely trapped. If help didn't come, they would die down here, starving and frozen, just like the crew of the *Beagle* did thirty years ago.

Lin gave no hint of the fear Peyton felt. "Revised recommendations, Chief?"

"Doubt they'll press the attack immediately, ma'am. They know we heard it. They want us to panic, tire ourselves out."

"I concur." Lin turned to Nigel and Peyton. "Let's get some rest. We'll soon need it."

Nigel rolled his eyes. "Sure. No problem. There's just one tiny little thing bothering me about the revised *recommendations*. We—are—*trapped* down here! I mean, are we even going to talk about that?"

"No, Doctor Greene, we're not. We will, however, solve that particular problem when the time comes."

"Great, great," he said, nodding theatrically. "Just, you know, speaking for myself here, I'd like a brief preview of this *magical solution* that will free us from this frozen prison at the bottom of the ocean. I'm just saying—it would help me sleep."

Lin shot a glance at Peyton, then focused on Nigel. "You'll have to trust me, Doctor Greene. And *after* we get out of here, you'll have to trust me a lot. So get used to it." She settled back under the blankets and pulled them to her chin. "Now I'm going to get some sleep. I suggest you all do the same."

A sly grin crossed Seaman Rodriguez's face as he slipped under the covers. Nigel followed reluctantly, and Peyton nestled close to her mother once again.

Lin clicked off the LED light. A few minutes passed in silence. To Peyton, they felt like hours. Every creak and sound was like an alarm. She listened, wondering each time if the attack had begun.

As her eyes adjusted to the darkness, broken only by the dim green glow from the monitor, she could make out her mother's face. Lin's eyes were open and determined.

"Penny for your thoughts," Peyton whispered, reciting the phrase her mother had said to her countless times.

"I wouldn't sell my thoughts for all the tea in China." Lin smiled. "But I'd *give* them to you." She paused. "Altamira."

"The cave. The picture with the ancient paintings."

Lin nodded.

"You think Doctor Kraus hid something there—for you to find."

"Probably."

"If…" Peyton swallowed. "*When* we get out of here, that's our destination?"

"No. Not at first."

"Where then?"

"Oxford."

Peyton knew her mother had done research at Oxford during the years they lived in London. As a child, she had always dreaded the days when her mother took the train to and from Oxford. She would depart early, before Peyton awoke, and would return home late, after Peyton had gone to bed. And she was always tired the next morning.

"Why?" she asked.

"The oath."

"The Latin phrase on the picture. What does it mean?"

"It's an oath taken before you can be admitted to the Bodleian Library. It's been signed and uttered by some of the most famous scientists and leaders in history."

"And by you?"

"Yes. I believe Kraus hid something there—for me to find. He wants me to start there."

Nigel sat up, not bothering to keep his voice low. "You can't be serious."

"Doctor Greene?" Lin said flatly.

"It's a needle in a haystack. I graduated from Oxford. There are millions of volumes at the Bod."

"I know what I'm looking for, Doctor Greene."

"What's that?"

"I'll tell you when we get there. Now I really am going to sleep."

In the Citium submersible *Ice Harvest*, Captain Furst opened his eyes and silenced the alarm. The two remaining men in his team roused as well. It was time to begin.

They cleared the floor and laid out the map of the *Beagle* Yuri Pachenko had supplied. After disconnecting the Shaws' submersible from the sub, they had reconnoitered the ship's perimeter, noting hull breaches, and updated the map, coloring the flooded sections in blue.

The lab complex was located in the center of the middle deck. The Citium had valued that space above all others in the vessel: it was shielded with redundant bulkheads and had a separate air and power supply. There was little question that the Shaws had retreated there. It was defensible, but Furst had the tools to overcome anything they threw at him. And the truth was, Lin and Peyton Shaw had nowhere to go. Killing or capturing them was simply a matter of time.

Furst pointed to a compartment on the same deck as the lab complex, nearly sixty feet away. "We'll insert here. Prep the rovers."

One of his men took a rover from the shelf and duct taped a handheld radio to the top, careful not to cover the camera. He repeated the task with the second rover, then held up his own radio. "Radio check."

The other man tested the plasma torch, then turned his attention to the ship's controls. They moved close to the sub and hovered. The horizontal docking tube extended and attached, its magnetic clamps echoing loudly. The water drained from the tube, and the man affixed his helmet. He turned to Furst, who had also donned his helmet in preparation for the frigid burst of air, and awaited the order.

Furst nodded. "Proceed, Chief."

The man opened the hatch, crawled to the hull, and lit the torch. They'd be in soon.

☣

The sound was like a gong tolling. Peyton sat up.

Adams was on his feet. Rodriguez too.

"What's—"

"They're breaching," Adams said. "Get ready."

☣

On the screen inside the *Ice Harvest*, Furst watched the rovers depart in opposite directions. Each was operated by one of his men, who stared at the night-vision video feed as they drove. The green-tinted view of the sub's passageways was like a documentary tour of a shipwreck.

"Got something."

On the left screen, Furst saw what looked like a blanket stretched across the corridor.

"Use the arm to lift it up and look under. Don't cross the threshold."

On the screen, the blanket lifted, revealing a wall of white.

The chief switched off night vision.

Three rows of crew bunks stretched out four deep. Bodies had been rolled to the back, the blankets removed. A dozen round LED lights the size of hockey pucks were spread out on the floor, with a few in each bunk.

"Pull the blanket down," Furst said. "And proceed."

His eyes moved over to the cans of smoke and tear gas they had set out for their plan. He'd have to adjust slightly.

"Trip wire," the other specialist called out. "Improvised."

Furst watched the rover's camera arm extend and pan.

"It's not live," the specialist said.

"Cut it down."

The next trip wire *was* live—rigged to what looked like C4. Smart—they had rigged the explosives deep in the ship, far enough from the hull.

Furst marked it on the map.

An hour later, the rovers had searched all the corridors they could. Each now sat at a locked hatch. The lab complex wasn't far beyond.

⚕

Chief Adams stared at the screen. "They've got a rover." He squinted. "Something strapped on top. Could be explosives."

"They're searching for us?" Peyton asked.

"Yes, ma'am," Adams replied. "And disabling our counter-measures."

"We could kill the rover," Rodriguez said.

Adams didn't take his eyes off the screen. "Too risky. Might be trying to draw us out."

"Draw us out?" Nigel asked, clearly disturbed.

"They could be waiting near the rover, ready to attack."

Peyton was again impressed with Adams. Even under pressure, he was focused and clear-headed.

Adams studied the screen. "Okay, make that two rovers."

"Where does that leave us?" Lin asked.

"We wait for now."

⚕

Furst and his men snaked through the passageways, deploying trip lines of their own, careful to avoid the enemy explosives they'd identified. They were almost ready.

⚕

The sound of metal on metal captured everyone's attention. Adams rotated the monitor so they could see it. In the corridor where the first rover still sat, a can was rolling toward it, smoke billowing from one end.

"Tear gas," Adams muttered.

Another can rolled down the passageway where the second rover waited. Then a second can rolled out in both corridors, belching a thicker cloud. Smoke. The camera's view of the corridor was completely blocked, and all they could hear was a soft hissing.

"They're trying to box us in," Adams said.

"It seems they're doing a good job," Nigel spat.

Lin shot him a look that landed like a slap to the face. The British scientist fell silent.

"Mister Adams?"

"We can wait, make our stand here."

"Or?"

"Or we go out there, fight at a place and time of our choosing."

"And then what?"

Adams shook his head. "One thing we know for sure: there's only one way off this sub and back to the surface."

"Their submersible."

"Yes, ma'am."

"What are you proposing?" Peyton said.

"Rodriguez and I will take the fight to them. The three of you will take a different route, search for their vessel and escape."

Silence fell over the group.

"There's no other way," Adams said. "They're going to blow one or both of those hatches next. They'll use the rovers, and tear gas, and smoke, and they'll keep tightening the noose on us. We'll all have to suit up soon. We'll have a few hours of oxygen left—assuming a bullet doesn't puncture our suits. Time is not on our side. We have to make a move."

"Making a move could be dangerous," Lin said. "We have to assume they've placed their own booby traps throughout the ship."

Adams nodded.

"And even if you and Seaman Rodriguez neutralize the enemy, we face a difficult task getting out. We need a clear route. There's another solution here, one we've overlooked."

Adams raised his eyebrows.

"The item strapped to the rover."

"I'm assuming it's an explosive—for use on the hatch."

"A reasonable bet, but I count it as unlikely," Lin said. "Our adversary would be averse to sacrificing a rover—they need them to clear beyond the hatch."

"Then…"

"It's a radio."

Peyton didn't follow her mother's line of reasoning.

"There's another way out," Lin said. "For all of us. But it will require Peyton and I to risk our lives."

She glanced at Peyton, seeking support.

Adams shook his head, as if disgusted by the idea. "Negative, ma'am. Our first priority—"

"I'm in," Peyton. "I'm tired of leaving people to die."

Peyton followed her mother through the passageway, their helmet lights carving beams into the darkness. Adams had put up a good fight, but he'd soon realized how futile it was to argue with Lin Shaw when her mind was made up.

"Many years ago, in Rio de Janeiro," Lin said over the comm, "Yuri and I were kidnapped. Beaten, held for ransom. Your father rescued us. He came alone and, five minutes later, he walked out with both of us, without a shot fired. He was very brave that night." She paused. "I still think that's why Yuri couldn't bring himself to kill your father all those years ago, on the night he sank the *Beagle*. He sent men to kill him, but when your father escaped, Yuri let him go. I believe he realized then how much your father meant to him."

Peyton had already read this story in the pages her father had left behind for her and Desmond, but she didn't interrupt. This sounded like a confession the older woman needed to make.

"After Rio, your father insisted that every person leaving the ship be equipped with some sort of personal defense device." She stopped at a closet and pried the frozen doors open. "These are those devices. They're going to save our lives. And the rest of our team. But you have to be careful, Peyton. If you're careless, it will be *your* life you take."

Peyton sat with her back to the wall, her helmet at her side, waiting, wondering if her mother was right. Wondering if she could do her part to save them. She had never been so nervous in all her life. She was about to fight to the death. She felt like throwing up, but she wanted to be brave. She had to—for Desmond, for her mother, and for the three men down there counting on her.

A gravelly voice rang out in the silence, broadcasting from the radio on the rover. The voice was picked up by the cameras at the two hatches.

"Doctor Lin Shaw. Doctor Peyton Shaw. We're not here to harm you. We got off on the wrong foot on the ship. I'm not sure what my men did or said to upset you. I regret the loss of life."

He waited.

"We don't want anyone else to get hurt. I mean that. If we were going to kill you, we would have simply left. We're here because we want to bring you back *unharmed*. Those were my orders. Those directions came from Yuri *and Desmond*."

Peyton and Lin locked eyes. Lin shook her head.

"It's true. Desmond has recovered his memories. He knows the truth now. Peyton, he sent us here to bring you and your mother back. He's very worried. The world is going to change soon."

Peyton's mind raced. *What if it's true?*

"Our adversary is clearly well-trained in the art of deception," Lin said.

Like clockwork, her mother always knew what Peyton was thinking.

"Listen, doctors. If you've got other people with you, they can come too. But first, the two of you need to meet us in the mess deck. Come alone, unarmed. We know the route you're going to take. We've got cameras. And a rover. We'll be following you. Don't deviate. If anyone else comes along, they'll be blown to bits."

A pause.

"You have five minutes to get to the mess deck. If you're not there, we're coming in after you. Please, doctors. Make the smart choice. Nobody has to get hurt."

Lin stood with her helmet held at her side, like an astronaut getting ready to step out onto a foreign planet. "It's time, Peyton."

Peyton could barely feel her body as she got to her feet. She was shaking.

Lin placed her hands on Peyton's shoulders. "One step at a time. Stay focused. Don't think about it. Just take the next step."

She picked up Peyton's helmet and put it on her, then donned her own.

Peyton tried to slow her breathing. The sound was loud in the helmet.

"Focus on my voice, Peyton."

Her mother brought her helmet to Peyton's. They touched. Lin stared at her.

"You can do this."

CHAPTER 12

THE XI PANDEMIC had hit the *USS Carl Vinson* especially hard. Of the aircraft carrier's typical five-thousand-person crew, nearly a thousand had died. Those remaining all wanted one thing: payback.

They had been searching the Pacific Ocean for weeks, trying to locate the Citium base of operations. Around the clock, planes took off and landed, and their search results were mapped, the grid slowly filling in.

In the bowels of the ship, in a small stateroom, Avery Price assembled her rifle. She stared at it, then reset the timer and began breaking it apart again. The exercise reminded her of her training in Northern Virginia. The focused, repetitive action was like meditation for her.

During their off hours, other members of the crew lifted weights, watched movies on their laptops, emailed home, played video games, or knocked boots in their bunks—despite the regulations against it. Avery did none of those things. She thought about Desmond, and when she couldn't help it, wondered if they were torturing him. And most of all, she wondered if he had remembered. She desperately hoped the *Carl Vinson* was the ship that found him. She had unfinished business with him—and the men who had taken him. Desmond had sacrificed himself for her, traded his life for hers. She didn't like being in anyone's debt. But it was more than that. A lot more than that.

The clock on the wall read nearly fourteen hundred hours when an alarm blared from the ceiling, and a naval officer said, "General quarters. General quarters. All hands man your battle stations."

Yes, Avery thought. *We've found the Citium.*

Minutes later, she stood on the ship's bridge. The comm officers were in a frenzy. The XO was barking orders over the shipboard radio.

Captain Barrow stood still, staring into the middle of the tempest as if deep in thought.

"I'll lead the strike team," Avery said. "The corpsman just cleared me," she lied.

"What?"

"My boots hit the ground first—"

"We haven't found them, Price. Comm's down." Barrow turned to the XO. "Execute course change, Commander."

Course change. Avery glanced around. "Where're we going?"

"Our rally point. Standing orders in case of a global comm failure. Now get out of here, Price."

"You think this is an attack."

Barrow was losing patience. "Yes. A virus infected our equipment." He squinted. "Wait. Your jacket said you were a programmer before. Get down to—"

Avery realized what was happening—and who was truly under attack. She had to get to Peyton and Lin Shaw.

"I need a helo and a special ops team."

He laughed. "Get out. Now."

"Listen to me, Captain. Disabling the internet and global comms is part of the Citium plan."

"Apparently." He nodded to a tall, muscular sailor standing at parade rest by the hatch. "See that Miss Price makes her way back to her quarters—"

"Captain."

The sailor gripped her arm.

She grabbed his hand and twisted his thumb until he winced,

but his grip didn't break. "You don't want to do that," she said calmly. She focused on the captain. "Allow me to speak for ten seconds, sir. You need to hear this."

Barrow gave a quick nod to the man gripping Avery's arm. He let his hand fall away.

"Ours isn't the only Rubicon operation. There's another one— above the Arctic Circle. A partnership with the Russians. If we're in a blackout, there's a reason. The other mission is likely under attack. We need to send a team to investigate."

"I have my orders, Miss Price. And I take them seriously. Every person and every aircraft could be needed to defend the United States."

He motioned to the sailor. "Make sure she's in her quarters until further notice."

CHAPTER 13

LIN INSISTED ON walking twenty feet ahead. The beams from Peyton's helmet shone into the darkness, revealing only a faint glimpse of her mother's lithe form. She knew her mother well, and why the older woman was putting herself out front: to protect Peyton. Her mother was placing herself in front of her daughter—in case there were more booby traps.

Lin's voice was calm over Peyton's helmet speaker. "Stay where you are."

"What's wrong?"

"I'm at the hatch."

Lin grunted. The roar of steel on steel echoed in the dark passage, like an ancient vault being opened.

Smoke and gas billowed into the passageway. It dispersed and settled near the deck like a layer of fog.

"Let's resume," Lin said.

Peyton tried to control her nerves as she walked through the mist. Each step could be her last. She stumbled and braced herself against a wall.

Lin whispered, "I see the rover. Peyton, join me so they can see us both."

Peyton turned the corner and found her mother standing in the sea of smoke up to her knees, the beams of her helmet pointed down at the rover, boring a hole through the cloud. She stopped beside her. The rover spun on one track like a toy tank, drove around them, and stopped at the hatch. It was standing watch—for anyone following behind them.

Lin resumed walking. Peyton followed, her heart beating faster with every step. A trickle of sweat ran down her forehead, into her eyes.

The smoke dispersed as they went.

A message had been scrawled on a piece of paper taped to the bulkhead up ahead.

REMOVE HELMETS

Lin removed hers first, extinguishing the two beams of light.

Peyton reached up and placed her gloved finger on her helmet's latch. This was the most dangerous part of the plan. Once the helmets were off, their adversary could use tear gas or mace. Or take them down a hundred other ways.

It didn't matter. There was no turning back.

She unlatched the helmet and slipped it off. The freezing air assaulted her face and flowed into the suit, the smell slightly acidic with a hint of gun smoke.

They stood in darkness, waiting. Footfalls echoed ahead. Then behind. Two. Maybe three. If there were three, that would be a problem. She and her mother had planned on two. They could only handle two.

A narrow beam of light came on, like a train in a tunnel.

Peyton was blinded for a moment. When her eyes adjusted, she could make out two figures behind the light.

"Take the suits off, ladies." She recognized the gravelly voice from the radio.

"It's too cold," Lin said, emotionless.

"Then you better hurry."

Lin hesitated, then glanced at Peyton and began removing her suit.

Moment of truth.

Peyton's hands shook as she took off the bulky garment. She

didn't know if it was her nerves or the cold, but with each passing second, she shivered more.

When the suit fell to the ground, she stood in her boots and a layer of insulated clothes over thermal underwear. The gun she had hidden under the bulky clothes bulged at her waist. She felt naked, as if they could see the weapon clearly. The gun hidden below Lin's clothes was even more obvious.

The man's tone turned playful. "You ladies are more voluptuous than we expected." The levity left his voice. "You reach for those guns and we'll shoot you. I won't warn you again."

A pause. No one moved.

"Now lift your arms and hold them straight out. Lin, turn around, face away, and march backward toward me. Peyton, stay where you are. Don't move."

Lin turned and walked backward, careful not to trip over the suits on the floor. She stared at Peyton, her eyes shining, unblinking. In her mind, Peyton could hear her mother's unspoken words. *Be brave, darling.*

A hand gripped Peyton's side, right below her breast, reached under her shirt, and yanked the gun free, holster and all. It fell to the metal floor.

A second man approached Lin from behind and removed her gun.

So there were three men. The two who had disarmed them, plus the gravelly-voiced man holding the light.

The man behind her reached around and ran his hands down her chest. Hands gripped Lin as well.

The older woman acted first. She spun, grabbed the man's neck, and squeezed.

A bolt of terror went through Peyton. Just as quickly, her instincts took over. She pressed her thumb into the ring on her index finger, exposing the three needles on the bottom. She lashed out at the man. Her hand connected with his neck, right at his carotid artery.

Behind her, she heard the other soldier gasping for air as the toxin from Lin's ring paralyzed him.

The man holding Peyton released his grip and collapsed to his knees. He glared with malice in the dim light.

"You b—"

Foam flowed from his mouth as he fell forward.

Peyton depressed the button on the ring and slid it off. It hit the floor with a clink. It was a single-use device, but she didn't want to risk injecting herself, in case there was any residual poison.

Behind her, the beam of light jerked wildly, like a strobe in a night club. Lin screamed.

Peyton turned. In the flashes of light, she saw that the soldier who had frisked Lin was lying still, but the man with the light was now struggling to hold Lin's arms. He swung the light, hitting her in the face. She screamed, a ragged, bone-chilling sound, and fell to the floor, flailing, crawling toward the gun. The man fell on top of her, reaching for her arms.

"Peyton!" she spat, flecks of blood flying from her mouth. "Please, Peyton."

The man pinned Lin with his elbows and wrapped his hands around her throat.

Peyton staggered forward. Lin's holster and gun lay at her feet. She bent and drew the weapon out, barely able to hold it straight with her shaking hands.

Lin's eyes bulged.

"Let her go." Peyton's voice shook as much as her hands.

The man didn't look up.

"Do no harm, Doc."

Lin's arms fell limp.

"Drop the gun and no one gets hurt."

Lin stared at her daughter, pleading with her eyes. She had seconds to live.

Peyton placed her other hand on the gun, steadying her grip. She pulled the trigger.

CHAPTER 14

THE SOUND OF heels clacking on the library floor drew Desmond's attention. Jennifer sauntered toward him. She wore a navy dress that was tight around her hips, and a white blouse, low-cut and loose around her chest. A tan cardigan hung over her shoulders, her auburn hair falling around it.

She stopped at the long table by the three-story window and set a small, gift-wrapped package in front of Desmond.

He raised his eyebrows.

"A little Christmas gift," she said, shrugging sheepishly.

"I..." He had lost all track of time, didn't even know it was Christmas.

"Just open it, Des."

He pulled the package close, and smiled when he saw the wrapping paper: it was a series of printed pages with screen captures and the logo from the TV series *Alias*.

"Thought you might like the homemade wrapping paper."

"I do. Love that show," he said. He peeled the pages off, revealing three paperback books, all by Phillip Pullman: *The Golden Compass*, *The Subtle Knife*, and *The Amber Spyglass*. The complete trilogy was entitled *His Dark Materials*.

"I figure you can't spend *every* waking hour reading non-fiction in this library. You need some relief."

True. He turned the books over, taking in the covers, then looked up. "I don't have anything—"

"I don't need anything."

He glanced at the books again.

"You know, you also don't have to take all your meals here," she said. "Might do you good to get out."

It would. She was right. But he also knew it would end badly for her. In his mind's eye, he saw them sitting down to dinner—not at a fancy place, but a cozy one, somewhere relaxed, where they could wear whatever they wanted and talk and stay as long as they wanted. He saw them discussing the books she gave him, then each of them talking about where they were from, him dancing around the truth about why he'd left Oklahoma for California. Things would progress from there. And like his relationship with Peyton, it would hit a dead end. That's what he was: an emotional dead end. He was toxic. He would hurt her like he had Peyton. He was lonely, and craved companionship, but he couldn't do it— wouldn't hurt her.

"I'd like to," he said, measuring each word. "But I can't."

She smiled. "You can't read and sleep *all* the time."

"I'm here for a reason."

"So am I."

He thought she was talking about him. He opened his mouth to respond, but she pulled a chair out, sat, and spoke before he could.

"I'm a grad student at Stanford. In physics."

"Oh."

"I'm here for the same reason as you."

He squinted. "You are?"

"My professor is a member of the Citium. I want to join. Most of all," she motioned to the stacks of books on the table, "I want to be admitted to this library. I want to know what they've found. I envy you. You must be very important to them."

Desmond shook his head. "Yuri invited me here—"

"For a reason."

Desmond nodded.

"He wants something from you."

"I have no doubt of that."

They stared at each other, the buzzing lights the only sound in the cavernous space.

"I want something too," Desmond said. "When I was a child, something happened that changed me. I didn't realize it for a long time. Until I fell in love."

"What happened?"

"I discovered that I wasn't capable of loving her the way she loved me. That's why I'm here. I want to be able to change myself. That's what Yuri's promised me."

She stood and smiled, not a happy or amused smile, but one of sympathy and concern. "I hope you find what you need."

CHAPTER 15

THE SHOT WAS deafening in the cramped passageway. Despite Peyton's shaking hands, it hit the man in the shoulder, propelling him off of Lin, into the bulkhead. He screamed, then turned and dove for Peyton.

She staggered back, tripped over the lifeless soldier at her feet, and fell on her rear. But she held tight to the gun.

The wounded man leapt on top of her like a feral animal, grabbing for the gun with his good hand. He grasped her forearm and slammed it into the metal floor. On the second strike, the gun clattered away.

The man crawled over her, dragging his torso over her face, crushing her. The floor felt like a block of ice grinding into the back of her head. He reached for the gun.

Peyton punched him on both sides, but he barely moved, the blows harmless against his body armor. She brought her knee up into his groin. He arched his back, screamed, and glowered at her, hate in his eyes. Peyton squirmed, trying to get away, but she was trapped.

He raised his fist, and his mouth twisted into a grin. He waited, letting the fear grip her, as if he was absorbing power from her, feeding on her fear. Peyton could only raise her arms above her face.

She heard him laugh. In the dim light, she saw her mother lying ten feet away, unmoving. Possibly dead.

A crack silenced his laughter. The man's head exploded like a dropped watermelon. The echo of the gunshot seemed to follow a second later.

His body snapped back, then toppled forward.

Peyton twisted to the side, her face narrowly avoiding the waterfall of blood spilling down. The man landed with a disgusting thud, still pinning her down. She pushed up with her elbows and tried to crawl out, but he was too heavy, and she was too exhausted.

She heard footsteps in the darkness. Hands lifted the dead body up and off her, and threw it aside.

Helmet lights shone down. Through the open visor, she saw Adams, stone-faced, searching her for wounds. Rodriguez appeared over Adams's shoulder.

"I'm okay," Peyton said, panting, shivering. "My mom."

Rodriguez moved over to Lin and knelt beside her. "She's alive."

Peyton felt the tension drain out of her. In its place, she realized how cold she was.

"How many?" Adams asked, his head moving back and forth, scanning the passageway, his gun held at the ready.

How many what? Peyton couldn't seem to process the question, as if the cold was freezing her mind.

Adams glanced down. "Enemy combatants." He paused. "How many troops do they have, Doctor Shaw?"

"We just saw these three."

"Did they reference others? Provide other information?"

Peyton shook her head.

Adams moved over to Rodriguez. "Let's evac."

The two SEALs gathered the suits and women in their arms and made a hasty retreat.

Drifting through the halls in Adams's arms, Peyton suddenly felt so exhausted. The adrenaline was gone, weariness left in its place. Her mother was alive. And she was safe.

☣

Peyton opened her eyes. She was trapped. Tied up, her arms pinned to her sides, her entire body wrapped tightly, only a slit left for her mouth and nose. She was blindfolded, too; only a faint glow of light was visible through the cloth over her eyes.

"Hey."

Her voice was a ragged whisper, her mouth and throat like sandpaper. She tried to swallow.

"Hey."

Movement. A click.

A hand removed the cover from her eyes. The light blinded her.

"Oh, sorry." Nigel's voice. "How're you feeling?"

"Terrible," she muttered. Her chest ached. She felt drained.

"Do you…"

"Water."

"Oh, right."

He returned with a canteen, tipped it, and Peyton chugged. The cool water filled her mouth, then ran over and down the side of her face.

"Sorry, sorry."

Peyton still couldn't move her arms. "Untie me, Nigel."

He looked confused. "You're not—oh. Right. The *commandos* rolled you and your mom up in blankets, like burritos, to warm you up." He set the light down and slipped out of sight. "Hang on."

Seconds later, Peyton was free and sitting up.

Lin lay beside her, sleeping. Peyton hated to wake her, but she had to examine her for internal bleeding.

"Can you help me unwrap her? I want to check her injuries. She took a beating back there."

"Adams and I already examined her."

"And neither of you are physicians."

Nigel helped her unwrap Lin, who stirred but didn't wake. Peyton wondered if she had a concussion.

Bruises and red marks ringed her neck. Peyton checked her head for bumps or swelling. No signs of a subdural hematoma. Pulse was normal. She pulled her mother's shirt up and scanned for bruises and broken ribs. None. The skin was pale and pasty.

It also told a story. Two long scars and three short ones crisscrossed Lin Shaw's abdomen. A puckered wound—the remnant of a gunshot—lay on her right side. Lin had always worn one-piece bathing suits and had never revealed her midsection, even at home. Now Peyton knew why.

Nigel glanced from Lin to Peyton. "What?"

Peyton pulled the shirt down. "She's okay. Just tired."

There was still so much she didn't know about her mother. And the more she learned, the more questions she had.

Adams and Rodriguez returned an hour later. They were hungry, as were Peyton and Nigel. Lin was still asleep, so they ate in silence, waiting for Lin to awaken. She didn't so much as stir. Peyton was starting to worry. Finally the older woman's breathing increased and she opened her bloodshot eyes.

At the sight of Peyton, a flicker of a smile crossed her lips—an unusual show of emotion for the older woman. Just as quickly, it was gone, like a light flipped off.

"Status?" her voice was hoarse.

Peyton held the canteen to her mother's lips while Adams gave a concise report. They had found the Citium submersible and checked it for booby traps. Adams had studied the controls and was confident he could operate it.

Lin sat up, her arms shaking. Peyton handed her an MRE, and Lin ate with an unsteady hand, chewing robotically. "Bring the map," she said when the tray was half gone.

She studied the diagram of the sub and pointed at a compartment two decks above them. "Supplies here."

"Supplies?" Adams asked.

"Expedition gear." She took another bite.

Adams marked the compartment. "So we're going to the surface?"

"Only chance."

Nigel threw his hands up. "Only chance of what? Freezing? Getting bombed?"

"Rescue," Lin said.

"She's right," Adams said. "If a rescue plane flies over, or a drone, they'll have no clue we're down here."

"And if the Citium finds us first?"

"She never said we were *all* going to the surface," Adams said. "Rodriguez and I will take shifts manning the surface."

"No," Lin said. "We stick together. The submersible could break down."

Nigel rolled his eyes. "They'll kill—"

"They won't, Doctor Greene." The strength had returned to Lin's voice. "They won't know who's in the tents—us or their people. We'll strip the uniforms off their men. Adams and Rodriguez will wear them, and they can treat us as prisoners if our adversaries arrive."

Nigel was unconvinced. "Why not just take the submersible out? They launched from *somewhere*. We keep going until we clear the ice, then surface and call for help."

Lin raised an eyebrow. "And starve to death while we wait? The submersible can only carry so much of our rations. It's a dead end." She studied the map. "The food stores are in the mess deck."

"That food's been down here thirty years. Most will be spoiled," Adams said.

"It will have been frozen, and not much of it was perishable, even in the *Beagle*'s day." Lin folded up the map, silently closing the matter. "Let's get started."

⚕

Peyton, Lin, and Nigel stayed below, recuperating, while the two Navy SEALS retrieved the expedition gear and food, took it to the surface, and set up camp. Only when everything was ready did they all leave the *Beagle* behind.

Peyton had dreaded what she would see on the surface—and it was as bad as she feared. The *Arktika* was gone. There was a hole in the ice where it had been, a watery graveyard where the charred remnants of lifeboats floated, grave markers of the *Arktika*'s crew and scientists. And beyond the tents and expedition gear from the *Beagle*, the ice was barren as far as she could see.

She took a moment to inspect the equipment and the two tents. Everything was old but functional, and space heaters had already warmed the tents. Peyton wouldn't exactly be comfortable inside, but she would also be in no danger of losing her fingers and toes. The SEALs had spread LED lights around the camp, forming circles like a bull's-eye. Peyton hoped the rescuers would see it.

She looked to the sky. The aurora was gone, as if the violence and death had driven the spirit away.

Inside their tent, she and her mother ate by the light of an LED bar. They had food for a few weeks, and batteries for the heaters to last a little longer. There was no solar power to recharge them. If help didn't come by then, they'd have to make a hard choice. If the Citium arrived sooner, there would be nowhere to run.

☣

On the bridge of the *Invisible Sun*, Captain Vasilov listened as her communications officer tried the radio again.

"*Ice Harvest*, this is *Invisible Sun*. Do you read?"

Nothing.

Her first officer leaned over. "Could've gotten caught in the crossfire."

"Doubtful. They knew the strike was coming." To the radio tech, she said, "Satellite status?"

"Flyover in seventy-five minutes."

"They could have gotten jammed up in the *Beagle*," the first officer said. "You want to launch the other DSV?"

"Yes. And the helo. Just in case they made it to the surface and their radio is out."

Or if they had been killed. There would be a price to pay for that.

CHAPTER 16

THE NEXT TIME Yuri arrived, Desmond was ready. As usual, he was sitting at the long table by the library's window. But this time he had prepared seven hardcover books. Each lay open in front of him, turned to pages featuring artists' illustrations of prehistoric humans and columns of text showing the details of scientific studies.

Yuri gazed at the books. "I take it you found the answer?"

"We're the Borg."

Yuri's eyebrows knitted together.

"The Borg." Desmond paused, waiting for recognition that never came. "From Star Trek: The Next Generation? You, know, 'We are the Borg. You will be assimilated. Resistance is futile.'"

"I'm not familiar."

"Right." *I should have known.* "Anyway. We assimilated or killed the other human species."

A small smile crossed Yuri's lips. "Go on."

"These are research notes from the *Beagle*. They found archaic bones—Neanderthals in Europe, remnants of another human species in the Denisova cave in Siberia, and bones from *floresiensis* on an Indonesian island. They sequenced the samples. And found something extremely surprising."

Desmond waited, but Yuri said nothing.

"Overlap," Des continued. "DNA from each of these three species is present in modern humans. As our ancestors spread across the world, they wiped out their competition, but that wasn't all: they interbred, too. Europeans share up to 2.8 percent of their DNA with Neanderthals. Chinese, only 0.1 percent. In the islands of the South Pacific, like Papua New Guinea, current inhabitants share up to 2.74 percent of their genomes with Neanderthals. Plus, these islanders have between 1 and 6 percent Denisovan DNA. The researchers on the *Beagle* also theorized that that the Aboriginal Australians interbred with another human species, though they haven't found any remains of that other species yet."

"Good," Yuri said. "It's very good work. And the other half of the mystery?"

Desmond shook his head. "I assumed it was because humans can't interbreed with any of the other primates."

"That's true, but there's a more important reason the chimps, gorillas, and bonobos are still alive."

Desmond exhaled. He had hoped his research phase was finished.

"There's a larger picture here, Desmond. One that will change your entire understanding of the human race."

"Can't wait."

"You're getting frustrated."

"Yes."

"Patience."

"Has never worked for me. Look, I came here because I thought you could help me. I wasn't looking for this... bizarre one-person grad school."

"This is your path."

Desmond stared at the older man. "Well, I need to know that it's going to lead where I want to go. I don't think that's too much to ask. For all I know, this is all some sick joke you're playing on me."

"I don't joke, Desmond."

Desmond sat silently.

"You want to know where this road leads?" Yuri stood. "Follow me." He walked out of the library, not bothering to look back to see if Desmond was following.

They donned their winter coats and got on the elevator. As the doors closed, Desmond nodded at Jennifer, who smiled, a hungry expression that communicated much more. On the street, Yuri led Desmond through the crowded sidewalks of downtown San Francisco. It seemed like everyone in the city was either rushing home from work or out buying last-minute Christmas presents.

They stopped outside a high-end restaurant with wide plate glass windows that looked out onto the street. Snow was beginning to fall. The streetlamps and headlights reflected off the flurries, making them look almost phosphorescent.

"I know what you want, Desmond."

Yuri shifted his gaze from Desmond to the people passing them, then to the restaurant window. White linens covered the tables. Real candles burned inside glass vases. The back wall was lined with half-circle booths, most with wine buckets on silver stands, beads of water forming from the ice inside.

Desmond stopped abruptly, his gaze fixed on a table in the middle of the restaurant. Peyton sat there, a half-empty glass of white wine in front of her, a picked-over piece of fish on her plate, and a placid, almost somber expression on her face. Her dark brown hair looked almost exactly the way it had the day he had driven away.

Peyton's mother sat to her left, and her sister, Madison, and Madison's husband both sat across from her. Peyton had no date. Wore no ring.

Desmond felt a thrill run through him. Then a pang of guilt.

Yuri's soft voice almost startled him.

"You want to know that all of this leads back to her."

Desmond couldn't find the words to respond.

"You want to know that you'll be together when this is over."

Desmond turned to face the older man. He had never even said Peyton's name to Yuri. "What is this?" he asked.

"Proof."

"Of what?"

"That we do our research too, Desmond. Proof that I know exactly what you want. Who you are. What you're capable of. And who you're here for." Yuri paused. "She's waiting for you. But time is running out. You have to dedicate yourself."

"You're manipulating me."

"Yes, but for the right reason. You have a role to play."

"What's *your* role?"

"People. I know what they'll do."

"Oh yeah? What am I going to do?"

Yuri broke eye contact, and his voice was barely audible over the din of people around them. "You'll shake your head, go back to the library, and turn it upside down looking for the answers. You'll find them, and you'll know the truth. We are humanity's only hope. And yours."

☣

Conner listened as the National Guard troops tried the handle on each door to the van.

"Locked," the soldier said. "Looks abandoned."

"Fox Company," a woman's voice said over his radio. "We've got another abandoned van here. Also locked."

Another voice came on the line. "Check the wheel wells and under the tires for keys. If you find them, bring the vehicles back. We could use them for supplies. If not, disable them."

Conner turned his head, whispered. "Time, Doctor?"

"I don't—"

"Guess."

"A few more minutes."

They didn't have a few more minutes. If their vehicles were disabled, they would have to get others, and if the troops searching the area were disabling *all* abandoned vehicles...

Conner activated his comm. "Team two, I need a diversion. Now."

He listened, heard nothing.

A voice outside, on the radio. "Bravo Company. Shots fired near Sand Hill and Saga Way. We're investigating. Request backup."

Boots pounded the pavement. Humvees cranked, tires squealed. Conner waited.

A few minutes later, the platoon leader from Conner's fourth vehicle whispered over the comm. "We're surrounded by hostiles. They're trying to open the van. Orders?"

"Team three," Conner said. "Create another diversion. Quickly. Something louder this time."

In moments, he heard the boom of an explosion. He waited, then: "Two, sit-rep?"

"They left a small platoon. Nothing we can't handle. Should we retake the vehicle and move?"

"Negative. Hold position."

Conner lay there, waiting. They couldn't play this game much longer. Fight or run.

"Sir," the doctor whispered. "Brain waves are back to normal."

"You're sure?" Conner wouldn't risk his brother's life. He'd sacrifice his own first.

"Positive. The memory is finished."

Conner sat up, turned on the satellite phone, and opened the Labyrinth Reality app. When the Citium had disabled the internet worldwide, they had taken great care to isolate the server powering this app. If it were to go down, so would their entire plan.

A prompt asked him how he would like to enter the Labyrinth: as the hero or the Minotaur. As he had before, he tapped *hero*, and another dialog appeared:

Searching for Entrance...

A few seconds later, it read:

1 Entrance Located.

Conner tapped the screen, and the map appeared. It was centered on an address nearby, in Menlo Park, on Windsor Drive—a short residential street that ran between Santa Cruz Avenue and Middle Avenue, near Stanford.

He activated his comm. "All units, we've got a new location. We're moving out. Major Goins, coordinate efforts to liberate our units that are pinned down."

The comm line erupted in chatter. The mercenaries in Conner's van returned. Operatives from the fourth van set a third diversion, this one much larger: a fire in an office building off Monte Rosa Drive. Conner had to resist an urge to admonish them for choosing to set a fire. He could not show weakness—and the fire was the right diversion.

As the van pulled back onto Sand Hill Road, he saw the first plumes of smoke go up. His mouth went dry.

He tried to focus. The location. It seemed vaguely familiar, but he couldn't place it.

He drew out his phone and texted the address to Yuri.

Do you know this address?

A second later, Yuri's response flashed on his screen:

Yes. It was Lin Shaw's home address.

CHAPTER 17

PEYTON AWOKE TO what sounded like popcorn in the micro-wave. It was rhythmic, the pops evenly spaced, and growing louder. As awareness took hold, she realized what it was: a helicopter's rotors.

She tossed off the stack of blankets and reached for the tent's zipper.

"Peyton," her mother called.

She ignored her and rushed outside.

The helicopter hovered a hundred feet away. The aurora borealis had returned, its purple and green glowing bands barely lighting the black vessel in the sky.

Peyton waved her arms. "Hey!"

Adams emerged from his tent, rifle in hand. "Get back inside!"

When Peyton looked up, the helicopter was moving off.

Adams watched it, then strode over to Peyton. The cold was taking hold now, seeping through her clothes.

"Stay inside next time," he said.

"It could have been rescue." She was shivering now.

"Rescuers would have landed."

Peyton knew he was right. She turned and re-entered the tent, with Adams behind her.

"Who was it?" Lin asked.

Adams shook his head. "Didn't get a good look."

Peyton slipped back under the covers. "What will they do?"

"They'll find a place to touch down. Test the ice first, make sure it holds. Then they'll disembark and hike here."

"And?"

"And then they'll attack."

☣

Two hours later, Adams came to Peyton and Lin's tent. He and Rodriguez had set makeshift traps around the camp's perimeter, and they had been alternating guard shifts, but there had been no movement.

"What are they waiting on?" Lin asked.

"Hard to say. Tire us out. Starve us out, maybe." The SEAL was munching on a stick of beef jerky.

"Options?" Lin asked.

"None. We wait."

☣

Peyton heard gunshots outside the tent, then Adams and Rodriguez shouting. She knew she should stay inside, but she couldn't resist peeling the flap back and peeking.

Adams held his rifle at the ready, and was panning left and right. Rodriguez was running full speed, his boots pounding the ice. Beyond the last ring of LED lights, a figure was fleeing, zigzagging. Rodriguez pulled up and took a shot, but the figure kept running, swallowed by the darkness.

Rodriguez watched for several minutes, then began trudging back. Along the way, he stooped and picked something up.

When he arrived at Peyton and Lin's tent, he ducked through the opening and tossed the item at Lin's feet. It was a stake, with a radio taped to it, along with a handwritten note wrapped in plastic.

My name is Avery Price. I'm here for Lin and Peyton Shaw. If they are your prisoners, I am willing to negotiate. If you aren't willing to negotiate, be advised: my team and I will recover them either way. Call me.

"I know her," Peyton said. "She rescued Desmond and me from the *Kentaro Maru*."

Adams rubbed his eyelids. The man was clearly exhausted. "She may have turned. Or is being coerced."

"I know Avery as well," Lin said.

Peyton was shocked. She studied her mother.

"But I don't know what side she's truly on. Let's play this out," Lin said. "Let her talk to someone she trusts." She handed the radio to her daughter.

Peyton clicked the button. "Avery, it's Peyton. Do you read?"

"I read you, Doc. You okay?"

"We're okay. I've got my mom here too."

A pause on the line.

"What's your status?" Avery asked.

"A Citium team sank the icebreaker and chased us to the *Beagle*. We... came out on top down there. We've been waiting for rescue."

"Copy that. Who's with you?"

Adams put his hand over the radio. "Say seven SEALs at the camp and two satellite camps with snipers."

Peyton shook her head. "This is Avery—"

"We take nothing for granted."

Peyton relayed the false report.

"The soldier I saw during the flyover was wearing Citium cold weather gear," Avery said.

"Yes. We assumed they would arrive first—after their people failed to check in."

"Safe assumption. I'm going to ask you a question."

Peyton paused. "Okay."

"After we escaped from the *Kentaro Maru*, you and I fought about something. What was it? Before you answer, know this: if you're a captive, lie. If you don't answer, I'll know for sure."

Peyton smiled. She and Avery *had* fought—in fact, the two had hated each other initially. But Avery had saved Peyton's life.

And after Avery was injured at the battle on the Isle, Peyton had helped save the younger woman's life.

"Hannah. She needed a hospital. We fought over her."

"Yeah, we did, Doc."

"But it turned out okay," Peyton said.

"So will this," Avery said. "I'll come in. Unarmed. Tell your guys not to shoot me."

Ten minutes later, Avery was sitting in the tent, everyone gathered around her.

It was the first time Peyton had seen Avery and Lin together. There was an air of familiarity there, along with something else— mutual caution. Suspicion.

"What's happening out there?" Lin asked Avery.

"I don't know any more than you all. The US military had standing orders to rally to the continental US in the event of a major comms breakdown."

"Where are you operating from?" Adams asked. "A carrier?"

Avery hesitated. "Ah, yeah. But we don't want to go back."

Peyton raised her eyebrows.

"Captain and I had a disagreement about this particular mission."

Peyton shook her head. "You stole the helo?"

"Requisitioned it." Avery shrugged. "Without authorization."

Peyton was starting to like Avery more and more.

"We need to evacuate," Adams said. "I don't like being out in the open here."

"I agree," said Lin.

"What did you find down there?" Avery asked. "Please tell me it's something we can use to stop Yuri." She paused, not making eye contact with Peyton. "And find Desmond."

Peyton looked to her mother.

"Bones from extinct species—as we suspected," Lin said. "Including a human ancestor previously unknown to us. We sequenced genomes of the samples."

"Was the data lost with the *Arktika*?"

Nigel gripped his bag. "No. We got it out."

"As soon as we get to a high-speed internet connection, we need to upload the data," Lin said.

"Upload to where?" Avery asked.

"A data center."

"I got that," Avery muttered. "*Whose* data center?"

"My associates."

Avery leaned forward. "It's Phaethon Genetics, isn't it? During the outbreak, you collected DNA samples and sequenced them at Phaethon. You're storing all the data there, aren't you?" When Lin didn't respond, Avery continued. "In fact, that was your plan all along. That's why you wanted Phaethon to build its own data center. All those queries, they weren't about our mission—curing disease. You were just getting ready for this. Phaethon was a front for your Citium research."

Peyton held up her hands. "Wait—you two worked together at Phaethon?" Her mother's company had hundreds of employees. When Avery first told Peyton her story, Peyton had just assumed their paths had never crossed.

"On occasion," Lin said quietly.

But Avery was angry now. "So all that stuff about 'let's find the genetic basis of disease' was just a cover. Everybody in the company was living a lie."

"You're being dramatic, Avery." Lin looked away. "Now we need to—"

"I want to know what you're doing. I deserve to know. And I'm your only way out of here."

Rodriguez let his hand fall to his side, to the handle of his gun. "I can fly a helo."

Avery's eyes flashed on him. Her hand went to her own gun.

"Stop." Lin's voice was like a hammer blow. "Both of you. We are all leaving here together." To Avery, she said, "Yes. It was a cover. But for all the right reasons. I believe you're familiar with that concept."

"I want to know the reason that was so right."

"Two thousand years ago, the Citium was founded to answer a simple question: What is humanity's destiny?"

Avery rolled her eyes. "You've got to be kidding me. You're a true believer."

"I am a believer in science. And I believe we are on the verge of the greatest discovery in history. The answer is written in our genes, a code that will unlock the mysteries of our existence. And lead us out of the darkness."

Avery exhaled heavily and scratched her head. "I'm ready to fly out of the darkness here, so why don't you give me the English version of what you're talking about."

"In English?" Lin raised an eyebrow. "The universe has a purpose. We have a role to play. It's not magic, or religious mysticism. It's a scientific process that has been going on since our universe was born—a process that will result in its end."

"And you're telling me our genes reveal what, exactly?"

"They are a medium. For a message."

Avery squinted. "A message from whom?"

"I don't know," Lin said flatly.

"Aliens?"

"You're comparing apples to oranges."

"What does that even mean, Lin?"

"It means that your question is out of context, and more importantly, we're out of time. I leave you with this: since our species emerged, our genes have been shifting. Several turning points in human history hastened these shifts. The cognitive revolution. Agriculture. Cities. The scientific revolution. They were necessary steps along the way. And each of these turning points left a bread crumb in our DNA. Think about it. It's the perfect medium for a message."

"And you found those DNA samples on the *Beagle*. Now what?"

"Only some of them. I believe the rest of the samples were hidden."

"Why do you think that?"

"I suggest we discuss that en route."

Avery got up. "Fine. En route to where?"

"Oxford."

"Mississippi."

"England."

"Okay, this helo is definitely not going to get to England."
Avery thought for a moment. "I refueled at Post–Rogers Memorial
Airport on the way here. I saw a few planes."

"Any you can fly?" Adams asked.

"I can fly anything."

CHAPTER 18

CONNER HAD ORDERED the vans to avoid Sand Hill Road. With the X1 treatment camp at Stanford, the thoroughfare would be crawling with mixed units of National Guard, Army, and FEMA employees. So they drove slowly through the residential roads of Sharon Heights, their headlights off, only the moonlight and occasional streetlamp lighting their way.

They staggered their arrival. The scout van was the first to turn left off Middle Avenue onto Windsor.

On his laptop screen, Conner watched the vehicle's video feed. The street was lined with houses built in the sixties, though a few had been torn down and replaced with larger homes that looked slightly out of place. In a few years they would probably be the majority.

Lin Shaw's home was one of the originals. It was a ranch with a double garage, stucco exterior, and a shingle roof that was showing its age.

As planned, the scout van drove by once. Save for a smattering of lights inside a few homes, the street was quiet, not a soul in sight. Conner knew that some of the residents were in the Stanford Treatment Center. Others had died. Many had fled—into the California mountains, or for those with the means, offshore to private islands. The ones left had ridden out the pandemic at home. With the recently enacted curfew, they would be peeking out their windows at any movement on the street.

The scout van parked several houses down from Lin's, and

three of Conner's men got out. In their unmarked black uniforms, they strode down the street with purpose, as if they belonged there.

The view on Conner's laptop split, and he saw a feed from the lead soldier's helmet cam. He knocked on a door. Curtains in the window to the right were drawn back, and a woman's face appeared, eyebrows raised. A click, and the door swung open, catching on a chain.

"Yes?"

She was middle-aged, with wavy brown hair and dark bags under her eyes.

"Evening, ma'am. We're just canvassing the neighborhood making sure everyone heard about the curfew."

She swallowed, seemed a little more at ease. "Yes, we heard."

"Good. Can we do anything for you?"

She shook her head. "They brought food this morning." She hesitated. "Our internet's down. So is everyone else's I've talked to—uh, during the day."

"We're aware of that. Hope to get it fixed soon."

"Thank God. My daughter is in Seattle and we haven't heard anything. Phones don't work either."

"That's connected to the internet issue. It'll all be over soon." The man's words brought a smile to Conner's face. "We're going to be conducting operations on the street, so you'll see some of my men and some other vans."

"Is everything—"

"Nothing to worry about, ma'am. Just routine. Have a good night, now."

The next house was right beside Lin Shaw's home. It looked deserted, and no one came to the door when the soldier knocked. He walked around the house, jumped the chain-link fence, and used his knife to open a double-hung window. He searched the two-story residence quickly, confirmed it was empty, then opened the front door and let his team in. They set up a base of operations in the breakfast room off the kitchen, at the back of the house, out of view of anyone walking down the street.

They opened a crate, drew out what looked like a camera with a telephoto lens, and connected it to a laptop.

On his laptop, Conner watched them sweep the camera back and forth, revealing an infrared view of Lin Shaw's home. There was nothing living inside. Still, Conner wasn't taking any chances where Lin Shaw was involved. Or Desmond. The home could be booby-trapped, rigged to blow, or some kind of failsafe to facilitate Desmond's rescue.

Conner watched his team jump the fence between the two homes and set up a recreational camping tent that wouldn't seem out of place in this residential neighborhood. The men placed the tent against the home's rear wall and crowded inside, out of sight.

One soldier drilled a hole in the wall, then used a hacksaw to make it larger, just big enough for a man to squeeze through. He reached into his black bag and took out a small rover. It was perfect for the search: rubber tracks, a long arm, and a 360-degree camera. The man slid it through the hole and manipulated it with the remote control.

The rover crept through the home, revealing it in the green glow of night vision. The sink was filled with dirty dishes. Clothes were strewn across the bed. The alarm wasn't set. All were indications of someone leaving in a hurry—or of someone who had wanted it to look that way.

Methodically, the rover worked its way through the home. There were no cameras, no wiring to the doors or windows, just the standard alarm contacts.

"Permission to breach?" the soldier asked over the comm.

"Granted," Conner replied.

The men crawled through the hole, still wary of using a door or window. Within seconds, they had searched and secured the home.

"Entry point?"

"Garage," Conner said. "Keep the lights off."

"Copy."

Conner's van pulled away from the curb and crept through

Menlo Park. When they arrived at Lin's home, they backed onto the driveway and into the garage. The door closed behind them.

"Should we unload?" Dr. Park asked.

"No. We need to stay mobile. But you should recharge your equipment."

Conner pulled out the phone and studied the Labyrinth Reality app.

Downloading...

Extension cords were strung from outlets inside the home to Dr. Park's equipment. Conner then waited while his troops canvassed the rest of the street and took up positions in abandoned homes at each end.

The phone beeped.

Download Complete

Conner turned to the doctor, who was studying his laptop.

"Brain waves just changed," Park said. "Another one is starting."

"How long?"

"Not as long as the other one. An hour maybe."

Conner got out and walked through the home, to the bay window in the living room. In the distance, he saw the light of the fire that burned at Sand Hill Road, the thick column of smoke rising to the moon. It was coming their way. For the second time in his life, he was trapped inside a home, a wildfire barreling toward him.

CHAPTER 19

AVERY BANKED THE helicopter and swept its exterior lights over the darkened airport. From the back, Peyton peered out. Post–Rogers Memorial Airport had only a single runway and no signs of life. She spotted two helicopters and five planes.

The airport was a few miles outside Barrow, Alaska, the northernmost city in the United States. The city was small even before the X1 outbreak—less than five thousand inhabitants—and Peyton wondered how many they had now. They were over two hundred miles north of the Arctic Circle, which meant the sun wouldn't rise again for another month. She felt as though she had lived in darkness for years; the sun was a distant memory.

They landed, and stepped out into the cold December night. Avery paced ahead of the group to look the planes over. She strode quickly past the four single-engine prop planes and headed straight for the jet, which had a logo for an oil and gas exploration company Peyton didn't recognize.

"It'll do," she said.

"How far away is Oxford?" Peyton asked.

"Don't know. London is four thousand miles, give or take."

Lin studied the plane. "Oxford's close to London. I used to ride the train there twice a week. What's the jet's range?"

"It's a G5. Over six thousand nautical miles, roughly twelve thousand kilometers. It's fast, too—up to six hundred and seventy miles per hour. Ninety percent the speed of sound."

Adams eyed her suspiciously, as if she were kidding.

"Rubicon used to own one," she explained.

They fueled it up and transferred their gear. The inside of the craft was worn; Peyton estimated that it was probably twenty years old. But it started immediately and felt surefooted on the runway.

As soon as they were at altitude, Avery engaged the autopilot and walked back into the cabin, where her five passengers were gathered. "All right," she said. "What did I miss?"

"The freezing part," Nigel muttered.

Lin ignored him. "As we said at camp, we found bones on the *Beagle*, but not nearly as many as I expected." She waited for everyone to focus on her. "We did find a clue, however."

Avery pinched the bridge of her nose. "Okay. I'll bite. I'll take Cryptic Things You Found on a Sunken Submarine for a thousand." She leaned in theatrically. "Please tell me it's a Daily Double."

"I'm glad you're enjoying yourself, Avery," Lin said. "We lost a lot of people back there, so it's not as easy for us."

The statement stopped Avery cold.

Peyton was amazed at her mother's ability to control the situation. In a single breath, she had focused everyone and made them feel what she wanted them to feel.

Lin continued without looking up. "In an office deep inside the *Beagle*, Peyton and I found a picture of a cave painting." She drew it out and passed it around. "Read the back."

When it reached Peyton, she read it again.

> *Do fidem me nullum librum*
> *A Liddell*

Avery handed the page back to Lin. "I took Latin in the eleventh grade, but I got a B. So... gonna need a little help here."

"Only the first part is Latin," Lin said. "It's the beginning of an oath. A very old one. *Do fidem me nullum librum vel instrumentum aliamve quam rem ad bibliothecam pertinentem...* It's an oath I took. For almost a thousand years, it was a covenant agreed to by some of the greatest humans who ever lived. And by those who had the potential to join them.

"The people who have spoken or signed this oath have won fifty-eight Nobel prizes. In every category. Twenty-seven prime ministers of the UK have signed or said the words. Margaret Thatcher. Tony Blair. David Cameron. Theresa May. The prime ministers of Australia and Canada. Sir Walter Raleigh. Lawrence of Arabia. Einstein. Schrödinger."

"Impossible," Avery said.

"It's true. The list is even longer when it comes to writers. T.S. Elliot. Graham Greene. Christopher Hitchens. Aldous Huxley. J.R.R. Tolkien. Phillip Pullman. C.S. Lewis. Even philosophers like John Locke and William of Ockham."

"As in Ockham's razor?" Avery asked.

"The same," Lin replied.

"What kind of oath?" Nigel asked.

"One to protect knowledge."

"How?"

"By not burning books."

Lin's statement drew silence from the others.

"It's a vow that was required before admittance to a library." Lin folded the page and tucked it away. "One of the oldest libraries in Europe, built nearly a thousand years ago. It's the largest library in the UK, after the British Library. Under British law it can request a copy of every book printed in the UK. Irish Law gives it the same rights in the Republic of Ireland."

"The Bodleian," Nigel said. "Oxford University's main library."

"Yes."

"What's the oath?" Peyton asked.

"Not to carry a flame inside the library. In the centuries before electricity, the Bod closed at sundown. No candles allowed. No cigarettes. No chance of burning the stacks of priceless books inside."

"What's the second part? Nigel asked. A Liddell?"

"It's a reference to a work by an author who took the oath. A professor at the university. He first originated the term 'Looking

Glass.' The Citium took inspiration from him in their great project. He wrote under the pen name Lewis Carroll to protect his true identity. I believe his book is what we're looking for: *Alice's Adventures In Wonderland*."

CHAPTER 20

THE NIGHT HE saw Peyton at the restaurant in San Francisco, Desmond barely slept. He kept replaying the moment in his mind, the look on Yuri's face as they stood outside on the street in the falling snow. Something was wrong about it. The thought gnawed at him. There was a connection—there had to be. But he couldn't see it.

He got up, splashed water on his face, and exited his condo. He expected to see Jennifer sitting at the desk in the lobby off the elevator, but a young Asian man sat there instead, studying a laptop screen.

At the sight of Desmond, the man stood. "Morning, sir."

"Morning..."

"Huan."

"Nice to meet you." Desmond paused. "Is Jennifer off today?"

"Who?"

"Jennifer. Nelson. She usually works the day shift."

"I don't know, sir. I've never met her." Huan paused. "Can I get you anything?"

"No. Thanks, Huan."

Desmond once again sat at the long table next to the towering window in the library, pondering the question of why early humans, during their march across the world, had wiped out Neanderthals, Denisovans, *floresiensis*, and every other hominin species, but had allowed primates like chimpanzees, gorillas, and bonobos to live.

Yet try as he might, Desmond couldn't focus on the question. His mind kept drifting back to the scene in the restaurant. Peyton's face. Lin, sitting there, placid, almost a mirror of Yuri. *Focus.*

Desmond stood, climbed the winding metal staircase to the library's third floor, and stopped at the archives of the Citium conclaves. He pulled out a volume from the late sixties, scanned it, then pulled out another. He found the presentation he needed.

It was a piece.

On the second floor, he found the expedition logs from the *Beagle.* Multiple volumes. He carried the books down five at a time, stacked them high on the table, and pored through them.

Two days later, he had found the answer to Yuri's question.

The echo of the voice in the tall room startled him. "You look like a man who's discovered something." Yuri walked to the table and sat. "Let's hear it."

Desmond cleared his throat. "Our species is the greatest mass murderer in the planet's history."

"Motive?"

"Calories and protein."

Yuri gave a rare smile, but it was quickly gone. "Explain."

"The other human species—Neanderthals, Denisovans, *floresiensis*—were competitors for calories. The primates in the jungle, not so much. The apes consume far fewer calories than we do. Chimpanzees and bonobos need about 400 calories a day, gorillas about 635, and orangutans 820. That's despite them being far larger than us. The reason is our brains. A pound of brain tissue uses twenty times the amount of energy a pound of muscle does.

"But more importantly, those other primates are mostly herbivores—bananas, nuts, et cetera. That meant they weren't competitors for the ultimate fuel our bigger brains needed: meat. And especially cooked meat. Our pursuit of meat is what drove us out of Africa and all the way to Australia. And it had a huge impact on the planet—nothing less than a global extinction event."

"Extinction of what?"

"Megafauna—large animals. Every time behaviorally modern humans moved into an area, the megafauna went extinct. It happened 45,000 years ago when those ancient humans reached Australia. When they arrived, they found thousand-pound kangaroos, two-ton wombats, twenty-five-foot-long lizards, four-hundred-pound flightless birds, three-hundred-pound marsupial lions, and tortoises the size of a car. And then, in a very short amount of time, more than 85 percent of the animals weighing over a hundred pounds went extinct. This wasn't an isolated incident."

Yuri's face was expressionless. "Go on."

Desmond opened one of the expedition logs from the *Beagle*. "All around the world, the researchers found remains of species we killed off. This global die-off is called the Quaternary extinction event. And they proved," he pointed to the book, "definitively, that our ancestors caused it. A global holocaust, not just of other humans, but of every large mammal on Earth, with only a few exceptions. Even today, we humans account for 350 million tons of biomass on this planet. That's three times the biomass of all the sheep, chickens, whales, and elephants—combined. This planet has become an ecology almost completely dedicated to fueling our massive calorie-hogging brains."

"And what happened when the megafauna were gone?"

"Crisis. Our population receded. And then we kept going, expanding—that's what drove our ancestors across the Bering Strait, to the far edges of South America and the Pacific Islands, and all the way to Hawaii and Easter Island. Food.

"When it was gone, human populations stagnated. That's the answer in Australia. They got there, killed the large game, and settled into an equilibrium. They missed the great innovation that swept the rest of the world, the next major calorie boost: agriculture. The agricultural revolution—growing grains like rice and wheat—provided an almost unlimited source of calories. And we didn't even have to hunt it down. Which is why, starting around 12,000 years ago, the first cities emerged—they were all centered around agriculture. Human civilization exploded from there. Trade. *Writing*. Laws. Coinage. Agriculture paved the way for all of it. And it's all about powering our massive brains."

Desmond paused. "And that's what the early Australians missed. They were still hunter-gatherers when the rest of the world found them. They never developed agriculture, which meant they never developed cities, or city lifestyle, which was conducive to thought and research and invention."

"Good, Desmond. Very good work. But you're still missing a piece."

Desmond leaned back in his chair.

"Why us?" Yuri said.

"Us...?"

"Why aren't we Neanderthals? They had larger brains than us. Bigger bodies. Stronger muscles. And they were very well adapted, having survived for half a million years on at least two continents before we wiped them out. Now that's something." Yuri pulled the stack of books closer and flipped through them one by one, scanning the tables of contents. Finally, he opened one and turned it to face Desmond. It was a log of an expedition to Germany in 1973.

Desmond was surprised. "You've read these books?"

"I have studied these books more than any person alive." Yuri looked down at the black-and-white pictures of an archaeological dig, of the bones uncovered. "It was a dangerous expedition. East Germany was very difficult to get into at the time. And even harder to get out of—especially if you were transporting something. I had to use my contacts in Russia to get us in."

"You were *there*? On the *Beagle*?"

"The day she launched... and shortly before she sank."

"Your name—"

"Isn't in these logs. Or the conclave archives. The names have all been changed. If our enemies found this library, it could be dangerous for us."

Desmond opened his mouth to ask another question, but Yuri cut him off.

"Focus on the mystery at hand, Desmond. Not the Citium's history." He pointed to the page. "On this expedition, we found caves inhabited by Neanderthals fifty thousand years ago.

Evidence of stone hearths. Ritual burials. Stone tools. We saw evidence that elderly members of the tribe—some of whom were sick, likely had been for years—were cared for. This species was very much like us. The mystery is why we had such an overwhelming advantage over them."

"Behavioral modernity—"

"Is the answer, but what specifically, Desmond? Think about it. If you didn't know the answer, if we were standing on a hill fifty thousand years ago watching a tribe of our ancestors in one valley and a tribe of Neanderthals in the next, which would you bet on to take over the world? We know who wins—because we're here to talk about it. But back then, both groups looked behaviorally advanced. Dig deeper. The answer is here."

When Yuri was gone, Desmond sat for a long time, thinking. He opened the expedition log and read the report, trying to determine Yuri's code name in the books. Dr. Nilats? Yes—that was it. He could tell by the tone of the man's reports. And the name, Nilats—it was Stalin backwards. Yuri had grown up in the Soviet Union in the years after World War Two, so Stalin was a man who no doubt had caused him a lot of pain. He was a man Yuri wanted to be the opposite of.

Desmond skimmed the rest of the expedition report, which contained accounts from archaeologists, geneticists, and biologists. On the last page, his mouth went dry. He read the next expedition report, then the next. His mind flashed back to that night on the sidewalk, to Peyton and her mother sitting in the restaurant. It couldn't be.

He read every log again, not stopping, like a man possessed. Finally, he pushed his chair back and rubbed at his eyes. He needed some fresh air, and to calm his nerves. He put on a jogging suit and marched to the elevator.

Huan stood as he approached. "Sir, can I get you anything?"

"Just gonna get some fresh air, Huan. Thanks."

He ran toward the sea, the air crisp and cool in his lungs. The smell of fish grew stronger as he approached the wharf. The crowds changed from locals to tourists, pointing and taking pictures of Alcatraz and the sun setting over the Golden Gate Bridge. And with each step, he couldn't shake the feeling that he was being watched. He slowed to a walk, glancing behind him and all around.

It was past eight o'clock when he returned. The run had helped clear his mind. He was almost certain of his theory now. But he had to know for sure.

He showered, dressed, donned his coat, and grabbed his wallet.

He walked several blocks from the building, checking over his shoulder periodically. Why was he being so paranoid? His theory would explain how Yuri knew that Peyton and Lin were at the restaurant—but that didn't mean they were watching *him*.

He hailed a cab on Bay Street.

"Menlo Park. Windsor Drive."

The man typed the address into a TomTom navigation unit hanging from the inside of the windshield, then pulled away into the night.

It was almost an hour later when the cab stopped at the address on the quiet residential street. Desmond paid the cabbie, told him to wait, and walked to the front door, his heart beating fast, a lump in his throat. He almost turned back. He'd be humiliated if he was wrong.

He knocked. A light flicked on. Footsteps. The peephole darkened as an eye peered out. The door swung open, revealing Lin Shaw, dressed in a pantsuit, as if she had only recently arrived home from work.

"Desmond."

"Can I come in?"

"Of course."

Desmond had only been to Lin's home a few times. It was neat, and decorated in a neutral, almost generic way, as if it were staged for sale. He knew Lin spent almost all of her time at Stanford and her company, working on her genetics research.

"The name changes threw me off," he said.

"I'm sorry?"

"You were on the *Beagle*. You're a member of the Citium. I read the reports. It was subtle, but I could hear your voice in them. And the dates coincide with what Peyton told me about you—and her father. Was he on the *Beagle* when it sank? The dates match."

Lin sat in an armchair by the bay window and motioned for Desmond to sit on the couch.

He remained standing.

"Sit down, Desmond." Her voice was flat, commanding.

He sat down and leaned forward, elbows on his thighs.

"Why are you here?"

Desmond had always liked that about Lin: she cut to the chase.

"I assumed that Yuri recruited me because I had been asking questions about the Citium. I found the organization while working at a startup. SciNet."

He waited, hoping Lin would volunteer information. She simply stared at him.

"But I don't think that's true," he continued. "I think you told him to recruit me."

Desmond searched her face. She gave away nothing.

"I want to know why." He paused. "I think I deserve that."

Lin finally looked away. She sighed. "Before Yuri recruited you, we removed all the photos from the logs—of him, me, and Peyton's father. I assumed you wouldn't put it together. I rarely underestimate people, Desmond."

"Why? Why me?"

"Peyton."

"Peyton?"

"You broke her heart."

The words hit Desmond with the force of an elephant rifle. "I never meant—"

"I know you didn't. What happened... was circumstances beyond your control." Lin's voice fell to a whisper. "I know about that. I know what it's like to lose the love of your life. She hasn't been the same since you left."

"I—"

"Listen, Desmond. She never will be. And neither will you. But you *can* be. The Looking Glass can heal those wounds."

"So it's true, what Yuri promised me?"

"Yes."

"And that's why you had me recruited."

"Yes."

"What do you want?"

"What every parent wants: for my daughter to be happy. For her life to be better than mine."

They sat in silence then. Finally, Desmond spoke. "Should I tell Yuri... that we talked?"

Lin exhaled through her nose. "Don't bother. Yuri Pachenko is always a step ahead—of everyone. I suspect he already knows you're here. And I don't know this for a fact, but I'd bet he's listening to us right now."

"So, what do I do?"

"Go back and finish. If you give up, you're giving up on her."

CHAPTER 21

CONNER COULD SMELL the smoke from the growing blaze in the distance. The chatter over the radio told a story of chaos and disorder. The fire was spreading from home to home, and people were evacuating—breaking curfew—to escape before it reached them.

Through the bay window in the living room, he saw a garage door open. A black BMW pulled onto the street and sped away.

He made his way to the garage, where the van's back doors sat open. Dr. Park was inside, staring at a flat screen with wavy lines in blue, green, and red.

"How long?"

Park didn't look up. "Not long. Twenty, maybe thirty minutes."

Conner wondered if they had that long.

He retreated back into the home, through the kitchen, and into Lin Shaw's bedroom. On the dresser was a picture of Peyton, Andrew, Madison, and Lin at the Grand Canyon. An apt metaphor for the person not pictured: the children's father, Lin's husband, William.

Conner picked up the picture—and stopped. He felt something on the back—a piece of metal. He turned over the frame.

A key was taped to the back.

It was small, the right size for a padlock, or perhaps a safe. The head and shoulder were painted white, while the shaft, teeth, and tip were plain silver. Why?

He pulled drawers from the dresser and emptied them, searching for a padlock or safe. He pulled the covers off the bed and flipped the mattress. He rifled through the closet. Nothing.

He went to the window and scanned the back yard for a garden shed or storage building. Nothing there either. He went from room to room, ransacking the house.

Where was the last place anyone would look?

He walked into the hall, reached for the cord, and pulled down the stairs to the attic. They wobbled and creaked as he climbed. He pulled the string connected to the exposed light bulb. Empty. Nothing up here but exposed rafters, a buzzing HVAC unit, and blown-in insulation.

He walked back down the stairs, frustrated.

If the key was to a safe, he would have found it by now. Had Lin Shaw left the key just to mess with anyone who invaded her home? He wouldn't put it past her. But he wasn't ready to give up.

He walked back into the bedroom.

The room had no walk-in closet, just two strip closets hidden behind louvered folding doors, standard for the era. He compared the insides. Yes—there was a difference. The one on the right had extra white molding, like what would surround a window or door. The strips ran along the back corners, where the side walls met the back wall.

Now he was getting somewhere.

He tossed the clothes on the floor, pushed against the back wall. It gave, just a little, but too much for regular drywall on studs. He searched the entire back wall, but there was no keyhole.

A small, two-level shoe rack lay on the floor. He threw it out, revealing only the narrow planks of the hardwood floor.

Conner settled back onto his haunches. As his eyes moved over the white, wooden base molding, he stopped. One part didn't reflect light like the rest. He ran his hand over it, and felt the wood turn to metal—a round disc. A small piece of computer paper had been clear taped in the middle. He tore it off.

A keyhole.

He put the tip of the key on the face of the lock and scratched, revealing silver metal. He smiled. Very clever. Before painting the lock to match the trim, Lin had inserted the key, so as not to get paint inside the keyhole. That explained the strange paint pattern on the key.

He slid the key in, and heard a click as he turned the cylinder. He pushed against the back wall. It didn't swing wide, only cracked a few inches, but it was enough for Conner to squeeze through.

A string hung down from a light bulb, just like in the attic. He turned it on, then stared, mesmerized, at what he saw. He quickly closed the wall behind him and squatted to examine the items Lin had hidden. For good reason.

In the corner, an old military uniform was folded up. Conner knew it hadn't been worn in over seventy years; the nation that issued it no longer existed. But the Nazi uniform was unmistakable.

Beside the garment sat a shoebox. Conner carefully removed the lid. A stack of photographs lay inside, mostly black and white, with creases like cracks in concrete, worn ends, and rounded corners. Most were of a middle-aged man, Caucasian, European descent.

On the wall, a world map had been spread out and dotted with colored pushpins. The pins marked locations outside major cities, but Conner didn't recognize their significance. He drew out his phone, snapped pictures of everything in the tiny room, and uploaded them to the Citium server.

Then he dialed a phone number.

"Yes," Yuri said, emotionless as always.

"I found something at Lin Shaw's house. You need to see it."

CHAPTER 22

THE VAST SITUATION room was teeming with activity. Yuri's people were performing admirably, moving the pieces into place. Soon the Looking Glass would come online, and his life's work would be complete.

Yuri stepped through, avoiding the empty coffee cups that littered the floor like debris washed up on a beach, and entered the conference room, where Melissa Whitmeyer and two other ops techs were waiting.

As soon as he sat down, the red-haired woman began her report.

"The dev team estimates they're halfway finished on Rapture Control. They wish to remind us that estimating completion progress is not an exact science."

She waited for Yuri, who simply nodded.

Whitmeyer turned the page and exhaled. This was bad news; Yuri sensed it.

"We just heard from Captain Vasilov on the *Invisible Sun*. They've searched the surface and the *Beagle*. The incursion team she sent is dead." Whitmeyer paused. "She's identified evac locations and is preparing to search them, beginning with Post–Rogers—"

"Tell her not to bother. Lin Shaw is gone. And we can assume she found what she was searching for on the *Beagle*."

"We've activated our assets embedded in governments. No reports of contact yet."

"There won't be. Lin is too smart for that. She'll stay off the radar until she needs to surface."

"Where does that leave us?"

"Chasing her is futile," Yuri said. "We need to figure out where she's going—and be there waiting. And we need to figure out what exactly she's working on. She no doubt has collaborators. If her project is a threat to the Looking Glass, even containing her might not be enough."

"Suggestions?"

"Dig deep into her past. I want a list of all the locations that might have meaning for her. All the locations that are tied to those scientists who died on the *Beagle*. Find the intersection points. I want small teams to stake out the locations. Don't ask, just send them as soon as you identify potential targets. And I want a tactical team prepped and ready to go on a moment's notice."

CHAPTER 23

THE PLANE FLEW through the darkness toward the North Pole. The shortest route to Oxford was over the top of the Earth, past Greenland and Iceland.

Peyton sat in a chair facing a long couch that held her mother, Avery, and Nigel. The two SEALs stood, hovering nearby.

"Lewis Carroll. Author of *Alice in Wonderland*," Avery said. "Though the sequel seems more relevant: *Through the Looking-Glass*. But how did you get to Lewis Carroll from 'A Liddell'?"

"A Liddell is *Alice* Liddell," Lin said. "She was the inspiration behind the novel. She was a girl at the time Carroll wrote the book. Her father was the dean of Christ Church, a college within the university. And Carroll—his real name was Charles Lutwidge Dodgson—studied at Oxford and became a professor there. He was a polymath—a writer, logician, mathematician, photographer, even an Anglican deacon."

"Yeah," Nigel said. "Didn't know all that. Here's what I do know: he's dead. Has been for a while. Like since the 1800s."

"True enough," Lin said. "But the Bodleian has been around far longer than that. Since the 1200s. And it's famous for keeping rare and first-edition books. If I'm right, we're looking for one of those first editions. A rare first edition of *Alice's Adventures In Wonderland*."

Off the coast of Greenland, the sun broke above the horizon. Peyton watched the soft orange glow turn to rays of white. It blinded her at first, and a throb of pain came next, quickly, like fingers pressing on her eyeballs. She squeezed her eyes shut and felt the warmth touch her face. She hadn't seen the sun for a month and hadn't realized until now how much she had missed it.

The last month had revealed so much about her life she hadn't known. The truth about her father and brother. Her mother's involvement in the Citium. Desmond's. It was like she had lived her life in darkness. Now the truth was coming to light. It hurt at first, but she was slowly beginning to open her eyes. She saw the sun on the horizon. And she was ready for it.

CHAPTER 24

IN THE WINTER of 2003, Desmond spent every waking minute in the library overlooking San Francisco Bay. Yuri arrived weekly, and Desmond always had a new wrinkle to his answer to the mysterious question.

"We walked upright. Primates don't. Chimps. Bonobos. Gorillas. It's more than just appearance."

Yuri sat quietly under the multi-level chandelier, waiting.

Desmond continued. "Walking upright had a huge impact on our evolution. The female birth canal became narrower at the exact same time that our brains were getting larger. This obstetric dilemma had a huge impact on our offspring. We developed openings in the skull called fontanelles that essentially allow babies' heads to compress during birth. The anterior fontanelle actually stays open for two years after birth, allowing the brain to expand further. That's completely different from chimpanzees and bonobos. In their offspring, brain growth occurs mostly in the womb. The anterior fontanelle is closed at around the time of birth. Their brain growth is already done.

"Which is why, if you compare our babies to those of apes, the apes' babies are far more developed. You'd have to gestate a human baby for eighteen to twenty-one months to achieve similar development at birth. Compared to other species, our offspring are born almost completely helpless. They need their parents, so those parents bond with them. As a result, we form villages, social structures to protect our young. Family units. Evolution met that biological challenge—that obstetric dilemma—with a cultural, societal solution. One that makes us human."

He waited, hoping, but Yuri shook his head.

"It's a piece, but not the key, Desmond. Dig deeper."

Desmond did. He read day and night. Months went by. Christmas passed. Then New Year. Looking out the window, he expected to see the Golden Gate Bridge coated in snow, but it was the same shade of burned red he'd seen the first time he'd come here. He'd never get used to seeing the years turn without snow on the ground. San Francisco, despite its latitude, seemed to exist in a bubble. The winters were mild and the summers were dry, as if it didn't observe the rules of nature.

February rolled around. Valentine's Day. It always reminded him of Peyton. He wondered if she had met someone. If she was happy. If Lin had been wrong. A part of him hoped she was. Another part hoped she wasn't.

The next day, Yuri sat in the library, waiting.

"Communication," Desmond said. "On the *Beagle*, they examined Neanderthal fossils. Their throats were different. They couldn't make sounds like us. So they never developed complex language. We did."

"You're getting closer."

Yuri walked out, and Desmond threw a book at the wall.

Huan ran in. "Sir?"

"Just getting my exercise, Huan."

"Can I get you any—"

"No. Thank you."

Desmond changed in his room and rode the elevator to street level. He ran through Telegraph Hill, past Union Square, and out of the financial district. Somewhere in the Mission District, he stopped thinking about the question.

The answer came to him not long after.

☣

He called Yuri the next morning. "I've got it."

"I'm on my way," the older man said.

Instead of sitting, as he usually did, Yuri stood, the morning light beaming in through the towering window.

"Story," Desmond said.

Yuri sat.

"Fiction. That's what we had that they didn't."

"Continue."

Desmond threw open a book with expedition notes from the *Beagle*. "This is from a place in Spain. It's called the Cave of Altamira. These paintings were made thirty-five thousand years ago."

"Steppe bison," Yuri said.

"You're familiar?"

"I was there when we excavated it," he said quietly. "But they aren't fiction. These beasts existed at the time the artists painted them."

"True. Our real breakthrough was imagination—specifically the ability to imagine something that didn't exist." Desmond stood. "The Neanderthals had fire. They buried their dead, cared for their sick. Walked upright like us. Made stone tools. But these were mostly reactive adaptations. We *imagined*. In our mind's eye, we saw things that didn't exist. We imagined what the world would be like when they *did* exist.

"You asked me about the early Australians. Why did they reach the island when the Neanderthals never had? When the Denisovans never had? Imagination. They imagined a device that would carry them across the sea. A raft maybe, perhaps a simple boat. And they created it, and sailed. They found a land with abundant calories to power those massive brains, those biological computers that rendered new realities in their minds, simulations of the future they could choose from."

Yuri smiled. It was a genuine gesture, unlike anything Desmond had ever seen from the older man. "Yes, Desmond."

"So... that's it? What you wanted me to find?" Desmond said. "The quintessential human trait: imagination, fiction, simulation. Powered by energy our brain could use."

"Yes. It's what makes us completely different from any species before us on this planet. It has been the singular key to all of our progress. And it's part of a pattern. It points to the path of our species."

"I don't understand."

"You will." Yuri stood. "When you answer one final question." Desmond shook his head.

"Patience." Yuri took a step away. "The pieces will fit together. But first, I have something for you. A reward."

"What kind of reward?"

"A trip."

"Where?"

"It would seem, for you, that all roads lead back to Australia."

They left that night, on a private plane, chartered from SFO. They flew for seventeen hours, playing chess on the table between the plush seats, taking turns sleeping on the couch, Desmond asking questions occasionally, Yuri always brushing them off.

To Desmond's surprise, it was night when they landed. They had flown into the sunset, their path rotating with the Earth.

Yuri said nothing about their destination, though the airport directories told Desmond he was in Adelaide. The last time he had walked through this terminal, Peyton had been with him, on a journey to retrace his past, hoping he found resolution. That had failed. Was Yuri trying the same thing? The outcome would be the same.

He had been here exactly one other time—as a child, on the day he left Australia for America. Another woman he loved had held his hand that day: Charlotte, towering tall above him, her smile the only light in the darkness of his life.

That darkness had never truly ended. And as he followed Yuri through the airport, he wondered if it ever would. If he was on a fool's errand. If there were truly answers here. But Lin Shaw had assured him that he could be with Peyton. That was all he wanted. That was enough for him to follow Yuri's road, wherever it led.

A car was waiting outside the airport. The drivers were professionals—dark suits, bulges under the armpits. Desmond was surprised, but he sat in the back and said nothing. They stopped in the country, outside a cemetery in a small town Desmond knew well. The sun was rising over the hills as they stepped out and weaved through the grave markers, Yuri carrying an item covered in a black trash bag.

"Do you know what today is?" Yuri whispered.

Desmond realized instantly. "The anniversary. Twenty years since the bushfires." The fires that had killed his family—and changed his life.

Yuri's pace slowed, and he pulled the black bag off the item he carried, revealing a wreath. He handed it to Desmond as they came to a stop.

Desmond stood there a long moment, the heat of the sun warming his face, a summer breeze blowing past him. He stooped, placed the wreath on the grave marker, and read the names. Alistair Anderson Hughes. 16 February 1983. Elizabeth Bancroft Hughes. 16 February 1983.

"Look closely," Yuri whispered. "For what you don't see."

Desmond glanced back at Yuri, studied the man's impassive face, then focused on the grave markers. There were two, where he expected to see three: larger ones for his parents and a small one for his infant brother. "Conner," he whispered.

He looked back at Yuri. "He's buried elsewhere?"

"That would be an assumption. We don't make assumptions. We form hypotheses. And test them."

"Two possibilities," Desmond said. "He's buried elsewhere— or he isn't buried at all."

"Correct."

Desmond rose. "What do you know, Yuri?"

Yuri turned and walked back toward the car, the sun on his back. It took every ounce of will Desmond possessed not to run and tackle the man and hold him down until he revealed exactly

what had happened to Conner. The two gun-wielding men looming at the car were only a minor deterrent; Desmond would
have fought an entire army for the answer. But he knew Yuri
would never yield under force. He was made of the same stuff as
Desmond: strength forged in fire.

They rode back to Adelaide in silence, to a hotel in the city
center area. Desmond's suite was large, with a living room and a
desk with a laptop and internet access.

"Answer one more question," Yuri said, "and you'll be a
member of the Citium. And I'll help you discover what happened
to Conner."

Desmond knew this wasn't a negotiation, that Yuri wasn't making an offer. These were his terms. He sat at the desk. "The library
is back in San Francisco."

"You won't need it for this question. Just the internet. And
your intelligence. The answer to this final riddle is in plain sight,
though few see it."

Desmond took a pen and pad from the desk.

"In July of 1405," Yuri began, "a Chinese fleet under the command of Zheng He departed from Suzhou for a tour around the
Pacific Ocean. The scale of the expedition was massive. Over
three hundred ships, almost twenty-eight thousand crewmen,
mostly military. They visited much of Southeast Asia, including
Brunei, Java, and Thailand. They stopped in India, the Horn of
Africa, and Arabia.

"China in 1405 was home to sixty-five million people. England
had only two million. China was the largest economy in the
world at that time. India was second. And the Chinese fleets were
much more advanced than those of any European power. Their
largest ship was four hundred feet long and had a four-tiered
deck. By comparison, Christopher Columbus's largest ship, the
Santa María, was roughly fifty-eight feet long.

"In 1400, if you were asked to guess which nation would
colonize Australia, you probably wouldn't have looked to Western
Europe. Yet it was the Dutch who landed there first—in 1606. And
Britain who established the first colony—in 1788. Why? It's not

an isolated incident. Western European nations came to dominate the world—economically, militarily, and culturally. Why? What made the British and Spanish explorers so different?"

CHAPTER 25

CONNER RETURNED TO the hidden room in Lin Shaw's home with a duffel bag and carefully placed the items inside it. His instincts told him that the pictures, and especially the map, could be useful at some point. They might even hold the key to understanding the motive behind Lin's betrayal.

A voice came over the comm. "Zero. Unit two. We've got incoming X1 troops." Conner and his men had taken to referring to the mixed units of National Guard, Army, FEMA, and Navy units as "X1 troops," since no other moniker seemed to fit. "They're evacuating the homes along Santa Cruz."

Conner raced to the living room. Through the bay window, he saw that the wildfire had grown, and was expanding by the minute.

"Status?" he whispered, nearly paralyzed.

"Sir?"

"The fire!" he roared. "You idiots. What is the status of that bloody fire you set?"

A pause. "We did a drone flyover ten minutes—"

"Status!"

"It's contained south of Sand Hill. They've set up a firewall around Stanford."

"We're not *at* Stanford, are we?"

"No, sir. North of Sand Hill, the fire is rolling through the neighborhoods. It's too big to stop."

Conner froze. "How long until it reaches us?"

"Twenty minutes. Maybe a little more or less."

Conner raced back to the garage. Dr. Park was still sitting in the van with the rear doors open. A screen displayed Desmond's brain wave patterns.

Park had apparently been listening to the radio exchange, and anticipated Conner's question. He shrugged. "I don't know."

"Doctor."

"It'll be close."

"How close?"

"Minutes. I'd say it's fifty-fifty we get out before the fire."

Conner wanted to retreat then and there. But he couldn't. Wouldn't. He looked at his brother lying on the hospital bed. He was helpless, at the mercy of the coming fire, just as Conner had been a long time ago.

Desmond had tried to save him that day. He had failed, but he *had* saved Conner twenty years later. Conner now had to do the same for his older brother—and the memories buried in the Labyrinth were his only hope of that.

He activated his comm. "Units two, three, and four. Fall back to West Atherton. Take up covered positions. Unit one, converge on my position and prepare to leave. And stay out of sight."

Ten minutes later, the temperature was rising in the home. Conner sat in the garage, sweating, focusing on his breathing, trying not to imagine the inferno marching toward him.

To his surprise, a knock sounded on the front door.

☣

Desmond didn't wait on Yuri to find Conner. In Australia, he hired the country's best private detective to research what had happened to his brother after the fire. Then he hired the second best. Again and again, they hit dead ends. They requested money for lawyers to get public records, specialists to advise, but they made little progress. He pressed them harder.

When he wasn't searching for Conner, he pondered Yuri's final riddle. At the heart of the question was how the world had come to be the way it was. Specifically, why had Great Britain colonized

Australia instead of Russia, or China, Japan, or India? All were substantial powers in 1606 when the Dutch landed in Australia, yet none of the Asian nations had found the island continent. It was also Western Europe who colonized the Americas and the Pacific Islands, spreading their language and culture, and with it their system of laws and economic principles. Why?

Desmond began with an obvious difference: religion. But when he presented his theory, Yuri simply shook his head. "This isn't about religion."

Desmond dug deeper. He compared the geography and climate. Then he realized the key to this mystery might be found in the answer to the previous mystery. The human race had bested its competitors—the Neanderthals, Denisovans, and *floresiensis*— because it *thought* differently. How had the British, Spanish, and Dutch thought differently?

The answer became clear immediately.

☣

Yuri sat in Desmond's hotel room with his legs crossed and his hands in his lap. Desmond stood before the floor-to-ceiling window overlooking the green expanse of trees and grass and walking trails that made up Victoria Park.

"Capitalism," Desmond said. "It powered the West—incentivized exploration, exploitation even."

Yuri nodded. "It's half of the answer."

Desmond didn't have the other half.

When Yuri left, Desmond grabbed the lamp from the desk table, held it up to throw it at the door, but stopped at the last second. He wanted to take a drink.

Instead he went for a walk. He was learning more than the facts Yuri had led him to. He was learning patience. And discipline.

His phone rang. A thrill went through him when he heard the private investigator's voice. The man's name was Arlo, and the New Zealander spoke with a thick accent and gruff voice. "Think I got something, Desy."

They sat in a coffee shop off Grenfell Street, the steamers screeching in the background. Patrons with dogs crowded the small cafe, staring at laptops and paperback novels and, nonchalantly, each other.

The shaggy-haired man laid a manila envelope on the round table and drew out a series of photocopies of handwritten notes on hospital forms. Intake details. Surgeries. Medications. The name on the forms was "Joe Bloggs"—the Australian equivalent of John Doe. Age estimated at twelve months.

"Two days after the fire, a couple rescue workers came round to your old homestead, takin' a survey an' all that. Found this little guy under a flipped-over refrigerator of all places. Burned remains of a woman next to it—"

"Please be quiet," Desmond whispered.

He read the hospital notes, each word a dagger cutting through his heart. The urge to get up and walk away was nearly irresistible, but it was second to his desire to read more and learn the truth.

The ER doctor who had admitted the infant had placed him in the pediatric intensive care unit. Their primary concerns were noted: *Severe dehydration. Third-degree burns on 40 percent of his body. Two instances of fourth-degree burns: right thigh and right triceps.*

Desmond stared at the final words: *Prognosis poor.*

The care team administered fluids. Removed dead tissue. Dressed the wounds. Tried to get his weight back up.

On the fourth day, the attending's notes turned more positive. *Still critical, but stable. Responsive to treatment.*

They moved him to Adelaide Children's Hospital, where he convalesced for two months. He cried constantly when conscious. They sedated him and did their best to heal the burn marks across his face and body. The charge nurse's words rang off the page: *It's both a blessing and a curse that he's so young. At least he won't remember the horror of his wounds.*

Arlo was getting antsy. "Oy," he called to the barista. "'Bout an Irish coffee?"

She muttered something Desmond couldn't make out.

Arlo leaned forward. "'E was a fighter, Desy."

Desmond turned the last page, which noted that the patient had been remanded to an orphanage outside the city.

"Where is he now?"

Arlo sat back. "Don't know."

"What else do you have?"

"That's it."

"This is *it*?"

"Well, thought you'd want to know straightaway."

Desmond did. But the news that his brother had indeed survived the fire only made him even hungrier to know more.

"Find him, Arlo. Or find out what happened."

The weathered man fixed Desmond with a fake sympathetic grin. Finally, he exhaled theatrically, as if regretting the bad news he was about to deliver. "Look, that there weren't exactly easy to come by. Had to search half the hospitals in South Australia. This little manhunt of yours is getting right expensive, Desy. I mean, my time and expenses is already going on three large."

Arlo glanced away, waiting. Desmond knew the routine. The man was testing his client to see how deep his pockets were—and how far he was willing to extend his arms.

"I'll give you two weeks," Desmond said. "And ten thousand Australian when you find him or a death certificate."

Arlo spread out his hands. "Hey, I bill by the hour. I can't control where the case takes me—"

"I pay for results. If the ten thousand doesn't work for you, we'll settle up now."

Arlo glanced away, as if struggling with the decision. "Aw, all right. At this point I just want to see you reunited with your baby brother."

☣

Every day that went by was agony for Desmond, knowing his brother was alive, that he had suffered, and was likely still suffering, possibly alone.

He slept little. His mind was a record on repeat, replaying that day twenty years ago, standing in front of his childhood home, the flames licking the walls and climbing the roof while he screamed his brother's name. He knew the truth now: if he had waited, if he hadn't rushed into the fire, he could have searched the remains for Conner, possibly gotten him to the hospital sooner. They could have been together. Grown up together. How would it have changed their lives? What had happened to Conner? The questions and guilt haunted him.

He tried to focus on Yuri's final mystery, but couldn't concentrate.

So, as he had in San Francisco, he turned to exercise for escape. He ran in the Adelaide Park Lands, pushing himself harder each day, to the point when the endorphins shut down his mind and freed him.

Days went by. Arlo didn't call.

Desmond ran every morning and again in the afternoon. In the spring rain and in the blazing South Australian sun.

On a clear Sunday morning, at the end of a seven-mile run, realization struck him when he least expected it. He hadn't even been thinking about Yuri's question, but the answer came, unbidden. Every piece of Yuri's puzzle fit together, they were like images in a vast panoramic landscape Desmond had been staring at his whole life, but had only ever seen in parts. Now his eyes were wide open.

He drew out his phone and dialed Yuri.

"Yes?"

"I know what the Western Europeans had, why they colonized America, and Australia, and India, Hong Kong, and Africa five hundred years ago."

Silence on the line.

"They had *you*, Yuri."

CHAPTER 26

THE GULFSTREAM JET banked hard and dove, throwing Peyton into the central aisle. Lin was up first. She ran to the cockpit where Avery was shouting into the radio. Peyton saw the Royal Air Force jets a second later.

She caught the gist of the conversation in clips and phrases as the plane leveled out and flew away from the Scottish mainland. Apparently the Rubicon program had established relationships with governments around the world. Avery was verified via the RAF ground operator, and the jets soon fell in beside them and acted as an escort.

Through the oval window, Peyton got her first look at civilization in a month. Or what was left of it. In the midday light, she saw only deserted highways littered with burned cars. Military vehicles were massed around schools and stadiums and hospitals, like swarms of bees dotting the green expanse and nearly empty cities. A few cars moved along the smaller roads—people going out for supplies, no doubt. But for the most part, the world below appeared to have ground to a halt. Everyone was hunkered down.

Green fields surrounded the Oxford airport. Like Post–Rogers, it had only a single runway. Two dozen armored troop carriers and canvas-backed trucks were parked at the terminal.

As soon as they landed, twenty troops marched out onto the tarmac to greet them. They were dressed in camo and body armor, with beige berets featuring a black patch. The patch showed a sword between wings, with a phrase below: *Who Dares Wins.* SAS troops. Whoever Avery had made contact with had requested the very best to accompany them.

Inside the terminal, they made ten copies of the data Nigel had rescued from the *Arktika.* Lin refused to tell her hosts exactly what the data was, what she intended to do with it, or even whom she was working with. She simply asked them to transport copies to the governments of the US, Canada, Australia, Germany, and Russia, and to hold five copies at different locations in the UK. She wasn't taking any chances.

When the data was on its way, Lin and the others—and their SAS escort—loaded into Land Rovers and drove into Oxford. Peyton took in every detail. Despite spending the first six years of her life in London, she had never visited Oxford. It was a quaint town, filled with old stone buildings with Gothic architecture. Ivy grew up the walls, crawling toward the steep-pitched slate roofs. The village was almost medieval, like something out of a fairy tale, an ancient town frozen in time.

As they turned onto Catte Street, it began to rain, a slow drizzle that blotted out the sun like a curtain being drawn. The city seemed to shrink around them as haze filled the streets.

The convoy stopped at the Old Bodleian Library, and Peyton stepped out into the cold December day. A gust of wind carried a chill, though it was nothing compared to the bone-penetrating gales in the Arctic. And despite the cold, there was no snow on the roofs.

There were also no people in sight, only a few abandoned bicycles leaning against the iron fence across the street. Christmas was in a few days, but no wreaths hung in the windows, no garlands, no strings of lights. In this town devoted to tradition, survival had taken priority.

The Bodleian's Great Gate lay ahead. At five stories tall, it was the largest gate tower in England. It was also called the Tower of the Five Orders of Architecture, owing to its Tuscan, Doric, Ionic, Corinthian, and Composite decorative elements. Peyton took in the beautiful stone structure as they marched past its heavy wooden double doors. A ticket booth for tours sat deserted, and beyond, the Old Schools Quadrangle was also empty.

Their footsteps echoed in the stone courtyard as they crossed, altering their course only to go around a bronze statue of the Earl of Pembroke, who was the chancellor of the university from 1617 to 1630.

Another set of wooden double doors led to the library's vast entrance hall. Large circular information desks lay at each end. A tall man who looked to be about sixty introduced himself as the Bodleian's librarian. Ten younger assistant librarians crowded behind him, taking in the SAS troops and Peyton's party with expressions of surprise and curiosity.

On the plane, Lin, Peyton, and Avery had discussed how to find a first edition of *Alice's Adventures In Wonderland*. Normally, they would have used SOLO—Search Oxford Libraries Online. But Avery's Rubicon contact had confirmed that SOLO had gone offline when the internet routers had been compromised. The contact had asked for the title they were looking for, but Lin had been emphatic that they not reveal it. It was Lin's decision instead that they would select three librarians at random to accompany Peyton, Avery, and herself as they searched for the books. Nigel would remain behind with the SAS troops and Navy SEALs. Lin still didn't trust him enough to include him in the search.

Lin didn't introduce herself or say anything about what they were doing here. She scanned the librarians and pointed at three of them: two men and a woman. Together, they made their way out of the entrance hall.

The room they entered was breathtaking. It reminded Peyton of a medieval church. On each side were five wide windows, at least twelve feet across and twenty feet high, with Gothic arches and stained-glass panes. The ceiling was ribbed in stone. Peyton felt like she was walking through the belly of a giant whale, seeing its back and spine from the inside. The ribs met in star formations that flowed toward the floor like stone icicles hanging from the ceiling.

And something about the place was familiar. "What's this part of the library called?" she asked the librarian walking next to her, a girl about her age with brown hair and glasses that were slightly too large for her face.

"It's the Divinity School. It was built in the 1400s. It's the oldest surviving purpose-built university building."

Peyton nodded.

Another librarian, a young man with black hair said, "It was in Harry Potter. The infirmary."

That was how Peyton knew it.

The female librarian shook her head, clearly perturbed that pop culture was coming to define this historic place.

They stopped in the middle of the room, and Lin said, "What we're about to do here is very important. Many lives are at stake. You must not reveal anything I'm about to tell you or what occurs after."

The librarians went wide-eyed. Lin waited for everyone to nod.

"We're looking for a book. A first edition of *Alice's Adventures In Wonderland*."

The female librarian spoke up. "Which first edition?"

"What do you mean?" Lin asked.

"Well, the first print run was planned for two thousand books. But they were scrapped at Carroll's direction."

"Elaborate."

"The publisher, The Clarendon Press, now MacMillan, sent Carroll fifty advance copies in June of 1865—copies the author could give away. But when the illustrator, John Tenniel, saw them, he told Carroll that he was dissatisfied with the way his drawings were printed. Carroll asked for the advance copies he had sent out to be returned, and he told the publisher to sell the rest of the two thousand books as waste paper."

"He was a perfectionist," Lin said, almost to herself.

"Yes. 'First Alice,' as the editions are called, are exceedingly rare. Sixteen of the known copies are in institutions. Another five are in private hands. Christie's auctioned a copy last year. Bidding reached almost two million dollars, but it failed to sell."

"Yes," Lin said. "That's the edition we're looking for. Are there any copies here at Oxford?"

"Of course. Carroll was one of the dons of the university. It was written here. There's a copy at the library in Lady Margaret Hall. Another in the closed stacks at Weston. And the last is upstairs, in the Duke Humfrey's Library."

"Good. We'll form three teams—each led by one of the three of us," Lin motioned to Peyton and Avery, "and accompanied by a librarian."

Lin assigned Peyton to the upstairs location, and Peyton knew why: safety. Most of the SAS troops were located here, and going outside was a risk; Yuri or his men could already be in Oxford, waiting to ambush them.

The female librarian, who introduced herself as Eleanor, led Peyton upstairs. The Duke Humfrey's Library was incredible. Stacks of books on dark-stained wood shelves stretched the length of a two-story room. The hazy, midday light blazed through the window. Peyton recognized this place as well, and she placed it this time: this was the library used in the Harry Potter movies. The setting had served as a turning point in so many of the stories. Tom Riddle, the series' antagonist, had entered the restricted section to find *Secrets of the Darkest Art*, a book that revealed how to live after death through horcruxes. Harry had visited the restricted section too, often wearing his invisibility cloak. Peyton felt almost like a character from the books, someone caught in a vast fight between good and evil.

"Here it is," Eleanor said.

She spread a cloth on a nearby table and donned white cloth gloves. She withdrew a silver key from her pocket, opened a glass cabinet, and gently withdrew a small red volume. There were no words on the cover, just an emblem in the center: a circle, engraved in gold, containing the silhouette of a girl with flowing hair holding a pig. Three golden lines ran around the cover's edges.

Gripping it with both hands, Eleanor turned the book so Peyton could see the back cover, which also had a round golden emblem, this one containing an illustration of a Cheshire cat. She then set the book on the table and glanced at Peyton, who nodded for her to proceed.

Eleanor opened the book.

The title page read:

ALICE'S
ADVENTURES IN WONDERLAND

BY
LEWIS CARROLL

WITH FORTY-TWO ILLUSTRATIONS
BY
JOHN TENNIEL

Eleanor continued turning the pages gently, past the table of contents and to the first page of chapter one, which was obscured by a see-through piece of trace paper. It looked as though someone had begun tracing something, but stopped. Eleanor turned past the loose page, revealing the illustration and text below it.

The chapter heading read: DOWN THE RABBIT-HOLE. The illustration featured a rabbit standing upright wearing a waistcoat and holding an umbrella. He was peering at a pocket-watch.

"I've never seen an original copy with vellum pages," Eleanor said.

It was a beautiful volume, but Peyton was more interested in that sheet of trace paper. "Can you hold that paper up to the light?" she asked.

Eleanor removed the semi-transparent page from the book and held it so the light from the two-story window shone through it.

Peyton activated her comm. "We've got something here."

Her mother responded instantly. "Say nothing more over the radio. Avery, retrieve your book, but don't open it. We'll meet back at the Divinity School."

Eleanor carefully returned the trace paper to the book. "Should we go back down, or...?"

"No. We've got time. Keep going."

Eleanor continued turning pages. There were more pieces of trace paper—one for each illustration at the beginning of the first five chapters.

"What are these?" Eleanor asked.

"I don't know." But Peyton had a sense of it now. Dr. Paul Kraus had left this here—these were his bread crumbs. What they meant, she didn't know.

☣

When all three teams had gathered in the ornate room in the

Divinity School, Lin dismissed the librarians and SAS troops, requesting that they remain sequestered in the Duke Humfrey's Library above. The two Navy SEALs led Nigel into the room, where the three first-edition *Alice* copies lay on a long table.

"We searched the other two," Lin said. "No markings or notes." She held up the first page of trace paper Peyton had found. "This is what Kraus wanted us to find."

Avery was unimpressed. "An incomplete drawing?"

"It's complete enough," Lin murmured.

She took a sheet of paper from her coat pocket and began drawing. Peyton didn't recognize what it was at first, but when Lin sketched the Strait of Gibraltar, she realized Lin was making a map of Western Europe.

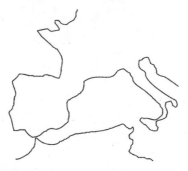

Lin placed the trace paper on top of her crudely drawn map. The lines met for the most part.

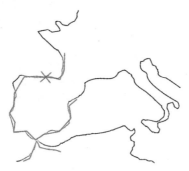

"A map," Nigel said. "We'll need to get a detailed—"

"I know where this is," Lin said.

The group fell silent.

"It's in northern Spain, outside Santillana del Mar. There's a cave there that once changed our understanding of human history. And I think it's about too once again."

"The Cave of Altamira," Nigel said.

"Yes. I believe that cave is our rabbit hole."

CHAPTER 27

YURI'S PLANE WAS flying thirty thousand feet above the Atlantic when his sat phone rang. It was Melissa Whitmeyer, the Citium's best remaining analyst.

"We're tracking Lin Shaw's plane off the coast of Spain. It's losing altitude."

"Likely destination?"

"Santander."

That didn't make sense. Unless—

Whitmeyer answered his unspoken question. "We checked. There's no record of Shaw ever visiting there."

"What about Kraus?"

Keyboard keys clacking.

"No. The *Beagle* never stopped there either."

"Interesting."

"We'll be out of sat range in thirty minutes. Shaw might know that. She could be stopping to change planes."

"Next flyover?"

"Two hours. We've got most of the satellites tasked to coordinate the Looking Glass transfer in rural areas."

That was a problem. If he couldn't figure out where Lin Shaw was going, he was going to lose her.

"Keep digging. On Shaw *and* Kraus. And activate everyone we have in Western Europe. I want the planes on the tarmac and ready."

CHAPTER 28

THEY LANDED IN Santander, a port city on Spain's northern coast, and drove southwest on the A-67. Their entourage had grown. The SAS troops had followed them to Spain, and been joined by just as many soldiers from the Spanish Army's Special Operations Command. Adams and Rodriguez were still with them, as was Nigel.

Peyton stared out the SUV's window at the rolling green countryside. It was beautiful, almost like a rainforest: damp and cloudy, with lush vegetation unrestrained by civilization. The terrain grew mountainous as they moved inland. One of the Spanish special forces remarked that Spain was the second most mountainous country in Europe. Only Switzerland had more mountains. Peyton was happy to have the conversation; the others all seemed lost in thought, perhaps contemplating what they'd find at the Cave of Altamira.

The sun was setting when they arrived at the cave complex. Vehicles broke from the convoy as they entered. One blocked the access road, while two others barricaded the entrances and exits to the car park. The remainder parked at the visitor center, which was set into the hill and had a flat roof covered in grass, making it almost disappear into the landscape.

Lin forbid any of the SAS or Spanish troops from accompanying them into the cave, so they set about establishing a defensive perimeter and making camp inside the visitor center. The museum section of the visitor center had a large room with rough stone walls and ceilings, replicating the cave Altamira's prehistoric residents had inhabited, and its plate glass windows looked out on the green, hilly countryside beyond. The troops seemed to like it; they unrolled their sleeping bags there and laid down their packs. Their piles of munitions and supplies contrasted bizarrely with the exhibits and informational placards.

Lin led their group up the paved walkway toward the cave mouth as the last rays of sunlight retreated over the hills. The entrance to the cave was rectangular and framed with timbers, like an open doorway into a grassy hill. Large mature trees towered on both sides.

Inside, they flicked on their lanterns. The two SEALs were the only guards they had brought with them. Their defensive plan relied entirely on the troops surrounding the entrance and visitor center.

The temperature dropped quickly as they ventured deeper into the cave. The narrow passageway soon opened into a large chamber with a long glass case that held stones and informational cards. There was a small alleyway to the right, another vast chamber to the left, and two large openings dead ahead. One wall held colorful silhouettes of handprints in red and black, as if the Altamirans were waving at them across thousands of years. Other walls held paintings of what looked like horses, goats, and wild boars. On the ceiling was a large mural of a herd of steppe bison.

Peyton found the art breathtaking, almost otherworldly. The others also appeared to be transfixed—except for Lin, who had set her lantern on the long glass case and taken the book from her pack. Peyton was a little worried about the moisture in the cave affecting the rare tome, but with the fate of humanity on the line, she decided to let it slide.

"Now then," Lin said. "Peyton found the map to Altamira at the start of chapter one. I think the symmetry of our expedition and the story is lost on none of us. Alice follows the White Rabbit down the rabbit hole, landing herself in a large room with many doors. Those doors are either too large or too small. She grows and shrinks, in both cases too much so to fit through the doors and passageways. Altamira has over a thousand meters of known tunnels, and they indeed shrink and expand. The going ahead will likely be difficult."

"You've been here before?" Peyton asked.

Lin didn't look up. "Yes."

"When?"

"A long time ago." Peyton sensed that her mother was eager to avoid further questions.

Lin gently turned the pages to the sheet of trace paper at the start of the second chapter. She peeled it back, revealing the illustration beneath.

The title below the illustration read, THE POOL OF TEARS. The first line of the text read, "Curiouser and curiouser!"

Lin had acquired a map of the cave's tunnels in the visitor center. She pulled it out now and placed the trace paper over it. "As I thought," she said. "It's another map."

She led them to the back of the room, where an alcove branched to the left and a wide passageway lay to the right. They took the passage, and kept left at a fork. The walls and ceiling were adorned with more paintings, animals in flocks and some alone. They had walked about three hundred feet when Lin stopped and studied the trace paper atop the map.

"It's close."

She held her lantern up and searched, walking slowly. She stooped and stared at a narrow opening in the wall. "Through here."

They not only had to stoop, but soon, crawl. The rock grew damper the farther they traveled. Suddenly, the tunnel opened into an irregular-shaped chamber, like a skewed pentagon.

"Dead end," Nigel muttered.

Lin walked along the perimeter of the room. "Doubtful."

"In the book," Avery said, "Alice grows tall and hits her head on the ceiling. Her tears pool, and when she shrinks, she swims out."

Peyton studied her, surprised.

Avery shrugged. "My dad used to read it to me."

"Cute," Nigel said. "What does it mean?"

Lin had stopped at a small indentation in the stone wall. "Bring a canteen."

Adams stepped over to her, canteen uncapped and held out.

Peyton peered around him. In the lantern's dim light, she saw Lin reach into a ledge and grab a small object. A figurine of a mouse.

"Alice meets a mouse as she swims through her own tears," Avery said.

Lin nodded absently and tipped the canteen slightly, pouring water into the crevice where she had found the mouse. She paused every few seconds and listened. Peyton listened too, hearing only water trickling beyond and dripping. But after the seventh time Lin stopped pouring, a click sounded beyond the stone wall.

Peyton understood then: the crevice must lead to a tank that, when filled, activated a mechanism that unlocked the hidden door.

Lin pushed against the wall. It gave, revealing a hidden room beyond.

CHAPTER 29

CONNER PEERED THROUGH the peephole in the front door. XI soldiers stood outside, two on the stoop, two others cupping hands at their temples and gazing through the bay window.

The man on the stoop activated his radio. "One forty-five is empty."

They walked across the lawn to the next home. They were simply evacuating the street, clearing residents in the path of the fire.

Conner exhaled. He would have to wait for the troops to move on—and for Desmond's memory to complete. But they were safe for now.

Yuri was waiting in the hotel when Desmond arrived, sitting in an armchair by the floor-to-ceiling windows. Desmond sat in the other chair, ignoring the fact that he was soaking with sweat from his morning run.

"I see it, Yuri. All of it. I know what it means."

As usual, the older man's voice was emotionless. "Start at the beginning, Desmond. It's important. This is your final test."

"Test before what?" Desmond wanted to hear him say it.

"Admission to the Citium. And the things you want."

"The things you promised me? Peyton. My brother."

"Yes."

Desmond stood. He felt like a PhD student defending his thesis.

In many ways, that's what Yuri's bizarre training had been like: grad school for some master of the universe course.

"Western Europe took over the world five hundred years ago. They had an advantage none of the rest of the world understood. They had you, Yuri."

"I'm old, but I'm not that old."

"Not you per se—but people like you. The Citium. Scientists. Thinkers."

"Start at the beginning, Desmond."

"All right." He took a moment, gathered his thoughts. "There have been three pivotal events in human history. These... anomalies created the world we live in. Your three questions—their purpose was for me to find these events and understand them. And I know why. Because they are the key to understanding the future—what's going to happen to the entire human race."

Yuri nodded. "Go on."

"The first event occurred somewhere between seventy and forty-five thousand years ago. Somewhere on Earth, a human developed a new ability. A cognitive breakthrough. They possessed a mind that thought differently. That human had the ability to imagine something that didn't already exist. Our predecessors created tools, but those were mostly reactive, incremental steps that were almost obvious. This event signified the birth of fiction—a mind that could literally simulate a reality that didn't exist. A reality radically different from the human's own. This human could render possible futures, imagine what life would be like *if* something existed. That was the transcendental mutation."

"Evidence?"

Desmond smiled. "All roads lead to Australia. That's what your first question was about: concrete evidence, perhaps our earliest, of a human imagining a fictive future *and making it a reality*. Not just painting it on a cave wall. Somewhere in South Asia, roughly fifty thousand years ago, a prehistoric human, whose name we will never know, stood on a beach, stared at the ocean, and imagined something they had never seen before, a device that had never before existed on Earth: a boat. An invention that would carry their people to a land they had never seen, a place they didn't know for a fact was even there. We know only that this person did in fact build that boat or raft and crossed vast expanses of open sea with their people. And they landed here, in Australia, becoming the first human to ever set foot on this continent.

"The reward was unimaginable. Big game. An endless buffet of animals that were attuned to their environment, but were completely unprepared for the invaders. And that's the irony of these intrepid Australians—the original colonists of this continent. They missed the second revolution: agriculture. They feasted on the megafauna, contributed to the Quaternary extinction event the *Beagle* found evidence of. But when the food was gone, their populations stayed small. Fragmented, each tribe adapting to its environment. They plateaued. When the next invaders arrived, fifty thousand years later, they were the prey."

"Why?"

"Agriculture, and the cities it brought with it, brought further changes to human brains, and especially culture. Beginning twelve thousand years ago, for the first time in history, our ancestors planted roots, literally and figuratively. Instead of chasing game and gathering their sustenance, never knowing where their next meal would come from, we had a sustainable source of calories, renewable and controllable."

"Consequences?" Yuri asked.

"Massive. Human society saw its biggest change in history. Up until this point, all of our ancestors had been tribal. Small groups, mostly migratory. We were at the mercy of our food supply. Every human on Earth coasted on fumes, literally chasing our next meal to feed our over-sized brains.

"But those enormous brains should never have existed. They're a mystery, a biological anomaly."

"Explain."

"The human brain uses way too much of the caloric energy a human takes in. For millions of years, the brain would have been an evolutionary *dis*advantage—that is, up until this transcendental mutation, the advent of imagination, came about. Imagination, fictive simulation, is what propelled our species across the planet—literally—and enabled us to conquer it. But for thousands of years after we developed fictive simulation, we were still struggling to survive—and to power the massive resource hog."

Yuri raised his eyebrows. "Resource hog?"

"In the extreme. Consider this. Earth is roughly 4.5 billion years old. Life, in some form, has existed for 3.8 billion years—beginning with single-cell prokaryotic life, bacteria perhaps. Since then, the history of life on this planet has been a series of fits and starts—a biological roulette wheel testing combinations that would ultimately arrive at this device, the human brain, a biological computer, something that by the laws of nature shouldn't exist. The human brain consumes 20 percent of the calories we ingest, but it accounts for only 2 percent of our weight. No species in the history of the planet has ever dedicated so much of the calories they consume to their brains.

"But the advantage it provided was unimaginable. We are the first species to ever command the planet, to imagine what it could be and reshape it based on the images in our minds.

"And it was agriculture that enabled this intellectual revolution to scale up. Grain and livestock provided a renewable, sustainable source of power for our biological computers. Cities networked them together, enabled minds to share ideas and focus on innovation like never before. And this revolution—the advent of cities—came with consequences, some bad, but some very, very good. Before agriculture, our ancestors had never organized themselves in permanent, high-density settlements. The formation of cities resulted in a concentration of brainpower. It's like…"

Desmond grasped for an analogy and found one from his own past. "It's like the personal computer. In the eighties, they got more powerful all the time. But they were isolated. They sat in our homes, running programs and games, but their data stayed local. That changed when local area networks became ubiquitous. The servers stored data, clients ran productivity programs, and workers could collaborate and share ideas. Efficiency went up. The speed of commerce accelerated."

Yuri stood to join Desmond at the window, smiling. Desmond was filled with energy. He felt that he was on the cusp of a breakthrough. Here, in the place where his life had disintegrated, he sensed that he was on the verge of making a discovery that would help him put it back together. Peyton. His brother. His own limitations.

"The third seminal event that turned the history of humanity was another cognitive revolution. A new kind of software for operating the human mind. You asked how the Western Europeans were different from the rest of the world. Why the Spanish conquered Central and South America. Why the British flag flew across the world. The examples are incredible. In 1519, Hernán Cortés landed in Mexico with no more than 550 men. Within two years, he had defeated the Aztec empire, which had almost five *million* inhabitants. The Aztecs' capital, Tenochtitlan, now Mexico City, had over two hundred thousand residents, roughly the same size as Europe's two largest cities: Paris and Naples. In the war, the Spanish and their allies lost a thousand men. The Aztecs, over two hundred thousand.

"Pizarro conquered the Incan empire with even fewer soldiers —168.

"The British in India were even more remarkable. In the nineteenth and early twentieth century, India had over three hundred million inhabitants, yet the British ruled it with about five thousand officials and less than seventy thousand soldiers. Remarkable."

Desmond sat back down. "The key to this success? People like you, Yuri. Individuals dedicated to science."

"The Chinese and Indians had scientists."

"True. But science is only half of European colonists' breakthrough. Capitalism is the other half. This combination of *scientific capitalism* is what drove them. Capitalism provided a platform—a societal construct, if you will—for distributing value across a population, in particular to reward minds that imagined and implemented things that brought advantage to others. Case in point: a Spanish conquistador who established a new trade route enriched himself as well as the monarchy that supported him and that monarch's subjects. Even more to the point, consider the Dutch East India Company—one of the first joint stock companies in history. They issued shares to investors, gave them part of the profit, distributed the risk across a larger pool of people. This dual system is the most powerful construct to date: capitalism to manage risk and share rewards; science to expand efficiency and resources."

Desmond paused. "The Citium. It wasn't just the atomic bomb they created. It was all the things before. In those archives in San Francisco, there are mentions of the electric telegraph, the steam turbine, and even bigger discoveries like gravity and natural selection. The world we live in is the product of scientific capitalism."

"The consequence?"

"Globalization."

"Implication?"

"Our fate is reflected in our most famous invention: the computer. Those local area networks that sprang up like cities in the eighties and nineties got connected at the turn of the century by the internet. Just like European colonization connected the globe. Globalization is to the human race what the internet is to computers—a method for sharing resources and ideas. Ideas can now move around the world in nanoseconds. We have a platform for enabling the strongest minds to transform their thoughts into reality—and deploy that reality for the good of the masses.

"If you think about it, vision—fictive simulation—remains the most powerful human ability. Look at the Forbes list of the richest people. The individuals listed are very different, but they all share one trait: vision. The ability to imagine a future that doesn't exist—to imagine what the world would be like if something changed, if a product or service existed. And these people's fortunes were made because their visions were *accurate*—they correctly predicted that something that didn't already exist both *could be* created and *would be* valuable to a specific group of people.

"Take Bill Gates. He saw the power of the personal computer, but so did thousands of others. But his vision *also* told him that there would be many computer makers, and many software makers, and that there would need to be a ubiquitous operating system that every computer used so that it could run any software. That same sort of fictive simulation occurs every day in companies everywhere; right now there are internet companies like Amazon and eBay who are imagining what life will be like with their products. The question is whether their simulations are right. But if they are, they'll be worth a huge amount of money. In every walk of life—business, politics, military, art, fashion, everything—the quintessential ability is simulating the future accurately."

Desmond stopped there, sure that he had satisfied Yuri's great test.

The older man sat back down. "Now tell me what comes next."

"What?"

"Desmond, we are on the cusp of a fourth and final revolution. Consider this: in February of 1966, the Soviet Union soft-landed a space probe on the moon. Humanity has been launching programs ever since. NASA launched Voyager 1 in September of 1977. In 2012 it became the first satellite to reach interstellar space. At some point, Voyager will fall into the gravity well of a planet, or asteroid, or even another planet's moon. Possibly a black hole. The point is that it *will* crash somewhere—maybe on a place like our moon, but orbiting another planet, very far away." Yuri smiled. "And if that's true, then why has it not happened here—on our moon, which is over four and a half billion years old? The greatest mystery in the world is why our moon isn't covered with space junk."

"Space junk?"

"Interstellar probes—like Voyager 1—from other sentient species across the universe, launched long before we evolved, launched long before there was even life on our world."

Desmond turned the question over in his mind. It was incredible. A mystery in plain sight—of staggering implications.

"What are you telling me?"

"I'm showing you evidence of our future. An event we can't avoid. One that's closer than you realize. Right now, Desmond, there are humans who think differently. I'm one of them. And I believe *you're* one of them, just as I said to you months ago. You are awake.

"Very soon, the next revolution will begin. It will be more profound than the emergence of fiction. Or agriculture. Or the scientific revolution, or global capitalism, or the internet—though they were all necessary precursors. This revolution will change everything. Forever. And we are creating it. The *Citium* is creating it. Look closely. Consider what you've learned. The next step is inevitable. Do you see it? It's written in the pattern of history."

Desmond pondered Yuri's words, what he'd learned, the long arc of human history. In his mind's eye, he saw a pattern now, pieces fitting together, the wide view—as if his eyes had been mere inches from a painting, but now he had stepped back and could see it all, understand it.

The pieces were there, in history—the stepping stones that had created the modern world. The first event: brains that operated like simulation machines. Then agriculture and cities to power them. Cities to network them together. Ships to trade goods and ideas, then railroads, the electric telegraph, telephone lines, fax machines, dial-up modems, fiber-optic lines. Faster and broader networks, facilitating access to calories and the exchange of information. He saw it all, and for the first time, he saw where it was going.

He glimpsed the Looking Glass, and he was in awe.

CHAPTER 30

CONNER SAT IN Lin Shaw's kitchen, the refrigerator and freezer door open, the blast of cold air barely dampening the heat from the blaze. Sweat dripped from his face onto his body armor.

Major Goins entered and squatted down in front of him. "Sir, we have to go."

"We stay, Major."

"Sir—"

"You have your orders."

Goins marched into the garage. Conner heard muffled voices, men arguing with Goins' orders, threatening to mutiny and leave.

The conflict steeled Conner. He thrived on opposition. It had been the key to his survival as a child.

He walked to the doorway, watched as the men fell silent.

His voice was calm. "We'll be leaving shortly."

A tall, short-haired man with a scar on his chin glanced at the five mercenaries gathered behind him. "Will that be *before* or *after* we burn to death?"

Conner let his hand fall to the gun holster at his side. "If you open your mouth again, it will be after I kill you."

Silence. The man's gaze softened and fell to the concrete floor. With each second the roar of the fire grew louder, like a wind tunnel being turned up.

"Load up," Conner said. "I'll be driving."

That was the only way to guarantee the van didn't leave before he was ready.

As they filed into the van, he leaned close to Dr. Park and whispered, "Time, Doctor?"

"Minutes. Not long."

Conner got behind the wheel, buckled up, and rolled the windows down.

A voice called over the radio. "Zero, Unit two. We've got a problem. X1s are using El Camino Real as a firebreak—they've got air support dumping suppressant on the road. It's impassable. They're doing the same on Valparaiso Avenue. They've got checkpoints set up. They're cataloging evacuees and routing them to Stanford. Flame-retardant barricades are set up at the other intersections."

"Use the drone," Conner said. "Find a weak checkpoint and converge a block from there. Wait for us. We'll breach it together."

Assuming the fire didn't arrive first.

If Conner did make it to the checkpoint, he knew everything would change: the X1 troops would know for sure a sophisticated adversary was operating in their theater. They would likely assume that Conner's team had set the fire. The X1 units would then turn Menlo Park upside down looking for them. He hoped the next Labyrinth location was far away.

To Desmond, the world looked completely different than it had just a second before. The past made sense. The future was clear.

In the hotel room overlooking Victoria Park in Adelaide, Yuri finally spoke. "Tell me what you see, Desmond. What is our destiny?"

"A world where only one thing matters: the strength of your mind. Where it doesn't matter where you're from or what you look like. A world where all wounds can be healed, even the ones in our minds. Where a person can start over."

"You understand now." Yuri stood, and Desmond followed suit. "We're building that world. Will you help us?"

"Until the end."

Yuri nodded.

"How?" Desmond asked. "Tell me exactly how the Looking Glass will function."

Yuri spoke at length, describing the one Citium conclave that had been removed from the archives. He described a device of breathtaking ambition. Desmond asked question after question, and each time, Yuri had an answer. Much of the technology would still need to be created, but there was a roadmap to do just that.

"Where do I fit in?" Desmond asked.

"Soon. You'll know soon."

"Then where do we start?"

"With the ones we love. The ones we'll save."

In his mind's eye, Desmond saw a smiling face, framed by dark hair, lit by the glow of the moon behind her. He saw them lying on a blanket in the sand dunes, wind whistling off the sea, Peyton kissing him with reckless abandon. Then he saw a baby's face, sitting in a high chair, smiling at him. The memory of Conner was the last he had.

"Would you like to see your brother again?"

"Yes. More than anything in this world."

☣

They rented a car, and Desmond drove while Yuri recited directions from memory. The route took them north, out of Adelaide, into industrial areas and high-crime suburbs. Well-kept neighborhoods turned to dive bars and run-down strip malls, then warehouses and body shops. They entered Port Adelaide. Desmond took it all in. There were signs for the rubbish dump north of A9. The fisherman's wharf. Train and bus stations.

"You knew," Desmond said. "He was here all along." What he didn't say was, *And you let me search in vain.*

But Yuri answered the unspoken accusation. "It's natural. You couldn't help but look for him. I would have."

"What happened to him after the hospital?"

Yuri stared through the windshield. "Turn left here."

The apartment building was in bad shape, with tarps over several sections of roof. Motorcycles and old beat-up muscle cars sat in the parking spaces.

"Park near the back," Yuri said.

Desmond did so and turned the car off. He pulled the door handle.

"Stay."

Desmond glanced at Yuri, who whispered, "You need to see him first."

Desmond pulled the door closed, now worried. He watched the apartment complex's outdoor staircase as people filed out and headed to work.

"Not long now," Yuri said.

Desmond wondered if he would recognize Conner. It had been twenty years. He had been a baby then. But Desmond had read the reports. *Third-degree burns over 30 percent of his body.* Sadly, his brother would be easy to pick out. And he was.

On that overcast day in late May, in the early days of the South Australian winter, Desmond saw his brother for the first time as an adult.

Conner trudged up the stairs from his garden apartment, grungy, long hair hanging down over his face. Thick burn scars covered his right cheek, chin, and forehead. Mottled flesh pulled at his right eye, making him look like a photograph that had been rained on, the image partially washed away, the damage irreversible.

He lit a cigarette and swapped it from hand to hand as he pulled on a hooded sweatshirt, covering the red marks and bruises in the crook of his elbow. As he walked away, Desmond realized something.

"He's why you chose me, isn't he? You knew, even before you came to my office."

"He's only half the reason."

Desmond waited.

"There's a piece of the Looking Glass that only a mind like yours can create."

"What is it?"

"Rendition."

Desmond saw it then—the true sequence of events, how everything was connected. Him and Peyton. Lin Shaw had seen her daughter's despair, had gone to Yuri, suggested they bring Desmond in and use the Looking Glass to help both of them. Yuri had researched Desmond, discovered that he could be useful—and more, that he could be controlled. But Yuri likely concluded that Peyton wouldn't provide enough leverage to control Desmond; after all, romantic love could be fickle. Conner was the key.

Desmond felt that he understood Yuri a little more then. The man had said before that his specialty was knowing what people would do, but the truth was darker than that—Yuri needed to control people. That's how he knew what they would do. The revelation brought Desmond pause, but even then, he knew he was already committed. He couldn't walk away from his brother. And Yuri might hold the only hope of healing his wounds.

As Conner slipped out of view, Yuri said, "He's like us, Desmond. A victim of circumstances. But it's not too late for him. The Looking Glass is his only hope." He paused, let the words sink in. "We have that power."

"What happens now?" Desmond asked.

"I need something else from you."

Desmond waited.

"I need to know you'll finish what we start. We'll have to cross bridges that will make you uncomfortable."

Desmond stared at the older man, this visionary who was literally holding out the promise of saving his brother's life. "I walked through fire to try to save him once. I'll do it again—even if it burns me alive this time."

CHAPTER 31

TO DESMOND'S SURPRISE, they didn't contact Conner. He paid the private detectives, including Arlo, and told them the search was over. He stayed in Adelaide, and so did Yuri. They rented condos in the city center and began planning.

They sat in the living room, Yuri drinking tea, Desmond fidgeting, anxious to get on with it.

"Where do we start?" Desmond asked.

"Delphi."

"What?"

"The Temple at Delphi," Yuri said. "The words printed above the entrance: *Know Thyself*. That's the key to understanding Conner's path. He has spent his life reacting to his environment, fleeing pain, minimizing his suffering, never truly discovering who he is."

"Okay," Desmond said slowly. "How do we help him discover who he is?"

"We take him out of his environment." Yuri laid a folder on the coffee table.

Desmond rifled through it. To his surprise, it was the financial statements for an Australian web hosting company named Yellow Brick Road. "I don't follow."

"We need a crucible in which to burn away the things this world has poisoned Conner with. A way to discover his strengths and weaknesses."

"Right. But a web hosting company?"

"In the coming years, internet infrastructure will become increasingly important—like the railroads during the industrial revolution. They're also essential to the Looking Glass." Yuri placed another folder on the coffee table. Another company profile—one Desmond recognized. Rook Web Hosting.

"You'll invest in Rook via Icarus Capital," Yuri said.

Desmond looked up.

"Icarus will become a Citium subsidiary. We'll divest irrelevant companies and focus on companies relevant to the Looking Glass."

Yuri had just asked Desmond for his entire fortune as casually as if he were asking Desmond for a cup of coffee. And Desmond was willing to give it. Anything for Conner.

"You'll join Rook's board," Yuri continued. "And Rook will purchase this Australian company, Yellow Brick Road. You'll oversee Yellow Brick's integration with Rook, under the guise of a concerned board member. I believe you're familiar with IT infrastructure."

"Very."

"You'll make suggestions. One will be to have the network engineers focus on what they do best—programming routers, rebuilding servers, and software patches."

Desmond could see where this was going. "And we'll hire a small group of manual laborers to move the servers, unpack new equipment, maintain the cages, even pull wire. A job Conner could do."

"Yes."

"Then what?"

"Then we heal him. We'll introduce voluntary drug rehab as an employee benefit. If he doesn't go, we'll begin drug testing and make rehab mandatory."

"What if he doesn't go to rehab?"

"He will. By then he won't want to lose his job and everything that comes with it."

Yuri handed a brochure to Desmond. It was for a treatment center called Red Dunes. "This is where we'll do the real work.

Get him healthy again. Classes on how to keep his addiction in check. And we'll have skill-building courses. We'll see what's inside him, and we'll nurture that."

Desmond flipped through the brochure. The facility was in an old English-style country home with a stone exterior, limestone lintels over the windows, and green vines growing up the sides to a gray slate roof. It was a bit run-down on the outside, but the interior was updated—not lavish, but clean and cozy. They grew their own fruits and vegetables—the home was set on two hundred acres—and bought meat from local farmers. Cooking was one of the courses, as were gardening, sewing, even computer programming.

"Do we own it?"

"Red Dunes? It's a non-profit. But I made a sizable contribution last week when I met with the executive director. They'll form a partnership with Rook and take *very* good care of the people we send." Yuri paused. "When he returns to work, Conner will be a new person. He'll be the person he was supposed to be. And you'll guide his career."

Emotion overwhelmed Desmond. Hope. Gratitude. He swallowed and said the only thing he could manage. "Thank you."

Desmond watched Yuri's plan unfolded exactly as predicted. He knew that Yuri was doing this not only to help Conner—and Desmond—but to prove that he could be trusted. And that his plans became reality.

Conner took the job at Rook Hosting—for the money, Desmond assumed. At first, he injected most of that money into his arm, and tucked the rest into the bikini bottoms and bra straps of strippers. After a while, he began saving a bit of it and slowly made a few changes. He moved out of North Adelaide, closer to his job in the city center. He bought some clothes. With each passing week, he became a little more attached to the job that provided for his new lifestyle. Attached enough to go to rehab when asked.

During that time, Desmond was receiving an education of his own—on the Citium and its many branches. Companies. Subsidiaries. Non-profits. Research projects. It was a web seemingly without end, a labyrinth of which he had glimpsed only pieces during his time at SciNet.

Twice Desmond asked Yuri if he should begin on his portion of the Looking Glass, and both times, he got the same response: "Focus on your brother for now."

Yuri gave Desmond a dossier on Conner that was much more detailed than what Desmond had been able to assemble. It traced the young man's journey through the South Australian foster system. Most of the records were unofficial, simply recollections of people who had worked there and cared for the young boy. They described a child who was curious and happy as an infant and toddler. That was followed by a troubled childhood. He was laughed at. Picked on. He was constantly getting in fights, listed as a troublemaker, always one of the first to be transferred when a new spot became available at another home.

He bounced around for years. He was the child no one wanted—including the adoptive parents who visited the homes. Desmond imagined Conner lining up or sitting in the playroom, his badly scarred face twisting into a smile for the first few families who came to call. Then learning to remain stoic, to expect rejection. Desmond's heart broke all over again as he read the notes. His memories of his brother were of a happy-go-lucky, kind-hearted child. An innocent with his whole life ahead of him. And it had been snatched away by a twist of fate. It wasn't fair. Conner had done nothing to deserve the life he was given.

Desmond replayed the fire in his mind. If only he had kept going, crossed the wall of fire, gotten to the home, he could have gotten Conner out. If only he had been stronger. Had more will. If only he had stayed home that day. Or come home earlier. He had been so wrapped up in building that stupid fort.

In foster care, Conner found escape in video games, much like Desmond had retreated into books as a child. Most of the homes had some sort of game system—mostly used, donated by some family who had upgraded. Conner started on the Atari, moved to the Nintendo, and then the Super Nintendo. He was only at peace when he was sitting in front of the TV, lost in a role-playing game or strategy game. Despite his real-world record of fighting and disorder, he disliked any games with excessive violence. He never cared for Mortal Kombat, Contra, Ninja Gaiden, or even racing games like R.C. Pro-Am. His favorites were epic role-playing games where a young hero sets out from a broken land to save his people. In games like Dragon Warrior, he spent hours gaining experience points, leveling his players up, and saving money to buy better armor and weapons. He made allies, and beat the game over and over. The game console was his only companion, and the foster home administrators were happy to leave him to it.

Yuri's notes solved another mystery Desmond hadn't thought about for a long time: the fate of his beloved dog, Rudolph. He assumed the fire had claimed him as well, but it hadn't. In fact, Rudolph was partially responsible for saving Conner. The aid workers had found the kelpie barking at the burned remains of the home. One of the aid workers who found Conner went on to adopt the dog. The records ended there, but the news brought a rare smile to Desmond's face.

He was surprised to learn that Conner had been adopted at the age of fourteen. But there was no information on Anderson and Beatrix McClain. In its place was a handwritten note:

Desmond, see me for details —Yuri

As soon as Desmond saw that, he walked to Yuri's condo. "The McClains. The file is empty."

"It won't tell you anything you don't already know about Conner," Yuri said.

"What will it tell me about *them*?"

Yuri broke eye contact. "That they were bad people."

Desmond had assumed as much. There were two types of people who adopted troubled children: devils and saints. Desmond had hoped that the McClains were the better of the two.

"Where are they now?"

"Six feet under," Yuri said quietly.

"How?"

"Car accident."

Desmond already knew the older man so well. He was holding back. Desmond was glad.

"What did Conner do after?"

"He left. He was seventeen anyway, knew what the foster system had to offer him." Yuri walked into the living room and sat. "He left to find his own way in life, just like you." He sighed. "He just wasn't as lucky."

"He had a harder lot," Desmond said. "And I bet life on the docks in Adelaide wasn't half as easy as writing code in San Francisco."

"Perhaps. But we both know the years before you left Oklahoma weren't easy for you either. Orville Hughes wasn't a model parent."

"You can say that again," Desmond muttered.

"What you can't do," Yuri said, "is blame yourself. There's a big difference between a reason and an excuse. There's a reason why Conner's life was hard. And yours, too. But you never let it be an excuse. Responsibility is the difference. You took responsibility for your own actions. You made your choices. So did he. So have I. You can't blame yourself for what happened to him."

A silent moment passed.

"He's still young, Desmond. And he has you."

"And apparently you."

"The three of us have each other now."

"I'm thankful for that."

Desmond was also thankful that Yuri had redacted the history of Conner's life with the McClains. There was enough pain written in the rest of the file. Desmond was ready for his younger brother to put it all behind him.

That began in rehab. Desmond watched the video feeds, of Conner in the group sessions, his evasive answers, his tortured sleep that grew more restless with each night. His determination when withdrawal symptoms overwhelmed him. It was agonizing to watch. And impossible not to.

With the help of methadone, Conner finally broke free of his heroin addiction. The change in him was radical: he was like a person waking up from a deep sleep and a long nightmare. His demeanor changed. His mind was sharper. He was alive again. But the pain remained, as did his feelings of isolation, of not fitting in with the world. He had no friends. No family. His only solace had been the drug that had made him forget it all. And now he no longer had that. Desmond wanted desperately to drive to the treatment center, embrace his brother, and tell him the truth. Tell him that everything would soon be all right, that he wasn't alone.

Yuri urged him not to.

"Follow the plan, Desmond."

On the videos, he watched as Conner opened up in the group sessions. He connected with the others going through treatment, people as wounded as him. And in them, he found companions. He finally made human connections. It was a floodgate opening, parts of his mind that had lain dormant his entire life. He was a different person, and he was discovering who that person was. As Yuri had predicted, he was living the words written at Delphi— coming to know himself. Inside him was a strong resolve. A will to never touch drugs again, to never fall in the hole that had trapped him his entire adult life.

Yuri and Desmond encouraged the Red Dunes administrators to introduce Conner to a variety of classes and trades, to test his affinities. Unlike Desmond, Conner didn't excel at computer programming, or math, or any science field. He did, however, have a knack for strategy—no doubt honed by those countless hours playing video games.

"That's the key," Yuri said over dinner at a sushi restaurant.

"I don't follow," Desmond said.

"Rook Web Hosting will power the world's internet and data infrastructure one day."

Desmond ate a bite of sushi. It was good, almost as good as his favorite spot in San Francisco.

"Do you know what the key to Rook's success is?" Yuri didn't wait for Desmond to respond. "Resource allocation."

Desmond raised his eyebrows.

"The company needs a leader who's obsessive about the capabilities of every server, router, switch, and tape backup. Who can look at network demand around the world and allocate resources to regions likely to grow. Who can make the right choices about hardware in the data center and do accurate capacity forecasting."

Desmond understood. "Like a strategy game."

Yuri nodded.

"So it all comes back to hit points, magic points, leveling up those data centers, and upgrading the weapons and armor."

"In a sense."

Desmond put his chopsticks down. "You knew, didn't you?"

"I suspected what role Conner would play."

And he played that role well. In the following months, Conner joined Rook's South Australia purchasing team. He ended up saving the company half a million dollars by purchasing cheaper hardware that performed just as well for the same requirements. He did an audit of their existing hardware, sold off pieces they didn't need, and repurposed what was left. He spent every waking minute obsessing over four key stats: revenue, power consumed, network utilization, and hardware cost. His goal in life was to optimize those numbers, driving the company to the next level. He was made head of operations in Australia, and the following week, he and Desmond met for the first time.

Desmond was nervous as he entered the board room at Rook's Australian headquarters in Sydney. He had considered several approaches to meeting Conner, including doing it in private and coming clean. He'd decided against that one.

Desmond strode into a room with an impressive view of the city's downtown. He shook hands with each of the executives. When he came to Conner, their eyes met briefly, and Desmond knew he held Conner's hand a little too long. But his brother didn't seem to notice. Maybe he was used to people lingering on his face longer than was comfortable, holding the handshake while they stared.

Desmond barely listened to the presentation—except when Conner spoke. They were building a new data center in Melbourne. A possible acquisition in Christchurch, New Zealand. When the meeting ended, Desmond stood and promised to preview their requests to the board. As he walked out, he heard Conner call to him. "Mister Hughes."

Desmond's mouth ran dry. He turned.

Conner approached in a slow jog and held something out. "You forgot your pen."

Desmond was speechless for a moment. He reached out and took the pen. Conner turned and began walking away.

"Thank you, Conner," Desmond called, a little too loudly.

Yuri was waiting at Desmond's condo when he arrived home.

"And?" the man said simply.

Desmond shrugged. "We were strangers. But only he knew that. It was super, *super* awkward."

"For you, Desmond. Only for you."

"I have to tell him."

"Not yet."

Desmond shook his head. "Why?"

"Because he needs time to find himself. He's rebuilding his life. You know what that's like. He needs to do this for himself. He needs time and space to discover who he is and become the man he was always supposed to be. If you tell him now, it will distract him from his own life and career. It will confuse him. Wait, Desmond. I urge you."

Desmond relented.

And Yuri was right. From a distance, he watched Conner's successes and failures at Rook Web Hosting. His mind was incredibly well tuned for analytics, planning, and strategy. And in his own way, he was a charismatic leader. He was dogged when he set a goal. He didn't accept excuses—or care what people thought of him. He had thick skin, developed from years of rejection and ridicule.

Two years after he'd joined Rook, the board voted to make him CEO after the company's leader retired. Desmond made sure he was the last to vote. It was unanimous. Conner deserved the job.

Desmond was glad he had waited to contact him. But he couldn't resist any more. He invited Conner to his home in San Francisco—under the guise of discussing Rook's future plans.

And so, on a warm summer day in June of 2005, Desmond sat in his living room, waiting to introduce himself to his only living relative—the brother he had lost and found and brought back from the dead. He was nervous and overjoyed and counting down every second.

Five minutes early, the doorbell rang.

CHAPTER 32

YURI'S PLANE WAS in a holding pattern off the coast of Spain when his phone rang.

"We've got something," Whitmeyer said.

"Go ahead."

"In 1943, Kraus led an expedition to the Cave of Altamira."

Yuri had never heard of it.

Whitmeyer shuffled some papers. "We only know because it was mentioned at Nuremberg in the trial of another Nazi scientist. He claimed to have been with Kraus during the period, but Kraus denied it, and Kraus's trip was confirmed by a border guard called to testify."

"Interesting. What's in the cave?"

"Cave paintings. Some of the oldest ever found in Europe. It's a UNESCO World Heritage Site now."

"That's it—that's where she's going. Figure out a rally point somewhere outside the site. Be discreet. And send everyone we've got in the region. This is a fight we have to win."

CHAPTER 33

LIN STEPPED INSIDE the hidden room in the Cave of Altamira, holding her electric light out in front of her. From behind her, Peyton saw stacks of metal crates—just like the ones they had found on the *Beagle*, with round metal discs on the end that provided a view inside.

Lin stooped and slid one of the discs aside, then moved to several more, peering in each crate for only a second or two. "Bones," she whispered.

Peyton saw a glimmer of excitement cross her mother's face, like a child on Christmas morning. Lin Shaw had been searching for this room for thirty years. It was the culmination of her life's work. The missing piece.

One by one, the others slipped through the crevice and deployed their lights around the small room, which Peyton estimated to be no larger than fifteen feet across. The walls were stone, and she could see now that the stone door had been added to this natural alcove to close it off.

"Should we carry them out?" Adams asked.

"No," Lin said quickly. "We need to find the inventory. There should be a list of everything that's here."

Nigel glanced around. "Maybe it's in one of the cases."

Lin took out the first edition of *Alice's Adventures In Wonderland* and set it on one of the crates. "Kraus left five pages of trace paper in the book. We've only used two."

"After Alice is carried away by the pool of tears," Avery said, "she washes up on a bank. She and her random group of companions do a Caucus race to get dry."

Chief Adams scrunched his eyebrows. "What's a Caucus race?"

"One of Carroll's inventions," Lin said, her eyes focused on the book. "It means they ran around in circles with no clear winner."

"Well, I don't favor us running around in circles," Nigel said.

"Thank you, Doctor Greene. We'll keep that in mind."

Lin turned the book to the beginning of the third chapter. The opening illustration showed a mouse standing on his hind legs, hands held out. Alice and twelve animals, including a Lory Parrot, a duck, a Dodo Bird, a lobster, and a beaver, stood around the mouse in a circle.

Lin pulled out the page of trace paper.

She overlaid it with the cave map, and the lines intersected.

"Another hidden room?" Avery asked.

"Doubtful," Lin murmured.

"Why?" Peyton asked.

"Because he wouldn't have done that."

Peyton got the sense that there was a deeper relationship between her mother and Dr. Paul Kraus.

Lin flipped through the book, speed-reading it. She skipped over the other sheets of trace paper, leaving them in place. The others stood silently, waiting, awkwardness growing. Lin ignored them. It was simply the way she was made. Peyton knew her mother that well: the woman assumed—perhaps correctly—that hers was the strongest mind present and that she alone had the ability to unravel Kraus's clues. Engaging in a discussion would only waste time and divert her focus.

Lin took the fourth piece of trace paper and held it to the map. It connected with a location deep in the cave, off a narrow passage.

"Another location," Avery said.

"So it would seem," Lin said, but Peyton could tell she didn't believe the words, that the response was simply a way to avoid further conversation.

Lin placed the fifth and final piece of trace paper on the map. It intersected with a location even deeper in the cave.

"Maybe there are more clues at these locations," Nigel said.

"Unlikely," Lin replied quietly, still deep in thought.

She stacked all five of the trace pages together and stared at them.

Peyton could sense the group getting anxious, perhaps annoyed at being in the dark.

"What are you thinking, Mom?"

Lin turned to her and made eye contact, as if realizing the others were there for the first time.

"Carroll's story has several meanings for Kraus. It was the allegory the Citium used in the 1950s when it embarked on the Looking Glass project. Kraus was one of the leaders of the organization at the time. He believed the nuclear bomb and the nuclear age itself were a sort of rabbit hole the human race had fallen down, that we were entering a strange, unpredictable era in which extinction was a real possibility."

She motioned to the book. "The novel begins with Alice being bored and following a White Rabbit into the rabbit hole."

"The atomic bomb is the White Rabbit?" Avery said.

"No. To us, it symbolized technology in general. As do the other clever characters in the story. The blue Caterpillar smoking a hookah, who questions Alice about her identity crisis, is another representation of technology—one that is impartial, but forces us to discover who we are. The Caterpillar tells her that one side of the mushroom makes her larger and the other side makes her small."

"And the ones that mother gives you don't do anything at all," Avery whispered to Adams, who smiled and shook his head.

"What it means," Lin said with force, "is that technology both shrinks and expands our world. The telegraph and railroads were rapidly bringing people together when Carroll published the story, and the steam engine was enabling the construction of vast cities and supporting industrial agriculture that helped our population explode. When the book was written, in 1865, there were roughly 1.3 billion people in the world. Since then, the population has grown by 6.2 billion. The largest increase in history, perhaps, for any large species."

Lin assembled the trace paper pages. "But the story was about more than that to us. We believed even literary scholars didn't truly understand *Alice's Adventures In Wonderland*. They thought it was simply a new type of fantasy novel, an accomplishment in the literary nonsense genre. It's about Alice descending into a world that is very much like hers, but she is constantly changing—growing too large and small, as though she doesn't truly understand her own capabilities or how the things in the world will affect her. She is lost and wants to get home. She is eventually put on trial for growing too large—for taking the very air the other animals breathe."

"Like a mass extinction," Nigel said slowly. "The Quaternary extinction. Or the mass extinction currently happening on Earth."

"Exactly. Carroll was a polymath who was keenly aware of the changes happening on Earth."

"So what does it all mean?" Avery asked.

"To know that, you would have to understand Kraus."

"The way you do," Peyton said. There was something more going on here, a piece she had missed. She was sure of it.

"Yes." Lin held the stacked pieces of trace paper up to a lantern, her back to the group. "Kraus believed that his work was the way out of the proverbial rabbit hole humanity had fallen into. He believed the key was science, and in particular genetics: understanding how the human genome had changed over time. He believed that in our genomes, we would find bread crumbs that lead to an ultimate truth. To him, the genomes of our ancestors were like layers, and when we found the key layers, he believed they would form a picture—an answer that would be our only hope of escaping the rabbit hole."

She turned, revealing the five translucent pages in front of the lantern. The lines connected, some darker and lighter, just like the cave paintings, forming the image of a doe.

"This is what we're looking for. The inventory will be hidden there."

CHAPTER 34

DOCTOR PARK HAD never been so scared in his entire life. Sweat rolled down his face. The heartbeat monitor was the only sound in the van, a countdown to their fiery death.

He never would have imagined himself here, of all places. He had worked hard his whole life, nearly died from exhaustion during his residency. Recovered during his fellowship and dedicated his life to medical research. He had landed his dream job at Rapture Therapeutics, a company on the cutting edge of neurological medicine. He was making the world a better place. Doing important work. Or so he thought.

When the X1-Mandera virus threatened to decimate the world's population, he was herded into the conference room at Rapture Headquarters and told that the company had a contingency plan for such catastrophes—that employees were free to go home, but that if they stayed, they'd be evacuated to safety. It was an easy decision: be an anonymous name and number on the government relief rolls, or go to a private, company-owned island and wait it out. He thought he was saved.

He soon learned that he was trapped. And when Desmond Hughes arrived on the island—with a modified Rapture Therapeutics implant—Park became a forced participant in Conner McClain's quest to discover the location of Rendition.

"Doctor!" Conner yelled from the driver's seat.

Park studied the brain waves on the monitor. He opened his

mouth, then stopped. The waves were collapsing. "He's coming out!"

Conner cranked the van.

One of the mercenaries bailed out of the back and punched the garage door opener. The double door didn't budge.

"Power's out!" Conner screamed. "Roll it up manually!"

The man ran to the front of the van, pulled the garage door's emergency release rope, and lifted it. A wave of heat barreled in.

Park coughed, struggling to get a deep breath. He felt like he was in an oven. Could barely think.

The soldier climbed back into the van. Doors slammed. The van's tires barked, screeched as they swerved left onto the road.

Through the windshield, Park saw a wall of black. It was night now. No, it wasn't. The smoke from the blaze was blotting out the sun. Flames spread out thirty feet away, dancing on roofs, jumping to trees, painting the cars and driveways in black soot.

"Location!" Conner yelled. He waited a few seconds, then screamed the question even louder.

Location of what? Park thought.

"Doctor," Conner growled. "I need that location."

The app. Labyrinth. Conner had given Park the satellite-enabled smartphone. He opened the Labyrinth Reality app and quickly ran through the prompts.

Searching for entrance...

Conner shouted his question again.

The location appeared on the screen. A Menlo Park address. Less than three miles away.

"It's close," Park said, his voice coming out quietly, barely above a whisper.

Conner let out a torrent of obscenities.

Park read out the address, which was on Austin Avenue. "I'm mapping it."

"Don't bother," Conner said. "I know it."

Over the radio, he said, "Unit two, take down that checkpoint, and prepare to follow after we pass."

"Copy that, Zero." Orders followed over the comm line as the Citium operatives took up positions.

Park listened over the radio as Conner's other men captured the X1 soldiers at the checkpoint. He was glad Conner's men didn't kill them—these people were just doing their jobs, in the wrong place at the wrong time. The Citium had told him they didn't desire any more loss of life than was necessary, and he wanted to believe that was true.

All three vans were waiting when they passed the checkpoint, as were two Army Humvees. The five vehicles fell in behind them.

They drove at high speed through mostly deserted neighborhoods. The sun grew brighter as they cleared the smoke cloud. It felt as though they were driving out of a massive tunnel.

Conner brought the car to a stop at a two-story house surrounded by yellow police tape. The walls were stone, the windows clad in steel. The roof featured high-pitched gables, and its gray slate tiles were textured and uneven, as if they had been placed on a house in Europe hundreds of years ago.

In the front seat, Major Goins said to Conner, "Same approach as the Shaw home?"

"Don't bother," Conner replied, backing into the driveway and severing the police tape. "We searched it two months ago."

Goins squinted at Conner, who slammed the van into park and opened his door.

"This is Desmond's house."

The Citium troops bounded through the yard, over the boxwood hedges, and opened a window. A few seconds later, the black, wrought-iron gates opened onto the home's motor court. It was paved with an exposed aggregate, making it look like small stones that had been encased in cement. The vans backed in, followed by the Humvees.

On the smartphone, Park clicked the button to enter the Labyrinth.

Downloading...

Five minutes later the screen blinked again.

Download Complete

On the computer screen, Park saw Desmond's brain waves change. He had entered a dream state. The memory was beginning.

☣

Desmond wiped his sweaty palms on his pants as he walked to the door. The morning sun blazed through the leaded glass, shadowing the figure on the stoop and blurring his features.

Desmond opened the door. "Hello, Conner."

Conner extended his hand and spoke with a thick Australian accent. "Morning, Mister Hughes."

Desmond had asked him repeatedly to call him by his first name. Conner had never heeded the instructions.

Conner stepped inside and glanced up at the chandelier hanging in the two-story foyer. "I love your home. It's an English manor, right?"

"It is."

"It's in amazing condition. You renovate it?"

"Built new actually, by the previous owner."

"Incredible. The detail outside. Looks authentic, like it came out of the ground two hundred years ago."

"They were meticulous. I bought the place after the dot-com crash five years ago. Mostly for the land. Was thinking it would become condos in the future, or even a tear-down and subdivide."

Conner raised his eyebrows. "You'd tear *this* down?"

Desmond smiled, happy for the small talk. "I figure the future is about urban density."

Conner nodded. "Probably right. Reminds me of all the old estate homes in Australia. They didn't quite know what to do with them after the colonial era."

Desmond knew what they had done with *some* of them. One became a pediatric hospital where Conner had been taken after the bushfire, badly burned and on the edge of death. Others had served as orphanages, where his scars made him an outcast, a child constantly passed over by the parents coming to visit.

"Would you like a tour?" Desmond said.

"Sure."

Off the foyer, they wandered left, down the gallery hall. Desmond had mostly left the previous owner's art in place. He had hung only two photos of his own—both for this specific moment. He paused at the first, which showed him, age six, standing in front of an oil well, Orville Hughes towering over him, a mean scowl on his face.

"This you?"

"It is."

"Your dad?"

"No, my uncle. Orville. He adopted me when I was five."

Conner simply nodded. Desmond had hoped he would open up some, mention that he was adopted too, but only silence followed.

Desmond moved to the second framed photo, which he had also taken from Orville's home. It was black and white and creased across the middle. Orville and his brother, Allister Hughes, stood in front of a fireplace, both in their teens, both with close-cropped hair and hard expressions.

"Your uncle again?" Conner asked.

"Yes. The younger boy is my father." *Our* father, Desmond wanted to say. He watched, but Conner made no reaction.

"They were born in England," Desmond said. "Orphaned during the war. They came to Australia as part of a program run by the Christian Brothers. They weren't very kind to most of the children they adopted. Forced labor. Abuse."

Desmond waited, watching his brother through his peripheral vision. *Does he know?*

But Conner's tone was expressionless, and when he spoke, his words were emotionless, as if he were reading a speech. "That's a shame. Orphans are perhaps the most vulnerable people on Earth.

They have no one to defend them—except for their keepers. If their guardians abuse them, then they have no one at all—except their fellow orphans."

Those fellow orphans had ostracized Conner. He had truly been alone.

"Well," Conner added, his tone brightening, "it would seem," he motioned to the home, "that things turned out pretty well for you. And I can tell you that all is well at Rook." He placed a hand on his messenger bag. "I brought updated financials and data center reports if you'd like to see them."

"Maybe later," Desmond said softly.

He led Conner through an opening with pocket doors, into a paneled study. "Like anything to drink?"

"No thank you."

Desmond motioned for Conner to sit in a club chair, and he sat across from him. "I'd like to tell you a bit more about myself."

Conner squinted, confused, but quickly made his expression blank again.

"As I said, I was five when my uncle adopted me. I was born in Australia." He paused, hoping Conner would react. Nothing. "My parents both died in the Ash Wednesday bushfires." The corners of Conner's eyes tightened, but he remained silent. He looked like a dam on the verge of breaking.

Desmond leaned forward. "I grew up on a ranch. The day of the fire, I was playing far away from the home, in the woods. I smelled the smoke. The blaze... it was like it was walking across the ridges in the distance. I ran as fast as I could back to the house. But it was already on fire. Roof burning. Fences, too. Like a ring of fire. I tried to get through it."

He slipped his shoes off, revealing his scarred feet, then pulled his pants legs up. The scars were thick and mottled, like tree roots growing up his legs.

Conner's eyes widened.

"I don't know if it was the pain or the asphyxiation," Desmond said, "but I passed out. Relief workers found me. Saved me."

He paused, but Conner said nothing.

"They contacted my next of kin. Orville. He adopted me. Didn't want to. I assumed all my family was dead. I didn't learn the truth until a few years ago, when I went back to Australia, to my parents' grave, and saw that there was no marker for my baby brother. So I searched—and I found him. I had some help. My partner, Yuri Pachenko, helped me buy a hosting company, Yellow Brick Road. And we hired my brother. And I watched in wonder and joy as he transformed. What you've accomplished is incredible, Conner."

Conner leapt to his feet, alarm on his face. "What is this?"

"I wanted to tell you—"

"You're lying."

"I'm not. You were Conner Hughes before you were adopted."

"It's a common name."

"It's our name. You're my brother, Conner."

"Impossible."

Desmond leaned forward. "It's true."

Conner grimaced. "What do you want from me?"

"Nothing. You're the only family I have. I just want—"

"Excuse me." Conner turned, grabbed his bag, and marched out.

Desmond followed. "Conner, wait."

Conner never turned, or slowed, or looked back. The door slammed as he left.

Desmond sat in the study after that, replaying the scene in his mind, playing out what-ifs, imagining how he could have done things differently.

He called Yuri, whose advice was simply, "Patience, Desmond."

Desmond tried to be patient. He couldn't work—his mind was too busy. He tried to read, but failed at that too. He exercised, then went out to the yard. He pulled every weed in sight. Trimmed the bushes. Then the trees.

He didn't hear the doorbell ring. The sun was setting when the wooden gate to the back yard creaked open. Conner took two steps into the yard and stopped. Desmond walked over to him, covered in grass stains, with dirt on his hands and sweat pouring down his face.

Conner's tone was flat. "Why didn't you tell me?"

"I wanted to. I thought giving you space was better."

"You had me promoted—"

"No. I promise you, Conner. That was all you. *You* earned that. The company, hiring you, it was just a way to get you clean and healthy, to offer you a chance at a better life. The chance that fire took from you."

Conner glanced away. His expression softened. Desmond thought he saw the start of a tear at the corner of the eye that was pulled by the scarred flesh. "What do we do now?" he whispered.

Desmond shrugged. "I don't know. I just want to get to know you."

Conner nodded.

"You hungry?" Desmond asked. "I was gonna order some take-out."

For the first time that day, Conner smiled. "Yeah. Sounds good."

They talked into the wee hours of the morning. Told stories about Orville Hughes and Desmond's escape to San Francisco, about Conner's youth in the foster homes. There were plenty of dark chapters, and some funny ones. When Conner rose to leave, both men's eyes were bloodshot from crying. They didn't shake hands. Conner didn't call Desmond "Mister Hughes." They hugged in the foyer.

"No more secrets," Conner said.

"I promise you."

Conner reached for the door.

"Can you come back tomorrow?" Desmond asked.

"Of course."

"Good. There's something else I want to tell you about. A project that could be very important to you."

"Is it important to you?"

"Extremely."

"What is it?"

"It's called the Looking Glass."

☣

Conner stepped out of the van into the motor court. Desmond still lay on the hospital bed in the back of the van, the machines hooked to him, the display updating in real time as the memory unspooled. Soon, Conner would have his brother back. They would sort this out together.

He took the service entrance into the house, walked through the back hall, past the mud room and laundry room, and into the gallery hall. The frame that had held the picture of Desmond and Orville was empty—they had taken the photo, scanned it, and shown it to him a month ago on the *Kentaro Maru*, hoping it would jog his memory—and the home had been turned upside down by Citium operatives looking for clues about where Desmond had hidden Rendition. It wasn't here.

Conner looked into the paneled study. Eleven years ago, his life had changed in that room. When he thought about what his brother had done for him, his heart broke. Desmond had tried to save him—had risked his life, burned himself. And then he had rescued him from the darkness his life had once been. He desperately wanted his brother back.

A voice came over his earpiece. "Zero, we've got comm chatter. X1s are looking for their troops missing from the checkpoint."

"On my way."

CHAPTER 35

AVERY WAS SEARCHING near the mouth of the Cave of Altamira when her sat phone rang. She was surprised it even worked. She answered without looking.

"Price."

"Ma'am. Austin Avenue location. I have a status update."

Until now, Avery had heard nothing from the surveillance unit she had posted outside Desmond's home. Hadn't expected to, either. She paced to the mouth of the cave, instinctively moving toward better reception. The moon glowed behind the clouded night sky as she leaned against the timber-framed opening.

"Proceed."

"House was breached five minutes ago."

"By whom?"

"Unknown. All perps are wearing unmarked body armor."

"Troop strength?"

"Four paneled vans and two X1 Humvees. We've seen five total operatives. Estimate there are between fifteen and thirty total."

"Gear?"

"Looks like Citium field gear based on the tactical dossier."

"Current status?"

"The vehicles are in the motor court. Two idling."

Avery paused. She knew Citium operatives had already searched Desmond's home. Why were they there? It hit her a second later.

"Ma'am?"

"I'm still here." Her surveillance team was small—just three special operators, rotating through eight-hour shifts. Not enough to raid the house. Or even cordon it. "Hold position for now. If they leave, you are to follow as discreetly as possible."

"Copy that."

She severed the connection and made a call she had dreaded.

David Ward answered on the first ring.

"David—"

"Avery, my God, where are you? What the hell happened after you left Oxford?"

"Lin Shaw didn't want anyone to know our destination. Listen, McClain is in the US—outside San Francisco."

"How do you know?"

"I put a team outside Desmond's house. I think Conner McClain is there—with Desmond—right now."

"But you don't know."

"I know *someone* is there," Avery said. "And I can think of only one reason why."

"A Labyrinth location."

"Exactly. Desmond is the key to everything. Without Rendition, they're up the creek."

"It's a lot of speculation."

"I'm right."

Ward sighed. "What do you want me to do?"

"Raid the house. In force."

"Have you lost your mind? It could be looters—"

"It's not. I can feel it."

David's tone softened. "I know what he means to you, Avery."

"It's not about that."

"Sure it's not," he said sarcastically. His tone became serious again. "We'll get him back. How about you? Need backup?"

"No. I don't think we're on the Citium's radar. I agree with Lin Shaw for once. The fewer people who know our location, the better. I'll call you when I have something."

"And I'll call you when we have him."

Through the night-vision binoculars, Yuri watched the blonde-haired operative slip the phone back inside her body armor and walk back into the cave.

He glanced at the Citium Security operative beside him.

"Begin your assault, Captain."

CHAPTER 36

CONNER ARRIVED EARLY the next day, and Desmond was glad. They sat for hours, in the paneled study, sharing stories. Despite growing up three thousand miles away from each other, on different continents, with different parents, they found they were a great deal alike. Both strong-willed, driven, and stubborn at times. Both had been hurt. Neither had recovered.

They withheld nothing. Each shared their past unfiltered. To a stranger, they might have altered a detail, provided a reason—or an excuse—for their actions. With each other, they were recklessly honest, certain the other wouldn't judge and would still love them even knowing everything they had done.

For Desmond, it was an outlet. A person to trust, an anchor in the rough sea of life. Something he hadn't had since Peyton. He didn't realize how much he had missed it. He told Conner about killing Dale Epply, about how he discovered that he couldn't love Peyton the way she loved him, the pain, his depression. Everything.

Finally, Conner asked the question Desmond had been waiting for.

"The Looking Glass—what is it?"

"A solution."

"To what?"

"To what ails us, brother."

"Is that all?"

"No. That's not even the half of it."

Conner smiled, twisting the scars on the side of his face into a grotesque mountain of mottled flesh, his happiness a sharp contrast to his rough expression. "Wish you'd be a little more cryptic."

"I recently learned that true knowledge must be earned, not given. Come on, I want to show you something."

They drove north, out of Menlo Park, through San Mateo and past Daly City, into San Francisco. Desmond followed the same route Yuri had taken: through Golden Gate Park, past the Presidio, and into downtown. He parked in the same deck and rode the elevator up to the suite of condos on the twenty-fifth floor. He nodded at the concierge behind the raised dais, then pushed open the pocket doors to the library.

Conner gazed around the massive three-story library. "I'm surprised you ever left—given your near obsession with reading."

"I didn't for a while." Desmond walked deeper into the room. "But I found what I was looking for."

"Which was?"

"Answers."

"Answers to what?"

"Questions that reveal the true nature of our existence, truths that peel back the layers of the modern world, laying reality bare."

"Okay."

"These questions are an education unlike any other. And they lead to the Looking Glass. But I can't give you the answers. You have to find them for yourself. If you're willing to try."

"I'll never stop."

"Good."

Desmond closed the doors, and they sat at one of the long tables by the window.

"There are apartments here in the suite," Desmond said. "You could relocate from Australia. Work from the Rook offices here."

Conner nodded. "Don't exactly have anything tying me to Sydney. And... my only family is here." He smiled. "That'll take some getting used to: having family."

"Yeah. It's a nice change."

"You're more important to me than Rook. I could quit. Dedicate my time to what you're doing here."

"No. Rook's part of what we're building. And you've worked hard to get where you are."

Conner nodded. "Okay. Where do we start?"

"With a question. For us, all roads lead to Australia." Desmond stood. "Forty-five thousand years ago, something remarkable happened. A tribe of humans made boats and sailed the open sea for hundreds of miles. For the first time in history, humans set foot on the continent of Australia. They were the most advanced people on Earth at that time. Yet when the Dutch arrived in 1606, the indigenous Australians were far behind them technologically. The question is: why? What happened to those people—the first human sailors?"

Desmond watched as Conner worked his way through the stacks and volumes in the library, just as he himself had done a few years earlier. Conner lived in the same apartment he had, and spent every hour outside of work in the library. He peppered Desmond with theories and questions. And as Yuri had done with him, Desmond sat patiently with Conner, guiding and instructing. With each answered question, Desmond provided another.

It took Conner longer to find the answers than it had Desmond, but eighteen months after he moved to San Francisco, Conner arrived at the revelation. The following day, Desmond returned with Yuri at his side.

"Conner, I'd like you to meet someone very special to me. Yuri brought me into the Citium. He led me to you. And the Looking Glass. He's going to be our partner."

Yuri took Conner's hand in his. In that silent moment in the library, a thread seemed to connect the three of them, woven from their shared past of pain and their desire for a better life.

They sat, and Conner spoke first. "Where do we begin?"

"We plan for the future," Yuri said. "In the coming years,

cyber-attacks will become common. Governments and large corporations will try to strengthen their defenses in-house. When they fail, I want them to turn to us. To Rook."

"Sure," Conner said. "Cybersecurity is a core strength. We host plenty of financial institutions, some international pharma, and insurers. Our uptime is industry-leading. We've got it all: generators, fail-over capabilities, disaster recovery."

"We need to go further," Yuri said. "Proprietary software and hardware—only available to a select few customers."

Conner shook his head. "We don't develop software at the moment."

Yuri raised an eyebrow at Desmond.

"I'll dig around," Desmond said, "look for a security startup we can buy. Capital has been hard to get since the collapse, so we should have attractive options."

"Good," Yuri said. "In addition to network security, I want a software solution for natural disasters. An end-to-end solution for emergency response agencies. A way for them to organize and communicate with affected populations."

"That's definitely doable," Conner said. "But I think we'll need to rebrand. We're just a web host now. You're talking about software solutions, services, hardware. And we'll need to attract scientists working on cutting-edge quantum computing for the Looking Glass component."

"Fine. I'll leave all that to you." To Desmond, Yuri said, "Where are we with Rendition?"

"It's coming along. Not nearly as fast as I'd like."

"It never is."

☣

They met every week after that. They sat around the table in the library, each giving their update on their piece of the Looking Glass.

Conner renamed his business "Rook Quantum Sciences." Desmond helped him acquire a cybersecurity startup. They made progress bit by bit, the three of them assembling a large puzzle, the pieces slowly falling into place. Months turned to years, and in the summer of 2010, Yuri made a request of Desmond.

"I'd like you to join the board of a Citium company."

"Sure. Which one?"

"Phaethon Genetics."

The name sounded familiar. Yuri placed it for him.

"It's Lin Shaw's company."

"What's the focus?"

"On the surface... identifying the genetic basis of diseases and sequencing viruses."

"And under the surface?"

"I suspect only Lin Shaw knows that."

"What's *my* focus there?"

"Figuring out hers."

Desmond smiled. "I suspect you have better spies than me on your roster."

"No one she trusts more. And no one *I* trust more."

Desmond had never told Yuri about going to Lin Shaw's home that night, but Yuri's words confirmed that he already knew. It was just as well. As with Conner, Desmond wanted no secrets between him and his mentor.

He attended the first board meeting at Phaethon the following week. He was intrigued by their work. The potential was incredible. Phaethon was dedicated to identifying the genes and epigenetic triggers that caused disease. Phaethon envisioned a world where diagnoses were made by a combination of symptomatic reporting and DNA sequencing. Remedies could be synthesized at home, like a cup of coffee. Every kitchen would have a 3D medical printer that would dispense a cure as soon as symptoms arose.

He was most affected by Lin Shaw's passion for the project. In the board room in Menlo Park, she stood in front of the projector, a double helix glowing behind her.

"We are living in a transcendental moment in human history. Our generation can be the first to cure disease. Not one malady, or a few. *All* diseases. Human history has seen turning points.

Agriculture. The Enlightenment. World War Two. But none like this. The end of disease will herald a new kind of golden age for humanity."

She looked directly at Desmond. "And today, we're one step closer. I'd like you all to welcome Desmond Hughes. Desmond is an investor in predominantly IT startups, some of which I'm sure you're familiar with." She read a few of the names. "In particular, I believe Desmond will be very helpful with our growing pains in the data center. He has experience with scaling up big data operations, especially in the scientific space. He was one of the lead developers of SciNet, which I know some of you remember. He's also a board member of Rook Quantum Sciences—one of the world's leading ultra-secure web hosts.

"So. Welcome, Desmond. We're looking forward to your input on the IT and finance side, and of course anything you see fit to feed in on."

When the meeting broke, Lin held out her arm to Desmond. "Care for a tour?"

☣

"This is our biggest pain point," Lin said. They stood in the middle of the data center.

"You could outsource it to Rook."

"True. But it would complicate things for us. We promise our clients that the data they give us will never leave our custody. And even if we didn't, we still want control. We need to be able build out as needed, when we want to."

"All right. I'll talk with my brother. Maybe they can consult, help you scale up and advise you on hiring the right people."

"Good."

On the elevator, Lin said, "There's another Rook project we'd like to integrate with—their emergency response system."

Desmond bunched his eyebrows.

"We can sequence genetic samples faster than any company in the world. In outbreak responses, we could analyze patient samples, sequence viruses and identify mutations, possibly even help with contact tracing—on a genetic level."

"What are you asking?"

"For sales help. We'd like the Rook sales force to carry Phaethon's outbreak response solution in the door and bundle it with their emergency data response services."

"I'll run it by Conner."

"Thank you."

They walked past a sea of cubicles. Narrow corridors ran between them, a maze with rows of heads slightly bowed, staring at screens, headphones on. It was like a labyrinthine garden of hedgerows made of plastic.

Lin closed the glass door to her office and sat behind the desk. For the first time that day, her tone softened.

"It's good to see you, Desmond."

"You too."

"Yuri doesn't need to worry."

Desmond exhaled through his nose. Lin Shaw was direct. Fearless.

Her frankness inspired Desmond to ask the question he had wanted to since Yuri asked him to be on the board, the question he dreaded hearing the answer to.

"How is she?"

Lin didn't move a muscle. "As well as she can be."

The answer was like a shot of morphine: it stung at first, then a bizarre numbness settled over Desmond, like his mind was blocked, keeping him from the pain that was still there. He couldn't think straight. He sat, as if in a trance.

Lin broke the silence. "It will heal all wounds, Desmond."

"It?"

"The Looking Glass."

☣

That night, Desmond did something he had sworn not to do. He opened Internet Explorer 7 and Googled Peyton Shaw.

The first hit was a page welcoming her EIS class at the CDC. It featured a picture of a crowd of roughly a hundred people standing in front of a glass building. She was in the back row, not smiling. Seeing her was like falling down a hole. He clicked the next link, then the next, going deeper down the trail. He paused on a picture of her on the Johns Hopkins website, where she was listed as a resident physician. He saw so much of Lin Shaw in Peyton: the delicate, Chinese features, porcelain skin, dark hair. And something he hadn't seen when they were together: the start of crow's-feet at the corners of her eyes. Worry lines. Her smile was serious, her gaze focused. Gone was the carefree girl he'd met at a Halloween party twelve years ago. That broke his heart all over again.

He kept searching but didn't find what he feared most: an engagement announcement. There was no wedding website telling a story of how she'd met her soulmate, mentioning their shared pet, no write-up detailing the bridal party or the wedding venue. The revelation made him both happy and sad. He wondered if she was waiting—or if he had turned her into what he'd become: a person unable to truly love.

He was so engrossed in his search that he didn't hear the door open. Or the footsteps behind him. Conner's voice startled him.

"You know that's not healthy."

Desmond turned back, away from the screen. "I know."

Conner pulled up a chair from the long table. "What happened?"

"I saw her mother today."

"And?"

"We talked about her. I couldn't resist."

"Are you going to contact her?"

"No," Desmond said quickly. "I can't. I want to. But…"

Conner nodded. "You said you wanted to talk about Rook."

"Yeah. It's actually related to Lin's company. They need some help."

Desmond oversaw Rook's collaboration with Phaethon and watched as their data center scaled up. He dedicated his remaining time to building Rendition. The work was conducted through a front called Rendition Games, and the project seemed to drag on. Yuri urged patience, but Desmond and Conner only grew more eager to see the Looking Glass completed.

On a warm summer day in 2015, Desmond's life changed again, unexpectedly. Phaethon's biostatistics group had been constantly clashing with the business and science sides of the company, and Desmond was brought in to try to make peace. He failed miserably.

The head of biostats was a man in his sixties named Herman. Herman had a PhD in the field, wore round wire-rimmed glasses, and seemed to always speak in an acerbic tone.

Herman interlocked his fingers, placed his hands on the desk, and exhaled. "The problem is quite simple. I do not have the manpower to program reports to satisfy their every whim and curiosity—in the outrageous time frames given."

"Then prioritize," the CFO said. "I'm getting on a plane at eight a.m. tomorrow for an investor meeting. If I don't have those reports, there won't be any money for more resources—for anybody."

"And how long have you known about this meeting?"

"I don't know."

"We received your request yesterday. I will simply assume the meeting has been scheduled for longer."

The CFO rolled his eyes.

"Poor planning on your part does not constitute an emergency on my part."

Desmond stared at him. "Really?"

Herman didn't respond.

"You work for a tech company," Desmond said. "*Everything* is an emergency. If you don't like emergencies, this isn't the place for you. There are plenty of places with no emergencies. Would that be better for you?" He glared at the man, challenging him.

Silence filled the room.

Finally, Herman said, "Mister Hughes. With all due respect,

when *everything* is an emergency, *nothing* is an emergency. Everything is urgent."

One of the clinical project managers spoke up. "Well, I agree, but... our client has an FDA reporting deadline coming up."

Herman had brought three of his employees with him: two overweight men, one on each side, both of whom shared his stone-faced expression, and a younger blonde woman with dazzling blue eyes. Thus far, the woman had been relegated to a hardback chair against the wall, behind those around the conference table. But now she stood, leaned forward, and whispered in Herman's ear. He didn't even look back, just shooed her away. She didn't budge. Instead, she whispered more forcefully, though the words were still a little too quiet for Desmond to hear. Herman turned and glared at her. Still she didn't flinch, like a fighter sizing up an opponent.

Herman swiveled his head back to the group. "We're aware of *all* of your requirements. Was there anything else? As you know, my overworked people need to get back to some urgent reports."

The next morning, Desmond awoke to find two emails from a name he didn't recognize: Avery Price. One was addressed to the CFO, and contained a secure link to the report he had requested. The other was to the project manager—with a link to the FDA report she needed. The first email was sent at 2:38 a.m., the second email four hours later.

There were also responses of thanks from the recipients. Desmond replied as well, requesting a meeting—only to get an automatic notification that his message to Avery Price had bounced.

At the Phaethon Genetics office, he stopped at the first cubicle in biostats. "Hi."

A short-haired, twenty-something guy pulled off his headphones. "What's up?"

"I'm looking for Avery Price."

The guy raised his eyebrows.

"He's a biostats programmer—"

"No he's not."

"Actually, I'm pretty sure—"

"He's a she, man. And she got canned this morning."

"What for?"

The guy raised up from his chair to peek over the cubicle walls. Then he whispered to Desmond, "Going off the reservation."

"What does that mean?"

The guy sat back down. "Wait, who are you again?"

Desmond took a step back. "Forget it."

He had spent enough time at Phaethon to have an office, and a login to the network. He opened the Oracle HR program and looked up Avery Price. A picture of her stared back at him with cold, arresting eyes. This was the woman he'd seen in the meeting, whispering in Herman's ear. He scanned her bio. She was a graduate of UNC-Chapel Hill where she'd been on the tennis team. Most recent job was at a VC firm called Rubicon Ventures, doing due diligence.

Her employment status read: Terminated for Cause. There was a footnote: theft of company time and direct insubordination. Desmond typed the address into Google Maps on his iPhone. Just as the route appeared, a figure ducked in his doorway. Lin Shaw.

"How'd it go with biostats?"

"Not well."

"Solution?"

"Not sure." He glanced at the directions. "I'm working on something though."

☣

Conner was standing in Desmond's bedroom when he heard the first pop. Then another.

One of his men spoke over the comm. "Zero, we're under attack. They're shooting the tires."

Conner pressed the mic button on his collarbone. "Back up to the garages. All units, covering fire!"

CHAPTER 37

THE CAMPAIGN SIGNS were in every window. Hillary. Pelosi. The 2016 election seemed to get more brutal each day.

Desmond drove past them into one of the more run-down parts of San Francisco. Or *formerly* run-down. It was slowly changing, becoming gentrified, the cars now mostly Priuses and Teslas. The morning sun burned against his shoulder as he climbed to the second floor of the apartment building and knocked on the door.

Nothing.

He knocked again.

Still no answer.

He took out his phone and dialed the number listed in Avery's employee profile.

A groggy voice answered. "Price."

"Hi. It's Desmond Hughes. We've never met—"

"What do you want?"

"Um. I'm on the board of Phaethon Genetics."

Silence.

"I know you were terminated today."

Movement in the background, like sheets rustling.

"I'd like to talk. In person. About the reports you sent this morning."

Swooshing, like fabric being pulled across the phone's receiver. "Where?"

"Ah. Actually... I'm at your apartment."

A second later, the door swung open. Her hair was wild, the blonde strands sticking out like Einstein's gray mop.

"Hi," she said.

"Hi." He couldn't help but take her in. She wore a shirt, long and tight around her body, and boxer shorts. Nothing else.

"I'm going to need your full name for the restraining order."

His eyebrows shot up.

She released the door, letting it swing open. "Just messing with you. Come on in." Her accent was southern, not thick, but noticeable.

The place was furnished like the apartments of practically every startup founder he knew. An IKEA couch. A flat-screen TV sat on the box it had come in. A faux distressed wood coffee table. The strange medley of magazines was different, though: *TENNIS, The Economist, Time, Us Weekly*, and the Alzheimer's Foundation of America's *Care Quarterly*. The recycle bin was filled with empty Gatorade G2 bottles, and the necks of two wine bottles protruded from the pile, as if they had washed up on a plastic beach.

"Love what you've done with the place."

"Maid's late this morning. I usually entertain board members in the evening."

Desmond let out a laugh. She was bold. He wondered if it was because she was recently fired or if it was simply her nature. Either way, it was refreshing. As a board member, he found that most employees spoke to him in carefully measured, mentally rehearsed words.

"Want something to drink?" She walked into the small kitchen, opened the refrigerator, and peered in. She pulled out a bottle of Cupcake chardonnay, eyed it, found it nearly empty, and took out another bottle as well, Yellow Tail. She rinsed a coffee mug in the sink, dumped in the Cupcake wine, and began unscrewing the Yellow Tail to top it off.

Desmond held up a hand to stop her. "I have a better idea."

She didn't look up, merely focused on the pour as if she were in a lab mixing the contents of two beakers. "You have a better idea than wine at nine a.m. on the morning I got fired?" She glanced up. "It would need to be *really* good."

He walked over, took the wine bottle from her hand. "It's pretty good." He screwed the cap back on. "How about we go get some breakfast, talk, you get your job back, and your old boss gets put in his place."

"Okay. But for the record, I was going to say no until that last part."

"Noted." He glanced at her hair again. "I can wait if you want to shower or—"

She walked past him, toward the bedroom. "I'm not really that kind of girl."

Before he could react, she was through the door, pulling her shirt off, her back turned to him, but the profile of her bare figure in full view. His eyes lingered a second before he was able to pull them away. He turned and took a few steps into the living room. Maybe she was still a little drunk. Or an exhibitionist. Or both.

She emerged wearing gym shorts, a T-shirt that read Carolina Tennis, and a white cap over her untamed blonde hair. A green plastic wrist coil wrapped around her right wrist, curling like she'd gotten caught in an old phone cord. A single key hung from it.

"Figure this will keep you from taking me anywhere too fancy."

He smiled. "I'm not really that kind of guy."

☣

The breakfast place was filled with hung-over Stanford students, a few professors, and locals on their way to work. Desmond and Avery fit right in.

Avery ordered half the menu—eggs, hash browns, pancakes, and toast. Desmond wondered if she had a hollow leg.

"What happened?" he asked.

She folded the toast, lathered it with strawberry jelly, and mauled it. "Pulled an all-nighter, did my job, got a call at eight a.m. telling me not to come in—indefinitely. Fired, just like that."

"Why were you fired?"

"Paranoia."

She was finally slowing down. The pancakes seemed to be a hill she couldn't climb. Nevertheless, she was applying butter and syrup, as if greasing the path.

"I don't understand."

"What's happening at Phaethon happens to every company. We saw it all the time at Rubicon at the companies we invested in. The founders and first hires are people with a 'can do' attitude. Everybody's on the same page. 'Get 'er done' mentality."

Desmond laughed.

"It's a popular saying back home in North Carolina."

"I know it."

Avery looked skeptical.

"I grew up in Oklahoma."

"Really." She took another bite of pancakes, yawned without covering her mouth. The all-nighter was catching up to her.

"So what's the real problem at Phaethon?" Desmond asked.

"People have different priorities now. Like Herman. He's upper-middle management. His priority is keeping his job, maybe moving up a bit. Making himself more indispensable to the company. Increasing his power. Adding to his head count—and thus justifying a higher salary. He wants—needs—the other units to rely on him."

"And if we replaced him?"

She shrugged, put the fork down. "Things would improve for a while. But you'd get more of the same. People adapt to their environment."

"So we change the environment."

"That's right."

"How?"

Avery exhaled. "For one, probably 80 percent of the reports requested are just variations on a few templates. You write two pieces of custom software: one for the business side, one for the scientists. Then give them a small analytics and reporting group—and train some of their staff on the system. Empower them to run their own reports."

"And for the ones they can't run?"

"Biostats will still have to program those." She picked up the fork and took another run at the stack of pancakes. "But it won't be an issue. Half the people in that group don't need to be managed. You tell them what to do and they'll get it done. They're good. Might need a little help translating the requirements from their *customers*, is all—and the biz group and scientists are their customers, and they should start looking at it that way." She set the fork down again and looked around for the waitress as if she were going to flag her down.

"I already paid."

She nodded. "Wonderful. I'm recently unemployed."

"About that."

She squinted.

"How would you feel about being *re*-employed. As you say, biostats doesn't need a manager. They need a translator for the customers' needs."

She leaned back. "Kind of hard to get excited about going back into the lion's den on the day I got my head bitten off."

"I'll take care of the lions."

☣

The drive back to Avery's apartment was less than ten minutes, but she was asleep in the passenger seat within three.

When they arrived, Desmond reached over, shook her shoulder, and waited. He tried again, but she was dead to the world. He slipped the wrist coil with the key off her hand, walked around, opened the door, and lifted her up. He carried her to the second floor, careful not to move too quickly. Inside the apartment, he considered laying her out on the IKEA couch, but he had slept on a few of those. So, although it felt like a mild invasion of her privacy, he pushed the door to the bedroom open, revealing a queen bed on rails with no headboard. Two Kindles lay on the bedside table, one charging.

As he put her down, she stirred. That made him nervous for some reason. He waited, but she didn't move again.

He pulled the blackout curtains tight, wrote a note, and left it on the counter: *Key under the mat.*

In the Phaethon Genetics conference room, Desmond sat beside the CFO and Lin Shaw, who was Phaethon's Chief Science Officer. The only other attendee was Herman. When Desmond finished describing how the division would be split into three groups, the older man looked incredulous.

"You expect me to go from managing one group to managing three—spread across three divisions, sitting on two different floors? That's ridiculous."

"No," Desmond said, "we don't. We expect you to use your PhD in biostats and your programming background to help build the more complex reports assigned to the streamlined reporting group."

The man's mouth fell open. "I'm being demoted? You think I'm going to go sit in a cube next to the people I used to manage and write code again?"

"If you're not willing to sit alongside the people working for you—and do the same work you're asking them to do—there's no place for you here. We're a company of doers, not managers."

Herman huffed, glanced away. "Well, who's going to translate the requirements? And more importantly, who's going to prioritize the work? It'll be chaos."

"The customers will prioritize the work. It's their call. Each report will be assigned an estimated time to complete." Desmond nodded toward Lin. "Science gets 70 percent of the hours available, business the other thirty. Each group internally prioritizes their own jobs based on their own needs and time estimates."

"And the specs?"

Desmond had been waiting for that question. "We have someone in mind for that."

Herman leaned forward.

"You know her actually. Avery Price."

☣

Avery flourished in her new role. She was hard-working, dedi-cated, and no-nonsense. She was all about the work. Despite her conduct at her first meeting with Desmond, he saw that she was quite professional at the office.

Several opportunities arose to promote her, but she declined each one. "I don't want to be in charge," she said. "I want to do the work." She negotiated for more stock options instead of a higher salary. She reminded Desmond so much of himself at SciNet.

He spent more and more time with her. She was often his first point of contact when the board wanted special reports. She programmed a lot of them herself and never missed a deadline.

He was leaving the Phaethon office late on a Friday when he saw the task light on in her cubicle. He walked over, found her with her headphones on, hunched over, a window with a SQL server database diagram open, lines drawn between the tables listing the columns, like a family tree showing the relationships. She pulled a line across, creating a primary-foreign key relationship.

He knocked on the cube's steel frame. She turned and pulled the headphones off. She had black bags under her eyes.

"Hey," he said.

"Hey yourself."

"Leaving soon?"

"Doubtful."

"What're you working on?"

"Report for Lin Shaw." She motioned to some handwritten notes on a pad. Desmond recognized the names of a few genes and SNPs. The specs called for data sets by age groups, gender, race, and associated medical conditions.

"Looks intense."

"It is. I'm almost too fried."

"Come on." He motioned to the conference room. "I'll help you." She grinned as if he was kidding.

"I was a programmer once. I can still write a SQL query."

They ordered Chinese food, sat at the conference table side by side, their laptops open, and split up the work. They put their datasets together, the pieces sliding into place slowly at first, then more quickly as they found a rhythm between them.

While they waited for a particularly complex query to execute, Desmond asked, "Why do you push yourself so hard?"

She didn't look him in the eye. "I don't know."

"Okay. Make something up."

She laughed and ate a piece of sweet and sour chicken, which was almost cold now. "I guess the way I grew up. Hard work was a virtue sort of thing."

"Yeah, I know what you mean."

The query finished. Desmond scanned the results window. Duplicate rows. He searched the query text, then grabbed the mouse. "This left outer join needs to be an inner join—"

"I see it." She brushed his hand off the mouse. He paused at the touch, felt his breathing accelerate. She clicked the text and typed, not making eye contact. Clearly she didn't feel the same thing. She was determined to finish the query herself. She clicked execute again.

"So what drew you to Phaethon?"

"Money."

Desmond shook his head. "Do you always lie when someone asks you a personal question?"

She cocked her head back in mock contemplation. "I'm detecting a circular reference in your query."

He laughed out loud. Geek humor always got him. "No, seriously. Why do you always dodge?"

"Hard to say."

"And why is it hard to say?"

"Data set's too small." She shrugged. "I don't get many personal questions."

"In that case, let's try the query again. You work really hard here. But you could do that anywhere. Why here? Why this company? Come on, it won't kill you to answer."

She looked him in the eye. "All right. I believe in what

Phaethon's doing. Finding the genetic basis of disease. It will have a huge impact."

"True. Is that it? There's no... personal stakes for you?"

The query finished. It was right this time. She copied and pasted the results into an Excel spreadsheet. He thought she was going to ignore the question, but she responded, her focus firmly on the screen.

"My dad."

Desmond said nothing, giving her time.

"He has Alzheimer's."

He felt like he saw the first true piece of Avery then. It was so much more personal than seeing her apartment the morning they first met, or even when she'd pulled her shirt off and changed in plain view. And he felt a new kind of connection to her. He knew what it was like to pursue something to help a sick family member. More than anything, he wanted to tell her about the Looking Glass then, to tell her that she was indeed working on something that would help her father, and so many others.

Two weeks later, Avery walked into his office. Her demeanor was different. Gone was the humble self-confidence. She seemed... almost shy. Nervous.

"What's up?"

"I—" She scratched behind her ear. "I'd like to ask a favor."

"Anything."

She inhaled. "I judge this startup competition at my alma mater."

"UNC."

"Right." She swallowed. "So, there's this startup, CityForge, it's about helping villages in the third world become cities. Anyway, I was thinking, if you were up for it, and you had time, which you probably don't—"

"I do."

"It's okay if you don't."

"What do you need?"

"Well, I was hoping you could, um, talk with the founders, maybe give them some pointers. I could set up a conference call—"

Desmond held up his hand. "Avery, do you have any idea how many requests for calls I get from people with the next great startup idea?"

She opened her mouth, but he cut her off.

"Just messing with you."

She laughed, releasing some of her nervousness.

"Payback for that restraining order comment a few months ago."

"Touché, Mister Hughes."

"Look, I'd be glad to. In fact, urbanization is a focus for Icarus Capital. Cities are important to what we're doing."

"They're a non-profit."

"Fine by me. I'm not that into profit these days."

☣

Desmond read their business plan and was impressed. CityForge had a great idea. It wasn't strictly part of the Looking Glass, but urbanization was a helpful precursor. He decided to fly the two founders out to San Francisco for dinner. He insisted Avery come along.

It was the first time he had been back to her apartment since their first meeting that morning months ago. He knocked on the door and waited. A moth circled a glowing yellow bulb, knocking against the metal shade.

The door swung wide. Avery stood in a black, form-fitting dress, her hair down, the blonde locks seeming to glow against the fabric. Her blue eyes sparkled. A silver necklace hung around her neck with a locket he had never seen her wear. He was speechless.

She glanced down at herself. "I had to borrow the dress."

"I'm... glad you did."

She grabbed a clutch off the console table. "Don't get used to it."

He laughed as she locked the door.

The dinner was marvelous. He listened mostly, and talked to the founders about how important their work was. Avery drank two glasses of wine and facilitated the conversation. Desmond realized it was the first time they had been together outside the context of Phaethon. It felt like something they were doing together, as if they were partners, co-mentors to the young entrepreneurs. He agreed to join the CityForge board, and to make an investment of $150,000.

When he parked at Avery's apartment complex again, he got out to walk her up, almost without thinking about it.

"Door-to-door service, huh?"

He fell in beside her. "Oh, I'd feel terrible if you got lost."

"I'm sure."

She unlocked the door and turned, a coy grin forming on her lips. "This wasn't a date, you know?"

Desmond held up his hands. "Whoa. Who said anything about this being a date? Wait, are you saying it *was* a date?"

She pushed the door open. "Good night, Des." She stepped inside, glanced back. "And thanks."

"For what?"

"For helping those guys."

"They're good guys."

"Yeah. There were three good guys there tonight."

CHAPTER 38

LIN LED PEYTON through the Cave of Altamira's winding passageways, her lantern held high, the light and shadow playing on the stone walls. Each time they approached a cave painting, Peyton paused, but Lin trudged on, eyes fixed on the uneven ground.

At the hidden chamber, they had divided into three groups: Peyton and Lin, Avery and Nigel, and the two SEALs, who had remained to guard the sealed cases.

In the dim light, Peyton saw a cave painting ahead on their left. Four legs, a large body, no antlers. A doe.

"Mom, look."

"It's not it," Lin said without even turning her head to look. A second later, she said, "It's just ahead."

Peyton held her response, but she was certain now: her mother knew exactly where she was going. A theory formed in her mind. She would soon test it.

The passage opened slightly into a small chamber with more paintings on the walls and a few scattered on the ceiling. Lin walked straight to the back-left corner of the room and stopped, squinting, clearly surprised. She held up the lantern and illuminated a painting of a doe, standing proud, its lines drawn in black and red. Beside it stood a buck with seven points, painted completely black. Below the two adult deer stood a fawn, less than half the size of its parents.

Now Peyton was sure.

Lin squatted and held a hand out to the fawn, ran her finger across it. The black came away like soot from a fireplace. Peyton was taken aback at her mother's brazen desecration of this ancient site.

"Mom—"

"It's not original," Lin said quickly. Almost to herself, she whispered, "It wasn't here before."

Peyton moved to her mother and squatted in front of the painting. "It wasn't here when you visited before."

Lin continued wiping away at the fawn, which was disappearing line by line, starting at the bottom, like a curtain being lifted.

Peyton pressed the point. "When you visited with Doctor Paul Kraus."

Lin kept wiping. Just a little of the fawn remained. Then it was gone.

"Who was your father."

Lin's eyes snapped to Peyton. "That took you long enough."

CHAPTER 39

"HE'S MY GRANDFATHER," Peyton said, coming to grips with the revelation.

"Yes," Lin said. Her hands were covered in the black charcoal paint.

"He was a Nazi."

"He was not. He was a German, but not a Nazi. Your grandfather was a good man. One caught on the wrong side of a war that consumed the world."

"He brought you here."

"In 1941."

"That's why he chose this hiding place, isn't it? Altamira is special to you."

"And to him. This is a very, very remarkable place, Peyton. It is perhaps the oldest evidence we have of the cognitive revolution. It was a singularity whose impact is still rippling through our reality."

Peyton studied the cave painting, of the doe and buck standing above the now-erased fawn. "What happened here in 1941?"

Lin took a deep breath. "Papa woke me up late one summer night and told me to pack only the things I couldn't live without. Well, I was a child, so you know what that meant: dolls, a dollhouse, a train set. I had a lot of toys; I was an only child, and they had doted on me. And books, of course. I had just learned to read, and I couldn't get enough of them. *Grimm's Fairy Tales* was my favorite. And *Alice's Adventures In Wonderland*."

Peyton smiled. "You're Alice."

"So it would seem. I surprised him. I packed all of my books. The suitcase was bursting at the seams and far too heavy for me to lift. When Papa saw my suitcase filled with books, the toys in a pile off to one side, he was so proud. He emptied his own luggage and filled it with my toys. He knew what was coming and that I would need them.

"We left on a night train out of Berlin, westbound toward France, which had already fallen and been under German control for over a year. The British had escaped the previous summer at Dunkirk. The border crossing between France and Germany was uneventful. But when we reached the Spanish border, they interrogated us. To the border guards, we looked like another German family escaping. But Papa talked our way through it." She paused as if remembering something.

"And you came here? To this cave?"

"Yes. He led an expedition here. It was a cover though. One morning he woke me up early, led me inside the cave, and showed me the paintings. That was a special moment—the first time he had given me a glimpse of his research and how his mind worked."

Lin looked at the cave painting. "Our journey ended here. The original painting was only a doe."

"He added the stag and fawn."

Lin nodded. "They symbolize our family. He was protecting us. We left on a ship bound for Hong Kong that day."

"Why Hong Kong?"

"My parents thought we'd be safe there. They were wrong. My mother—your grandmother—was a scientist too, and a Chinese national with dual British citizenship. Her family had lived in Hong Kong for fifty years. Her brother was still there. The city had been under British control since 1841. It was called the Pearl of the Orient—a major trading hub, financial center, and a strategic location with a deep harbor.

"In 1941, the Chinese and Japanese had already been at war for four years, and it was bloody. The Battle of Shanghai involved almost a million combatants. Chiang Kai-shek lost his best troops and officers there. They never recovered. The following month, the Japanese took Nanking, the Chinese capital at the time. And what they did there... was inhuman. After the losses, the Chinese were on the defensive. China and Germany were still allies at this time; the Germans had trained the best Chinese officers. And the German military advisors advised their ally to use perhaps their only weapon against the Japanese invaders: land. China's interior is vast; conquering it would stretch out the Japanese supply lines and divide their army."

"I thought Japan and Germany were allies in the Second World War?"

"Eventually. The relationship between Japan and Germany was somewhat antagonistic before the war. Japan had been a British ally in the First World War, had fought against German troops in Asia, and had taken all of Germany's territory. Japan was also a signatory to the Treaty of Versailles that punished Germany for the war. But six months after Shanghai and Nanking fell, Germany switched its alliance, recalled its advisors, and stopped giving military aid to China."

Lin studied the painting of the buck and doe. "Anyway, when we arrived in Hong Kong, the Sino-Japanese War had bogged down for years, with seemingly endless battles on the Chinese mainland. My parents assumed that the Japanese would never attack the British, as that would divide their focus; China was a big enough prize. With Mother's only family in Hong Kong and British troops guarding the city, she and Papa both thought we'd be safe there, that the British would never give up the city and that the Chinese would fight to retake it if they did. These were reasonable assumptions, but they were wrong. On both counts."

Lin rubbed the black soot on her fingers, as if she were trying to wipe away dried blood. "Five months after we arrived, on December seventh, 1941, the Japanese attacked Pearl Harbor. The next day, they invaded Hong Kong. The British and Canadian forces fought for eighteen days, but they were outnumbered and surrounded. We were bombed day and night from the air, stormed on the ground, and shelled from the sea. The last troops surrendered on Christmas Day. We called it Black Christmas. The occupation was... Well, it was humanity at its worst. They starved us, tortured us, and some of us they just loaded on trucks and boats and carted off to be used as slave labor. When the Japanese invaded, there were 1.6 million people living in Hong Kong. When the war was over and the British returned in 1945, there were less than 600,000. A million people dead or gone. Nearly two out of every three. My mother was one of them."

Lin studied the painting of the doe for a moment, then reached out and began wiping away the buck beside her. "When my uncle returned me to Germany in 1946, my father wasn't the same man. He was a shell. He blamed himself for my mother's death, for making the wrong choice on where to send us. Maybe the war had changed him, too. It had changed me. I was only five years older, but I was no longer a child. I hadn't been a child since..." She looked around. "This place, this cave, in this very corridor, is where he told me I was going away. This is where my childhood ended."

Peyton wanted to reach out and embrace her mother, but she knew her better than that. Lin Shaw needed space as she revealed this secret she had carried for so long.

"After the war," Lin continued, "there was only the Looking Glass for him. He saw it as his way to atone. His duty. Our relationship wasn't like that of a father and daughter; we were more like partners in this great work. We had seen how evil and dark the world could be. We wanted to end that forever."

The buck was gone, and her hands were covered in the dark soot now. She took a cloth from her pack and began wiping it away.

"That was our bond, and the thread that ran through everyone in the Citium back then. In Stalingrad, Yuri had gone through an experience similar to my own in Hong Kong, though on a larger scale. We shared our stories and found that, at least back then, we saw the same world and were dedicated to the same cause. Your father had lost both of his parents in the war too. Going through what we did... it changes you. You can't help but change. You have to. To survive. But some of us, like Yuri, had wounds deeper than they seemed. He proved capable of things I never imagined."

She traced a finger over the cave wall, where the fawn had been. "No matter what happens after this, Peyton, you must promise me that you will do whatever it takes to stop Yuri. No matter the cost."

Peyton studied her mother. "What do you mean—what happens after this?"

"As I said, my childhood ended here. My life was dark and difficult after. I believe Papa had another reason for hiding his inventory list here: he's telling me that my life is about to change again. Darkness lies ahead. Hardship. He's telling me that I will have to make difficult choices—like he did. And that they might not be the right ones."

She pressed her fingers into the wall, and it gave, flakes of plaster raining down. Peyton's eyes widened as she realized it was actually just a plaster layer, and behind it was a foam block. Lin pulled out the block, took a folding knife from her pack, and cut the foam away, revealing a sealed plastic box.

She opened it with a pop. A sheaf of loose pages lay inside.

"Like him, I'll try to protect you, Peyton. But you may have to finish this."

Peyton glanced at the smeared lines of the painting, at the buck that had been wiped away, at the child that had been ripped open, the secrets the father had left inside now pulled out into the open. And the doe, painted so many years ago, staring at her, just like her mother.

"Promise me, Peyton."

"I promise."

CHAPTER 40

DESMOND DIDN'T KNOW when it happened, but something had changed inside him, like a season that had ended abruptly, a long winter that had broken. Everything seemed new again. Exciting. He looked forward to going to Phaethon Genetics, especially to meetings he knew Avery would be attending. He found excuses to join projects she was on. And he thought about her in the hours in between.

Yuri often asked him about Lin Shaw, and his response was always the same: "Nothing suspicious."

Desmond arrived one morning for a meeting at Rendition Games to find that the prototype of the device he had devoted a decade to developing finally worked. He and Yuri celebrated that night at Desmond's home. Conner was there too. It was like the three of them had landed on the beach of a new world. They all felt that anything was possible, that they had turned the corner on an impossible task. Desmond soon learned there was more work to do.

"What's your plan for testing it?" Yuri asked.

Desmond hadn't given that much thought. He had been singularly obsessed with making it work. "Not sure. I was thinking we'd start with animal trials. Primates. If it looks good, move on to human studies. Run an ad for volunteers. Maybe—"

"And how would we explain what we're doing?"

"Maybe a neurological study, or—"

"That would open us up to regulatory approval. Oversight.

And even if it didn't, it would, at the very least, expose part of what we're doing." Yuri drew a folder from his briefcase and pushed it across the coffee table.

Desmond opened the folder. It included a profile of a company called Pacific Sea Freight, along with travel routes for one particular cargo ship. "I don't understand."

"We need a place to test Rendition. A large space—out of the way, beyond prying eyes. A secure location."

"A sea freighter?"

"It's ideal if you think about it."

Desmond scratched at his hairline. "Well, not really. What if the subjects experience adverse events? We should be near a hospital."

"Even more to my point. The subjects need to be *very* close to medical help—and not just some crowded ER room with over-worked staff. Specialists trained to deal with the sorts of issues that might arise."

"I don't follow."

"We'll transform the ship into a floating hospital and laboratory." Yuri put his fingers together and steepled them. "And it offers a third advantage."

Desmond waited.

"Recruitment. This ship," Yuri nodded down at the folder, "the *Kentaro Maru*, puts into ports around the world. We could recruit subjects with diverse genetics."

"They'd need to be informed of the risks. In fact, we need to figure out some idea of the risks before we even get started."

"Certainly. But we could also target specific populations. The terminally ill. Prisoners governments want to get rid of."

Desmond opened his mouth to object, but Yuri continued. "They and their families would be well paid. Again, we'd have health professionals close by in case anything happened. We need to move quickly now, Desmond. With the Looking Glass complete, we're more exposed. If someone is going to betray us, it will happen now."

Finally, Desmond nodded. "Okay."

"Good," Yuri said. "Let's talk about the specifics."

Desmond looked at the file. "Do we own this company, Pacific Sea Freight? The ship?"

"Yes. We have for about six months."

That didn't surprise him. Yuri was always a step ahead.

"Where's the *Kentaro Maru* now?"

"Docked in San Francisco. Fully staffed with contract medical personnel, drawn mostly from the third world, all bound by non-disclosure agreements. We're ready for the trial, Desmond. Right now."

"Well, it's going to take me a few days to wrap things up here—"

Yuri held up a hand. "I have a better idea."

Desmond raised his eyebrows.

"Stay. Let Conner and I take care of this."

"What?"

"Rook is complete. So is Rapture. Neither require our attention. We can test Rendition for you."

"No one knows Rendition better than me—"

"Are you sure? You were the architect, but the people who developed it are the ones we need to make adjustments. They should oversee the test. But there's an even better reason we need you here."

"And that is?"

"Lin Shaw."

"Lin—"

"Could be planning something, Desmond. If she is, she'll strike now. You're close to her. You're the only person in the Citium who's in a position to watch her."

Desmond exhaled and thought about Yuri's words.

"And there's something else." Yuri glanced at Conner. "This is an opportunity for Conner to take on more responsibility. We need somebody we trust to oversee the security on the ship."

Desmond shook his head.

Yuri ignored him. "Is that something you're interested in, Conner?"

"Of course," Conner said quickly. "I'll do whatever is needed."

Desmond argued, fought the plan, but in the end, he agreed.

Yuri seemed to have anticipated every objection and planned for each one, like a chess game he had already played out in his mind.

Yuri and Conner left the next day. Desmond was there at the pier to see them off, the wind blowing in his hair, the massive cargo ship towering in the bay, the Golden Gate Bridge looming in the background.

"Be careful out there."

Conner hugged his brother. "I'll get this done for you, Des. I promise. When I get back, it will start."

The first week brought nearly constant updates from the Rendition team and from Conner and Yuri. The first participants in the trials were recruited from islands in the South Pacific. The results were incredibly positive. No deaths. A few adverse events. The Rendition developers adjusted the device.

And so it went, for months, trial after trial, each port bringing new participants. The rest were held on the ship, told they would be released at the end of the project.

Updates became less frequent, but Desmond assumed all was well.

One Saturday afternoon, he went in to the Phaethon offices and found Avery camped out in the conference room, boxes of file folders open around her.

"Looks like an IRS audit in here."

She jumped at his voice and held a hand to her chest. "You scared me." She put the top back on the closest box.

"That's a first." He studied the folders. Personnel files. "What're you doing?"

She swallowed as she put the cover on another box. "Research project…"

She looked as if she hadn't slept in a week.

Something about the encounter bothered him, but he couldn't put his finger on it. Avery seemed to be spending every waking hour at the office, like a college student cramming for finals.

Halloween that year fell on a Friday, and the entire office dressed up. Politicians were well represented. There were three Hillary Clintons, just as many Nancy Pelosis, a few Barbara Boxers, no Donald Trumps, and seven Bernie Sanderses.

Some costumes skewed intellectual. The comptroller wore his usual dark business suit with one exception: the button-up white shirt and tie were replaced with a T-shirt with a line chart on it. The labels below listed the years, starting at 1980 and going up to 2015, a line for every five years. On the left were numbers: zero to twenty. He offered a reward of prime plus ten dollars, $13.50, to anyone who guessed what he was. Desmond instantly realized it, but refrained since the rest of the accounting department was obsessed with the mystery. Until lunch, that is, when he found the accountants crowded around the comptroller's table, practically grilling him, insisting he was the target fed funds rate.

"No. You're close, but that's not it."

Desmond stepped through the crowd. "Greg, if I'm not mistaken, you're the LIBOR rate."

The gray-haired man grinned. "How'd you figure it out?"

"September 2008. LIBOR spiked after Lehman collapsed. The only real divergence with the fed target rate in decades."

The CFO reached into his pocket and removed an envelope that contained thirteen dollars and fifty cents.

"You're a real geek, Desmond. You know that?"

"Yes. I'm aware of that."

The costume voted best was topical. A lab tech had ordered a custom T-shirt from Vistaprint with four images: Gene Roddenberry, Silent Bob, the numeral eight, and a red circle with a line through it. His modern hieroglyphs—representing gene-mute-8-shun, or gene mutation—were lauded throughout the company.

Seeing the costumes reminded Desmond of the house party in Palo Alto the night he had met Peyton, when they had worn matching Mulder and Scully costumes. That had been a good night. There weren't many that could touch it in his mind.

Like the comptroller, Desmond had also challenged people to

guess his outfit, and offered a hundred dollars to the first person to do so. He wore a suit tailored in a mid-1800s style, a green visor on his forehead, and thick chains that hung from his neck and wrapped around his torso. The outfit drew plenty of lookers, most of whom dropped by his office in pairs or trios, peering around the frame as if they were looking into an open tiger cage. Board members were scary animals.

Many of the guesses were the same. Harry Houdini. David Blaine. Some professional wrestlers he'd never heard of. He shook his head and turned back to his computer each time.

Avery stopped by in the late afternoon. She looked terrible— this time purposefully so. Her hair was a rat's nest, not unlike the first time he had visited her apartment. She had painted her mascara down her face, like Tammy Faye Bakker or a member of Kiss. She wore a teal skirt, tight-fitting, and a white T-shirt. On the front of the shirt the delta symbol was written three times in magic marker. She twirled to let him read the back of the shirt, which read: *Bad Decisions*.

That stumped him.

He stood for her, letting her take in his outfit.

"Seriously?"

He shrugged. "What?"

"It's like, almost intellectually self-mutilating."

"Does that mean you know who I am?"

"It means that I do."

He cocked his head, surprised. She pointed at his outfit.

"You're Jacob Marley, the business partner of Ebenezer Scrooge, immortalized in a certain novel titled *A Christmas Carol*. You are, how do I say this…"

"Lay it on me."

"Okay. You're dead."

"That's a shot to the heart."

"Indeed."

"Tell me more."

"You're tortured. A ghost, doomed to walk the Earth forever for your greedy, selfish, and uncaring attitude toward mankind.

You roam the world, unseen, but seeing others' pain, unable to help them. You realize your mistake. And it becomes your cross to bear. You lay it at Ebenezer's feet, and arrange for three ghosts to visit him: the ghosts of Christmas past, present, and future. If your partner, Ebenezer, can be redeemed, perhaps you'll finally know peace."

"Wow."

Avery shrugged. "Lucky guess."

"Unlikely. You must have been a lit major."

"Nah. Ira David Wood. He did a production of *A Christmas Carol* in Raleigh every year. It was great."

Desmond drew out the five twenty-dollar bills he had extracted from the ATM that morning.

Avery held up a hand. "Keep it."

"I'll donate it to charity."

"Grand. Do you... want to talk about your outfit?"

He squinted. "I thought we just did."

"No, like what it means."

"That I'm a lover of classic literature?"

"Clearly, but of all the characters in the history of stories, you picked Jacob Marley."

"And?"

"And he's a tragic figure. A businessman who realized his life's work had hurt others. But only after he died and was reborn— after he wandered the world and saw the full truth. He's a person on a mission to change his partners and pay for his crimes."

Desmond leaned back in his chair. "Oh. Well, I was thinking, I've got this old suit and some chains in the garage, and the visor I bought cheap at a second-hand store. So, no, I didn't really get that far in my analysis."

She smiled. "Well, it's worth thinking about. Just saying." She turned to leave.

"Hey."

She stopped.

"I didn't guess yours."

She turned back. "All right."

He studied her chest, the three deltas, tight against her body. He couldn't remember the words on the back.

"Turn for me."

The corners of her mouth twisted slightly, but she spun and showed him her backside.

Delta represented change. "Bad Decisions" was written on her back—they were *behind her*. And she had clearly been crying. Or in a fight.

"You're... making changes to leave bad decisions behind?"

"Close. Not quite."

"Three changes?"

"No changes, actually."

"Huh."

She shrugged. "Don't sweat it. Nobody's guessed it."

"What's the reward?"

"Mystery," she said over her shoulder as she walked away.

And a mystery she was.

At five o'clock, he stopped by her cubicle, and found her working on another query, with tables he recognized.

"Well," he said. "Anybody guess it?"

"Nope. You?"

"Nah. No classic literature aficionados around, apparently. What you working on?"

"Your health trait report."

"That can wait until Monday."

"I've got nothing else going on."

"No hot date on Halloween?"

"I don't date."

He exhaled a laugh. "Me either."

"I doubt that."

"It's true."

"And why is that?"

"Faults that are mine alone."

She pointed at the chains hanging from his neck. "Character flaws that doom you to wander the afterlife, trying in vain to atone for your shortcomings?"

He smiled. "Something like that."

"BS."

He studied her.

"I meant what I said a few months ago."

"That—"

"You're a good guy. Aren't many left."

"Right, well, I'll keep that in mind." He turned to leave.

"Hey." She stood up in her cube as she called after him.

He looked back without speaking.

"Yes," she said.

"What?"

"The answer is yes."

"Answer to what?"

"We'll have dinner at my place."

He smiled. "I told you I don't date."

"Which is the only reason I'm willing to have dinner with you."

"If we're having dinner, we're having it at my place. Because, well, your place is… your place. You know?"

"I know."

He wrote out the address for her and drove home, feeling a strange mix of excitement and nervousness.

The doorbell rang a few minutes after he entered the motor court. The pizza guy was young, polite, and dressed as the blue person from Avatar—the name escaped Desmond. He tipped the guy excessively and told him to be careful tonight.

Just as he was setting the boxes on the kitchen island, a knock sounded on the solid wood door. Desmond saw Avery's outline through the blurry, leaded glass as he went to greet her.

She glanced up, then left, into the dining room, and forward, taking in the expansive great room. "Jesus. It's like Martha Stewart renovated an abandoned insane asylum."

He howled with laughter, not a polite reaction, but a genuine heartfelt laugh. "Her fees were exorbitant."

"You must have hired her before prison."

"This place is an investment."

"Right."

He led her down the gallery hall, to the kitchen, where the boxes of pizza were waiting, along with a carafe of water and two bottles of wine.

"I've got water and wine, which I believe you like. As well as beer."

"I'll take beer."

He pulled open a refrigerator drawer. "I've got Amstel, Bud, Bud Light, Fat Tire—"

"I'll have what you're having."

"I'm just drinking water."

"Really?"

"I... don't drink. Used to."

"Me too."

"What?"

"I quit recently."

"Really?"

"Like four seconds ago."

He smiled. "All right. Water it is."

He poured two glasses, and they sat at the long island, eating pizza out of the boxes.

"What are you?" he asked.

She raised her eyebrows.

"The costume. I'll never get it."

"Oh. I'm the walk of shame."

He shook his head. "I have no idea what that means."

She scrunched her eyebrows skeptically. Then comprehension seemed to dawn on her. "Oh. That's right. You never went to college."

A flicker of insecurity ran through him. It was a foreign feeling, repulsive, like someone was accusing him of something he was innocent of.

"I was kind of poking fun at myself and other sorority girls."

He relaxed. A sorority was not something he associated Avery with. "Wait. Seriously? You were..."

She nodded. "I was."

"No way."

"It's not that bad."

"I know, but why—"

"Well, believe it or not, my various… *defense mechanisms* make it hard for me to make friends sometimes."

"You don't say."

She sighed theatrically. "I'm afraid it's true. This shell is hard to crack."

"And your looks no doubt add to the intimidation factor."

She took another bite of beef and pineapple pizza. "No comment. Anyway, being put into a situation where you have to be friends with people was like, kind of helpful."

"And you became a Delta, Delta, Delta."

She let out a laugh as she leaned forward.

"What?"

"We call it tri-delt."

"Okay, Princess Tri-Delt. What does the back mean?" He tried to remember. Bad decisions?

"It's like, you gussy yourself up, go to a mixer or a formal— these are events between a sorority and a frat—you walk in classy, have a few drinks, you're dancing, and the next thing you know you wake up, hair's out of whack, you're wearing some guy's T-shirt, and you're sneaking out before class, walking across the quad, back to your dorm or apartment, mascara running, looking like a tramp… you know, the walk of shame."

"That I definitely would not have gotten. I mean, it's a bit obscure."

"Says the guy dressed as a minor character in a novel a hundred and seventy years old."

"Touché."

They ate in silence a moment. Then he asked, "What do you do for fun?"

"I read."

"What do you read? Romance?"

"Don't have the heart for it."

"Good one."

"Crime fiction mostly."

That surprised him. "Why?"

"I think we read about things we don't have. Things we wonder about, want to see in the world. I think there's not enough justice in this world. Too many victims—without anyone to defend them."

"I agree with that."

"What do you read?"

"Books about ideas."

"Because that's what fascinates you."

"Yes." It was the only thing that fascinated him. Except for her. But he would never say that. He stared at her, but she didn't meet his gaze.

"And when you're not reading? What do you do on the weekend? When you're not writing SQL queries?"

"Not much."

"You don't seem like the idle type."

"Fair enough," she said. "I teach tennis."

"Where?"

"San Jose. Inner city."

He leaned back on the stool. "Really?"

She mimicked his expression, seemed defensive. "Really."

"I think it's cool."

She shrugged. "It's something to do."

"Right. Just something to do." He stared at her until she made eye contact. "Be honest. Why do you do it?"

She shrugged.

"It has to mean something to you or you wouldn't do it," he said.

"Equality."

"Equality?"

"On the court, it doesn't matter who you are. Where you came from. Who your parents are. It just matters what you can do. There's... justice." She took a drink of water.

"There's a line ref."

"And review."

"So there is."

"Venus and Serena Williams. They grew up south of here, in Compton, just outside LA. They started playing tennis when they were three."

"So tennis is like a Cinderella ball? Anybody can make it."

"Your words, not mine. But yes. Your skill is all that matters. And attitude. It's about mental and physical toughness."

Desmond stared at her, finally realizing who she was, what her values were, deep inside, the part beyond the sarcasm and defense mechanisms. He saw it and he liked it.

He set his glass down on the marble counter. "You want to see something cool?"

"I never say no to that."

They walked to the back staircase and descended to the basement, which held an empty wine cellar and some classic arcade games. Desmond marched into the tasting room, which was lined with empty wooden racks. The walls were clad in tumbled brick. Antique lanterns hung from the ceiling.

Avery held up a finger. "This is usually the part in the movie where bad things happen."

"You getting scared?"

"Terrified."

He chuckled as he moved to the back of the room. He pushed in a brick and leaned against the wall. The hidden door swung open with a groan, revealing a mesh steel catwalk enclosed by glass walls.

"This isn't like, a *Fifty Shades* room, is it?" She said, eyeing the room beyond.

"You mean a hidden room for pleasure and pain?" He held his hand out, ushering her inside. "See for yourself."

She squinted at him as she stepped through the opening. On the catwalk, a smile slowly formed. "A racquetball court?"

"They built it under the garage." He studied her. "Do you play?"

"Not really. I have. A couple of times."

"I hear it's like riding a bike."

"I'm sure."

He smiled. "If you're not comfortable with your skill level—"

"Don't get carried away, Mister."

"I can loan you some gym shorts—"

"I have clothes in my car."

Ten minutes later, she walked back onto the catwalk wearing a white sports bra and gray shorts.

He couldn't help but stare. She was stunning. Fit—but it was something else about her. The way she looked at him, how she carried herself.

"Prepare to be schooled," she called down.

He smiled. "I stand ready for my lessons, headmistress."

She never broke eye contact as she descended the steel stairs. "Punishment for failure will be swift. And painful."

"I expect nothing less."

They volleyed for serve.

She won.

The ball echoed off the walls, and they danced around each other. Desmond was more powerful, but Avery was faster, and her precision was greater, her serves falling in the unreturnable corners. His forehands were lightning, the crack seeming to sound after the ball whizzed by. The room was cool when they began, but an hour later, it felt like a sauna. Sweat poured down Desmond's face. His shirt was spotted with patches where he'd dried himself. Avery practically glistened, her blonde hair, which was pulled into a ponytail, almost dripping. Three red welts on her legs marked times she had been too slow to dodge Desmond's strikes. Her stomach was like dunes in the desert, the light reflecting off the valleys and ridges.

When it was fourteen to twelve, her way, she paused at the serving line. "FYI, this is the part where you lose."

"I've got you right where I want you."

She served, and he returned, a thunderous volley that sent her reeling back into him, their bodies intertwining, both so soaked they almost slipped off of each other. They hit the wood floor together, sliding then rolling toward the back wall, racquets flying out of their hands.

He came up on top. Her chest heaved, and she stared at him.

Her hair spilled onto the wooden floor like golden silk. He had never been so sure of anything in his life. He lowered himself, kissed her, and she wrapped her arms around him.

It felt like the world exploded and nothing would ever be the same.

CHAPTER 41

THE GUNSHOTS FOCUSED Conner. He screamed into the radio, "Get those vans back into the garages. Now!"

He barreled down the central hall of Desmond's massive home. Two of his men were standing in the great room, exposed to the three French doors that opened onto the back yard.

"Back! Get back—"

Sniper fire shattered the glass and dropped one of the men. The other cowered behind the couch and soldier-crawled into the hall.

"Second floor units!" Conner called. "We've got snipers in the back yard. Return fire!"

A second later he heard a massive explosion. Charred planks of wood and cedar shakes rained down on the yard and pool—the remnants of the neighbor's elaborate tree house scattered in every direction.

Conner raced to the back staircase, up to the second floor, and kept going, through the insulated door to the attic. At the dormer, he waddled forward and peeked out.

The street was blocked on both sides by armored troop carriers. They had heavy artillery behind them. He counted two dozen armored Humvees.

He was outnumbered, outgunned, and perhaps most importantly, trapped.

He took out the radio they had taken from the X1 troops captured at the checkpoint.

"To the commander of the X1 troops out there. I have five of your men. I repeat. I have your people. If you fire another shot into this home—if you even set foot on the lawn—I will kill one and throw him out."

A man with a deep, gruff voice responded. "To whom am I speaking?"

The troops outside stopped moving. They were listening.

"Call me the man in the stone castle."

A pause.

"Yeah, well, I don't have time for a name that long. How 'bout I just call you Conner. McClain."

How? How could they know? A mole in his organization? Park? Doubtful. Could one of the X1 troops have gotten a message out? Unlikely. He looked across the street. Yes—it had to be a surveillance team. If that was true, they would have seen him arrive and observed his troop strength. What a mess.

He heard rhythmic popping above. Helicopters. Not ideal.

The gruff voice continued. "I'll take your silence as confirmation. I'm Major Charles Latham, United States Army, commanding a combined X1 force that is willing, ready, and able to do whatever it takes to recover our people. So why don't you send them on out, and we'll be on our way. You can have a house party or burn the place down for all we care."

It was a pretty good lie. Conner sort of liked his adversary.

"Major, be advised, we're not here for a house party, and if you don't withdraw your troops *right now*, the only way those X1s are leaving is in pieces."

Conner activated his mic as he raced down the stairs. "Unit two, launch the drones."

"Now, now," Latham said. "Let's not resort to threats. We both know you'll be leaving the same way they do. Let's choose the alive option. Speaking of which, I'm going to need confirmation that they are, in fact, still alive."

Conner stepped into the garage, where the vans were parked and the X1 troops were tied up. The highest-ranking prisoner was a lieutenant with short black hair and olive skin. Conner yanked his gag off. "Name and rank only. You go off script, and I'll kick you in the nuts. Got it?"

His captive nodded.

Conner activated the radio. "Stand by, Major."

He held the radio to the lieutenant. His captive spoke quickly.

"Lieutenant Jacob Danielson, US Marine Corps, twenty-five troops in the garage—"

Conner released the radio button and sighed. "Well played, Lieutenant." He couldn't very well kick the man in the testicles for doing his job.

He was about to head back into the house when Major Goins caught up with him. He glanced back to make sure he was out of earshot of the X1s. "Sir?" he said. "We're pretty jammed up here."

"Indeed."

"What's the plan?"

"It's very simple, Major. We're going to deal with it."

Latham's voice crackled on the radio. "Thank you, Conner. Another show of good faith would go a long way. Release the lieutenant, and I promise we won't shoot any more of your men."

Conner examined the available vehicles. Both vans in the garage had a flat tire. The two vans outside were shot up pretty bad, and probably wouldn't run. The Humvee in the garage and the one in the motor court were in good shape though. The only other vehicle was Desmond's Tesla sedan, plugged in and charging.

He stepped into one of the vans. A bank of screens in the back showed drone footage. He studied his adversary's troop alignment. Textbook cordon and siege formation. They would breach soon.

He held the radio button down. "That's a compelling offer, Major, but I'm afraid you're going to have to do better than that. First, you get those Strykers out of here. Second, you move your Humvees back a hundred feet. Do that, and we'll send your loquacious lieutenant out. And be advised, we have eyes in the sky—don't waste time lying."

Conner returned to Major Goins and spoke softly, but loud enough so that the lieutenant could hear. "Here's what we're going to do. Put the spare tires on these two vans. Get them running. Split our prisoners up, one in each vehicle—the two vans and the two Humvees, plus the Tesla. As soon as we're ready, we're going to send a Humvee out the front. The rest of our vehicles will follow the other Humvee out the back, onto Stockbridge. They're not set up there. We'll make a run for it. And if they shoot or try to stop us, they'll risk killing their own people."

Goins nodded. "I like it."

"Make it happen." He glanced at the lieutenant. "As soon as they pull the Humvees back and get rid of the ATCs, cut him loose."

"Sir?"

"You heard me."

Fifteen minutes later, the vans were ready to go. In the back of the second van, Dr. Park was studying the monitor.

"How long?"

"Soon," Park said. "Maybe ten minutes."

Conner turned to Goins. "Load up. Get ready."

When the kiss finished, Desmond paused, unsure what to do—and what he wanted. Avery was not. She raised her head and kissed him with fervor, her arms wrapped around him, holding him close, her strength surprising him. That strength seemed to feed him, like some part of her flowed into his body, reawakening a hunger that had lain dormant for thirteen years.

He kissed her back, and she gripped him tighter and rolled on top of him. She grinned as she looked down and ran a hand through his sweaty hair, her own blonde hair hanging down as she lowered her face to his.

He waited until her lips were almost to his, then pushed off the hard floor, rolling her over. He threw his leg over her, took her hands in his, and pressed them to the floor, the sweat making them glide, then catch, streaking, the skin on wood crying out like a wild animal caught in a trap.

He kissed her, slow then fast. He relaxed his hands and she

brought her right leg up, planted it against the floor and rolled him over again. Even in the dives and watering holes in Texas and Louisiana, he had never been with a woman as physical—or as strong—as her. It thrilled him.

She broke from his lips and straightened, straddling him. With one hand, she reached under the sports bra and ripped it up and over her head. She pushed his T-shirt up, revealing his bare chest as she lowered hers to him, rubbing her wet skin on his. She slipped out of her shorts as he pulled his off and his brain stopped working completely.

☣

They lay on the hard floor, staring at the court's buzzing lights until the warm beads of sweat on their skin turned cold. He wondered if she regretted it. The act had happened so fast, as if they had been exploring a cave and had fallen down a shaft, desperately hanging on to each other, not knowing where the bottom was. Now they were at the end, where the lovemaking had led them, both staring up, not acknowledging each other, not sure exactly how to get back to the place they were before, or if they ever would.

He didn't know if he regretted it. He expected to, but he didn't feel that, just the opposite. He felt more content than he could remember. He decided to gage her.

"What are you thinking about?"

She smiled. "The fact that my Halloween costume has actually become a self-fulfilling prophecy."

He rolled onto his side and looked at her.

"I have become the walk of shame. I went to a little get-together at what, frankly, sort of looks like a frat house. Things got out of hand. I got laid. And now, I'm going to be walking back to my car, hair disheveled, slightly skanky looking."

He shrugged and held the pose. "You're not *that* skanky looking."

She punched him, harder than he expected, forcing him onto his back. She was on top of him again, leaning in to kiss.

"Wait."

She stared into his eyes.

"Do you… are you ashamed?"

"No, Des. Not even a little."

"No bad decisions behind you?"

"Not recently."

She kissed him and they started up, but he held her at arm's length. "If we don't get off this floor you're going to be bruised all over."

She smiled, mischief in her cold blue eyes. "I'm okay with that."

He got on top of her. "I'm not."

He scooped her up in his arms, hefted her, and walked toward the staircase.

She leaned her head back, roared with laughter.

"What?"

She wiggled free, landed like a cat who had jumped from a tree. "Sorry, my romance allergy was acting up."

He wanted to strangle her and yet, bizarrely, he was even more attracted to her. "I carried you to bed once."

She squinted and seemed to remember the morning he had come to her apartment, when she was exhausted from pulling an all-nighter, half-drunk after learning that she had been fired, and ended up passing out after consuming an inhuman amount of breakfast.

"Oh, that. Well, it's not like it was consensual."

He opened his mouth, alarmed.

"And I never said thanks. But it was nice to wake up in my bed." She stooped and grabbed her clothes, but to his surprise, didn't put them on. She strode up the stairs and sauntered across the catwalk, still naked, without a hint of self-consciousness, like some Roman goddess who ruled the Earth.

She paused at the door and peered down.

"You coming?"

CHAPTER 42

DESMOND HADN'T EXPECTED it, but Avery spent the night. She slept naked, and that kept him up for a while. But he did sleep—eventually.

He awoke first, and he was glad. He watched her, amazed at how some people looked different when they were asleep. Avery looked more delicate. Younger.

He was sore from using muscles that had grown weak with disuse, and not just in his body. She was his first since Peyton. He wasn't like most men; he hadn't missed the sex. Maybe it was because he had sown so many wild oats in his younger years, in the rough and tumble time he'd spent with Orville.

He couldn't help but wonder what was next. He tried not to.

In the kitchen, he set about cooking breakfast, a large spread—pancakes, eggs, grits, and toast. The same meal she had devoured that first morning they had met.

She emerged with one of his shirts on—a starched white button-up. And nothing else. Her hair was wild, golden, spilling onto the stark white cloth like a gold mine spilling into a field of snow. The mascara from her Halloween outfit was faded from the sweat, but the outline was still there.

She pulled several sheets from the paper towel roll, layered them four times, and placed them on the stool. Then she sat, taking in the plates of food.

"I have something to admit."

He froze, spatula in hand.

"I don't have my wallet."

He exhaled, a laugh forming.

"And even if I did, I don't have any cash."

"Avery—"

"I'm afraid your tip will have to be a sexual favor."

He let the spatula fall to his side. "We accept all forms of payment here at Hughes Manor."

Desmond expected things to change, but they didn't. At Phaethon Genetics, it was as if nothing had ever happened between them. It drove him crazy. And the fact that it drove him crazy—the fact that he thought about it all—drove him crazier. She was a stone wall at work.

After hours was a different story. She would text, always on days when she was done with her work, no deadline, and always with a simple question: *What r u doing?* or *Plans tonight?* or *Dinner?* or *Rematch?*

He always said yes—because he wanted to, and because he didn't play games, and because, frankly, he had nothing else going on. Rendition was done. He was waiting on Yuri and Conner to finish the trials. He didn't understand what was taking them so long.

He and Avery settled into a pattern. They spent a few nights each week together and most of the weekend. They played racquetball, they had sex in every room in the house, and they played cards— gin rummy mostly, her favorite game—in the library. They talked, but she never let him in. He tried. He came close once, on a Friday night when they were in his bed, both covered in sweat, the moon full, shining through the steel-clad windows.

"Tell me about your parents."

She stared at the vaulted ceiling. "Not much to tell."

"Tell me anyway."

"My mom is dead."

"How?"

"Car accident."

"When?"

"My freshman year in college."

"My parents died when I was five. It turns your whole world upside down."

"Yeah."

He searched for the words. "It's like... they were the Rock of Gibraltar. Unmovable objects. Constants in your life. Gone in the blink of an eye."

"On the way to the grocery store."

"At home. Doing nothing. Herding sheep."

She exhaled. "I realized how dangerous the world was then. How anything could change. Any time."

"Your father?"

"Alive."

"You keep up with him?"

"I try."

He rolled to his side, looked at her.

"He has Alzheimer's."

"That's what drew you to Phaethon."

"Among other things."

She was a black box, one he desperately wanted to get inside. The physical part had been the easiest. The real work was ahead.

With each passing day, he watched as she changed. The worry lines on her face grew deeper. She texted him more often. Sex started at the door, her pushing him into the foyer, ripping her clothes off, like she needed it, like it was a drug that could cure her illness.

They finished in the study one night, and he turned to her. "What's going on with you?"

"Nothing."

"Don't lie to me."

"Would you lie to me?"

He thought for a moment. "Yes." Before she could reply, he added, "To protect you."

Her expression changed then, to one he had never seen, a vulnerable expression, scared almost.

"Then you understand. I *have* lied to you. But every lie I've told you was to protect you."

He stood, naked, the stacks of books behind him, the sconces glowing. "What are you talking about?"

She got up and faced him. "Do you trust me?"

"Yes."

"If I told you something that… changed everything you believe, would you still trust me?"

"Avery, what are you talking about?"

"What if I had proof—if I showed you the world was not what you thought it was?"

He took a step back, took her in, seeing her with new eyes. *What is this?* Was it personal—an admission like, *I'm pregnant*, or *I was married before*, or *I have a child*? No. It wasn't any of those things. Or probably not. It felt different. More like business.

"I think we're past vague generalities, Avery."

"Are we?"

"Pretty sure."

"Then tell me: what do you do?"

"What?"

"What do you *do*?"

"I'm an investor in high-tech companies—"

"A person can read that on your website. What do you really do? What are you really working on, Des?"

A chill ran through him. He took another step back, as if realizing he was in the presence of an enemy. "What are you asking me?"

His phone buzzed on the card table. He was torn between staring at her and picking it up. Finally, he broke eye contact and glanced at the screen. A message from Conner. That surprised him.

Need to meet. At pier eighty. On Kentaru Maru. Urgent.

"I need to go," he said absently.

"Why?"

"My brother. He's back."

"Where is he?"

He turned to her. "Why do you care?"

Her intense expression softened. "Please tell me, Des. And don't ask me why."

He knew it then: his life was at a crossroads. Telling her would cross a line beyond which nothing would ever be the same.

She stood stark naked in his study, surrounded by the books that he loved, that he had kept in his private collection. He knew one thing: he trusted her. She was genuine and pure, and in the darkest reaches of his mind he knew that she would never hurt an innocent person. And he knew that Conner would, and so would Yuri—because the world had made them that way.

And so he told her where Conner was, and before he could say another word, she had scooped up her clothes and left, running, not looking back.

He knew the truth then: she was somehow his enemy. What he didn't know was why she had been sleeping with him.

"He's out of the memory," Dr. Park said.

Conner leaned into the back of the van. "Is there another location?"

Park tapped the smartphone. "Yes. It's... What the—"

"Save it, Doctor." Conner turned to Major Goins. "Begin."

The major began barking orders, and the garage sprang into frenzied action. His men shoved the X1 troops they had captured into the vans and the Humvees.

Many of Conner's men were still spread throughout the house. Now the windows shattered as they fired, full auto, spraying the X1 vehicles on the street. They launched two rocket-propelled grenades, both of which found their targets, leaving the enemy's two camo-clad Humvees in flames. Conner's men then raced to the garage and climbed into their vehicles.

The Humvee in the motor court roared forward first, barreling past the open motor court doors onto Austin Avenue, charging head-on at the blockade of X1 vehicles. The second Humvee went next, but it cut a donut in the motor court, slipped around the house, and bounced through the back yard, flattening an aluminum fence as it trounced into a neighbor's yard. One van followed in its wake, then the Tesla sedan.

That left one van remaining in the garage.

To Goins, Conner said, "Good luck, Major."

Conner climbed into the van, gathered Desmond in his arms, and with Dr. Park and two soldiers surrounding him, stepped out and walked back into Desmond's home. Desmond hung limp, helpless, the tubes running from him capped. Conner descended the back staircase, into the dank basement, with its red brick walls lined with empty wine racks and classic arcade machines: Pac-Man, Donkey Kong, Galaga. Conner stopped at the hidden door and pushed the brick in. Above, he heard the van crank and power out of the garage.

He was first through the dark opening. The soldier's lights guided his way into the man-made cavern. Dr. Park pulled the hidden door closed behind them, and the mercenaries released their sacks full of MREs, water, and weapons. They had enough to last for days. Conner hoped it wouldn't take that long.

From the catwalk, he looked down at the cavernous space, lit by the beams of their helmet lights. The racquetball court's wood floor shimmered like an underwater lake.

They descended and hid under the catwalk, just in case someone entered and did a cursory search.

An hour later, Conner heard footsteps above, in the garage. He looked at his men, held a single finger to his lips, and clicked off his light.

CHAPTER 43

YURI'S MEN WERE efficient and deadly. They activated the radio and satellite jamming arrays and rushed the visitor center. The reports from their suppressed rifles echoed across the green rolling fields as they moved through the parking lot and into the building.

Yuri watched from a distance, through long-range binoculars, the muzzle flares like camera flashes in the floor-to-ceiling windows.

When the all-clear was called, he walked across the hills with his personal security contingent, through the parking lot littered with dead bodies, and into the visitor center, where a small group of British and Spanish forces were tied and gagged. They'd be needed for radio communication—and as bargaining chips if it came to it.

The commanding officer of the Citium Security forces was a Brazilian named Pablo Machado. Yuri walked close to the man. "You didn't find them?"

"They either left or they're in the cave," Machado said in a hushed voice. "We're about to start interrogating—"

"Don't bother. By the time we get it out of them, it will be too late."

"So we're going in?"

"Yes. Assemble a small team. Your best. And hurry."

☣

Deep inside the Cave of Altamira, Lin activated her radio. "Avery, come in."

"I'm here."

"We found it. Return to the rally point."

"Copy that."

Lin resealed the plastic container and handed it to Peyton. Without a word, she stood and began hiking away from the cave painting of the doe, now standing alone, the buck and fawn smeared from the stone.

As Peyton walked behind her mother, through the cave's dark corridors, holding the secrets her grandfather had buried so long ago, she felt that something had changed between them. Her mother's secrets were out in the open now. All except for one: the truth about the code buried in the human genome. She wondered if that would be next. Or if her mother would continue to shut her out.

Avery and Nigel were waiting on them in the hidden room. Despite the chill in the cave, Nigel's brow was drenched in sweat and his cheeks were red.

Chief Adams stepped forward. "We're thirty minutes past due on our routine comm check."

"Proceed," Lin said.

Adams motioned to Rodriguez, who left in a jog.

Lin called after him. "Tell them to send teams to carry these crates out."

"Does that mean you found it?" Nigel asked.

"We did." Lin took the container from Peyton and opened the top, the sound like popping a wine cork. She took out the first page and scanned it. The words were German, handwritten. She flipped to the next page, then quickly rifled through the entire sheaf.

"Mom, what is it?"

Lin glanced over, as if remembering the others were there. "An inventory. As suspected." She motioned to the crates. "They're the missing pieces."

Nigel huffed. "Missing pieces of *what* exactly? I for one would like to know exactly what's in there."

"We don't have time—"

"Mom. You owe us that much. And besides, if we're separated... I think it's better if we all know what's going on."

"Very well. We'll talk until the teams arrive." Almost to herself, she whispered, "Where to begin?"

She set the pages back in the container.

"First, you have to realize that Kraus came to his conclusion about the human genome over time. He had other theories that preceded it. His initial theory was that the rate of human evolution was accelerating."

"Punctuated equilibrium," Nigel said, nodding. "He believed we're in the midst of speciation."

"What's punctuated equilibrium?" Avery asked.

Nigel turned to her. "Seriously?"

"Sorry, I taught tennis in college, not evolutionary biology. Is it like a deviated septum? I can show you what that is."

Nigel's eyes grew wide.

Peyton held up a hand. "Why don't you tell us, Mom?"

"Punctuated equilibrium," Lin said, "is a theory proposed in 1972 by Niles Eldredge and Stephen Jay Gould. Before that time, evolutionary biologists had debated how new species developed. Most thought it happened gradually over time—what we call phyletic gradual evolution. But the fossil record doesn't support that. It shows that when a species emerges, it is generally stable, with little genetic change, for long stretches of time. When evolution does occur, it happens rapidly—new species branch off in a relatively short period of time. On a geological scale, anyway."

"Why?" Peyton asked.

"The trigger events for these periods of rapid evolution are a subject of debate. We know it happens when an organism is transported to a new environment."

"They're forced to adapt to survive," Avery said.

"That's right. Or if the species stays put and their environment changes, as occurred during the Quaternary extinction."

"That's what they were studying on the *Beagle*," Peyton said.

"Indeed. The researchers found evidence that the Quaternary

extinction was caused by two factors. The first was natural climate change on a global scale, specifically the end of the last glacial period, known popularly as the last ice age. If you want to get technical, we're still in an ice age, one that has lasted millions of years—we're just in an interglacial period at the moment. Anyway, at the time of the Quaternary extinction, the warming of the planet and retreating glaciers put many species at risk. Large animals that had evolved for cold weather died out, and those that survived fell prey to humans invading their environment. It's hard to imagine the scale of this climate change. The ice sheets that covered much of Asia, Europe, and North America stopped advancing and started retreating. Within a few hundred years, an unimaginable amount of ice had melted—enough to raise sea levels thirty feet in places. If all the ice in Greenland melted today, it wouldn't raise the oceans that much.

"The biggest consequence, however, was on sea currents. The flood of freshwater into the Northern Atlantic pushed back on the flow of warm water from the equator moving north. That warmer water was redirected south, toward Antarctica, shrinking the ice there and changing the circumpolar winds. In the course of a thousand years, most of the planet went from being a frozen wilderness to a fertile world perfect for our species. It was almost tailor-made for humans. We were alive at exactly the right time. And it changed us.

"That was Kraus's central theory. That the end of the last ice age kicked off a period of rapid evolution for our species. In the context of punctuated equilibrium, we call the splitting of a species 'cladogenesis.' Some scientists on the *Beagle* believed that the human race was splitting into two species, but the genetic evidence they gathered didn't support that. Kraus posited that one tribe developed a substantial genetic advantage—and it centered on how their minds worked. Art is the evidence of that change."

Lin motioned to the cave. "That's why he was so interested in this place. Altamira is one of the oldest examples of cave art and fictive thinking. Kraus believed that the advent of art was a transcendental moment in our evolution. He believed..." She glanced at the crates. "He believed it was like opening Pandora's box. Fictive thinking triggered a further acceleration in human evolution. If you compare our progress in the last thirty-five thousand years with the millions of years hominids inhabited the planet before, it's like we're a completely different type of organism. To him, there had to be a reason for such a dramatic shift—an environmental factor driving the change in our behavior. But we could find no environmental factor."

"That's why you needed the *Beagle*," Nigel said. "To take ice core, archaeological, and biological samples from around the world. In secret. You were trying to find evidence of environmental triggers in the past."

"Yes. Our first theory was HGT."

Nigel nodded.

"Okay," said Avery, "I'll bite. What's HGT?"

"Horizontal gene transfer," Lin said, "sometimes referred to as lateral gene transfer. Most of evolution occurs though vertical gene transfer—DNA being passed from parent to child. Horizontal transfer is when DNA is acquired from another living organism."

"It happens all the time in bacteria," Nigel said. "One bacteria develops an advantage and transfers it to another. That's how they become antibiotic resistant, among other things."

Lin nodded. "In our case, we thought perhaps there was some external source of DNA that was driving human evolution, almost like a symbiotic relationship—feeding us genes that advanced us."

"Like aliens?" Avery said, skeptical.

"No, nothing that dramatic. We thought perhaps some symbiotic bacteria or virus in the gut. When Kraus looked at the long arc of history, he saw some very strange patterns. In particular, a certain synchronicity. Take these cave paintings, for instance." She walked closer to the cave wall. "Cave paintings appeared at about the same time in multiple places in Europe and the Middle East. Why? How did fictive thinking—this evolutionary leap forward—occur almost simultaneously in independent populations separated by huge distances? The same thing happened with the development of agriculture, twelve thousand years ago. We found eleven different civilizations, completely isolated from each other, in which agriculture emerged independently, at almost exactly the same time. Or writing—the next great human breakthrough, as it allowed us to store data far more efficiently than we could through oral traditions. This, too, occurred at the same time, in at least three isolated groups.

"To Kraus, this synchronicity was the ultimate evidence that there was an incredibly powerful force sculpting humanity. He called it the Invisible Sun. To him, evolution was like this cave, each chamber leading to another. Art, then farming, then writing—these are the three principal chambers humanity has passed through, and each has left a genetic mark. Kraus believed that the last chamber, a final great leap for humanity, was yet to come."

"The code," Peyton said.

"Exactly. Kraus believed that when we found the genetic bread crumbs led by the march of evolution, that they would form a code, a key that would start the next great human revolution—this one far more profound than art, farming, or writing."

"What is it?" Avery asked.

"I don't know. He didn't either. And we didn't have the technology back then. Human genome sequencing was impossible. And even once it was possible, it's been cost-prohibitive until very recently."

"And now you're ready," Avery said. "You built Phaethon Genetics for just this moment. The recovery of these samples."

Lin studied the crates. "This moment is more important than any of you understand. The sacrifices that have been made. The giants whose shoulders we stand upon. We're on the precipice of something incredible."

An awkward silence stretched out. In that hidden room, in the dim light, Lin Shaw seemed almost possessed.

Boots pounded the cave floor. The makeshift door to the hidden room pushed in, and a hand forced it open wider.

Rodriguez slid through the opening, followed by three SAS

soldiers Peyton had never seen. Despite the chill in the cave, Rodriguez was sweating. And his gun was gone.

"Ma'am," he said. "We're ready to load out."

Adams moved his head quickly, as if seeing something, then relaxed. Lin stared at him, then Rodriguez.

Peyton sensed that something was wrong.

To her surprise, her mother said, "Proceed, Seaman Rodriguez."

CHAPTER 44

PEYTON SENSED A change happening in the room. It was as if one by one, the team was becoming aware of something—like prey learning that a predator was approaching. Lin appeared to realize first, then it moved like a wave to Adams and Avery. Nigel was muttering something, apparently unaware. Rodriguez was trying to communicate something to Adams with his eyes.

The hidden room deep inside the Cave of Altamira was cramped, but the three SAS troops were doing their best to spread out.

Suddenly, Lin slipped behind the closest SAS soldier. A split second later, Adams leapt on top of the operative beside him. Avery moved behind the last man, drawing a combat knife and placing it at his neck.

The room fell silent. No one moved.

Peyton realized her mother was holding a handgun at the back of the soldier's neck.

The man slowly let his hands drift out. "Ma'am," he said in a British accent. "I think there's been a misunderstanding—"

"Don't." Lin's voice echoed in the small space like a slap.

A silent second passed.

"The boots. I know they're Citium Security issue." To Peyton and Nigel, she said, "Take their weapons."

When they had taken their guns and knives and radios, Lin pushed at the back of the man's neck, prodding him to join the other two. "Is he here?" she demanded.

The man's face was stone. "Can't say I know who 'he' is."

"I'll take that as a yes."

"Ma'am?" Adams said.

"Yuri." Then to Rodriguez: "Report, Seaman."

His eyes drifted down to the floor, a look of embarrassment and disappointment settling over him. "I hiked to the radio cutoff and requested backup to help with transport. The operator used the breach code word in his response." He shook his head. "I turned and started running back, but they were already in the tunnel." He swallowed. "I should have—"

"Thank you, Seaman," Lin said.

Adams took out the cave map and pointed to a narrow passageway near the hidden room. "We'll set up a chokepoint here."

"No," Lin said. "We can't fight our way out of here."

"Is there another exit?"

"No. We're trapped. And outgunned. And ill-supplied for a siege. Those are the certainties."

CHAPTER 45

ADAMS INHALED AND straightened, like man who expected to soon face a firing squad. "What are your orders, ma'am?"

Lin placed her gun on the nearest crate. Her voice was quiet. "I'll handle this."

Nigel threw up his hands. "Oh, good. I feel relieved. Care to share any details? I'm particularly curious as to whether I will die in the process?"

Lin ignored Nigel's theatrics. She answered in a somber tone. "Unknown, Doctor Greene."

His eyes grew wide. "Well, what *do* you know?"

"As I said, I know we're trapped."

"Then what's your plan?" Nigel spat.

Avery's voice reflected Lin's calm. "Let's talk options."

Lin affixed the top to the plastic container she and Peyton had found. "There are none. There is no play here. Our adversary is a strategist with no peers. If not for his work in the Citium, he would likely be the world's leading expert in game theory. Any plan I can think of, he's already considered."

The room fell silent, the reality sinking in.

Peyton broke the silence. "Mom, when you said you'd handle this—"

"I'll go alone."

"No." Peyton closed her eyes. Less than a month ago, Yuri had killed her father. And before that, Yuri had kidnapped her brother and brainwashed him. She couldn't lose her mother too. "There has to be another way."

"There isn't. Yuri is here for me. *I'm* the threat to his work. He needs to capture *me*. He needs me to tell him my plan, and who I'm working with. In exchange, I'll ask for your freedom. At least for you all to be supplied and confined here until this... Looking Glass war is done." She exhaled. "Once he has me, he'll have no need for the rest of you."

"Exactly!" Nigel yelled. "He'll kill us all."

"I doubt that—"

"You *doubt* it?" Nigel turned to Adams. "This is clearly a military matter. Chief, we should be deferring to you. Please formulate—"

"I don't take orders from you, Doctor." Adams focused on Lin. "Ma'am?"

"When I leave, split up and hide. Rodriguez and these Citium operatives will accompany me—"

"Don't we need hostages?" Nigel asked, exasperated.

"No," Avery said, "we do not. We need to be able to fight, and we don't have the kit to run an underground prison camp."

"We could lock them in here."

"And let them destroy what we just found? Stick to science, Doctor." To Lin, Avery said, "Continue."

"Rodriguez will stay with one of the Citium operatives just inside the comm range. He'll relay the result of my negotiation with Yuri."

"Negotiation," Nigel muttered. "Surrender is more like it."

Lin ignored him. She stepped over to Peyton, gripped her shoulders, and looked her directly in the eyes, unblinking. "I love you very much."

Peyton was shocked. Her mother rarely showed affection, and never in front of others, especially anyone outside the family.

A wall within Peyton broke. A tear formed at the corner of her eye and rolled down her face. In any other moment, she would have wiped it away, embarrassed, but now she let it slide down, like the last grain of sand falling through an hourglass, a symbol of her time with her mother, which might be up.

Her voice was low and heavy with emotion. "I love you too."

Lin pulled her into a hug and held it. When she released Peyton, she walked to Adams, who stood straighter as she approached.

Even in the silent cave chamber, Peyton could barely hear her mother's voice. "Take care of my daughter, Chief. She is more important to me than anything in this room."

Peyton felt another tear escape her eye. And another. She avoided crying out loud, but just barely. Growing up, she had always come second to her mother's work. Missed soccer games, birthday parties, family time. Even her medical school graduation. Lin Shaw's work came first—and this room held the crowning achievement to that work. Lin Shaw had cajoled and killed and sacrificed for decades to find it. And now, in what might be the final chapter of her life, she had revealed what was truly important to her: Peyton.

Like any child, Peyton had always wondered where she stood in her mother's hierarchy of priorities. Now she knew, and it broke her heart all over again.

Lin turned to the group. "Let's proceed."

At the opening to the room, she paused but didn't look back. "Wait twenty seconds, then split up and hide. Use the earpieces for your radio to keep quiet."

With that, she slipped through the opening, and Peyton wondered if she would ever see her mother again.

☣

The cave paintings danced at the edge of the lantern light, making the animals seem alive. Lin remembered walking into this cave with her father. Her fascination with his work had been born here that day. One way or another, she would complete her own journey to finish his quest today. But there was far more at stake than that.

In front of her, the two Citium troops clad in SAS uniforms halted, one holding up a fisted hand. Lin and Rodriguez came to a stop, as did the other Citium mercenary behind them.

Figures moved in the shadows, emerging, guns held out, their bodies clad in black body armor, night-vision goggles flipped up, positioned on the top of their helmets like a unicorn's horn.

"Sit-rep," one of the black-clad operatives barked.

"They've surrendered," the SAS-clad operative said. "The woman wants to discuss terms with Pachenko."

Without a word, the mercenaries rushed to Lin and Rodriguez and frisked them.

A mercenary motioned to the Navy SEAL. "What's he doing here?"

"For the comm relay. The others are hiding until they hear from her. Keep an eye on him." The SAS-clad operative turned to Lin. "Let's go."

☣

The morning light spilling through the mouth of the cave was blinding. Lin paused to squeeze her eyes shut.

She heard boots pounding the stone ahead, drawing closer.

By degrees, she allowed her eyes to open. When the scene came into focus, she saw a dozen men crowding into the main chamber off the entrance, all wearing SAS or Spanish Army uniforms— except for the boots. No one had bothered to change out of the Citium-issued boots, perhaps for comfort, perhaps because finding the right fit would be like a massive game of musical chairs.

The first troops they had met in the cave had apparently radioed ahead and apprised the units here of the situation. They waved Lin forward.

Inside the visitor center, there was a stack of bodies—men and women in underwear—most with gunshot wounds to the torso. A still pool of blood encircled them, half in shadow, making it look black, like an oil spill. It was the most grotesque thing she had seen since the occupation of Hong Kong.

"Hello, Lin." Yuri's voice was emotionless, as if there were no water under the bridge between them—and she wasn't his prisoner.

Lin tried to control her breathing. Her voice came out harder than she wanted, her emotions betraying her. "I've come to talk."

"Then I will listen."

"In private."

Yuri squinted, studying her face.

Lin cleared her throat. "I'm willing to tell you what you want to know. Time is not on your side. That's what I can give you. I want her safety. That's all I want."

Yuri paused, then addressed the Citium operative who had brought Lin out of the cave. "Report, Captain."

"Yuri—"

"Please be quiet, Lin."

She listened while the man recounted everything that had happened.

Yuri appeared to think on this for a moment, then to another nearby soldier said, "Status on Bravo unit?"

The man activated his radio and conversed before reporting: "No movement. Shaw's SEAL hasn't said or done anything."

Yuri frowned. "Search her."

Two men ran their hands over her body, poking and kneading, patting and rubbing, indelicate, degrading actions. She stared ahead, face burning, hatred welling up. She had endured this before, but it had been a very long time. When it was done, the men said nothing, merely nodded to Yuri.

"Well then. Let's talk."

Yuri led her to a small office behind the information desk and closed the door behind them. Lin quickly took in the room, including all the items on the desk.

"This reminds me of Rio. The favelas."

Yuri was silent.

"We were prisoners then too. Held in a small room. Our bloody captors degrading us. The only difference now is that you're the madman on the other side of the gun, Yuri."

Lin watched, hoping he would crack a little—or even react to the words. He didn't.

"It's not too late to stop this."

A cold smile crossed Yuri's lips. "We both know it is. There's only one way forward for me. The Looking Glass has always been my only hope." He stepped closer to her. "And I just got one of the last pieces I need."

"But you're still missing one piece." Lin let a moment pass. "Rendition. Desmond Hughes is the only factor you misjudged in all this. He's different from you and Conner—more so than you realized. That must be hard for you."

"All's well that ends well." Yuri averted his eyes. "And besides, I have also recently acquired the key to controlling Desmond." The smile returned. "Peyton. And perhaps Avery. I wasn't here just for you."

"That's where you're wrong: you can't control him. He was willing to betray his brother. You think he won't sacrifice Peyton? Or Avery?"

"Why are you here, Lin?"

"I think you know by now."

CHAPTER 46

BY INSTINCT, PEYTON had wandered back to the narrow passage where she and her mother had found the cave painting of the doe. It stood proud in the lantern light. The wall beside it was smeared and gouged out, as if it had been gutted. That's how Peyton felt.

She hated waiting. She wanted to *do* something. But there was nothing to do.

She sat and clicked the light off. It was pitch black and damp, and every second felt like an eternity. It was like she was a speck of dust floating in endless black space, weightless, no light, no direction up, down, forward, or backward.

The earpiece crackled, and Rodriguez's voice came through in clips, deafening at first.

Peyton winced and focused. She wondered how long she had been hiding.

"I repeat, we have a resolution. Doctor Shaw has reached an agreement. All units come to location yellow."

Location yellow?

Rodriguez added, "That's the comm relay point. All units proceed now."

Peyton dreaded hearing what the resolution was—but hearing her mother was alive… It was a huge relief. And it gave her hope.

She clicked her light on. It was a like a supernova exploding. She waited and let her eyes adjust, then began hiking out. She turned a corner and, too late, saw a flash of movement from the corner of her eye. A hand wrapped around her, covering her mouth, and pulled her back.

Peyton struggled, but a voice she knew whispered in her ear: Adams. "Stay here, Doc."

She stopped moving.

He released his hand.

"Why?" she whispered.

"Location yellow. It's our pass phrase for all clear but stay alert."

"I can stay alert."

He moved around her. "I made a promise to your mother. I'll call you when I'm sure it's safe."

He turned her light off and slipped into the darkness, footsteps like a pebble falling down a well, the sound echoing and dwindling to silence.

Once again, she waited in darkness for what felt like an eternity.

Adams called over the comm, "Doctor Peyton Shaw, it's all clear. You can exit the cave."

Peyton wanted to run, but the ground was too uneven—and would be unforgiving if she fell. She hurried, the cave opening becoming lighter with each turn. To her surprise, she didn't meet a soul—not Avery, or Nigel, or Rodriguez, or any of the Citium troops.

She rounded a bend and stopped, letting her eyes adjust to the bright light. She held an arm up to shield her eyes as she hiked out. There was no one by the cave mouth, only cigarette butts and protein bar wrappers.

She made a beeline for the visitor center. The parking lot was filled with military vehicles, but completely devoid of soldiers.

She pushed the glass door open—and reeled back in horror. Bodies were stacked on top of each other like fallen tree limbs, a human brush pile atop a red-black pool of blood.

Peyton looked away, suppressed the urge to retch.

Beyond the bodies, more soldiers—these still living—lay face down, hands zip-tied behind their backs, feet bound too, strips of cloth tied around their eyes. In the cave exhibit, in the shadows, someone was hammering something. No, two people—there was an unsynchronized cadence, like blacksmiths striking two anvils.

Adams stood by the information desk, rifle in hand, a glint of triumph in his eyes. "We're secure here."

"How?"

He jerked his head toward a closed door behind the dais, where Rodriguez stood. Peyton followed him, and held her breath as the door swung open.

Yuri stood in the center of an office, his back arched, hands bound behind him and taped to his body. A blade was held at his neck, a line of blood below it, streaks running down like legs of red wine in a glass. Lin Shaw stood behind him, out of reach of his hands.

"She cut the head off the snake," Adams said. He shrugged. "Well, threatened to."

"Status?" Lin asked.

"They're tied. About done with the phones and radios."

"Good. Finish prepping our prisoner for transport."

Lin drew the blade away from Yuri's neck and shoved him toward Rodriguez, who caught the man, sat him in a chair, and began lashing him to it with duct tape.

Yuri looked at Lin. "Last chance."

"I'll pass."

"Rapture Control will be back online any second now. We'll have access to every person who received that cure." His eyes drifted to Peyton.

"Gag him too," Lin said as she walked past Peyton, into the lobby, and past the stacks of dead bodies and the rows of living ones.

Peyton and Adams followed her to the source of the hammering sound. Avery and Nigel were seated around a pile of radios and sat phones, raking them over one at a time and busting them with the butt of a couple of handguns. Peyton saw the gun's magazines lying nearby.

"How can I help?" she asked.

Adams drew his gun and ejected the magazine. "Feel like smashing something?"

"You have no idea." She took a seat next to Avery and began.

"Avery," Lin said. "Disable the vehicles."

Avery rose. "How many do we need?"

"Two. Just in case one breaks down."

"On it." Avery went out to the parking lot. Through the plate glass window, Peyton could see her popping hoods and fiddling around inside.

To Adams, Lin said, "Begin retrieving the cases."

With a nod, Adams headed off, and Lin went to assist Rodriguez.

Peyton kept her head down. She crushed a phone, grabbed another, and repeated. She expected more Spanish troops to arrive, but none came. "Are we getting reinforcements?" she asked Nigel as she crushed the hand piece to a radio.

"Lin decided against it. Security risk. She thinks maybe someone in the British or Spanish military gave away our location."

"Makes sense."

They resumed their orchestra of destruction in silence, each pausing only long enough to take a quick bathroom break. It was simple, satisfying work, and Peyton was glad for it.

Adams and Rodriguez came and went, moving the cases at an inhuman rate. They were drenched with sweat by the time they sat down in the lobby and tipped their canteens back. Avery had returned from the parking lot by then and washed up. She walked to the information desk, then disappeared from Peyton's view and yelled out, "Hey!"

Lin responded, but Peyton couldn't make out the words.

Adams and Rodriguez leapt to their feet, as did Nigel and Peyton. They ran toward the two women.

The door to the office stood open. The chair where Yuri had been tied up was empty. Strands of duct tape hung from it, the edges even where they had been cut.

"I tied him up tight," Rodriguez said, staring at the chair.

"It doesn't matter," Lin said. "He's gone. And we need to go too."

No one said what they all knew: Yuri hadn't freed himself. One of them had done it.

CHAPTER 47

CONNER AND HIS men had been hiding in the racquetball court under Desmond's garage for twenty hours. Empty MRE cartons dotted the catwalk. Two of the mercenaries were playing cards by helmet light. Dr. Park was asleep. Desmond lay under the catwalk, still sedated, his breathing shallow.

Conner opened a laptop and tried to connect to one of the drones.

Out of range.

He motioned to the closest Citium operative. "I'm going out."

He pushed the door open and waited. It was quiet. He ventured into the basement and activated the app again.

Out of range.

He walked up the back staircase, pausing every fourth step. The house was silent.

He crept down the central hall and plopped down in the great room. The drone footage finally appeared on his laptop. There was no sign of the X1 troops. As planned, the enemy combatants had pursued Conner's vans and Humvees. They had no doubt searched Desmond's estate, but they hadn't found the hidden room. After all, they wouldn't have been looking very hard for it, as they were sure their adversary had fled, just as the lieutenant had told them, relating the plan he had overheard Conner whispered to Major Goins.

He closed the laptop and returned to the racquetball court. He scooped Desmond up in his arms, and his men and Dr. Park followed him upstairs, through the back door, and under the cover of the old oak trees into a neighbor's yard. The neighbor's house was empty, as he'd suspected. The people on this street in Atherton owned homes in the mountains and on the coast—and on remote islands. Some even owned the islands themselves, and the private airstrips on them.

In the garage he found a Fisker Karma, plugged in, and a black Chevy Suburban.

"Take the gas guzzler," he said.

When Desmond was loaded in the back, he turned to Dr. Park. "Location?"

"It's near Bair Island. Hold on." Park studied the map. "It's the airport at San Carlos."

Conner considered that. It was the perfect place for an ambush. But he had no choice.

CHAPTER 48

THE TWO VEHICLES raced through the winding Spanish roads at high speed, Avery behind the wheel of the lead truck, Adams driving the other. Between the hills and curves, Peyton felt like she was on a roller coaster.

"Avery, if you drive any faster, we're going to travel back in time!"

"Wouldn't that be nice?" She pressed harder on the accelerator, and the engine screamed louder.

At the Santander airport, they loaded onto a Spanish Air Force jet while Lin and Adams conversed with a colonel commanding the forces there. Lin refused to take any additional troops with them. Soon Avery was in the cockpit, and they were once again in the air.

At cruising altitude, Avery engaged the autopilot and joined the others in the crew compartment. It was an open space with seats at the rear and reminded Peyton of a smaller version of the plane she and her EIS agents had taken from Atlanta to Nairobi a month ago. That felt like another lifetime. And on this flight, she felt like the student, her mother the teacher. A teacher reluctant to share her knowledge.

"A destination would be nice," Avery said. "Other than the American South."

Lin unrolled a sleeping bag and slipped inside. "Soon." She motioned for Peyton to bed down beside her.

Peyton unrolled another sleeping bag, and the others did the same. Adams and Rodriguez had arranged to take turns staying up to monitor the autopilot.

Everyone was dead tired, and in Peyton's estimation, Lin most of all. Her face was inches from Peyton's, and when Lin closed her eyes, the strength seemed to drain out of her. What she had done at Altamira had taken a toll on her, though she had hidden it well. There was so much Peyton wanted to ask her mother, but the questions would have to wait.

Just before she slipped off to sleep, Peyton noticed that her mother was hugging a bag, like a suitcase with shoulder straps. She was sure she hadn't taken it to Altamira. She must have gotten it there. But when? And what was inside?

CHAPTER 49

AVERY COULDN'T SLEEP, so she returned to the cockpit and suggested to Adams, who was currently on shift, that he catch some shuteye. He was happy to oblige; he was as exhausted as the rest of them.

Avery couldn't turn her mind off. She kept thinking about the siege at Desmond's home, imagining them storming it, Desmond getting shot in the crossfire. She wanted to be there more than anything in the world.

The sat phone buzzed, and she grabbed it. "Price."

"Avery." She knew immediately from David Ward's tone that it was bad news. "We lost 'em."

"You're kidding. How? I mean, you had them—"

"Conner McClain is good—"

"I don't want to hear how good he is. There are only two possibilities: he left the house or he's still there."

"We tracked down all the vehicles. It took almost ten hours—"

"Ten *hours?*"

"They used X1 troops as human shields. We couldn't fire. Had to run them down. They went in four different directions. We didn't find McClain or Hughes. We... interrogated his second in command. He insists McClain was in the last van. He wasn't."

"Then he's still in the house."

"We've searched it—top to bottom."

Top to bottom. For a moment she was back in the racquetball court, sweating, panting, volleying with Desmond, then rolling across the floor, him leaning down to kiss her and the wall inside her breaking down.

"Avery? You still there?"

"I'm here. There's a hidden room." She had assumed the stand-off would have ended in a firefight, never a game of hide-and-seek in the house. It never occurred to her to tell them about the racquetball court. She felt like such a fool.

"Yeah, the reading nook in the study. They found—"

"No. It's under the garage. A racquetball court. You access it from the basement—through the wine cellar. There's a false brick that opens the door."

"Hang on."

She could hear him making a call on another sat phone. Then he returned. "They missed it. I'll call you back."

Avery answered the second the sat phone rang.

"We searched the racquetball court," Ward said. "They're not there, but we found some MRE cartons, recently eaten. We think they slipped out after the search teams left the first time."

Avery thought for a moment. Desmond chose his home as a location for a reason. Why? To get help? To put himself on their radar? That was likely. If it was true, what would be his next stop? An escape route? Another location they both knew. One that offered options.

Only one place fit that description.

"I think I know where they're going. The San Carlos Airport."

"We'll deploy teams—"

"Don't. Let's not make the same mistake. Let it play out. You remember what Des told us there."

"Yeah."

"I want you there, David. Please."

"Hughes asked me the same thing. Look, Avery, things are in motion here. The whole world is coming unglued—"

"And you can't hold it together. We can't play defense. It's time to stop these people. Hughes is the key. Please. Go there—for me. I've never asked you for anything."

"You want me to take myself out of the middle of the action here, go there, and simply wait and hope Hughes shows up?"

"Yes. If you remember, he asked me to do that once. I didn't like it, but I did it. And it got us this far. Please, David. He asked you. And now *I'm* asking you. There's nobody I trust more. We need him."

"We? Or you?"

"Both, okay? I need him. I want to see him. But it's more than that. He's the key to everything."

A long pause. Avery thought about pressing the point, but one thing she knew about David Ward: he always pushed back at aggression.

"All right," he said finally. "I'll go. I'll give it twenty-four hours. I'm leaving after that."

Avery exhaled, relieved. "That's fair. Thank you, David."

CHAPTER 50

THE CHEVY SUBURBAN drove through the night, headlights off, the streets lit only by moonlight. The roads were eerily quiet, deserted, like a world after people.

From the back of the van, Dr. Park provided directions to the airport at San Carlos, his face illuminated by the smartphone. The phone was like a modern-day talisman, guiding their band to an artifact that would save their people and their cause. They had to know where Desmond had hidden Rendition. It was their only hope. Conner's only hope of getting his brother back.

The airport's gate was open, and the place looked deserted. Conner rolled down his window and inhaled the smell of San Francisco Bay. It was a mix of salt water and fresh water; nearly half of California's rivers and lakes drained to the sea here. The bay area was a symbol of the new world, and of the Citium itself: a nexus of thinkers, people creating a new society, their technology unleashed upon the world, for its betterment, whether the rest of humanity wanted it or not. The Citium would take the masses into the next world, kicking and screaming if they had to.

"Hangar twenty-seven," Park said, looking at the smartphone's screen.

The soldiers got out, broke in, and pulled the hangar doors wide open. Conner had expected to see a plane waiting—perhaps Desmond's escape plan. But he saw only corkboards littered with pages and photos, connected by strings. Tables ran in rows between the corkboard, empty except for a few cardboard boxes.

He moved behind the wheel and eased the SUV in. The hangar doors closed behind.

He got out and took in the strange scene, paying particular attention to the articles pinned to the boards. Pictures. Bios. News articles. He recognized them.

How was it possible?

From the vehicle, Dr. Park called, "We're getting a new feed. Memory is starting."

☣

On his phone, Desmond clicked the address Conner had sent him. The directions led to a pier in San Francisco.

Avery had left only a few minutes ago, the moment she had heard the address. Was she going there? He desperately wanted to know what was going on with her. He sensed that he had been lied to, and that hurt—particularly coming from her.

Questions about her dogged him as he drove north, out of Atherton, toward San Francisco.

☣

The *Kentaro Maru* was larger than he remembered. It sat tall in the water, long along the wharf. The gangplank was guarded by two Citium Security operatives.

One held up a hand as Desmond approached.

"I'm here to see Conner McClain."

"Name?"

"Desmond Hughes."

They checked over the radio. Instead of waving him on, they stood still. Two Citium Spec Ops members approached and asked Desmond to follow them.

On the ship's bridge, he waited, taking in the glowing floodlights scattered across the harbor.

"Hello, brother."

Desmond turned to find Conner in a merchant marine uniform for a company he didn't recognize: Terra Transworld. He saw the change in Conner immediately. A rigidity. A military composure. *What happened to him?*

Desmond was at a loss for words. Conner wasn't.

He held out his arm. "This way."

In the conference room, Conner closed the door. "I'm sorry I haven't been in touch."

"I'm not interested in apologies. Give me a reason."

"I'll do better than that. I'll show you a reason." Conner smiled for the first time. "We'll talk after."

He led Desmond into the bowels of the ship, past crewmembers covered in grease and carrying provisions. Based on the size of the packages, Desmond suspected they were preparing for a journey. In what looked like a modified locker room, Conner instructed Desmond to put on a biocontainment suit like a CDC employee might wear.

What has he done?

Desmond donned the garment in silence and followed his brother into the ship's hold, where rows of cubicles spread out. They were framed by metal posts and wrapped in sheet plastic. Yellow lights glowed inside, but the contents of the cubes were obscured. One group of suited personnel was pushing a cart down the aisles, stopping at each cube, ducking through the plastic flaps, and re-emerging with buckets, which they emptied.

Another group pushed a cart piled high with bodies.

"Conner," Desmond said, breathing hard. He waited, then realized the suit didn't have a radio.

Conner continued forward, leading him through the giant chamber, like a warehouse within the giant ship. At the other end, they entered a decontamination room. A spray engulfed the suits, then ceased, and they unzipped their suits and doffed them.

"What is this, Conner?"

"I'll explain everything, Des. It's why you're here."

They climbed a staircase and entered a conference room that

was filled with people. A large screen hung on the wall displaying a world map with red glowing dots. A plate glass window on one wall looked down on the hold full of glowing cubes, like Japanese lanterns floating on a concrete sea.

This is wrong.

Conner stood at the head of the room, confident, an almost possessed look in his eyes. His words rang out clear and strong, drawing the attention of every person in the room.

"Soon, the world will change. Stay the course. The coming days will be the most difficult of your life. But when this is finished, the world will know the truth: we saved the entire human race from extinction…"

When his speech was finished, the room cleared, leaving Desmond alone with Conner—except for the two security operatives by the door.

Desmond's voice came out soft, labored. "What have you done?"

"What had to be done."

"Conner." Desmond stared at him. "These are my Rendition subjects, aren't they? You've reused them like they were—"

"They're terminal, Des."

"That doesn't give you the right to—"

"They volunteered."

"What are you testing?"

"A distribution method."

"For what?"

Conner nodded to the two security operatives. They left and closed the door behind them.

"Rapture," he said.

Desmond's mouth fell open. "You can't be serious."

"This is the only way."

"What is it, Conner? What are you and Yuri doing?"

"What must be done."

"Is it a gene therapy? A retrovirus? Why?"

Conner was silent.

"You're not going to tell me? The truth and partnership ends here?"

"I'm asking you to let me handle this part of the project. Yuri has trusted me with it. I hope you will too."

"How many will die, Conner?"

"Very few." Conner shook his head. "People die every day—for things worth far less than the Looking Glass. Everything has a price. The Looking Glass is worth it."

Desmond opened his mouth to respond, but closed it. This was not his brother. "What happened to you?" It came out before he could stop it.

"Nothing has *happened* to me."

"I feel like I'm talking to a different person, Conner. You even look different."

"I've taken on new responsibilities."

Desmond squinted at him.

"I've been given command of Citium Security. I've been training."

"For what?"

Conner stepped closer to Desmond. "The beginning. It'll be painful, but don't worry, Des. I'll handle it. That's why we're a team—you, me, and Yuri. We each have a role to play. I'm asking you to let me play mine."

Desmond took a step back. "I need some time."

"Now *that* is something we don't have."

"What do you mean?"

"Things are in motion."

The words were like an alarm going off in Desmond's head.

He tried to come up with the words that would bring his brother back—make him see reason. But as Desmond stared at him, he realized that Conner was too far gone. He and his brother were different in one very important way—a way Yuri had understood. Understood and exploited. Conner's wounds ran deeper than Desmond's. Both brothers had been burned by the same fire, but Conner had suffered more, longer. He was vulnerable in the same way as Desmond, but on a deeper level. He was capable of being brainwashed. Used like a knife to slice the world open.

For the first time, Desmond saw Yuri's true nature—and he was afraid. The things the older man had said were true: the world was unfair, and cruel, and needed to change. But his solution was savage. A price too high to pay—for Desmond. But not for Conner.

And Yuri knew that. He had told Desmond as much. His specialty was reading people, knowing what they were capable of and what they would do. He moved the pieces, and he had positioned them perfectly.

Desmond was in a corner. There was only one way out. He had been here once before, on the day Dale Epply came to Orville's house, escorted him to the garden shed, and gave him the choice: kill or be killed.

He felt the weight of the decision upon him. He knew that his entire future would turn on this moment. He had dedicated his life to the Looking Glass. And Yuri's plan. But the price... it was too high. He hadn't signed up for *this*. He wouldn't sacrifice innocent lives. He would fight for those who couldn't fight for themselves. He would stop Yuri, even if it cost him his brother.

"I understand," Desmond whispered.

Conner exhaled. "Good. I knew you would, Des. I told Yuri that."

Desmond made his tone neutral. "What happens next?"

A smile curled at Conner's lips. "We have some work to do."

"What kind?"

"Stops to make."

"Where?"

"Just get Rendition ready. Won't be long now, brother."

As he drove away from the pier, Desmond's mind raced, playing scenarios out.

Confront Yuri. Bad play—Yuri had certainly already prepared for that.

Call the FBI. No. They'd be more likely to lock him up than help him.

Call the *Washington Post*. That could work. But not if they were starting from scratch. A story like this took time to research and verify, and as Conner had said, time was something he didn't have. He would need to find a journalist who had already scratched the surface of the Citium conspiracy—someone who would believe him, and publish quickly.

At stoplights, he searched on his phone, typing in the names of Citium subsidiaries and investment vehicles. He stopped short when he found an article published in *Der Spiegel* by a journalist named Garin Meyer. What the man had done was amazing. He had already connected many of the Citium subsidiaries, thinking they were some sort of organized crime syndicate—a new breed of twenty-first century high-tech companies colluding to rake in profits. And he was partly right, though those profits were being channeled to a cause—the Looking Glass.

Desmond knew he had to contact Meyer. But first, he had a stop to make.

He knocked on the door, nervous, suddenly unsure of the decision.

The light in the living room flicked on and the door opened, revealing Lin Shaw, still in her work clothes.

"Desmond. What can—"

"We need to talk. It's important."

She held the door open for him, closed it after him, but didn't welcome him deeper into the home.

Desmond decided it was time to roll the dice. "It's started."

"It?"

"Yuri. The Looking Glass. They're proceeding."

Lin didn't miss a beat. "How?"

"I think they're using some kind of pathogen or retrovirus. I couldn't find out."

Her eyes went wide—confirming that she didn't know. "Where will it start?"

"I don't know."

"What *do* you know, Desmond?"

"Only that they've been testing it on a ship."

She looked away, deep in thought.

"Can you stop him?" Desmond asked.

"No."

The word was like a gavel coming down. A final judgment. He had expected her to say yes—expected her to offer some solution.

"You have to—"

"Listen to me."

He exhaled.

"Really listen, okay?"

He nodded. "Okay."

"Yuri has been planning this for a very, very long time."

"I know."

"Do you want to stop him?"

"Yes."

"Are you sure?"

"Completely."

"Then do something he'll never expect."

Desmond shook his head. "Like what?"

"I don't know. Only you know that. Don't tell me. Don't tell anyone. That's the only way to ensure it works."

"You want me to destroy the Looking Glass."

"No. The Looking Glass is inevitable. It has always existed and must always exist."

The words shocked Desmond. He felt numb. The world around him stood still.

Lin stepped closer. "What is happening on this planet has happened on billions of worlds before. And it will happen on billions of worlds after ours."

"What are you saying?"

"The Looking Glass isn't what you and Yuri think it is. It is a singularity of far more importance."

He opened his mouth to respond, but couldn't find words.

"All that can change is who *controls* the Looking Glass. If you want to stop Yuri—the Citium—there's only one way to do it: from the inside."

He closed his eyes. "Lin, I can't—"

She opened the door. "Go, Desmond. I have to work to do."

He headed home, but never made it. Halfway there, a thought occurred to him. A vague notion at first, then a hypothesis, then a theory. It seemed outlandish, but it made sense—in context. Avery's question to him: *If I told you something that... changed everything you believe, would you still trust me?*

There was only one thing she could have been talking about. But if it was true... what was she? What was she to him?

He dialed her number. She answered on the first ring.

"You asked me if I was capable of changing what I believed, deep down."

"And?"

"I am."

He could hear shouting in the background, like traders on the floor of the stock exchange. No, they were calling out locations. And company names. Citium company names.

Footsteps, Avery walking away, the voices fading.

"I already have," he said.

"What are we talking about, Des?"

"People I know. I didn't—didn't know what they were capable of."

"What are they capable of?"

"My turn. What are we talking about, Avery?"

"Meet me."

"Where?"

"San Carlos. At the airport off Bayshore Freeway. Hangar twenty-five."

"What's there?"

"I am."

"Who else?"

Silence.

"Who do you work for, Avery?"

She exhaled. "I work for the people who can't defend themselves. All seven billion of them."

It wasn't an answer, and he knew he wouldn't get one.

He drove through the night, at high speed, past the airport gates, to the hangar, where two dozen black SUVs were parked and a throng of trench coat-clad men and women milled about. They stopped him a hundred feet from the hangar and demanded to know who he was and why he was here.

Avery jogged up to them and said, "He's with me."

They entered the hangar through a side door. And as Desmond stepped inside, his jaw dropped.

Wooden stands, holding sheets of plywood wrapped with corkboard, sat in a giant horseshoe, and they were covered, inch to inch, with information on the Citium. He saw his own photo. Yuri's. Conner's. The name Icarus Capital. Rook Quantum Sciences. Rendition Games. Every company the Citium owned. Their main investment vehicles were listed too: Citium Capital, Invisible Sun Securities. The entire web they had spun was diagrammed here—with red strings and pins showing the connections. And in the middle of the hangar, where an aircraft should have been, at least two dozen agents sat at long tables, bent over laptops or speaking into mobile phones.

"What is this?" Desmond asked.

"A mobile command center."

"For what?"

"Stopping a terrorist attack."

Desmond's head spun. His knees felt weak, like he was on a merry-go-round going two hundred miles an hour.

He was vaguely aware of Avery still standing there.

"They're not terrorists," he whispered.

"They?" a man's voice said, loud in the space. "Don't you mean *we*?"

Avery glanced back at him. "Desmond Hughes, this is David Ward, head of the Rubicon Group."

Ward was a tall man in a black suit with no tie. He nodded to a man in an FBI flak jacket. "Let's make it official in case it comes back to bite us."

The other man drew out his FBI badge and flashed it. "Mister Hughes, I'm Special Agent Reyes with the FBI. You're under arrest."

CHAPTER 51

AVERY THREW UP her hands. "Whoa, whoa, here. Let's take a step back, J. Edgar. Desmond is here of his own accord. To *assist* in this investigation."

She stared at Ward, who stared back. A battle of wills.

Ward broke eye contact first. He took the FBI man by the arm, led him away, and whispered something Desmond couldn't hear. Then to Avery, he shouted, "He's all yours, Agent Price."

Desmond's fear and shock morphed into rage. "You lied to me."

Avery didn't respond. She simply walked past him, out the door of the hangar, and into the night. When he caught up to her, she stared at him with those glowing blue eyes, like a creature ready to defend its ground, a predator just outside its den.

"You lied to me," he repeated.

Avery cocked her head. "I did? As in, I didn't tell you my work was part of a much larger project, a covert one? Is that what you mean?"

He said nothing.

"Any idea what that would be like, Des? Not telling the person you're closest to what you're really working on?"

"Avery." He wanted to press his point, but she was right. He had lied to her too. In a strange way, they were mirrors of each other, fighting on opposites sides, two people serving their cause by day, literally sleeping with the enemy by night. And their cold war was about to go hot.

She chewed the inside of her lip. "What's it gonna be? You want to debate water under the bridge, or you want to help us?"

"I want to know what's really going on."

"I could ask you the same thing."

"I asked first."

"Okay." She took a few more steps from the building—and the agents posted around it. "Yuri is moving pieces. Closing down Citium front companies. Transferring money. He's preparing for an operation. A large one. We think it could be his end game."

"Those are not crimes."

"True. But killing two hundred people is."

"What are you talking about?"

"The Citium conclave. The last one. When the scientists were slaughtered. Yuri did it."

"Impossible." He reeled at the words. It was as if the entire foundation of his knowledge about the Citium had been yanked out from under him. If Yuri had lied about the last conclave, what else had he lied about?

"It's true. That's how Rubicon"—she gestured back toward the hangar—"got started. Some of the scientists were worried that a Citium civil war was brewing. They contacted people like David Ward's predecessor. Hid evidence. And when they all disappeared, Rubicon was born. We've been investigating the Citium for thirty years."

"Yuri didn't kill those people. He... They were his friends. His colleagues."

"His competitors, Des. People whose Looking Glass projects would end his own. He'll do anything to protect his work."

He knew her words were true, but he grasped for any flaw in her logic, any way to destroy the hideous revelation.

"Lin Shaw," he said. "She was a Citium member back then. She's still alive. He didn't kill her."

Avery nodded. "Lin Shaw is an anomaly, a piece we don't understand yet."

"She's doing real work, Avery. Trying to find the genetic basis of disease. You've seen it. You've helped her. Explain that."

"We can't. We don't know what Lin's end game is, but we think it's separate from Yuri's."

"Then why is she alive? Was she colluding with him back then?"

"We don't know. Maybe. But we think he's controlling her somehow. Leverage of some kind."

His mind said a single name: *Peyton.*

He stared at the sky. "I need time—"

"Des. We don't have time."

"Then I need proof. You're talking about things that happened thirty years ago."

A sad expression crossed Avery's face. "Follow me."

Back inside, she stopped in front of a photo of a girl with flowing brown hair and a self-conscious smile. It was a face Desmond hadn't seen in thirteen years. Below it was a picture taken in the woods, of a hole dug with a shovel, the dirt piled in low mounds on each side, a body wrapped in plastic, the skin pale blue, like rubber. He recognized the hair.

He looked back at the smiling face. *Jennifer.* The sweet receptionist who had sat at the raised dais outside the Citium library. The girl who had brought him books and invited him to dinner.

"We recruited her at Stanford, after she was already working at the Citium." Avery's voice grew quiet. "She was doing digital dead drops. Somebody found out."

"How? Who?"

"We don't know. They were very careful."

Rage boiled inside him. His voice was barely louder than a growl. "Okay. I'm in. Now tell me what you know."

"Citium Security. It's Yuri's sharp end of the stick. The bulk of the contractors have no idea what kind of person they're working for. They're simply protecting high-value targets, executives at Citium companies who are traveling abroad, securing facilities in dangerous regions. Some corporate counter-espionage. The higher-ups are true believers—like Yuri, they'll do anything to see the Looking Glass completed. Same for a few special ops divisions." She glanced at the photo. "Like the one that did this."

Desmond's mind immediately replayed his interaction with

Conner, the military countenance his brother had taken on. *I've been given command of Citium Security. I've been training.* What had he made Conner do? What was Conner capable of? After what he'd been through, probably anything.

"What do you need from me?"

Avery stepped closer. "Where is Yuri?"

"I don't know. I haven't heard from him in months."

"Des."

"It's true."

"Your brother?"

"He's here. In San Francisco Bay."

Avery turned, motioned for the agents at the table.

"No." He took her by the arm. "You want my help, we do it my way."

She glared at him. "Right. *You're* going to tell *us* how to stop an international terror organization?"

"I'm going to tell you the terms of my involvement. And you're going to sell them to your boss." He glared right back. "You're good at that, aren't you? Getting your boss to do what you want?"

Her face was a mask of confusion and surprise, and then hurt, like a spear had been stabbed through her heart. He regretted his words instantly.

"Avery—"

The cool air coming off the bay was a stark contrast to the heat rising from her, her flushed red cheeks and blazing eyes. "I didn't mean for it to happen," she said.

"Avery, I know—"

"You pursued me just as much."

"Look." He grasped for words. "It's been... a weird day. I don't know who to trust. I need some time."

"Des—"

"I know, we don't have time." He tried to organize his thoughts. "Whatever you're planning—your head-on assault, Keystone Cops-style knock-down-the-doors-and-throw-everybody-in-the-paddy-wagon—it won't work. These people are too smart for that. Yuri is a master manipulator. And strategist. He looks at the board from his perspective, then he turns it around in his mind—and studies it from yours. I know because that's how he plays chess."

"This is not a chess game."

"Sure it is. And we're going to win."

"How? What do *you* know, Des?"

"I know he used me. And my brother. Because he could. Because we were both broken and desperately wanted to feel whole again. We would do anything for a cure to what ailed us. And most of all, because we were capable of building the pieces he needed. He planned it perfectly. The two of us can be used to control each other. I'm not okay with that."

"Then destroy the pieces, Des. You have Rendition."

"Won't work. They'll rebuild." Lin's words echoed in his mind, and almost without thinking, he repeated them. "The Looking Glass is inevitable."

She stepped closer. "What is it?"

"That's a longer discussion, Avery. And we don't have time."

"Then what's your plan?"

In his mind, he began laying out the pieces, arranging them, turning scenarios over. His priorities were in conflict. Save Conner. Stop Yuri. Take control of the Looking Glass—and keep it out of enemy hands. Figure out what he and Avery were. And him and Peyton, if too much time had passed for them. And if not... that complicated things.

But there was one certainty: Rendition was his greatest bargaining chip, perhaps his only tool to change what was coming. They would get it from him, one way or another. Unless he couldn't give it.

"I need to make a call."

He opened a web browser, found the number for a scientist at Rapture Therapeutics, and dialed. The man was in Berlin—a lucky break. He could work with him while he got the reporter at *Der Spiegel* up to speed.

Desmond made the call. It was noon in Berlin, and it sounded like the scientist was having lunch. After the pleasantries, Desmond cut to the chase.

"Doctor Jung, I have a Rapture implant. It's an older model." He opened his account on the Rapture website and read out the version. "Do you know it?"

"Quite well."

"I'd like to use it along with your memory therapy. Here's what I'd like to do…"

By the time he finished explaining, Jung had left the restaurant and was talking excitedly, thrilled at the idea of applying his work in a new way.

Desmond ended the call and dialed a local number. The programmer was still up, clacking away at a keyboard in the background. Everyone at Labyrinth Reality worked odd hours, and for once, Desmond was glad.

"Paul, I need you to create a private Labyrinth for me. With some custom features."

"What kind of custom features?"

When Desmond told him, he said, "Seriously? Is that even possible?"

"We won't know until we try it. You interested?"

"Yeah, man."

Desmond talked about the details with him for a few minutes, then hung up and walked back to Avery.

"What was that about?"

"A backup plan. In case things go south."

"And what's your primary plan?"

"We expose the Citium. Alert every government and every person who will listen. There will be nowhere on Earth for them to hide. We'll take control of the Citium—and the Looking Glass."

"Des—"

"There's a reporter in Berlin. He's already seen some of the pieces."

"I don't like this. What are you going to do with Rendition?"

"Hide it."

She motioned to the hangar. "They're never going to go for this. They're preparing to raid every Citium company on the planet."

"You think Yuri hasn't planned for that? It'll just get people hurt. We need to take them down from the inside."

"How?"

"I don't know Yuri's plan, but I know where Conner is—as I said, on a ship in the harbor. Whatever is going to happen, I think he'll direct it from there."

"So we take the ship—"

"No. Yuri will simply adjust. I'm going to get *you* on that ship."

"How?"

"By telling Conner the truth—half of it. That I want to help him and that I want to protect someone I care about. I want her on the ship, out of harm's way, when his plan unfolds. The only safe place is next to him."

She looked away, into the night. He waited for a reaction to his words, the closest he had ever come to professing his feelings for her.

She was all business. "What's on the ship?"

"A floating lab. Hospital. Test subjects."

"Testing what?"

"Rendition, originally. Now, I'm not sure."

"Okay. What do I do on the ship?"

"Wait for me. Help me when I get there."

Avery shook her head. "I'm not good at waiting."

"Then do what you can—try to get yourself in a position to help. Avery, this is the only way. Those are my terms."

They stood silently for a moment, the wind blowing their hair, the moon shining down, like two people standing in the calm before a storm.

"All right."

"Good."

"There's something else, Des."

He raised his eyebrows.

"We found it. The *Beagle*."

"Impossible."

"It's true. At Phaethon, I accessed Lin Shaw's hidden files. She had the ship's travel logs. We used them to organize a search grid.

We employed a new sea floor mapping technology to look for wreckage."

"What's down there? What's on board the *Beagle*?"

"We don't know. Lin's notes are cryptic, but she's obsessed with finding the *Beagle*. She talks about there being some alternative to the Looking Glass. Or a device that would neutralize it. A revelation that would change our understanding of the human species."

"An alternative to the Looking Glass?"

"So it would seem."

Desmond considered that.

Avery looked toward the bay. "Lin is an X factor here. We don't know why she survived the purge. Or what her goal is."

"She had me recruited to the Citium."

Avery's mouth fell open.

"For her daughter's sake."

Avery stared in disbelief.

"But I think we can trust her. And Conner—if we can break Yuri's mental hold on him."

"Des, we're playing a very dangerous game here. If you're wrong about any of these people..."

"If I am, we'll figure it out. If this is a game, then it's one we're playing together." He walked closer to her, their faces inches apart. "And we play very well together."

She smiled. "So we're partners now?"

"Yeah."

"You know, the thing about partners is, they look out for each other. Cover each other." She studied his face. "Tell each other everything."

She waited. When he didn't respond, she said, "Is there anything else I need to know?"

He debated telling her about his backup plan. But if it came to that, he needed her to be just as surprised as everyone else. That could save her life on the *Kentaro Maru*. It would also infuriate her. An angry, living Avery was better than a dead happy one.

"No," he said. "We're good, partner."

CHAPTER 52

INSIDE THE HANGAR, Desmond sat at the long table, listening. Avery was shouting and pointing at her boss and peers as she defended him, like a lawyer who was sure her client was innocent—and that the judge was in the prosecution's pocket.

Finally she looked them all in the eyes and said, "All right, bottom line: this guy is inside the Citium. He's got unlimited access. He's willing to try to stop them—if we turn him loose. *And* he's willing to put me in the middle of the action—undercover. You have nothing to lose. Even if he fails—even if *we* fail—you can still kick in doors and zip-tie the suspects. All we have—after *thirty years*—is a bunch of names and addresses and theories. Without Hughes, we've really got nothing."

"Incorrect, Agent," Ward said. "We have the ship in the harbor." He glanced down at the table. "The *Kentaro Maru*. We take it down, and we pull the thread and it all unravels."

Desmond spoke for the first time. "No, it won't. You pull the thread and you'll get a ball of yarn in your hand and a criminal in the wind. These people are prepared for you. And for people like you around the world. The Citium has firewalls. They compartmentalize everything. It's true, you can take the *Kentaro Maru*, but there are other ships, in other harbors, in cities around the world. You take the freighter, and the responsibilities will simply shift—and the timeline will accelerate. You will *set off* whatever they're planning. This whole thing will go off like a powder keg."

Ultimately, they relented.

Desmond had one final request. When he told them, Ward shook his head.

"Ridiculous. We're not a construction company."

"So hire one. This is non-negotiable."

"Why?"

"It's part of my backup plan."

"And the personnel?"

"Consider it an extended stakeout."

Ward didn't like it, but he agreed.

Desmond got up and walked to the bathroom in the hangar's small office. Ward and Avery followed. Desmond pointed at the far wall. "It needs to be here. Inconspicuous."

"All right."

"How long?" Desmond asked.

Ward threw up his hands. "Again, I'm not a construction—"

"I need it done in two weeks, max. Can you get it done?"

Avery stared at Ward, silently taking Desmond's side.

"We'll get it done," he muttered.

Avery and Ward filed out of the bathroom, leaving Desmond alone. He looked into the mirror over the small vanity.

"This is the end of the road."

It took him a moment to realize that he was talking to himself—that this was a message, sent from the past, from him to the future version of himself who would relive the memories.

"I can't show you any more," he said. "I can't tell you where Rendition is. If I did, they might find it."

He paused.

"You have to figure out what to do. How to stop Yuri." He looked down. "If you *should* stop Yuri. How to save Conner. What Lin's goal is." He stared into the mirror again. "I don't know the right answers. It's part of why I did what I did. I needed to buy myself some time. I needed distance—to try to see all the pieces objectively. You've seen them now. I know it's a hell of a burden to lay at your feet. I don't envy you. But you're the best person, the only person who can change what's happening."

☣

Conner awoke to voices talking excitedly. He sat up and let his sleeping bag fall down. The electric lanterns glowed in the dark hangar, the corkboard like a bizarre art show.

"I've checked twice…" Dr. Park was saying.

"Doctor," he called.

The slender man scurried over to him. "He's out of the memory."

"Location?"

Park's Adam's apple bobbed as he swallowed. "We don't have one. The app—"

"It's offline?"

"No. It's working. But it says, 'You've reached the center of the Labyrinth.' It won't give another location."

Conner thought about that. In Greek mythology, the Labyrinth was built by Daedalus to house the Minotaur—a half-man, half-beast. Daedalus had created the Labyrinth so intricately, so cleverly, that even he himself could barely escape it. The tale was a cautionary one—about geniuses creating devices with unintended consequences.

That Desmond had wrapped this silly mythology around his app didn't surprise Conner. Desmond had always been fascinated by ancient mythology. He'd even named his fund, Icarus Capital, for Daedalus's son, Icarus. Desmond loved old stories of all types, classic literature, dog-eared novels he found at used bookstores. Conner never saw the point. Looking in the past offered no help with the problems of the day. The present was what mattered, seeing the world and all its complexities as new, thinking fresh, solving the problems at hand without the blinders of history. There were no shortcuts, no ready-made templates and solutions to complex problems.

"Is that all, Doctor?"

Park looked down. "No. There's a button. It says, 'Open the Labyrinth.'"

Conner smiled. "Open it then."

Park clicked the button.

Nothing happened.

He realized his error a second later. "He's still under sedation."

"Turn the machine off," Conner said.

☣

Desmond opened his eyes. The light was blinding. He closed them again, mentally taking stock. His body was sore and weak. He felt groggy, like he'd been shot with an elephant dart.

He turned his head and cracked his eyes again, avoiding the buzzing lights overhead. He lay on a narrow table in an open space. A warehouse. No—as it came into focus he realized what it really was: a hangar. He knew this place.

He was splayed out on the same table where Avery had defended him, where the FBI agents had crowded around, working feverishly. They were gone now, the building deserted. But the corkboards and the pages were still there, displaying Yuri's web of deceit.

A face came into Desmond's field of vision. Scarred, mottled flesh. Someone he knew so well. Or so he'd thought.

Conner took Desmond's hand and pulled him up. He steadied him, his hands on both of Desmond's shoulders, and smiled, stretching the scars. "Welcome back, brother."

CHAPTER 53

PEYTON AWOKE TO the sensation of the plane losing altitude. The others were all awake except for Nigel, who was snoring intermittently.

She felt much better, more rested, though the sleeping bag had provided too little padding for her back's liking. She walked to the cockpit, where her mother and Adams were leaning through the doorway, and Avery was speaking into the radio.

"Confirmed, DFW ATC, proceeding to runway two."

Peyton knew the three-letter airport code: DFW was Dallas–Fort Worth. Apparently while Peyton had been sleeping Avery had cleared their entrance to US airspace and connected with her handler at the Rubicon Group. But why had they come here? Lin had no connections in the Dallas area that Peyton knew of.

On the ground, they were met by a contingent of X1 troops—mostly US Army with a few Marines. They offloaded the crates from the Cave of Altamira into a van with a FEMA logo on the side.

Lin took Peyton aside and spoke quietly. "I need you to deliver the cases. Alone."

"Deliver them where? To whom?"

"My colleagues. It has to be you, Peyton. You're the only one I trust. Please hurry."

Peyton exhaled. "We need to talk about what happened back there. One of the others let Yuri go."

"We'll worry about that later." She gave Peyton a folded piece of paper and an envelope. "Directions. Give the envelope to the gatekeeper."

Peyton hesitated, then asked a question she was scared to hear the answer to. But she had to know—just in case.

"Mom, back in the cave—what you said…" Peyton considered repeating her mother's words: *Take care of my daughter, Chief. She is more important to me than anything in this room.* But she couldn't. And it didn't matter. She knew from her mother's expression that the woman knew exactly what she was referring to. "That was for show, right? So that the Citium operatives would tell Yuri?"

"Yes."

The word hit Peyton hard.

"Taking Yuri was the only possible way out for us, Peyton. I had to get alone with him—I needed him to believe I was ready to negotiate."

Every word was a nail through Peyton's heart. The joy she had felt hours ago turned to pain.

Her mother grabbed her shoulders. "But that doesn't mean it wasn't true."

Peyton blinked. She opened her mouth to speak, but Lin ushered her toward the van. "Go, Peyton. Time is of the essence."

Behind the wheel, Peyton unfolded the page. It was a map with only a few roads marked. She really missed the internet—and GPS.

☣

DFW seemed to be one of the nerve centers of the government's post-pandemic relief efforts. Flights came and went every few minutes, and the airport was swarming with troops and cargo transports. It took Peyton ten minutes just to leave, and her papers were checked twice.

She took International Parkway south out of the airport, then 183 East to Highway 161 South, which turned into the George Bush Turnpike. The tolls were all electronic, but Peyton doubted anyone would get a bill.

The highway was nearly deserted save for military vehicles and transfer trucks. It was eerie, unnerving even. She took Interstate 20 East, then I-35E. The cityscape soon turned to countryside, skyscrapers replaced by barbed-wire fences around vast pastures.

She had been driving about an hour when she saw the signs for Waxahachie. She turned off the interstate at exit 399A, onto Cantrell Street, which turned into Buena Vista Road. A mobile home park lay on her left. Swings on the children's play sets swayed in the Texas prairie wind, but there wasn't a soul in sight. She passed barns, farms, and houses set back off the road.

She took the next turn, onto Perimeter Road. Six massive buildings stretched out before her, like a manufacturing plant set in the middle of a green field. The road was crumbling, neglected, left to bake in the Texas sun, its peeling pieces carried away by the wind. A chain-link gate ahead was manned. Peyton stopped, rolled down the window, and handed the man the envelope her mother had given her.

The logo on the man's uniform read "MedioSol"—Latin for "center of the sun." Peyton had never heard of it, but she knew it was her mother's work, a reference to the Invisible Sun her father had spent his life trying to find.

The guard grabbed the clip-on speaker microphone attached to his radio. "She's here to see Ferguson—on Shaw's orders."

The gate creaked as it rolled aside. Peyton was about to put the van in drive when an idea occurred to her. She held out her hand.

"I'm going to need that back."

The guard handed her the envelope, and she gunned the van along the uneven road.

When he was firmly in her rear view, she took the single page out of the envelope. Her mother's handwriting was neat and small.

She has the research from the Beagle. Hurry. She's my daughter. Protect her at all costs.

Another uniformed guard motioned her to the nearest building, where a wide roll-up door was opening. She pulled the van into the building, and the door closed behind her. The room looked like some sort of loading dock; forklifts and hand trucks lined the walls. Several workers in coveralls bearing the MedioSol logo entered from a side door and began unloading the van.

"Where are you taking that?" Peyton asked.

"Intake," one of the workers answered. He motioned to a door at the end of the room. "Doctor Ferguson's waiting for you."

Peyton didn't know the name.

The door led to a small, empty chamber with a door at the opposite end. As she entered, the door closed behind her. A blast of cold air ran over her, and she realized she was in a decontamination chamber.

The exit door clicked open, and Peyton walked through it. What she saw on the other side took her breath away.

Avery had spent the last hour debriefing, and she was sick of it. Finally, she walked out of the conference room, over the objections of the Rubicon-assigned FBI agent.

"Agent Price," the woman called, standing up.

"Be right back," Avery lied.

She found Lin Shaw standing in the X1 situation room, which was a repurposed air traffic control center.

"What's next?"

Lin turned to her. "Miss Price. I thought you were being debriefed."

"I'm briefless. So. What's the plan?"

"We wait."

"For Peyton to get back?"

"No."

Avery ground her teeth. Lin Shaw was as transparent as cinderblock wall.

"No what?"

"Peyton's not coming back."

CHAPTER 54

PEYTON'S FOOTSTEPS ECHOED on the concrete floor. The room was cold and dark and reminded her of Altamira, though this place was its technological opposite: a marvel of science and technology, not of ancient art. The room was tall, three stories, and the walls were glass. Beyond the glass, rows of server racks stretched out as far as she could see, their lights blinking green, red, and yellow. The place was massive, perhaps the size of twenty football fields put together. This datacenter had to be one of the largest in the world.

"Welcome."

The voice caught Peyton off guard. She turned to find a slender man with close-cut hair, wire-rimmed glasses, and a white lab coat.

"Sorry if I startled you." Based on the accent, Peyton guessed he was from Boston. "I'm Richard Ferguson. A colleague of your mother's."

"Colleague in what?"

He frowned. "You don't know?"

"I know she's looking for a code in the human genome. But she's never mentioned this place."

"Ah. That was probably prudent." He turned his back to her and headed toward another door. "I'm sure you'd like to shower and rest a bit. I imagine you've been through an ordeal."

Peyton didn't feel that "an ordeal" quite covered what she had been through. But she didn't want to shower, or rest. She wanted answers.

Beyond the door was a corridor that was more cramped than she expected. Colored wires, some thick, others as thin as Ethernet, hung in the ceiling like the veins of a mechanical beast. Large pipes, painted white, ran along the walls just above the door frames. Three letters were emblazoned every few feet: SSC.

"I'd rather talk," Peyton said, catching up to Ferguson.

"About?"

"What you're doing here. I want some answers."

"Certainly. I have some work to attend to first."

"You're going to work on the samples."

"Yes. They're very old. And delicate. I want to extract the DNA myself. And it needs to be done now—time is running out."

"Why?" Then Peyton realized the answer to her question. "Yuri. You're running out of time to stop him."

Ferguson stopped at a door and swiped his key card. It opened, revealing a room with a bed and a couch, about the size of a hotel room, with a window that looked out on a retention pond. "Correct. Now Miss Shaw, you'll have to excuse me."

"Sixty seconds. Please. Then I'll let you work." She looked through the doorway. "I won't go inside unless you talk to me."

He smiled. "Well, that leaves no doubt that you're Lin's daughter." He raised his eyebrows. "Not that we could spare the DNA testing equipment for the moment." He laughed at his own joke, almost giddy. Peyton realized that the arrival of the samples was like the ultimate Christmas present for him; she understood why he couldn't wait to sequence them.

She spoke quickly, knowing she had little time. "What is this place?"

"The Desertron."

"What?"

He shrugged. "Some people know the name. It was the unofficial designation. The formal name is the SSC, or Superconducting Super Collider."

Collider. That caught Peyton off guard. "Colliding..."

"Particles."

"Like CERN."

Ferguson soured at the mention, as if he had tasted a bad bit in his food. "Yes, like CERN—only this accelerator's ring is over three times larger than the LHC and uses three times as much power."

Peyton remembered hearing something about it now—when she was in middle school. "You're government?"

"No. The Desertron got canceled in 1993 due to budget cuts. Your mother convinced a consortium of investors—like-minded people—to purchase the facility and complete the work. It took almost twenty years. But it's operational."

"I don't follow. My mother's work is in genetics."

"True. But she believes the Invisible Sun operates at a quantum level, that it is a fundamental force in the universe, akin to gravity."

"A force that does what?"

"Directs the flow of particles. Specifically, particles that influence the conversion of matter to energy. That's the purpose of the universe, after all."

Peyton couldn't hide her shock.

Ferguson cocked his head. "Your mother didn't tell you any of this?"

"No," Peyton whispered.

"It's the Citium's fundamental theory. That the universe is a quantum machine that oscillates between matter and energy. The Big Bang wasn't a singular event—it was one in a cycle of many big bangs. At the end of this universe there will be only energy, then another big bang will occur, and so on. This has been going on for an infinite amount of time. And will continue for just as long."

Peyton felt lightheaded. She braced a hand against the wall. For some reason, she thought of Alice, growing tall and feeling trapped. The corridor seemed so small all of a sudden. She wanted to get outside.

Ferguson studied her. "Are you—did I upset you?"

Peyton shook her head, glancing down. "I… just give me a minute."

"Sorry. I haven't *told* anyone in a long time. We take this information for granted."

Peyton tried to focus. "So, the code, in the DNA samples. I don't understand how it's involved."

"Well, it's quite simple. We believe that in the past, this fundamental quantum force—the force of the Invisible Sun—exerted very little influence on our DNA. But as we evolved, developing more complex brains and increasing our calorie intake to power them, the quantum changes accelerated, like a feedback mechanism, changing our DNA at an increasing rate. There's only one known force that could affect changes at a subatomic level over great distance: quantum entanglement. The phenomenon Einstein called 'spooky action at a distance.'"

Ferguson saw the confusion on Peyton's face. "Let's see, how to explain. We believe the Invisible Sun is a quantum force that has existed since the Big Bang. It exerts a subatomic pull on all matter—but some matter connects with it more strongly. In particular, brain matter is strongly tethered to it, and as our minds became more powerful, this quantum force reacted more strongly in turn. The result was a feedback mechanism that changed our genome. We believe that over time, this quantum force left a pattern, a sort of *callback number* for us. Now that we have the archaic samples, we can establish a baseline over time and see that pattern. The code, your mother calls it."

"And what will you do with it?"

"Feed it into the accelerator, of course."

"To do what?"

"The Invisible Sun has been interacting with us for a very long time. For the first time, we're going to start generating similar subatomic particles. The running joke around here is that we're going to make the first quantum phone call. To us, the code in the human genome is like God's phone number."

CHAPTER 55

AWARENESS CAME GRADUALLY, like a sunrise, a ray at first: the realization that he was in the hangar at San Carlos Airport—and that this wasn't a memory. Desmond was awake and in the present.

Out of the corner of his eye, he saw corkboards littered with photos and pages. Strings connected the pins where FBI and Rubicon agents had tried to tie the pieces together, to unravel the Citium conspiracy. They had failed. And so had he. His last memory lingered in his mind: of him staring at his future self in the mirror, saying, "You have to figure out what to do."

Conner leaned closer. "You all right?"

Desmond nodded. His voice came out weak and horse. "Thirsty."

Conner spun and yelled at one of the two Citium special ops soldiers. "Get us some water!"

Desmond realized then how hungry he was. And sluggish. How long had he been sedated? Days? A week? With a shaking hand he reached up and touched his face, trying to measure the stubble. Three days' growth, give or take a day.

Conner handed him a canteen, and Desmond grabbed it, held it to his mouth, and let the water pour in and down his chin, onto his shirt.

Conner gripped Desmond's hand and steadied the canteen. "Easy, Des."

When the water ceased, Desmond panted. "Food."

Conner didn't turn or even say the words this time. The sound of plastic wrappers ripping echoed in the space, and a second later, one of the mercenaries was there, holding out a cold MRE, a spork dug into the home-style vegetables in sauce with noodles and chicken.

He sat up and braced himself, his legs dangling over the edge of the table. He took the tray and shoveled the tasteless meal into his mouth, pausing only to swallow, breathe, and take another bite.

When he was done, he stared up at the hangar ceiling, waiting for the sustenance to take hold. His hands were still shaking, his breathing heavy.

"Another one!" Conner yelled.

When Desmond finished, his eyes met Conner's.

"Thanks," he said.

"Still hungry?"

Desmond shook his head, which was pounding. "Just got a headache."

"Doctor—give us something."

A slender Asian man with round glasses and sweaty, disheveled hair approached, took a bottle from his backpack, and shook out two red pills, which Desmond swallowed down with a gulp from the canteen.

The two Citium operatives seemed to be the only other people in the hangar. Perhaps Conner had more troops stationed outside. It was unlikely that he would be here with such a small contingent.

"What do you remember?" Conner asked.

"A lot."

"Rendition?"

"I remember creating it." In his mind's eye, Desmond saw himself in his office, writing code, in a team room, drawing lines on a whiteboard, the developers gathered around him, the hardware and software teams arguing, working through issues. He saw the meetings with the integration teams from Rapture Therapeutics and Rook Quantum Sciences, his private meetings with Conner and Yuri, the things they didn't tell anyone else.

"Where is it?" Conner asked.

Desmond stared at his brother. "Let's talk. Just you and me."

Conner smiled. "Good. Okay." He motioned toward an office in the hangar.

Desmond slid to the edge of the table, lowered his feet to the ground, and stood, legs shaking. He had to hold the table for balance.

Conner grabbed his upper arm. "You need help?"

"No. Just—I just need a minute." He glanced at the corkboards. "Did you read them?"

Conner paused. "I did. They knew so much about us. The Citium subsidiaries, even me, you, and Yuri. Why didn't they act?"

Desmond swallowed. "I stopped them."

"What?"

"I told them I was going to do it. To wait."

Conner nodded. "Then in a way, you helped us."

Desmond couldn't think of a response. His head was still clouded from the sedatives. He took a tentative step, then another, Conner still holding him.

He stopped at a corkboard with pictures of a crime scene. The exterior of a large house in the country, framed by towering trees. A crushed gravel drive led to a fountain in front of the double doors. The pictures of the inside of the house were not so elegant. Dead bodies, lying on the floor—but with no signs of trauma, gunshots, or knife wounds.

"Did you see this?" Desmond asked.

"Yes. The last conclave."

"The purge."

"It's very sad," Conner said.

"Very." Desmond let his eyes wander down to a picture of a wine glass and the toxicology report next to it. "Yuri poisoned them. Makes sense. They were his friends and his competitors. He wanted a painless death for them, something at arm's length."

"There's no proof—"

"He survived, Conner."

"So did Lin."

"And her husband. William told me the truth about the purge. Yuri killed all these people so he could take control of the Citium."

"If he did, there's more to the story. They must have been a threat. He'd only kill if he had to."

"Like unleashing a pathogen on the world and killing millions."

Conner's eyes flashed. "That wasn't our fault. We offered the world the cure the day after the infection rate hit the tipping point. All we wanted was to distribute the cure, and Rapture with it."

"That's not all. You wanted control of world governments."

"What difference does it make? The Looking Glass will give us that anyway." Conner glanced back at the other three men. "Come on, Des." He apparently didn't want them to hear the conversation.

He led his brother to the office. Each step was easier for Desmond, his gait less labored.

Conner slammed the door behind them. "Now tell me: what do you remember?"

Desmond inhaled. "I remember going to Australia thirteen years ago and learning that you had lived. I remember the horror and joy of that moment. I remember the day I saw you leave your apartment. My heart broke that day—"

"Get on with it."

Desmond ignored the outburst. "I watch you from afar. Your transformation, Conner. What you accomplished, your strength, breaking that drug's hold on you. Your leadership at Rook. How hard you worked. You were an inspiration to me. I didn't realize it then. But I saw in the memories... what you did for me was every bit as profound as what I did for you."

Conner glanced around the office, unable to look Desmond in the eye. There were maintenance schedules on the wall, mandatory flight safety posters, a large-scale picture of a Cessna Citation sitting in a hangar, its doors open, a smiling pilot standing beside it.

"We don't have a lot of time here," Conner said. "We've had our differences, but that's over now. I know you don't agree with how we distributed Rapture. Fine. Let's just put it behind us.

Rapture *has* been distributed. Rook is ready and waiting. If you can recover Rendition, the Looking Glass will come online. That's always been our dream—our promise to each other. Now we can make it happen." He stepped closer. "Think about all the suffering happening around the world. We can end it. Right now. We can ensure humanity survives another thousand years—another *billion* years."

"It's not that simple any more."

"It is."

"Listen, Conner. Really *listen* to me. I saw what happened before the pandemic. The reason I hid my memories. It's not what you think."

Conner stared, confused.

"I went to see Lin Shaw after we met on the *Kentaro Maru*."

"And?"

"And she told me that the Looking Glass couldn't be stopped. That it was inevitable. That it had happened before on other worlds and would happen again—"

"We know that—"

"She *also* said that we—you, Yuri, and I—didn't understand what it really was."

"And *she* does?"

"She thinks so. She told me only one thing could change: who *controls* the Looking Glass."

Conner made the connection immediately. "So whatever she's doing, it would allow *her* to take control of the Looking Glass."

"I think we can assume that."

Conner paced across the office.

"She wanted me to stop Yuri," Desmond said.

"To keep him from controlling the Looking Glass, so that she could."

"Yes. But I think it's more than that. She knew what Yuri was capable of. The purge. The pandemic. Conner, he's not the person we thought he was."

"Yes he is. He brought us together. He helped you... bring me back. He's just like us: born in fire and raised in the ashes. He's dedicated his life to building a better world." Conner turned to his brother. "We're fighting a war, Des. The first battle was more bloody than we expected, but only because our enemy chose that. If they had relented—"

"Conner—"

"No." Conner shook his head. "Yuri placed his faith in us. He gave each of us a piece of the Looking Glass. We can't break faith with him. Not now. *I* won't. He's done too much for us. You have to see that, Des. You have to see that I wouldn't desert him any more than I would desert you."

Desmond did see it then: the full genius of Yuri's plan. He had assessed Conner McClain, like a piece on a chessboard, had seen his capabilities and his position, seen how he could be maneuvered. Conner's mind for strategy and tactics had enabled him to build Rook and to be a formidable commander of Citium Security and paramilitary forces. But most importantly, his devotion and loyalty to Yuri and Desmond was unbreakable.

"This is just a little bump in the road," Conner continued. "We knew there would be some. I talked with Yuri. He says he's already forgiven and forgotten. He's ready to finish this. So am I."

"*He's* forgiven *me?*"

"Can we move on, brother? Can we finish this—together? Please? You promised me, Des. You swore to me."

Desmond saw only one way out. A single choice that might change his life forever.

"Yes," he said. "We'll finish it. Together."

CHAPTER 56

"WHERE IS IT?" Conner asked.

Desmond stared out the window of the hangar's office. The two Citium Security operatives were leaning against a black Suburban. The slender Asian man was wandering around, reading the pages pinned to the corkboards.

"It's on a solid state drive," Desmond said. "In a safe deposit box."

"Where?"

"San Jose. At the Bank of the West. Box 2938."

Conner eyed him, as if trying to get a read. Desmond resisted the urge to swallow.

"Look, it's like thirty minutes from here. Let's go. I'll prove it to you."

"Where's the key?"

"No idea," Desmond said. "But you've proved quite adept at breaking into things lately. And the world is kind of over, so I figure no one will care."

Conner smiled, but Desmond sensed that his brother still didn't trust him fully. All the same, Conner walked to the door, opened it, and yelled to his men, "Load up!" He turned back to Desmond. "If you're lying to me..."

Desmond met his gaze and said nothing.

Conner broke eye contact and muttered, "All right, let's go."

"I need to use the bathroom." Desmond shrugged. "It's been a few days."

Conner touched his collarbone. "Grant, join us in the office." When the mercenary arrived, he said, "Keep watch."

Conner opened the bathroom door in the corner of the office, his right hand gripping the handle of his gun. He flipped the light on and walked inside. Desmond heard him take the ceramic lid off the toilet, open and close the cabinet doors under the vanity, then set the toilet lid back on. He heard boots on top of the toilet, ceiling tiles being lifted and tossed, and a light clicking on, then off.

Conner emerged. "All yours, Des."

He and the other man stayed in the office as Desmond entered. He closed the door and locked it behind him. In truth, he desperately had to use the bathroom, but he didn't have much time. Seconds at most.

He flushed the toilet to create some noise and began feeling along the corner of the back wall, hoping David Ward had been true to his word.

He found the indentation as the water drained from the bowl. He pushed, and the wall swung in. Whoever David Ward and the FBI had hired had done a great job. The seam between the wall and the hidden door was virtually invisible. It opened just enough for Desmond to slip through.

Before he did, he flushed once more, then turned on the faucet in the sink.

Just inside the hidden door, a small, motion-activated LED turned on, its light barely enough to illuminate the small space, which was about four feet wide and six feet deep. A round shaft led down, a metal ladder in its center. Desmond closed the door, gripped the rails, and descended with all the haste he could manage. His body was still shaky, but it was responding better with each passing second.

At the base of the ladder was a tunnel, round, with metal walls, like a giant iron sewer pipe with tiny LEDs on the ceiling.

Desmond ran for his life.

The Suburban was cranked, the men loaded inside, waiting. Conner stood in the office, listening to the running water.

"Des?" he called. How long has it been?

He began counting the seconds. At thirty, he walked to the bathroom door and listened, but heard only running water. He knocked. "Des?"

No response.

He tried the knob. Locked.

"Des? Answer me."

He counted five seconds.

He dreaded what came next, but he stepped back, his mind going blank, into an almost autopilot-like mode. His kick connected in the center of the hollow door, next to the knob. It exploded inward, hit the wall, bounced, and returned. The split-second peek confirmed that the room was empty.

He touched his collarbone. "Request backup. We've lost him."

He pulled his sidearm and entered the bathroom. It looked the same. He reached out with his left hand, still holding his gun, pressing the wall opposite the vanity and toilet.

A voice behind him. "Sir?"

"Check the ceiling!" he called, not turning.

The wall gave when he reached the corner. Just a slight movement. He stepped back and kicked hard. His foot went through the drywall and got caught. Balancing on one leg, he jerked his foot out and drew the Maglite from his belt. He switched it on and peered through the hole, taking in the small room and manhole.

He activated his comm. "I've got him."

Conner stood, thinking, his mind like a computer analyzing the situation. What does this mean?

Strong possibility: Desmond knew about this tunnel.

Evidence supporting: he had been here before—he knew what was on the corkboards when we he woke up.

Certainty: either the tunnel was here before Desmond visited the first time, and he was told about it... or it was built after, likely at his request.

Most likely possibility: Desmond planned this—as a trap door at the end of his memories.

Implication: the tunnel was made in the last few months.

What options do I have?

Chase him down, or go where he's going.

Chasing was always a bad option.

Which left only one question: what's his destination? The marshy waters of Bair Island Marine Park lay to the east, Bay Shore Freeway to the west. The tunnel would be unable to pass either, at least in the short amount of time they had to construct it.

Conclusion: the tunnel exited somewhere in the airport. Most likely at another hangar.

The operatives were at the door to the bathroom, guns held at the ready.

"Take the SUV, block the airport entrance!" They turned, and he called after them, "Shoot the tires on anything trying to exit. Be careful! Don't hit him!"

He clicked his light off. And stood silently. In the dim light of the bathroom, he stared through the opening in the drywall, hoping Des would re-emerge, hoping that maybe the tunnel went nowhere—that it was just a ruse to get them to move out, much like the ruse he himself had used to escape the X1 soldiers at Desmond's home.

Behind him, he heard the SUV crank and roar away.

He waited. No movement. No light.

He ran out of the office and found Dr. Park standing there looking wide-eyed, almost frantic. Park must have begun to realize that Conner didn't need him any more, now that Desmond had recovered all of his memories. And the scientist knew too much—including details about the location of the island that was the Citium's final stronghold.

Conner felt his hand drift down to the gun in his holster.

Park took a step back, furtively glancing around.

Conner knew what he should do. What Yuri would do. What needed to be done.

"Stay here, Doctor. I'm warning you."

He told himself that he would finish him when he got back, but as he ran out of the hangar, he knew it wasn't true. He pushed his legs as hard as they would go, running into the night across the grass, onto the tarmac. He unslung his rifle from his back and stood, waiting for a hangar door to open.

CHAPTER 57

THE TUNNEL SEEMED endless. Desmond's legs protested, but he pushed harder, his way lit only by the tiny beads of light above. Finally, he saw a ladder ahead. He slowed as he reached it, knowing time was precious, but that danger might be waiting.

He gripped the ladder and looked up. The dirt ended ten feet above at a concrete layer that was frayed at the edges, like the cheese topping on a slice of pizza that had been bitten into. He heard the faint murmur of voices, men arguing, then laughing.

He climbed the rungs quietly.

The exit from the hidden passage wasn't as polished as the entrance. Mounds of black dirt were piled on each side, hills left by the auger. The ceiling of a hangar loomed above. Desmond peeked over the edge and saw two men, overweight, one with a shaved head, the other with short hair, both sitting on cheap metal chairs at a folding table, studying playing cards fanned out in their hands.

One leaned back and spotted Desmond in his peripheral vision. He reeled back, the chair tripping him, sending him tumbling to the ground. The other man laughed, then realized something was wrong. He scanned, saw Desmond, and stood, drawing a side-arm and training it on Desmond. "Freeze. FBI."

Footfalls on the concrete, a third figure running, approaching.

Desmond held his hands up, didn't climb further. The third figure rounded the dirt mound. This man Desmond knew. David

Ward. Avery's boss—the same boss who had agreed to build the tunnel.

"We need to go," Desmond said.

Ward held his hand out, palm down, and the agent lowered his gun. The other agent was on his feet again, red-faced and embarrassed.

"How?" Ward asked.

"By plane. Right now."

Ward nodded to the two men, who raced to the hangar doors and pulled them open. A jet sat just beyond the hole in the concrete.

Ward helped Desmond climb over the dirt pile. "You screwed me over, Hughes."

Desmond looked at him. "I didn't."

"Don't lie."

"Look, I tried. I failed—"

"I'm only here because Avery Price thinks you're the key to stopping them."

So she had saved him once again. In the other hangar a month ago, then on the *Kentaro Maru*, and now here.

Desmond walked toward the plane. "Can we talk about how pissed you are in the air?"

Ward muttered something Desmond couldn't make out, but fell in behind him.

There were two black Ford Crown Victoria sedans sitting just inside the hangar door. A thought occurred to Desmond. Conner was likely already aware he had escaped—*and* that he hadn't gone far. To Ward, he said, "Can you fly the plane?"

The man glanced at it. Not a good sign. "Sure."

"Are you *sure*?"

"Why?"

"We need covering fire. Two men in a car making sure the runway is clear."

As if on cue, tires squealed from another hangar, and headlights beamed out into the night, picking up speed, like a panther released from a cage.

Ward called to the two agents and told them to load up. "Get your rifles, too."

He led Desmond up the plane's staircase, and they jogged to the cockpit. Ward squinted at the flight instruments. Another bad sign.

"You can—" Desmond began.

"Pull the stairs up, Hughes. And shut up."

Desmond heard the engines roar to life as he closed the door. He returned to the cockpit. "What can I do?"

"Just keep a watch for hostiles."

Desmond moved toward the co-pilot seat.

"No," Ward said. "Get back in the cabin."

Desmond studied him.

"Less chance of getting hit."

"Didn't know you cared."

Ward smiled. "I don't." He watched as the gauges on the panel ticked up. "Avery would kill me if anything happened to you."

"Right."

One of the Crown Victorias led them onto the tarmac, its lights off, the passenger window down, the short-haired man poised with an automatic rifle. Desmond saw Conner's Suburban parked at the entrance to the airport, blocking the gates. The two security operatives stood beside it, guns at the ready.

The plane was almost to the runway when the first shots ricocheted off the Crown Victoria. But the shots didn't come from the Suburban—the angle was wrong.

Desmond dashed to the opposite side of the plane, waited, and saw a muzzle flare from the grass on the Bair Island side.

"Shooter in the grass!" he shouted. "Bay side. Eleven o'clock."

More shots. The Crown Victoria sparked like a pack of firecrackers. A clang sounded off the plane's fuselage, then another.

"He's trying to shoot the tires!" Desmond called.

The airport had only one runway. He and Ward had to take off now or surrender.

A round of automatic gunfire sounded, this time from behind the plane, the bullets striking the tail fin.

"Hey!" Desmond turned toward the cockpit, but a massive explosion drowned him out. Through the window he saw the Crown Victoria engulfed in flames, the front-left corner lifting into the air. The car almost flipped, but settled back onto the ground.

A grenade—and an expert shot at that.

Ward swerved the plane. Desmond flew across the cabin, rolled off a seat, and hit the floor at the base of a couch. He heard more shots hitting the plane's metal skin.

The plane accelerated. From the floor, Desmond saw Ward pushing the throttle forward. He crawled up onto the nearest seat and peered out the windows. There were three shooters running down the tarmac, their rifles flaring. It reminded him of the orange lights flashing on switches in a data center in the Rook facility, with his brother at his side—the man now directing the shooting.

The wheels lifted off the ground. The aircraft wobbled. The engines roared, and the shooting stopped.

Desmond climbed over the seats to the back of the cabin for a better view. One of the shooters ran back to the burning Crown Victoria, where the agent in the passenger seat had climbed out. He pulled the man up and searched him. And then the darkness consumed the scene, and all Desmond could see were the beady runway lights. The Bayshore Freeway was dark and empty— something he had never seen as long as he had lived in the valley.

He walked to the cockpit, where he found Ward talking into a smartphone, giving orders and updates.

"Hey," Desmond whispered.

Ward held the phone to his shoulder.

"One of the agents got out of the car. They've got him—"

"I've got X1 units inbound."

Desmond didn't give that plan much success. Conner had proved himself quite adept at urban warfare.

"Does he know where we're going?"

Ward rolled his eyes. "Hughes, *I* don't even know where we're going."

"What?"

"Hold on."

Ward returned to his call, which apparently was with Rubicon ops.

Desmond settled into the co-pilot seat and studied the instrument panel. Fuel level was good. Not dropping. There were a dozen other readouts, only a few of which he understood.

When Ward ended the call, Desmond said, "So where—"

The man took a folded paper from his inside jacket pocket and handed it over.

Desmond opened it and read the single line of handwritten text. "What is this?"

"Apparently, it's a note from your past self to whatever the hell you are now. You gave it to me in that hangar back there a month ago when you asked us to dig your tunnel. Said it was for my eyes only. Not even Avery."

Desmond read the sentence again.

It lies in the bend, where blood turned to water and darkness turned to light.

"What does it mean?" Ward asked.

"I assume you've been trying to figure it out?"

"We have. Best at the CIA and FBI counterintelligence have been working on it."

"Best guesses?"

"The bend, mention of water and blood, they were thinking the Red River, maybe a location in Oklahoma. Couple of guys thought it was the Blood River in South Africa, the reference to the Zulu battle in 1838 and then 40, the Dutch alliance with the indigenous tribes the reference to the light and dark."

"Good theories," Desmond said. And they were. But they weren't correct.

"You don't know the answer?"

"I do. Fly east. To Oklahoma."

Thirty minutes later, Ward engaged the autopilot, stood, and walked out of the cockpit. Hughes was sprawled out on the couch that ran along the left wall of the cabin, sawing logs. Whatever his brother had done to him, it had left him shaken, weak, and sleepy.

Ward eyed the sleeping figure. Initially, Hughes had been a fulcrum with which Avery would split open the Citium and stop a conspiracy. But somewhere along the way, he had become an altogether different entity to her. Precious. Untouchable. An item she loved, nearly worshiped.

And it was Ward who had brought them together. He had recruited Avery right out of college, her mother dead, her father in assisted living, then round-the-clock care. She was pure of heart when she showed up at his office in Research Triangle Park, a truly good person. But the world had changed that. Her job had changed her, and he had given her that job.

And then this monster, Hughes, had changed her.

Now Ward didn't know where her allegiance lay—to the enigma snoring on the couch, or to him and the United States government. *Sex changes everything*, Ward thought. It was a variable counter-intelligence agencies and computer algorithms would never be able to factor in. Almost like a viral infection that rewires a brain, changes emotions, even alters the lens through which a person sees the world.

Perhaps it didn't matter. Hughes was their only way in. These people—the Citium—were a black box buried in a black box, and Ward had no choice but to follow this rabbit hole wherever it led. There was no other play. He needed Avery, and they needed Hughes.

And things were going to get messy.

He took out the sat phone and called his best agent, perhaps one of the best who ever lived.

CHAPTER 58

AS A BOY in Stalingrad, Yuri had learned to hide. To slow his breathing and remain quiet and listen. For years, he had lived like that, moving from one place to another as the siege dragged on and the city crumbled block by block, leaving dead bodies in its wake and driving the living back, like rats out of a sewer. That's what his childhood had felt like, and that's how he felt in that moment, hiding in the Cave of Altamira. But he did it then and he did it now, because he had to—in order to survive. He wasn't above doing whatever he had to. So he listened, and when he heard the vehicles crank, he listened more closely, waiting for the sound to fade into the distance.

He ran out, into the blinding afternoon sun, shielding his eyes as he moved to the visitor center. His men were alive—tied up and gagged. The phones and radios lay in a shredded heap. That was smart—and unfortunate for him.

"*Quien habla español?*" he yelled.

Several men writhed and lifted up, looked toward him as they screamed into the gags. He untied them. He needed locals, someone who knew the area.

"*Aeropuerto?*" one of the men asked.

"No," Yuri said quickly. "We need a car first. Then a boat. They'll soon be watching the airports." He motioned to the door. "Go. Split up and find a car. Return here, and I'll make sure you escape."

Thirty minutes later, Yuri and three of the mercenaries were riding in a Dacia Sandero, bouncing along the curving, hilly roads, heading toward the coast. At the small town of Suances, they found a yacht club. It was half empty, and the boats that remained had apparently been abandoned. There was an Azimut 50 among them, with almost five hundred gallons of fuel in the tank, and jugs of water in the lower deck. They gathered food from the other boats and a working sat phone.

As the vessel powered out of the harbor and into the Bay of Biscay, Yuri dialed the Citium Situation Room. He was quickly transferred to Melissa Whitmeyer. From the tone of her voice, he knew something was wrong—and it wasn't what had happened at Altamira.

"Sir, Mister McClain has been trying to get in touch with you."

Yuri sat down on the plush white leather sofa and stared at the teak floor. "Put him through."

Conner's voice was heavy with emotion. "I lost him."

"It's okay—"

"No. It's not."

"The tracker?" Yuri asked.

"Still in place, but..."

"Don't lose hope, Conner. This isn't over." Yuri paused. "Where is he now?"

"Heading east. Toward Oklahoma."

"He's going home. Maybe he hid Rendition there."

"Maybe. Where were you?"

"We have had a setback here."

Conner was silent a long moment. "He'll tell them where the island is."

"We don't know that. Hughes was drugged when he left the island. Even if he marked the stars, he couldn't find us."

"I lost the doctor, too—Park. He'll definitely tell them."

That was a problem. But Conner needed something else now, and Yuri knew exactly how to give it to him. "Listen to me.

None of that will matter soon. If we complete the Looking Glass, *nothing else* will matter. Focus, Conner. Now is our moment. We must win through. We always knew this would be difficult. We are being tested."

Conner's tone changed, the dread and worry fading away. "What do you want me to do?"

"Get to an airport. And be ready when I call you."

When Conner disconnected, Yuri dialed Whitmeyer again.

"I need a plane. And a new team."

"Santander is the closest—"

"No. That's where Shaw went. She'll have put them on alert."

"Stand by."

He heard her making calls in the background and typing on her keyboard. "I can get you a plane in Bilbao, but personnel is going to be a problem. We allocated everyone to Altamira. You could go back and—"

"I can't go back. Prep the plane. And keep an eye on Hughes's tracker. Is the biometrics working?"

"Yes. Heartbeat was through the roof during his escape. I think he's sleeping now."

"Good."

Yuri walked to the edge of the main deck and glanced up at the sun deck, where one of the Citium Security operatives was driving the boat, the other smoking a cigarette. The third man had gone down to the lower deck to one of the cabins to sleep.

"I have another tracker you need to activate," Yuri said quietly. "I want you to allocate all resources—and I mean *every* satellite we have or can get control of. We can't lose this one."

"Understood."

CHAPTER 59

AVERY WATCHED THE screens in horror. The situation room at the Dallas–Fort Worth airport was in chaos. Since the internet had gone down and martial law had been declared, the unease gripping the nation had grown by the day. Food rationing had added to the fear, and there were now riots across the nation, protests, even bands of paramilitary groups organizing, gearing up to fight. Those who had survived the X1 pandemic were afraid the next disaster was already starting—and that they might not survive this one.

The scenes made her realize how delicate the social fabric of the human race truly was. People's confidence in government and police—the order of things—was the glue that held society together. And that glue was coming unstuck. Once it was gone, instilling that trust again would be very difficult. The damage being done might soon be irreparable.

Her first call after landing at DFW had been to the Raleigh-Durham X1 ops center to check on her father. He was living in the camp at the Dean Dome in Chapel Hill, where David Ward had promised her that he would be taken care of, that his name was on the list of high-value individuals. Even without the crisis, he needed taking care of. Alzheimer's took more of him every time she visited.

"Agent Price," one of the operators said. "You've got a call."

She put on the headset. "Price."

Ward's voice was muffled by background noise—an airplane, Avery thought. "We've got him."

"Hughes? How? When?"

"He came through the tunnel a half hour ago. There's something else. He remembers everything. Meeting me at the airport, asking me to build the tunnel. Everything."

Everything, Avery thought. Including them. She had told herself that she didn't care if he remembered. But she did. Now that he had regained his memories, she could admit it to herself: she cared. A lot. And she wanted to see him. She wanted—needed—to sort out what they were. But there was a more pressing matter.

"Rendition?"

"He knows, or at least, he thinks he knows where he hid the key to finding it."

"Where are you now?"

"In the air."

"Destination?"

"We'll get to that. But we need to make a stop first." Ward hesitated. "We need to check him out."

"No—"

"I promise you he won't be harmed. Unless he makes us."

"I swear, if you hurt him or kill him, I'm done."

Silence on the line. Then: "Are you finished, Agent?"

Avery sighed. "Where can we meet?"

"What about Shaw? The older Shaw?"

"We've reached the end of the road here. She's waiting. I can tell."

"Waiting for what?"

"For whatever Desmond is going to do next. Or Yuri. I'm not sure."

A long pause, then Ward said, "So we either take her off the table or we keep her close."

"She still knows more than anyone else. But she has an agenda. I don't trust her."

"It's your call."

"Okay."

"There's something else. I know how you feel about him, Avery. I need to know you can set that aside. There's more at stake here."

Her tone turned combative. "What do you want me to say?"

"If we're standing in a room—him and me, hands raised, you on the other end of a Sig Sauer, who do you shoot?"

Avery exhaled into the phone's receiver. "I'd shoot him in the shoulder and kick you in the nuts."

Ward couldn't help but laugh.

"Probably punch you in the face for good measure," she added. "Let's hope it doesn't come up. Now, I'm going to need that location."

"Oklahoma City. Hurry."

When Avery disconnected the call, she found Lin standing close by, staring directly at her. The older woman motioned to a nearby conference room.

When they were alone inside, Lin closed the door and said, "Desmond?"

"He's escaped."

"Status?"

"We believe he knows where Rendition is. He's en route."

Lin stepped closer. "Good."

"Why do you need it? It's part of what *you're* doing too, isn't it? Your 'Looking Glass killer.'"

"Yes."

"Why?"

"Miss Price, we don't have—"

"What don't we have? Time?"

"Precisely."

"Well, you're going to make time. Because you have to. Because I'm the only way to get to Desmond. As of right now, I can have you confined to this facility."

"Don't be dramatic."

"I'm not. I'm tired of being a pawn in your games. Yuri's and Desmond's too. I'm tired of not knowing what's going on. You're going to tell me what Rendition is and why you need it—or you're not leaving this facility."

Lin broke eye contact. "Very well. Rendition was the last piece of the Looking Glass constructed. And arguably the most complex.

It was Desmond's project and life's work, as you likely know, given how close the two of you became." Lin studied Avery for a second, but the younger woman said nothing. "I want it for a very different reason than Yuri."

For the next ten minutes, Lin told Avery what the reason was, and what the Looking Glass was, and her alternative—the Rabbit Hole, she called it. It was driven by a particle accelerator about fifty miles from the Dallas area.

"That's where you sent the samples—and Peyton. To the accelerator?"

"Correct."

"When you say we need to rendezvous with Desmond, you mean..."

"You and I, Miss Price."

"Not Nigel, or Adams, or Rodriguez."

Lin nodded.

"Because one of them let Yuri loose," Avery said. "Or one of us. Or Peyton."

"It's only logical to leave them here," Lin said. "You and I will go."

In her mind's eye, Avery saw herself descending from the plane, Desmond waiting on the tarmac. It would be so different from their reunion on the *Kentaro Maru*. And with Yuri still at large, looming, no doubt searching for Desmond, a final conflict was likely. It could be her last chance to see him.

Peyton's last opportunity, too.

Avery considered that. Peyton had helped save Avery's life on the Isle of Citium. And despite their past disagreements, Peyton had always been straight with her. The woman deserved to see Desmond again, especially if it was her last chance, just like Avery's. Avery owed that to her—and to Desmond, no matter which one of them he chose.

"We're taking Peyton with us."

"No—"

"She comes along or you don't. Decide."

CHAPTER 60

DESMOND AWOKE LESS sore and groggy than before. The plane was dropping. Through the oval windows he saw a line of steel-and-glass buildings: dark tombstones in an urban graveyard. Desert beyond. Not Oklahoma City. He forced himself to move, up, off the couch, through the cabin and to the cockpit door, which was closed.

He threw it open and found David Ward at the controls, steering the small craft toward two rows of glowing lights.

"What are you doing?"

"Landing. Shut up."

"This isn't Oklahoma."

"Really? We'll have to fire the navigator."

Desmond slipped into the co-pilot seat. "I didn't realize you were so funny."

Through the windshield, Desmond saw a combination of things that made no sense to him: a pyramid, a pirate ship, and a volcano. It was like an escaped mental patient had taken all the things that fascinated him and put them on one street.

He realized a second later where he was: Vegas. But it was dark, the neon jungle deprived of power.

A few minutes later, the plane's wheels caught traction on the runway and the aircraft shuddered.

Ward unlatched his buckle.

Desmond followed suit. "What's the plan?"

"Follow me." Ward got up and walked back to the cabin.

"I'd rather not."

"You're a real pain, Hughes, you know that?"

"Yes, I know."

"I'll tell you what I know. I know I'm not a super genius like you and your brother. I'm just a lawyer who got pissed that the low-level criminals always got locked up and the super bad guy masterminds—like you—always got away with it. I know I'm in over my head. All of us are. We just work here—for the people of the United States. But I also know that *even I* would be smart enough to plan for the *possibility* that you might escape."

"A tracking device."

"Exactly."

Desmond got up. "Good call, Agent."

A convoy of SUVs was waiting on the tarmac, men and women fanned out around them, wearing suits and military uniforms.

They loaded up and raced through the city. From the back seat, Desmond gazed out the windows in shock. The place was a neon graveyard, an urban theme park gone dark and silent. Trash littered the street. Papers blew in the wind like tumbleweeds. It was his first glimpse of the post-X1 pandemic world.

"Where is everyone?"

Ward didn't make eye contact. "Hunkered down at home, in the shelters, some dead. Everybody's waiting."

"For what?"

"Whatever comes next. Some sign that the world is safe again. Or what the next crisis is."

At Sunrise Hospital, they ushered Desmond into a room with no windows and loaded him onto a table that slid into a large machine. Desmond didn't ask what the machine was, just lay there inside it until it was done with whatever it was doing.

The doctors and technicians came in, Ward behind them. An older doctor spoke for the group. He was slender and bald, with an impeccable tan and an unlined face. "There are two implants." He held up a scan showing a bone and a white oblong object. "The larger is in your upper thigh, close to your femur, likely inserted—"

"Can you remove it?"

The doctor was annoyed at being interrupted. "We can."

"Do it."

The doctor turned to Ward. "We'll need to put him under general anesthesia—"

"No." Desmond sat up on the table. "I've been under for days. I need a clear head."

"Mister Hughes, we'll be making a small incision through the adductor magnus—"

"I don't care. Use a local anesthetic."

"It will be painful. And we need you to be still—movement could be deadly. There's an important artery close by—"

"Let's get on with it." A thought occurred to Desmond. "You said there were two implants."

The doctor pulled out another scan, this one of a foot. "I believe we were meant to find the one in your thigh. It's in plain sight, and as I said, quite large. This one is far smaller and presents on an X-ray as a bone spur, which are somewhat common in the feet."

That was smart, something Conner would do. "Okay. I'm ready."

"Mister Hughes, the pain—"

"I can handle. Strap me down. Do whatever you have to. Just don't sedate me."

They led him to an OR with two beds, like what might be used for a transplant. The doctors worked quickly, taking the implant in the foot first. Desmond grimaced and Ward looked on impassively. They removed the small device, cleaned it, and showed it to Desmond. It was white on the outside, the color of bone.

A young man with a buzz cut, wearing a blue hospital gown and nothing else, walked through the swinging doors.

Ward stood. "On the table, Corporal."

The young man lay down on the second table and looked up at the overhead lights. A second team of doctors numbed his foot, made an incision, and began inserting the implant.

Desmond's doctors went slower for the larger implant. As promised, it hurt—a lot. Tears rolled down Desmond's face as they pulled out the oblong metal pill, but he didn't make a sound. He knew they were done when he heard the device hit a metal pan with a clink. The doctor nodded to him, and a younger doctor took his place to close the incision.

To Ward, the doctor said, "We will be placing the corporal under general anesthesia and beginning the operation as soon as you all clear the room."

"Understood."

When the incision was sealed and the bandage was firmly in place, Desmond rolled off the table. He grunted, the tender muscles protesting. Before limping out of the OR, he paused to look at the corporal lying on the table. Desmond felt like he should say something, but couldn't find the words. So he just nodded to the man, a silent acknowledgment of his bravery.

A new plane was waiting on the tarmac—a larger one, with Air Force insignia and two dozen camo-clad soldiers wearing body armor in the belly. They had Delta Force patches on their shoulders.

They assembled in a small briefing room behind the cockpit. An Army lieutenant colonel stood at the head of the table, a major, and a master sergeant at his side.

"Mister Hughes, I'm Lieutenant Colonel Nathan Andrews. Those are my men out there. And I need to know what we're walking into."

Desmond told them, and the colonel shook his head in disbelief.

"Sir," Desmond continued, "I suspect your men will see their share of action on this mission. But it won't be on the next stop. I'm fairly certain of that."

☣

They landed at Will Rogers World Airport in Oklahoma City, where more troops were waiting. And enough land combat vehicles to fight a war.

Desmond walked down the plane's ramp, Ward at his side. The sun was rising, the late December, early morning air cool on his skin. A faint puff of white fog left his mouth as he made his way toward the waiting SUVs.

The troops parted as he approached.

"There's somebody who wants to see you," Ward said.

Desmond assumed it was another meeting about the approach to the site. He was wrong.

A door opened on a vehicle at the head of the convoy. Desmond stopped in his tracks.

Avery stood on the tarmac, her blue eyes shining in the faint light of dawn. She wore military fatigues with no service branch or rank insignia, body armor over her torso and legs, and a rifle muzzle protruded at an angle from her back, like a sword sheathed on a medieval knight.

She didn't smile. She studied him, waiting for his reaction, her face a mask, seemingly like a dam about to break. Seeing her here wasn't like before—when they had met on the *Kentaro Maru*. Then she was just a woman he didn't know.

He knew her now, deep down inside, even the parts of her she hid from the world. She was brave and capable and strong in a way very few are. And more, she was a woman he had once loved. Still loved.

He remembered everything about her now—the hung-over girl he had carried up those stairs and into her apartment. Someone he had been happy with. His face must have revealed his recognition, because she blinked, exhaled, and smiled—relieved, happy. Her shoulders sagged as if the tension were flowing out of her.

He walked toward her, eyes locked, no idea what he was going to do. Hug her? Shake hands? Or just talk. Or kiss her? The romantic options would likely draw whistles and catcalls from the troops around them. The Avery he knew wouldn't care. What he didn't know was how she felt about *him*.

And there was Peyton to think about.

As soon as the thought came into his mind, the rear doors opened on a Suburban behind Avery, and two women stepped out. They were mirrors of each other, one older. Peyton on the right, Lin on the left.

Unlike Avery, Peyton's face wasn't a mask. She smiled at Desmond, and he saw moisture fill her eyes. He felt his own eyes cloud, and he squinted, trying to hold it back. A month ago, in the mess hall on the *Boxer*, they had made a promise to each other: that if they lived, they would start over—together. He was so certain then about what he wanted. He wasn't now. It was as if he had rediscovered Avery, and she was someone he cared about too.

In the first light of morning, in the cruel land where he had grown up, the two women stood on opposite sides, like book-ends, which he found fitting: Peyton was the anchor in his life before the Citium, Avery his joy and lifeline after. If he stood there for a thousand years he could never have chosen which woman to walk to first. They were in different categories, like forces of nature with no analog or comparison, both drawing him to them.

Fittingly, Lin Shaw walked between the two women. She had always been in the center of it all—she alone was the tie that bound all of them: Peyton, Desmond, Avery, and Yuri. And perhaps only she knew how it all would end.

The older woman seemed to sense the standoff. She walked to Desmond, gripped his shoulders, and smiled.

"It's good to see you, Desmond."

He nodded. "You too. I took your advice."

She raised an eyebrow.

"I did something no one would expect."

"That you did."

Avery and Peyton converged at the same time. Without thinking, Desmond held his arms out to both of them. As the two women reached him, Lin let her hands slip off his shoulders and stepped back, allowing Peyton and Avery to fall into the hug. Desmond squeezed tight, felt their arms reach around his back. They met, overlapping at first and then sliding next to each other.

Lin studied him for reactions, perhaps a clue about whom he would choose.

"Let's catch up en route," Ward said.

CHAPTER 61

THE CONVOY BARRELED through the deserted streets. First on I-240 East, then south on I-35. Deserted cars sat on the shoulder, some pushed into the guardrail where the X1 troops had cleared a path.

A Marine lieutenant drove. Ward sat in the passenger seat, Desmond and Lin in the back seat, and Peyton and Avery squeezed into the third row.

The signs for the exits for Norman, Oklahoma, reminded Desmond of Agnes.

"You want to tell us what the note means?" Ward asked.

The convoy took the next exit and turned onto Highway 9.

"No."

Ward exhaled heavily. He drew a copy of the note from inside his suit and read it aloud. "It lies in the bend, where blood turned to water and darkness turned to light."

Desmond waited. No one spoke. Peyton was the only one in the vehicle who might know what it meant. He could never reveal the details of the cryptic message—that would implicate him in a crime.

They drove through the outskirts of Noble, the small town he had visited so much as a child. Past the city, Desmond called to the driver, "The turn is up here."

They stopped at a gate to a pasture, opened it, and let the armored troop carriers proceed first. When they gave the all-clear, the SUVs moved in.

Desmond exited, and the group fell in behind him. He knew that he had been here at least twice in his life, although he could only remember the first time. It had been the darkest day of his life—a day when the darkness of his childhood and teens turned to light. That day he had killed a man and buried him here. He had washed the blood off in the Canadian river, letting the fresh, cool water carry away the last drops of evidence. He had driven west afterward, out of Oklahoma, to Silicon Valley. His life turned from darkness to light. He met Peyton a few months later.

He glanced back and found her staring at him, a look of solidarity that said, *I'll never tell what happened here—and I'm with you, no matter what you find.* He took a step forward, then another.

It was clever: hiding whatever he had here. He was the only person in the world who knew where this was. The exact location was etched in his brain like a bloodstain he couldn't wash out.

He paused at the gravesite. Grass had grown over it in the nineteen years since he had dug the hole, but Desmond knew that Dale Epply's body was there, right under the feet of the FBI and CIA agents surrounding him.

He walked past it, down to the river where he had cleansed himself. He saw it in the bend, just where the note had said it would be: loose dirt packed in a freshly dug hole, no larger than two feet in diameter at the top.

"I need a shovel."

"Negative, Hughes." Ward turned to the lieutenant. "Dig it up. Let's move back. Two-hundred-foot perimeter."

Desmond didn't fight them, he simply waited at the top of the hill.

The shovel clinked as it hit metal, and the soldier, wearing bomb gear, carefully reached down and used his hands to dig the object out. It was a round coffee can. The plastic lid was duct taped shut.

"Get the robot!"

"Ward, it's not an IED—"

"How do you know, Hughes? You remember putting it here? Didn't think so."

They watched the robot's activity on a laptop screen at the back of the Suburban. The robot's tracks halted just short of the can. Its metal arms extended, gripped the can, and peeled off the tape and the plastic lid. Its camera revealed the can's contents: a Ziploc bag holding a smartphone.

"The phone could be a bomb," Ward said.

A bomb tech standing beside him worked the robot's controls remotely. He opened the bag and, with some effort, using the robot's fingers, turned the sat phone on.

It wasn't password protected, and the home screen was unremarkable—except for the icon for the Labyrinth Reality app.

"This is a Labyrinth location," Desmond said.

Ward rubbed his temple. "What do you want to do here?"

"Really only one thing *to* do."

Desmond started down the hill, but stopped and turned when he heard footsteps behind him.

"Avery—"

"I'm coming with you."

"It could still be a bomb."

"I'll use you as a human shield."

He laughed and shook his head.

Peyton began toward them. Desmond held up his hand, but she kept coming.

"What's up?" she asked.

"Nothing," Desmond said. "We'll be right back."

"I'm coming too."

He glanced at the morning sun for a moment, knowing he was between a rock and a hard place. "All right then."

At the robot, he made them stay back ten feet while he picked up the phone. He opened the Labyrinth Reality app, and a prompt asked him if he wanted to join a private Labyrinth or a public space. He clicked private and entered the pass code he had memorized.

A message appeared.

Welcome to the Hall of Shadows Private Labyrinth.

Two icons appeared. To the left was a beast with the head of a bull and the body of a man. To the right was a warrior. And a question written below.

Declare yourself: Minotaur or Hero

The first time he had seen this prompt, that night in Berlin, Desmond truly hadn't know what he was. Now he did. It was fitting for him to answer the question here, in the field where he had buried Dale. He had done a monstrous thing that day—but he had been forced to. It was the same with the Citium. He understood now why he had picked this place. It was a final reminder to himself to stay the course. He might have to do terrible things, but there was light ahead.

Desmond knew what he was: the hero. He was the man he had hoped he was when he first entered the Labyrinth. And he had hidden Rendition to stop a monster: Yuri. Now it was time to find the Minotaur and slay him.

He clicked the icon, and another message appeared.

Searching for entrance...

And shortly after:

1 Entrance Located.
Labyrinth Entrance Reached
Downloading...

"It's starting, isn't it?" Peyton said. The wind was tugging at her dark hair. Her porcelain face looked so delicate and innocent here in the shade of the copse of trees by the river.

"Yes."

"Let's get back to the convoy," Avery said.

They hiked together, out of the woods and up the hill. The sun seemed to grow brighter with each step, as though they were all walking out of the darkness together. All three knew the past now, and their history together, and soon the world would turn to light—or, if they failed, to darkness.

At the Suburban, the phone buzzed and a message appeared.

Download Complete

To Ward, Desmond said, "Let's go."

"Where?"

"The airport."

"Then where?"

"Hopefully I'll know by the time we get there."

☣

In the memory, Desmond was once again at the hangar in San Carlos. Avery was at his side, fighting for him, arguing that releasing him was their only chance. David Ward led the opposing argument, insisting that letting a criminal go was ill-advised.

But Avery was tenacious and unrelenting, her verbal volleys as powerful as her serve in the racquetball court. She wore down her opposition, and they finally threw in the towel. She had done it, just like he'd known she could.

But that meant that if his plan didn't work, she would share some of the blame—and he needed to shield her from that. Plan for the possibility that he would fail. He took a pad from the table, thought for a moment, and wrote a single line.

He stood and approached David Ward. "Can I speak with you? In private?"

The man grunted, but followed Desmond to a corner of the warehouse out of earshot of the other agents.

"How soon can you build the tunnel?"

"How should I know, Hughes?"

"Please do it as soon as you can. I don't know when I'll need it."

"Is that it?"

"No. I want you to be there—"

"You've got a hell of lot of nerve, you know that? Telling me to be there like you're in charge now? Like—"

"I'm not telling you, Ward. I'm asking you. Please. Be there. I don't know how this is going to go. But that's my backup plan. And I need somebody there that I trust."

Ward smiled skeptically. "You trust *me*? You don't even know me."

"True, I don't. But she trusts you, and I trust her, so I trust you."

Ward stared.

"And she trusts *me*, which, by the way, is a reason why *you* should trust me."

"I've been doing this a while, Hughes. Long enough to see agents fall in love with their marks and get turned around."

"She's not turned around. And I'm not what you think I am. You'll see that before this is over." He handed Ward the page. "Here. If I show up in that tunnel, please promise me you'll give me this. And that you won't show it to another soul."

Ward read the line. "What is this, your favorite poem? A location?"

"Please. Promise me."

"Screw you—"

"This is part of the deal."

"I didn't like the deal before, why would I agree to more?"

"Because you know she'll fight you to the end, and so will I, and deep down, you know this is our best shot. You just don't like it. I don't like it either. Promise me, Ward."

The agent shook his head and folded the page, then tucked it in his inside coat pocket. "Yeah, I pinky swear."

Despite the sarcasm, that was good enough for Desmond. He walked to Avery and said, "You ready?"

She nodded.

They drove to her place, and she packed a bag while he paced between the living room and kitchen, talking non-stop, trying to think of anything that might help her.

"Yuri's an expert at reading people. If you come into contact with him, don't lie. If you have to, mix it with truth and be ready to run. Conner's an expert strategist and tactician. If you go up against him, don't go for your first plan. Dig deep, reach for something unexpected—"

Avery leaned her head out of the bedroom. "Des, I know all this. I've been studying these guys for years."

"Right. Okay. What else? On the ship, whatever you do, don't contact Rubicon or try to contact me. They'll be monitoring—"

She walked out of the bedroom wearing only a pair of slacks and a bra. She gripped him by the shoulders. "Des. Relax."

"Relax?"

"Okay. One of us has training for deep-cover, covert counter-intelligence operations. It's not you." She looked up at the ceiling as if grasping for the answer. "So that leaves…"

"Yeah, well, I get that. I just need to be doing something to help."

She reached into the bedroom and picked up a duffel bag. "You can carry my bag."

He took it from her, his hand closing over hers. Their eyes met.

"If something happens to you…"

She blinked. Her chest rose and fell faster, but her voice was even, almost a whisper. "Nothing's going to happen to me."

He let the bag fall to the floor and slipped his hand behind her neck, into her blonde hair, and pulled her close, kissing her with force, his hand moving to her side, up her stomach and under the bra.

She walked backward, through the minefield of clothes and shoes on her bedroom floor. She was naked by the time she fell into the bed. She spread her legs and he moved into her, and they made love quickly and passionately and forcefully, like two people trying to tell each other something without words, in the language of sex, never breaking eye contact. Sweat formed on their bodies as they rolled, him on top, then her, and finally both face down, her below him, both panting like wild animals, the tension gone.

"I needed that," he whispered.

"Yeah," she breathed.

She got up and spent a few minutes in the bathroom, then returned and dressed quickly.

Somehow, he felt about a million times better: more relaxed, more ready to confront the uncertainty that lay ahead.

The pier was dark, lit only by the moon and the pole lights, both overpowered by the fog and the dark.

He parked, but neither opened their doors. He tried to find the words he wanted to say. She looked down at the floorboard and fiddled with the zipper on her North Face jacket.

"Let's make a promise."

"Des."

"Not that kind of promise. A... plan. A date." He smiled. "Yes, I said it. After this is over, we're going to go away together. A trip to somewhere neither of us has ever been. No work. No global conspiracies. Just me and you, having fun. And sorting out what we are."

She took his hand. "Sorry, but I'd kind of like to keep my options open after this. Never know who I'll meet on the ship."

He opened his mouth to speak, but she cut him off. "Kidding. It sounds good to me. I could use a slowdown."

☣

When Avery had boarded the massive freighter, Desmond drew out his phone and dialed the lead developer for Rendition. He arranged an emergency meeting at a hotel. He couldn't risk going to the Rendition offices, or those of any Citium company. He called three other developers on team—everyone who could re-create the technology—and invited them as well. They were the last loose end he had to tie up.

CHAPTER 62

TO YURI'S SURPRISE, the escape from Spain happened without incident. There were no helicopters combing the countryside, and the guards at the Bilbao airport were bribe-able—diamonds still held their sparkle for those of loose morals, especially with governments and their currencies falling out of favor. People were looking for portable wealth, with intrinsic value anywhere they went.

The call he had waited for, the event that could save his cause, came when he was in the air off the coast of Spain.

For the first time since he had been working with her, Yuri heard relief in Melissa Whitmeyer's voice. "Rapture is online."

"All capabilities?"

"Affirmative. They just tested it on subjects here."

Yuri took in the view of the ocean below. They had done it. They had control now. Nothing could stop him. It was only a matter of time.

"Should we take down tier one targets?"

"No. Not yet. Launch the mesh first. Call me when it's done."

☣

Around the world, warehouses in rural areas rolled up their doors. Auto-launchers rolled out, onto the concrete and asphalt parking lots. They looked like giant rolling scaffolding machines.

They were forty-five feet wide, fifty feet tall, and forty feet long, with rubber tires roughly five feet tall, capable of turning independently. Thick steel columns rose into the air at each corner.

At the site in Lexington, Virginia, a technician used a tablet to drive the giant machine. When it was in place, he pressed a green button, and on three sides of the launcher, partitions descended—thick, white panels that would block the wind. The machine was programmed to track wind movement and turn so that its open side was downwind, the three partitions protecting its fragile contents.

The technicians inserted the package, and the first balloon began growing inside the launcher. The balloon's fabric was nearly translucent. As it took shape and reached toward the sky, it looked like a giant jellyfish about to take flight.

Twenty minutes later, the launcher released the balloon, and it floated free, toward the clouds. Hanging below it was a photovoltaic solar cell and a series of patch antennas capable of connecting to internet devices on the ground.

The balloons launched one after another every twenty minutes and drifted high into the sky, reaching the stratosphere eleven miles above sea level. They would stay in constant contact with each other and base stations around the world as they circumnavigated the globe. They could stay aloft for over three months, but their job would likely be done long before then. When the Looking Glass event was over, they would make a controlled descent to Earth and be retired, artifacts of the moment when the world changed forever.

CHAPTER 63

DESMOND WAITED NERVOUSLY in the hotel suite. One by one, the Rendition developers arrived and took a seat in the living room. There were three men and a woman, all in their twenties and thirties, two looking a little sleepy, one wired and still holding a Red Bull, and the last a little tipsy (some of the Rendition team had been taking much-needed down time since the completion).

"I'm sorry to call you all so late. I had no choice. I believe Rendition may soon be used by someone with all the wrong intentions."

The lead developer was an Indian-American named Raghav.

"Used to do what?" he asked.

"To hurt people. To control them."

The four developers looked confused.

"How?" Raghav asked.

Desmond stood and walked to the floor-to-ceiling windows. "I'm sorry, I can't tell you the details right now. Things are in motion. I need you to trust me. And I need your help. It won't be easy. It may be dangerous. I'm sorry, but I need each of you to answer right now. In or out. Will you help me?"

Confusion turned to worry.

The female developer, Melanie Lewis, said, "What exactly are you asking us to do?"

"We need to move Rendition. And you all need to hide."

Melanie shook her head. "Why should we hide?"

A heavyset developer named Langford sat next to her, drinking his Red Bull. He rolled his eyes. "It's obvious: when Rendition is gone, they'll come looking for us."

"Hide where?" Raghav asked.

Desmond sat back down. "That's the thing."

They all waited.

He searched for the words, rehearsed them in his mind. "It has to be somewhere they won't think to look. Somewhere safe. Off the grid."

Melanie bunched her eyebrows. "Like... what? Alaska?"

"I was thinking somewhere colder." Desmond inhaled. "Through Icarus Capital, I invest in a lot of companies. One is called Charter Antarctica. It's a combination of a cruise ship company and theme park."

"Antarctica?" Raghav said, shocked.

"Nice," Langford said. "Dude, you should have just led with the Antarctica part."

"I hate the cold," Melanie muttered.

The other developer, a redhead name Kevin, looked concerned. "I don't understand. Who's going to come looking for us?" He paused, but no one responded. "Government? Mafia?"

"It's no one like that," Desmond said. "It's someone who needs Rendition for an experiment. They're scientists, but I've recently learned they can be very ruthless."

"How long will we need to hide?" Kevin asked. "Months? Years?"

"*Years?*" Melanie echoed.

"What're we going to eat?" Langford asked. "Seals? Penguins? I'm not eating fish for a year—"

"Seals aren't fish," Melanie said. "They're mammals, you idiot."

"And penguins are birds," Kevin added. "But no way I'm eating them. Or dolphins. Whales, either." Before Melanie could say anything he shot her a look. "And yes, I know they're mammals."

Desmond held up his hands. "Nobody's eating any of that."

"How's it going to work, Des?" Raghav asked, clearly trying to focus the conversation.

"There's a small outpost, for the construction workers. They're building a hotel a few miles away. An ice hotel. Solar powered with geothermal heat."

Langford's eyes went wide. "Nice."

"The construction crews can only work in the summer—that's winter here. It's a small staff, maybe twelve people."

"Is the hotel close to being complete?" Raghav asked. "Can people live there yet?"

"I'm not sure. I'm only on the board and haven't gotten an update recently. The construction workers' habitat has plenty of room though."

"We'll I'm in," Langford said. "I'll even eat penguin."

"Me too," Kevin said. "Well, except for the penguin part."

"What if we don't go?" Melanie asked. Then, tentatively, she added, "Unless you're saying we have to—"

"I'm not," Desmond said quickly. "I'm hoping you will, though. If you don't, I strongly urge you to go into hiding somewhere else. You can't take your cell phone. No internet. No email. No calls."

Raghav looked at Melanie. "I'm going. And I think we need to stay together."

She nodded. "Okay."

They made arrangements after that. None of the four developers were married, but Raghav lived with his girlfriend, and Melanie had a sister in San Francisco. Desmond agreed that they could bring whomever they wanted, as long as they could leave tonight.

The four left, packed, and met Desmond at the harbor in Santa Cruz just before sunrise.

Raghav walked up to Desmond and dropped his bag. "What do we do when we get there?"

Desmond had spent the time after the hotel extracting the Rendition server and software from the office. It sat in a crate on the dock.

"How you pass the time is up to you. One request: don't set up a satellite connection or use a phone. Just in case."

"Okay." Raghav glanced uncertainly at the boat. It was thirty years old, but recently retrofit. It was a research and survey vessel, seventy feet long, with a crew of five, births for sixteen, and enough food and water for the trip. The hold was more than large enough for the Rendition equipment. It wouldn't win any races, or awards for luxury—but it also wouldn't draw much attention.

Desmond had considered chartering a private flight to the small landing strip at the construction site, but that would have left a paper trail. The boat was the best play. The captain owned the vessel and rented it mostly to universities and researchers in the bay area. He had agreed to stay at the Antarctica facility until Desmond arrived—at a cost of four thousand dollars per day. Desmond had paid him two hundred thousand up front for the trip and agreed to settle up at the end. The man was eager to get under way.

"There's one more thing," Desmond said to Raghav. "I'm going to Berlin next. I'll be meeting with a scientist named Manfred Jung. Jung is going to help me alter my Rapture implant."

"Okay."

"Afterwards, I believe Jung and his team might become a target —like you and yours. So I'm going to send them to the Charter Antarctica construction camp as well. Keep an eye out for them."

"Sure."

"And take care, Raghav. I'll see you soon."

☣

From the dock, Desmond watched the boat slip out of view. Somewhere else in the Pacific, Avery was sailing away, waiting for him.

The last few hours had been exhausting. The ships had sailed, but Desmond's work had just begun. He took out his mobile phone and dialed the number he had found earlier that night.

"Mister Meyer, my name is Desmond Hughes. I want to talk to you about your article. About the Citium."

"What about it?"

"You're right. It's a conspiracy. But you've only scratched the surface. I'm going to give you the biggest story of your life. Perhaps the biggest story in history…"

CHAPTER 64

THE JET WAS old, a little worn, but it ran well and had everything Yuri needed. He sat in a plush leather chair at a table, his laptop open, a map with a tracking dot on the screen.

It hadn't moved in hours.

Oklahoma City. Was that where Desmond had hidden it? Yuri counted that as unlikely.

His phone rang. Citium Central Ops.

Melissa Whitmeyer began her report without preamble. "Balloons are deployed."

"Coverage?"

"Combined with the existing internet infrastructure, we're at 72 percent globally. Over 90 percent in our primary nations."

Yuri exhaled. His moment was at hand. "Begin."

Whitmeyer paused. "I need you to—"

"To say it?" Yuri didn't blame her. "This is your official order, Miss Whitmeyer. Begin the Looking Glass transfer for vulnerable populations. You are also to target and execute our tier one adversaries."

"Confirmed."

"And when that's done, issue a message to their replacements: turn over Desmond Hughes, Lin Shaw, and Peyton Shaw—or you will meet the same fate."

CHAPTER 65

DESMOND AWOKE ON the floor, on top of a camouflaged sleeping bag. The air smelled of stale beer and fried food. He looked around. He was in a pub, the Cross Grain Brewhouse. It had a long bar with a brick wall and TVs, all of which were off. Two dozen wood-topped tables filled the place, condiments and rolls of paper towels sitting on top. Tall glass windows looked out on the runways of Will Rogers Airport.

Lin, Peyton, Avery, and David Ward sat at one of the tables, talking quietly, concerned looks on their faces, like a family in a hospital waiting room, anticipating news about a loved one's surgery.

Desmond sat up. Avery saw him first. She bolted out of the chair and was at his side in seconds, her hand around the back of his neck, helping him up.

"You all right?"

"Yeah. Just... still groggy and sore from the wringer Conner put me through."

Lin, Peyton, and Ward joined them.

"What happened?" Ward asked.

"In private," Desmond said.

Ward turned and led them through the airport, which was teeming with activity—troops and FEMA and federal and state agency personnel barreling through the corridors, the gates turned into makeshift briefing rooms. Desmond caught clips and phrases as they passed by: *containment, armed and dangerous, further rationing, improvised attacks.*

"What's going on?" Desmond asked.

Ward didn't look back. "The natives are getting restless." A few steps later, he added, "If you *can* stop these people, you need to do it now, Hughes."

Avery glanced at him, a question in her eyes. *Can you?*

He gave a solemn nod, and wondered if he believed it. Rendition was his life's work. It was Yuri's key to finishing the Looking Glass—a project Desmond had thought he wanted at one time. But he was willing to destroy it now—if it meant saving Avery, and Peyton, and so many others, even if it doomed Conner to the miserable life he desperately wanted to escape.

Ward led them past the Southwest Airlines ticket desk, into a room marked "YMCA Military Welcome Center." Men and women in uniform sat at round picnic tables, eating from paper plates, drinking tea and water from Styrofoam cups. In a small room off the welcome center, Ward closed the door and sat at a conference table.

"We're secure here."

"I remember," Desmond said.

"Rendition?" Lin asked quickly.

"Yes. I remember creating it, and where I hid it."

"Out with it, Hughes," Ward muttered.

"Antarctica."

Ward leaned back in the folding metal chair, pushing it onto two legs, and let his head fall back. He stared at the ceiling and then closed his eyes. "You have *got* to be kidding me."

"Explain," Lin said, her voice even, lacking Ward's frustration.

"One of my portfolio companies. Charter Antarctica. We were building a hotel there when the X1 pandemic broke out. I sent Rendition there on a private boat—along with all four programmers who could re-create it. And the Rapture scientist who altered my implant."

"So," Avery said. "We go there, destroy Rendition, and this is all over. The Looking Glass won't work without it."

"Exactly," Desmond said.

"You didn't destroy your creation before," Ward said. "When you could have. Why should I believe you'll do it now?"

"Because now I've seen what they're capable of. And what's at stake."

"You knew the stakes before—"

"This is pointless," Lin said. "Desmond is the only one who can take us to Rendition."

"Us?" Ward smiled. "There is no *us*. You and your daughter are staying here."

"That would put you at a disadvantage."

Ward raised an eyebrow. "Meaning?"

"No one alive knows Yuri Pachenko better than I do. I prevented a bloodbath at the Isle of Citium."

"And then you took us on a wild goose chase to the North Pole. We lost a lot of people up there and got basically nothing in return. No way we're going for a South Pole repeat."

"Apples and oranges, Mister Ward."

Avery held up her hands. "Stop it."

The room fell silent. Outside, Desmond could hear shouting. Boots pounding the floor, a stampede.

Avery pulled the door open. The welcome center was emptying, the troops leaving plates of barbecue and beans half-eaten, cups of tea still full.

"Something's wrong," Lin said.

They rushed out of the room, past the ticket counters and into the main concourse. There was a large projection screen set up at gate eighteen. It showed imagery from several drones from around the country, and perhaps around the world, judging by the varying amounts of sunlight. Balloons floated through the clouds. There were no baskets below. Each balloon carried only a solar cell with three panels and some kind of small metal device.

Ward grabbed a major in the Oklahoma National Guard by the upper arm. "What's happening?"

"Don't know. They just started appearing all over the world."

"So what? Why's everyone panicking?"

The man gritted his teeth. "We aren't panicking, sir. We've been activated. And people are dying."

Peyton stepped forward. "Who's dying?"

"Sick, mostly. Terminally ill," the major replied.

Desmond saw Avery's face fill with concern.

Another wave of discussion went through the troops gathered around the screen, a rumor spreading like a virus.

Desmond listened closely, and his mouth went dry when he realized what they were saying. The president of the United States was dead. Cerebral hemorrhage. So was the governor of Oklahoma—and every other state in the union.

A sergeant ran up to the major. "Sir, Colonel Weathers needs to see you right now."

The major left without another word.

Lin stepped into his place. "Mister Ward, we need to go, right now."

Ward shook his head.

She stepped closer to him and spoke quietly but with force. "Listen to me. Those balloons are Citium devices. Together with the internet, they are accessing Rapture nanites—the 'cure' you and your government distributed to stop the X_1 pandemic. *They* are in control now. And Yuri's next move will be to demand that the government hand us over. We need to go, the five us, alone. Right now."

CHAPTER 66

DESMOND'S EYES MET Peyton's, and he saw fear in them. That energized him. Her mother's words had rattled her. They needed to move.

"Ward, listen to her," he said.

Avery turned her head toward the end of the concourse, like a predator sensing a threat. Ten National Guard troops in camo were marching toward them. They passed deserted shops as they drew closer: Coffee Bean and Tea Leaf, Harold's Shoe Shine, EA Sports, CNBC.

Desmond got Avery's attention. "What's the best way out?"

"Lower level. Follow me."

Just like that, the decision was made. Avery broke from the group and began running, Lin behind her, then Peyton. Desmond glared at Ward, who shook his head.

One of the National Guardsmen called out, "Agent Ward!"

His voice echoed in the tall concourse, the sound bouncing off glass walls and hard floors.

Eyes turned to them.

Desmond and Ward joined the fleeing group.

Avery was almost to the escalator.

"Agent Ward! We need to speak with you!"

Avery took the stairs three at a time, prancing down the inactive escalator like a cat scaling a mountainside. Peyton and Lin struggled to keep up.

"Halt!"

Desmond pulled ahead of Ward, then paused to let him catch up.

Other troops were stirring now, joining the unit chasing them. Orders were called out, the meaning clear: stop them.

At the bottom of the escalator, he just glimpsed Avery barreling through an emergency exit beyond the baggage claim. Lin and Peyton were trailing far behind, and Desmond and Ward soon caught up with them. The four of them burst onto the tarmac together, a gust of cold wind greeting them.

Avery was already climbing the stairs to a Gulfstream jet, and the engines were running by the time the others reached it and pulled the staircase in.

The tarmac filled with troops as the jet taxied down the runway, but they didn't shoot. A fuel truck raced out and blocked the runway. Avery turned the jet and raced down another.

As the jet took off and gained altitude, Desmond looked across the aisle to find Peyton looking at him, worry in her expression. He wondered if he could protect her.

The laptop beeped. The tracking application displayed a message:

Target in Motion

Yuri watched the dot move away from Will Rogers Airport, southward.

He grabbed his sat phone and called Conner.

"It's begun. We need to meet."

Next he called Melissa Whitmeyer. "I need to know if there are any Rapture devices on that plane we can control."

CHAPTER 67

"TURN YOUR PHONES off!" Lin yelled.

All eyes turned to her.

"Do it! Right now. Your life may depend on it."

It turned out only Ward and Avery had phones. Both turned them off.

"Happy?" Ward said.

"I did that to protect you."

Ward got out of his chair and moved up the aisle, stopping at Desmond's chair, looming over him, still breathing hard from the frantic escape from the airport.

"Answers, Hughes. Right now."

"You'll get them." Desmond stood and brushed past the burly man. "First things first."

Avery was in the cockpit, holding her side, breathing hard and talking with air traffic control, trying to convince them it was all a big mistake, that she didn't in fact have Lin and Peyton Shaw and Desmond Hughes on board.

"Hey," Desmond whispered.

She glanced back and held her hand tighter to her side. He saw blood oozing out around it.

"You okay?" He stepped forward and took a closer look. There was a bandage over her abdomen. It was pink in the center and dark red at the edges.

"I'm fine. Just pulled a stitch."

"You're not *fine*."

"I am, Des. Relax. I just overexerted myself."

"You were shot?"

"Shrapnel from a bomb on the Isle."

He studied her. "That was a heck of a leap from the second story."

"Didn't have much choice. Thanks for covering me."

He smiled. "I'd cover you any time."

She deadpanned. "You wish."

He laughed. "Right."

She jerked her head and shouted into the radio. "Negative, OKC ATC, we cannot land at Chandler Field."

To him, she said, "What do you need?"

"Fuel and range?"

"Fully fueled. We'll get maybe sixty-five hundred miles, depending on how fast we push her."

The Charter Antarctica base camp was too far. "We'll have to refuel."

She worked the navigation system. "We need to get out of US airspace quickly. And probably avoid Mexico and Brazil."

"Best option?"

"Get to the Gulf..."

"And fly around South America?"

"Take too long," Avery said. "Where's your site in Antarctica?"

"Due south from Cape Town."

Avery studied the map. "We'll fly south through the Gulf and cross to the Pacific at Panama. We'll skirt the western edge of South America, go over the Andes, and land at Mar del Plata."

"What about Buenos Aires?"

"I don't favor it. More people, more military presence—and more likelihood of being captured."

"Right. What's the total distance on the flight path to Mar del Plata?"

Avery tapped the screen. "It'll be close: 5,960 miles. About ten or eleven hours in the air."

The plane would be about 90 percent out of fuel when they landed. Not ideal, but doable, assuming they didn't run into trouble.

"Okay. When you get the autopilot engaged, join us in the cabin. We need to talk."

She nodded and returned her focus to the flight instruments.

"Hey," he said quietly. "It's good to see you."

A coy smile crossed her lips. "I know it is."

Desmond couldn't help but shake his head as he walked back down the aisle. When he looked up, he found everyone studying him expectantly: Ward, Peyton, and Lin.

"We'll refuel in Argentina in about eleven hours," he announced.

Lin spoke first. "How far to your camp in Antarctica after that?"

Desmond had flown there from Buenos Aires a few times. Mar del Plata was close to Buenos Aires, the flight times likely the same. "Six hours, give or take."

"Well," Lin said, "seems we'll be on this plane for quite a while."

"Plenty of time to talk," said Ward.

"And we will. When Avery joins us."

Desmond walked to where Peyton was seated.

Lin eyed him a moment, then stood. To Ward, she said, "Let's take stock of our provisions, shall we, Mister Ward?" The two of them walked to the back of the plane, leaving Peyton and Desmond alone.

Peyton motioned to the seat beside her, and Desmond sat down. She held out her hand, palm up, and he took it and interlocked his fingers with hers. For a moment, he thought she was going to lean close to him, but she held her distance.

Her voice was soft, revealing a vulnerability he had only seen a few times. "After the battle on the Isle, when we didn't find you… I was so worried."

"Me too. They held me captive for a while. I wondered what happened to you. And Avery." The last part came out before he could even think about it.

She blinked several times. "You have a history with her."

He hesitated, unsure how to answer. He settled for the simple truth. "Yes."

"And now you remember it."

He nodded.

Her hand loosened and gradually let go of his. He felt himself hanging on, squeezing tighter than her.

"It's okay."

He didn't know whether she was urging him to let go—of her, or her hand, or both—or forgiving him. Or maybe just filling the painful silence.

"She and I—"

"You don't have to explain, Des." Peyton looked out the window. "We were together a long time ago. I only want you to be happy."

The truth was, he didn't know what he wanted. Whom he wanted to be with. It's like he was starting over in life—and the looming battle with Yuri was the only thing he could see.

"I want to talk about this when everything... is over. Can we do that?"

"Sure."

"After the Isle, what happened?"

"Avery was injured."

"In her abdomen."

Peyton nodded. "How did you know? Has she re-injured it?"

"Yes. She's bleeding."

Peyton moved to get up. "I need to take a look."

The relationship between the two women had certainly improved. Or maybe it was just Peyton being Peyton—always a doctor first. Or both.

"She's all right," Desmond said. "And I think she's got her hands full at the moment."

"Okay."

"What happened after?"

"My mom wanted to find the *Beagle*. And we did. In the Arctic. We searched it for weeks. Found bones from extinct species. Humans, animals. It was like Noah's Ark."

"What did she do with them?"

"Sequenced their DNA."

"Interesting."

"We found a message that led us to more bones—hidden in a cave in northern Spain. Her father, Doctor Paul Kraus, had hidden them there. He was a member of the Citium, one of the original architects of the Looking Glass—one of the people Yuri killed."

"You're kidding." Desmond remembered reading in the pages William Shaw left for them that Lin's father was on the *Beagle*, but he never knew any more about the man. "Why did he go to so much trouble to hide the bones?"

"Kraus believed they were bread crumbs, pieces of a larger puzzle—a code hidden in the human genome."

"What kind of code?"

"Evidence that evolution was a more complex process than previously believed. His theory was that it was interactive—that as humans developed consciousness and more powerful brains, evolution accelerated. New mutations appeared."

"How?"

"I don't know." Peyton thought a moment. "When we got the samples from Spain, she had me deliver them to a supercollider in Texas."

"Like the LHC at CERN?"

"Yes, but bigger."

"So you're saying the code in the human genome is somehow related to a quantum particle, or...?"

"Yes. I think somehow the pattern is the key to accessing a quantum process related to evolution."

Desmond turned the facts over in his mind. "And this is your mother's end game?"

"I don't know. It doesn't make sense to me."

It didn't make sense to Desmond either.

He realized Avery was standing in the aisle. Lin and Ward fell in behind her. The three took seats across from Desmond and Peyton.

"Okay," Ward said. "What exactly is the Looking Glass?"

CHAPTER 68

"THEY'VE LEFT US airspace," Yuri said.

On the other end of the line, Conner's voice became reflective. "Could be looking for asylum somewhere. A nation with limited internet access. Maybe try to convince them to fight."

"Perhaps, but I doubt that. Desmond and Lin both play to win. They're going for Rendition. If they destroy it... it would set us back years. Decades, perhaps."

"We need to know where they're going."

"I'm working on it."

"What's the status of Rook?"

"Operating perfectly. It works, Conner. Two million lives and counting. Waiting for Rendition."

☣

At CDC Headquarters in Atlanta, Elliott Shapiro and Phil Stevens were studying the fatality statistics. Reports were sporadic at first, but X1 treatment centers had alerted county and state health departments of increased mortality rates among their older population. There was a strong correlation between the mortalities and those affected by Parkinson's, Alzheimer's, and dementia. Casualties continued to rise at a steady rate—a pattern that was too consistent to be a natural phenomenon.

EIS agents were en route to investigate when the president of the United States and the governors of all fifty states collapsed.

Autopsies revealed the same cause of death in each case: brain aneurysms that ruptured, causing a subarachnoid hemorrhage. Death was nearly instantaneous. The event left little doubt that the fatalities were a coordinated attack. Assassinations. But why the elderly population affected with neurological disorders? An experiment, perhaps? A sort of trial balloon?

The warning came soon after: the vice president would be next, unless he handed over Peyton Shaw, Lin Shaw, and Desmond Hughes. The news had been a punch in the gut for Elliott.

"What do we do?" Phil asked.

"Start trials. Begin monitoring patients with neurological and other terminal illnesses. When they take the next group, maybe we'll learn something. There could be a key to slowing the process down, or stopping it."

In truth, Elliott counted that as unlikely. Their best chance of stopping this was the people their enemy was after: Peyton, Lin, and Desmond.

CHAPTER 69

"THE LOOKING GLASS," Desmond began, "is... a very complex device."

Ward rolled his eyes. "So give me the *Looking Glass for Idiots* version."

Desmond looked over at Lin.

"Perhaps I should begin," she said. "First, please realize that the Citium you all have come to know," she gestured to Ward and Avery, "is not the same organization I joined—in focus or methods."

"Yeah," Ward grumbled, "we know that. Ancient Greek philosophers on the island of Kitium, Zeno, blah, blah, blah. Just get to the part where you all ripped the world a new one and what to do about it."

"*We*," Lin motioned to Desmond, "didn't. The Citium is in a civil war. That war began in 1986 when almost every scientist was killed at the Citium conclave. That background is important for you to understand. You've only seen pieces of the whole, Mister Ward." Lin fixed Ward with a stare, silently daring him to challenge her.

Desmond sensed that she had an ulterior motive for telling this story: she wanted to explain herself to Peyton. It was as if she was confessing to her daughter—on the off chance that it was her last opportunity to do so.

"Central to their work," Lin continued, "was the theory that our world was not as it seemed. That the myths everyone believed—myths that explained existence—were merely place-holders, fictional explanations that gave people peace of mind until science could fill in the blanks.

"They watched as, one by one, those blanks were filled in. The sun was the center of our solar system. The Earth orbited around it. The moon orbited around the Earth. Gravity—an invisible glue—held them all together. And there were countless other solar systems and galaxies. Billions of suns and worlds. Some worlds were billions of years older than our own. This implied a simple truth, a statistical certainty: there was life beyond our world. And there had been millions, possibly billions of other civilizations long before us."

Lin took a deep breath. "But the most surprising revelation was that there was no evidence of those civilizations."

"No space junk," Peyton whispered, as if reciting from memory.

"Correct. The moon should be littered with probes from ancient civilizations—it has existed in its current state for billions of years. Yet it is bare. That paradox—now called the Fermi Paradox—consumed the group for a very long time. They believed that this was the greatest mystery of all time. Why are we alone? Where *is* everyone?"

"Are you telling us you figured it out?" Avery said.

"That's exactly what I'm telling you."

Avery's eyes went wide. "Didn't see *that* coming."

Lin continued. "Many theories were tested and discarded over the years. Finally, thanks to Occam's razor, the truth became clear: the path of advanced civilizations does not lead to space."

"You're saying they go extinct?" Ward asked.

"That was posited and explored. Indeed, it's a possibility. But surely extinction events wouldn't occur *100 percent* of the time—or even a majority of the time. We theorized instead that sentient species at some point make a discovery that enables them to survive—to continue their evolution and to secure themselves—without leaving their home world. A discovery that would make the rest of the universe utterly irrelevant to them."

"Interesting," Avery said.

"The *most* interesting part is that the universe seems finely tuned to exactly this purpose. Consider this: if a species that emerged ten billion years ago *had* left their home world, they would likely inhabit every viable planet in the universe right now. There would be no room for us—no chance of biological diversity."

"Impossible," Ward said.

"Hardly. The Big Bang occurred 13.8 billion years ago. We believe the first life-friendly star systems appeared 10.4 billion years ago. For perspective, the Earth is only 4.56 billion years old. The moon was formed 30 million years after that. On a cosmic scale, we're new kids on the block. The universe has supported biological life for a very long time. And as I said, it is tuned— tailor-made—for our kind of biological life. The Citium has always wondered why that is."

Peyton bunched her eyebrows. "You're saying the universe is a nursery for sentient species?"

"In effect. It is a medium, a chamber, but not just an isolated chamber. We believe our universe is a chamber in an endless ring of chambers. What we called the cycle of existence."

Ward closed his eyes and rubbed his eyelids. "Stop for a minute, I think my head's going to explode. And it's not the altitude."

"I'll simplify," Lin said. "Long-term, the survival of the human race depends on making this fundamental discovery—the same fundamental discovery that countless species have made before us."

"The Looking Glass," Ward said.

"Yes."

"Then what is all this chamber in a chamber, endless cycle stuff mean?"

"Let me put it this way, Mister Ward: we're already in a Looking Glass."

CHAPTER 70

YURI STUDIED THE map. The plane was turning south, hugging the coast of South America. The Gulfstream didn't have the range to make it to Australia, or even Hawaii; they would have to land somewhere in South America. But the Citium had very few assets on the continent, and Desmond had no investments there. They had checked Lin's ties as well and found none.

The conclusion was clear: it was a stop-over. Or a diversion to buy time. But time wasn't on their side, it was on his. Lin and Desmond would know that.

Yuri scrolled through Melissa Whitmeyer's analysis and recommendations. Desmond had a single investment with ties to the region: Charter Antarctica. That was it. Brilliant. It was off the grid—and beyond the reach of the X1 pathogen. No chance of being discovered.

He dialed the Citium Situation Room and requested Whitmeyer. "It's Antarctica," he said. "I'm sure of it."

He could hear her typing on her computer. "Best rendezvous point for you and Mister McClain is Buenos Aires."

Yuri got up, walked to the cockpit, and asked the pilot to alter their flight plan.

"I want the fastest jet you can find waiting for us," he said to Whitmeyer. "And a team of our best. It's imperative that we get to Antarctica first."

In the CDC's Emergency Operations Center, Elliott Shapiro was reviewing the latest casualty reports. The mortality rate was going down. It was as if they were reaching the end of an experiment—running out of eligible patients. Or pausing before they started the next phase.

The entire world was at their mercy. These people, whoever they were, had conquered the human race. Not with guns or airplanes or battleships, but with science so advanced it looked like magic.

CHAPTER 71

WARD SHOOK HIS head. "What do you mean, we're already in a Looking Glass?"

"What I mean," Lin said, "is that something happened before the Big Bang. That *something* was a Looking Glass event. It was likely very different from the Looking Glass we're creating."

"Why?" Peyton asked.

"Because the preceding Looking Glass was tuned for *its* universe, just as our universe—the physical laws—dictate the creation of a specific kind of Looking Glass here in *this* universe."

"Specific how?" Avery asked.

"One built for data processing and simulation."

Desmond glanced at the others. This was the part where the rubber met the road.

Lin pressed on. "If you look at the broad arc of history, it is toward greater data storage. Writing, agriculture, the information age—they all increased our data processing and storage capacity. And not only that, our ability to simulate realities. Consider the most successful people in the world—in any walk of life. They are the ones who can, in their own minds, imagine the future. This is what visionary business leaders do. And professional sports stars. Politicians. Writers. Investors. But we are currently limited by physical constraints."

"Our bodies," Peyton volunteered.

"Correct. Our minds are progressing faster than biological evolution can keep up with. The next step in humanity's journey is to free ourselves from our biological constraints—and eventually transcend the limits of this universe."

Peyton was stunned. "Are you serious?"

Lin stood and paced the aisle. "Entirely. Consider this: the human brain has one hundred billion neurons. There are roughly a quadrillion synapses—that's a million billion—interconnecting these neurons. For years now, organizations outside the Citium have had computers with the data storage and processing power to simulate human thought. But that's the easiest part of the equation. If you built a computer large enough, you still couldn't transfer yourself to the machine, because the brain is more than simply a data processing device. It is connected on a quantum level to some force that permeates the universe. That was the crux of Paul Kraus's work. That's how our tribe of humans was different. We are connected to the quantum fabric of this universe in a symbiotic relationship."

"Okay," said Peyton. "So you're talking about putting human consciousness in something *other* than the human brain. But if you can't store consciousness in a computer, then what sort of device would you use?"

Lin held a hand out to Desmond, silently yielding the floor.

"A quantum computer," he said.

Peyton stared at him blankly. "I don't know what that is."

"Me either," Avery mumbled.

"Goes without saying," Ward added.

"A quantum computer uses the state of subatomic particles to store information."

Ward nodded theatrically. "Jeez, why didn't you just say so, Hughes."

"Current computers are binary," Desmond said. "They store data in bits—digits that are either zero or one. Eight digits form a byte, a kilobyte is a thousand eight-digit pairs, a megabyte, a million. But quantum computers operate completely differently. They store data in qubits."

He was losing them, he could see it. He rubbed his eyebrows. He really wanted to take a nap.

"Existing computers use silicon, integrated circuits, and micro-processors. Quantum computers use quantum mechanics—they operate on the particles that are already here in the universe."

"And you developed a quantum computer?" Avery asked.

"Yes. Quantum computing has been theorized since the early eighties. The problem with building one has always been decoherence."

"Hughes," Ward grumbled, "I'm putting a moratorium on new words."

"Call it interference then. The problem with using subatomic particles as a storage medium is that they are in a constant state of flux—the universe is constantly interacting with them. That interference corrupts the superpositions of the qubits." Desmond spoke quickly, sensing another Ward blow-up. "Look, have you ever run a strong magnet over a hard drive? If so, you know that it erases it. That's what we had to deal with—it's as if the universe is essentially passing a magnet over our quantum computer constantly, scrambling our data within nanoseconds. We tried cooling the machine, but to operate it for any reasonable amount of time, we needed true shielding. That was the breakthrough at Rook Quantum Sciences."

"Rook," Avery said. "The quantum computer is Rook?"

"Yes."

"And the pandemic was Rapture," Peyton said.

"No, not the pandemic," Desmond said. "That was never part of the plan. The *cure* is Rapture. The focus at Rapture Therapeutics was always understanding the mind and developing ways to analyze and control brain function. That's what the original implants were about—that was what drew me to the company. I wanted it for PTSD and depression. The pandemic…" He looked at Ward, though it was Avery he was really speaking to. "I didn't know about that."

Ward said nothing. Avery's expression was a mask.

With a sigh, Desmond continued. "Rapture's research on PTSD and depression was real, but they were using that data in conjunction with other research for a larger goal: creating an implant that could successfully transfer a mind to Rook. A goal it achieved. However, once we created a working Rook transfer implant, the real challenge became clear: the population would never allow us to put implants in their brains. And besides, that would be too time-consuming and fraught with medical accidents and deaths. The nanorobots were our solution."

"The ones that cured the pathogen," Peyton said.

"Yes, but that was added later. Again, I was never told that would happen. The nanites' primary purpose is to migrate to the brain and transmit the data and quantum states to Rook—essentially transferring the human consciousnesses to Rook. The bodies left behind... well... they were to be euthanized after."

Stunned silence followed.

Finally Ward said, "This can't be happening."

"It *is* happening," Lin said. "You saw the monitors back at the airport. Millions have already been transferred to Rook."

"But it wasn't supposed to happen like this," Desmond said. "The plan was always to let people *choose* to enter the Looking Glass. But Yuri and Conner were too scared."

A defensiveness had entered his tone, and Peyton must have sensed it. "Tell us how it was supposed to work," she said softly.

Desmond nodded gratefully. "We were going to do a presentation—online and on TV. Tell everyone the truth—what the *Beagle* had found, our own research. The Looking Glass was going to be optional, the transfer gradual. We were going to start with vulnerable populations—anyone whose mind was weakened or at risk. Mentally ill. Patients with Parkinson's, Alzheimer's, and dementia. They were the key to testing Rook at scale."

A flicker of fear went through Avery's eyes. "Those people, the millions that have died, they had brain disorders?"

"If Yuri is still following that aspect of the plan."

"Where—" Avery stopped, thought a second. "What happened to them?"

"They're in Rook. Waiting."

"For what? What does it even mean to be 'in Rook'? Are they alive? Aware?"

"They're waiting for Rendition. Without Rendition, they are simply data in the machine. Alive, I guess. More like in stasis. Unaware. Rendition simulates reality—allows them to live again."

Avery put her face in her hands. "My God. This is the end of the human race."

"On the contrary," Lin said. "It's merely a step in an endless cycle. It's happened countless times before, and it will happen countless times after this."

CHAPTER 72

PEYTON LOOKED DESMOND in the eyes. She finally understood now. "That's why you hid Rendition. Without it, all Yuri and Conner can do is transfer and store the minds of everyone who received the Rapture nanites."

"That's right. It was my only play."

"Explain Rendition to us," Ward said. "How does it work, what exactly does it do?"

"I used Rendition Games as a front," Desmond said. "On the surface, it was a virtual reality gaming company. That allowed me to recruit the right programmers. I picked out the most talented ones, and told them the truth: we were creating a virtual-reality program—an incredibly realistic one, one that could simulate not just sight and sound but everything—that would run on a quantum computer. We used Rapture's brain-mapping data to simulate smell, taste, pain, pleasure. Everything."

Desmond paused. "And I used Rendition to regain my memories." He turned to Avery. "After I got you assigned to the *Kentaro Maru*, I contacted a scientist at Rapture Therapeutics, Manfred Jung. He led the Rapture research into memory archiving. I asked him if, in addition to transferring memories out, the Rapture implant in my brain could be used to receive memories and reintegrate them. He thought it was possible, though risky."

"And you used the Labyrinth Reality app as a transfer mechanism."

"That's right."

"If we destroy Rendition," Ward said, "it's all over, right? No more Looking Glass."

"Yes and no," Desmond said. "It'll set back the Looking Glass—years, at least. Maybe much more. But it's not 'all over.' The nanites have already been distributed, and Conner and Yuri have obviously re-created the control program for Rapture. That gives them instant 'assassination power' over almost every human on Earth. They can upload to Rook anyone who has the Rapture nanites in their body—assuming that person has an internet connection in range."

Peyton looked at her mother. "That's why you told us to deactivate our phones."

Lin nodded.

"But why would they transfer people to Rook," Avery asked, "if they don't have Rendition?"

"Clearly they're very confident they're going to get it. Without Rendition, Rook is useless."

"What about the balloons we saw?" Peyton asked. "What are they?"

"A solution to the rural internet problem," Desmond said. "Although I never thought it would be used to transfer minds to Rook. We just wanted to bring the world together—to educate people about the Looking Glass." He glanced at Avery. "It was one of the reasons I was interested in CityForge. Creating cities—and internet infrastructure—in the third world is imperative.

"The balloon implementation is based largely on Google's Project Loon. If I'm right, the balloons will circle the Earth, picking up anyone who's out of range of any other internet-enabled devices. The fact that Yuri has deployed them tells us he's planning on a full-scale transfer soon. I expect he'll do a small cohort first to ensure that Rook is operating correctly, then he'll scale up."

Peyton said, "I guess it's safe to assume Yuri won't upload himself or any of his critical personnel until he has Rendition."

"I think so." He thought a moment, then looked at Lin. "You were right, what you told me that night: the Looking Glass is inevitable; only one thing can change—who controls it."

"That needs to be us," Ward said. "So our goal is clear: we destroy Rendition and kill Yuri."

Up until now, Avery had seemed to recede within herself, her thoughts elsewhere. But now she looked up, eyes wide with alarm.

"If Rendition is destroyed... the minds in Rook, what happens to them?"

"Nothing," Desmond replied. "It's like data on a hard drive with no operating system. They are dead forever."

Ward exhaled heavily. "Our duty now is to the living." He looked at Avery. "We are going to kill Yuri and destroy Rendition."

Lin's voice broke the silence. "That's not quite enough, is it, Desmond?"

His eyebrows knitted together.

"Yuri isn't the only threat," she continued. "He's not the only one who orchestrated the pandemic, is he?"

Desmond grimaced and shook his head.

Lin turned to Ward. "Conner must be dealt with. As long as he's alive, the Citium will be a threat."

CHAPTER 73

WHEN THE PLANE'S door opened, Conner inhaled the fresh air. He felt like he had been on the jet for days. The sun was warm on his face and the smell of salt water wafted in the air. It was seventy-seven degrees in Buenos Aires, with not a cloud in the sky. After the cold, damp, overcast weather of the bay area in December, summer in the Southern Hemisphere was a welcome change.

Yuri was waiting in the terminal. He embraced Conner, then rested both hands on the younger man's shoulders. "Our day is here."

"The first cohort?"

"Stored flawlessly. We're proceeding with phase two."

Conner nodded. He had always been nervous about the go-live moment for Rook. Despite all the simulations and stress tests, there was truly no way to know if the machine could support millions of minds. Or billions.

"What's our count?"

"A hundred million and climbing."

"The balloons?"

"Are deployed. We lost a few to weather. A dozen shot down before we got control of governments." Yuri turned and led Conner to an airport lounge, where a scanner was waiting. "No matter. We still have enough to complete the transfer. We can always mop up with the drones." He held his hand out, palm up. "One last backup before. Just in case."

That was prudent. Danger awaited in Antarctica. Conner slipped into the machine and closed his eyes.

They boarded the plane thirty minutes later, and Yuri instructed the pilot to begin take-off. In the cabin, he sat across from Conner.

"You know what we have to do."

Conner knew what Yuri was asking him. He couldn't bring himself to think it, much less utter the words. Instead, he said, "Get Rendition and get out."

"He'll never stop. You know that. Neither will Lin Shaw."

Conner gazed out the window at the runway passing by, faster each second. "I can't kill my brother."

Sadness crept into Yuri's eyes. "I'd never ask you to."

"What are you asking me?"

"Not to stop me."

CHAPTER 74

AS THE PLANE turned east and flew over the Andes, everyone on board was trying to sleep—or pretending to sleep. They were all worrying about the same thing, and thinking very different thoughts.

☣

Desmond was thinking about what Lin had said: that Conner would have to die. He couldn't. Wouldn't. But what would be the cost of that?

Peyton's life? The rest of the world?

He knew it then: he couldn't lose her again. Or his brother.

☣

Peyton was trying to wrap her head around what she had heard. The Looking Glass was like a universe inside a universe—if she understood it correctly. What she had read in her father's writings finally made sense. He had said that after World War Two, the Citium had focused on creating a device that would answer their deepest questions—and make humanity safe from itself. The Looking Glass accomplished both. With Rendition, any catastrophe or war could simply be edited out—like removing a scene from a movie.

What she didn't understand was how her mother's device—the Rabbit Hole—was connected. How could a particle accelerator fit in with *any* of this?

She was sure of only one thing—her mother was still hiding something.

Lin Shaw saw all the pieces, and they were exactly where she wanted them. There was only one variable she couldn't factor in: Avery Price. The young woman had surprised her once. And she sensed that during the discussion, she had held something back.

Lin remembered something then—from Avery's initial job interview at Phaethon Genetics. It could be the key to controlling her— if it wasn't a lie.

Avery stared through the windshield, thinking about her father. If what Lin and Desmond had said was true, he was dead—or his body was. And his consciousness was inside Rook, in a sort of digital purgatory. Not alive, not dead.

Over the past few years, she had watched him slip away, little by little, as if his consciousness was being uploaded slowly, a shell left behind, the body alive but the mind gone. She wished now that she had spent more time with him. But she had dedicated her life to stopping the Citium and the Looking Glass.

Now was her only chance of seeing him again.

"Hey."

She jumped at the sound of Ward's voice.

He shushed her and closed the cockpit door.

"You scared me."

"Sorry." He plopped down beside her. "We need to talk."

"About?"

"You know what about. I don't buy that line they just fed us."

Avery squinted. "Which part?"

"The part about 'We can't stop the Looking Glass.'"

"We can?"

"Of course. Lin Shaw is playing us. She's got her daughter

wrapped around her finger, and who knows what Desmond Hughes is thinking."

"What are you saying?"

Ward broke eye contact. "When we get there, we destroy Rendition first. Then we take out everyone who can re-create it."

Desmond. Avery couldn't look at her boss.

"You understand what I'm saying?"

"Yeah."

"Do you remember what I asked you, Agent?" Ward was staring at her now. "I asked you if Hughes had a gun to my head, if you would shoot him."

"And I said I would shoot him in the shoulder and kick you in the balls."

"Be serious, Avery. He's got a gun to the head of every person on Earth. I know you love him. But you took an oath."

"We can do this without killing him."

"Maybe. But maybe not. I'm asking you right now—can you do it? I need to know."

Avery swallowed. "What's your plan?"

"Destroy Rendition. Take out its creators. Then we take Yuri and/or Conner. Interrogate them, figure out where Rapture Control and Rook are. We storm the beaches. Destroy both. Then the Looking Glass threat is over, the world goes back to normal, and everyone lives—and I mean flesh-and-blood life, not this upload to the quantum computer hocus pocus."

Avery knew this decision would change her life forever.

"This is what we signed up for, Agent. Sacrifice. The hardest part isn't giving your life for the cause, it's knowing what your sacrifice and decisions will do to those you love. Seeing it. *That's* the full price. The cost of being selfish is higher. Millions—no, *billions* of people are counting on us. We are the last line. No one will protect them. Not Yuri, or Conner, or Lin. It has to be us, here, now. I need to know if you're with me. Will you help me finish this? Will you do what you signed up to do?"

"I'll do whatever I have to."

CHAPTER 75

THE AIRPORT AT Mar del Plata was deserted. The planes were mostly gone. Those that were left looked old and broken down.

They found fuel though, and Avery and Ward stood guard while Peyton and Desmond connected the hose and operated the pump. Lin Shaw slept through the landing and the entire operation.

As they were taking off, Desmond wondered how anyone could sleep at a time like this. Unless she already knew what was going to happen.

The frozen continent was breathtaking. The ice below glittered like a sea of diamonds. As they descended, a long white habitat stretched out like a caterpillar crawling across a white desert. The runway was nothing more than hard-packed ice, an indentation barely noticeable from the air.

Desmond moved to the cockpit and pointed it out to Avery. "Is this going to be a problem?" he asked.

"I've landed on worse."

And she had—Desmond had witnessed it. He had supreme confidence in her. What he wasn't sure about was how things would turn out after they landed. He felt as though he were about to go over Niagara Falls in a barrel. The edge was looming, everything beyond uncertain and dangerous and unavoidable.

The building that ran along the runway was shaped like

a greenhouse with a field of solar cells nearby. The inside held barracks for the construction crew, living quarters, and supplies and equipment that couldn't stand the elements. Beside it, Charter Antarctica's fleet of snow vehicles sat idle. There were three snowmobiles and three PistenBully 300 Polar snowcats—large machines with tracks and instruments for moving ice and equipment. Each of the snowcats could be fitted with a pushing blade like a bulldozer, or a transportation bucket similar to a loader; one of them was already fitted with a radio-controlled hydraulic crane. The company had bought four of these large snow machines—so one of them was gone. Probably just left at the ice hotel.

The sun glared off the ice as they landed. The date was December 23—the summer solstice in the Southern Hemisphere—and the sun was at its zenith: 23.5 degrees in the sky. Every day after, it would descend toward the horizon until it finally set in March, during the vernal equinox. Darkness twenty-four hours a day would follow—for six months—until the sun rose once more in September, for the only time that year.

Desmond had first come to Antarctica a year after he and Peyton had broken up. He had stayed at a luxury resort that featured excursions to the South Pole and to a colony of emperor penguins. He had come to clear his mind and get away, but he had left with a lifelong love for this beautiful place—and a desire to help others experience it, not just the wealthy. That had been the mission of Charter Antarctica—to make this adventure available to anyone intrepid enough to undertake it, regardless of their means.

As soon as the plane rolled to a stop, Desmond opened the door and gritted his teeth as the cold embraced him. He, Avery, and Ward had debated their approach at length and had decided not to radio ahead, but rather to storm the building without notice. Desmond was wearing the cold weather gear from one of the Navy SEALs who had protected Peyton and Lin in the Arctic during their expedition to the *Beagle*. Ward wore the other SEAL's gear, and Avery had donned Peyton's. Peyton and Lin were bundled below blankets at the back of the cabin, trying to stay warm.

Desmond let the staircase slam into the ice, then descended, Ward and Avery close behind. His breath came out in white puffs as his feet crunched into the icy snow. Soon his lungs ached from the cold, and the crunching sound seemed louder in the still quietness around them.

Avery pulled ahead and burst through the door, rifle held up. The antechamber had rows of boots and heavy coats, but no fresh snow, no puddles of water below, and not a soul in sight. Ward was last through the door, which he slammed behind him. He doubled over, hands on his knees, panting. "Keep going," he managed between breaths.

Avery slipped through the next door, Desmond behind her.

They heard talking and laughing at the end of the hall. Avery crept along the narrow corridor. A tool room lay to their right. Empty. A supply room with cold weather gear sat open beside it—also unoccupied. A common bathroom and showers were on the left. Empty, water off. The doors to the bunk rooms on each side of the hall were open. Avery motioned for Desmond to pause.

With her rifle at the ready, she leaned slowly into the doorway, peeked quickly, then repeated it on the other side. Desmond could smell coffee now, and voices he recognized, though he couldn't place them.

Avery met his eyes and motioned for him to cover the bunk room on the right. Ward was coming up behind them, but she didn't engage him.

She crossed the doorway, sweeping her rifle across as she scanned the room. Desmond did the same on the opposite side. The bunks were empty except for a middle-aged man with a thick beard, streaked with gray, lying on the bottom bunk, a tiny light on, reading a paperback in his thermal underwear, like a child staying up past his bedtime. Desmond didn't recognize the man, but he was pretty sure he wasn't one of Yuri's Citium Security operatives. He looked right at home in Antarctica.

When the man realized Desmond was there, he dropped the book and reeled back, his mouth open. Desmond held a single finger to his lips and nodded for Ward to watch the man.

The other bunk room was empty, and Avery led the way down the corridor to the rec room. She and Desmond burst through the opening at the same time, guns held out.

A ripple of alarm went through the room's occupants: four construction crew members who were playing a game of Risk while a movie—*Into the Sea*—played in the background. They all froze, then slowly raised their hands. Desmond recognized one of the men: Lars Peterson, the construction foreman for the ice hotel.

"Who else is here?" he asked.

"Just us," Peterson said in a Scandinavian accent. "Well, and Jacobs is in his bunk."

"The people I sent here—where are they?"

Peterson furrowed his brow. "They left."

A bolt of fear ran through Desmond.

From the hall, Ward yelled, "Hey, what's our status?"

"Join us!" Desmond called back. "Bring Jacobs." To Peterson he asked, "When did they leave?"

"I don't know, a month ago. They heard about the outbreak on the radio and said they needed to get back to their families. Except for the young people and that scientist," Peterson added. "They're at the hotel playing their *video game*." He scoffed. "Not enough juice here."

Desmond spun to Avery. "The programmers are still here—only the boat crew left."

"How far is the hotel?"

"Twenty miles inland."

"Let's go," Ward said, already turning to leave.

To Peterson, Desmond said, "Lars, I need to borrow some cold weather gear and a snowcat."

"Of course." The man stood and began down the corridor to the supply room.

"Has anyone else been here?" Desmond asked as they walked.

"No, just the penguins and us." Peterson eyed Desmond's rifle, still looking a little disturbed by it. "We're... making solid progress on the hotel. We think next season—"

"Good," Desmond said. "This is about something else."

"It involves the young people?"

"Yes."

Peterson handed over the keys to a snowcat and gear for Peyton and Lin. The garments were a little large, but they would keep them warm. Ward complained about taking Peyton and Lin along, but Avery pointed out that if they left them behind, they could be used as hostages if Yuri arrived.

Desmond took Peterson aside and spoke quietly. "I need you to do something for us."

The man raised his eyebrows.

"Watch the runway. Take shifts outside. If anyone lands, I need you to radio us immediately. Then lock yourselves in the barracks."

Peterson grimaced. "Are we in danger?"

"I'm just being cautious. Will you do it?"

"Of course."

Desmond pushed the snowcat to its limits. The engine screamed, and the tracks threw up snow in its wake, like a monster truck powering through mud. The glimmering white hills rolled by in a flash, a background on repeat in a cartoon.

The enclosed cab was surprisingly comfortable. Ward sat in the passenger seat, Avery, Peyton, and Lin in the back. They listened as Desmond described the layout of the hotel. He didn't know its current status, but it was intended to be a ring, with a large lobby and open ballroom at the entrance. In the center of the ring was a solar power array that was disguised to look like a reflecting pool. A hallway ran the length of the ring on the inside, with the bedrooms all on the outside, so every guest could take in the views. Most were bunk rooms, like a giant hostel, but there were a few private suites. Desmond had insisted the architect design the structure to be both breathtaking and functional—to accommodate as many people as comfortably possible.

Ward opened the glove box and rummaged around. He took

out a sheaf of papers and unfolded one. "Does your hotel look like this?"

He was holding a blueprint of the floor plan. It made sense the construction crew would keep this handy.

"Yeah, that's it. But I think the far side of the ring is still under construction—based on the last report. The Rendition team is probably in the ballroom. It would be the warmest place because of the heat coming in through the ceiling."

"The construction foreman said they needed juice," Avery said. "For what?"

"Rendition. The developers brought the Rendition server from the office. It's like a small Rook array that allows an instance of Rendition to run. It takes a lot of power though. The solar array at the barracks isn't nearly as powerful as the one at the hotel. I think they're using the power to run the portable Rook server and load Rendition." He thought for a moment. "If they're using it when we arrive, we'll have to get them to exit the program."

"Why?" Avery asked.

"We designed the Looking Glass to enable those with root access to move back and forth—between it and the corporeal world. It was essential. After all, someone has to oversee the maintenance of the Rook array. Anyway, we never had time to program the eventuality of the Rook array spontaneously shutting off. It's one of the assumptions of the program: the underlying system will always be there. Long story short, pulling the plug could cause brain damage. I can go in using my Rapture implant and get them."

The group was silent. Ward shot Avery a look that Desmond couldn't quite read.

When the hotel appeared ahead, situated atop a ridge, Peyton, Lin, and Avery leaned forward to get a better view. The other snowcat was parked outside, and Desmond parked beside it. As they had done at the barracks, Desmond, Avery, and Ward got out and entered first.

The steel double doors creaked as Desmond pushed them open. The lobby was empty and eerily quiet. Desmond took off his goggles and pulled the insulated hood from his head.

The ice floor was pitted like travertine to provide traction. They crept across it carefully, rifle butts barely touching their shoulders. The ballroom loomed just ahead. Everyone at Charter Antarctica had taken to calling it "the rotunda" because of its domed glass ceiling and incredible acoustics.

In the middle of the room, in a six-foot-tall server rack, sat the Rendition server Raghav and his team had brought with them. Its face plates were obsidian, and they shimmered in the sunlight pouring through the ceiling.

Beside it, four cots stood in a row, each holding a programmer lying peacefully. No wires ran to the server—the implants communicated wirelessly—but Desmond knew from their breathing they were inside Rendition.

Movement out of the corner of his eye drew his attention, and he spun and trained his rifle on a man wearing a heavy parka and reading glasses. Dr. Manfred Jung.

Desmond lowered his rifle.

"Doctor."

"Hello, Desmond. It's good to see you again."

More footsteps behind them. Two women, both in their twenties. Desmond didn't recognize them, but assumed they were Raghav's girlfriend and Melanie's sister. The hall behind them was sealed with a temporary construction wall, hanging strips of thick plastic—most likely to keep the heat in.

Ward motioned to the machine in the center of the cavernous room. "That it?"

"Yeah," Desmond said.

"Rendition is loaded on there?"

"Yeah."

"That's the only copy."

"It is." He was getting annoyed with Ward's prodding. He needed to question the others. To Dr. Jung, he said, "How long have they—"

"Whoa!" Avery screamed.

Desmond spun and saw Ward pointing a gun at her. She was standing in front of the server, her hands held out.

Ward stepped closer to her. "Get out of the way, Avery."

Desmond trained his rifle on Ward and stepped closer. "Ward, you shoot that server, and those four people could die. Give me five minutes."

Ward kept his eyes on Avery. "I can't take that chance." A pause. "Get out of the way. I'm warning you, Agent. This is what we signed up for."

Desmond crept closer, to within four feet.

He lunged just as Ward pulled the trigger.

CHAPTER 76

FROM THE PLANE window, Conner peered down at the Gulfstream jet on the runway. "They beat us here."

"It doesn't matter," Yuri said. "What's important is who leaves." He pointed to his laptop. "The tracker says she's twenty miles away."

"At the hotel."

"Likely."

Conner activated the radio and instructed one of the three planes they'd brought to land and clear the habitat of hostiles.

☣

The ballroom was a hundred feet wide and long, with a thirty-foot-high glass ceiling and an ice floor. The crack of the gunshot was ear-splitting in the space.

Desmond collided with Ward a split second later. The older man's head cracked against the ice floor when they landed, Desmond on top. He punched Ward hard in the face, his knuckles crunching into the bone and soft flesh, the sound like boots digging into the snow. Ward's head rolled to the side. He wasn't unconscious, but he was close.

Desmond chanced a glance back. The two women and Jung were gone. The programmers remained on the cots, as if nothing were amiss. And Avery lay still, a pool of blood spreading out around her.

"Jung!" Desmond screamed.

The doctor's head popped out from the corridor.

"Help her!"

The man walked out briskly, knelt over Avery, and gently rolled her over. His eyes went wide.

Desmond was so focused on Avery he didn't see the blow coming. When Ward connected with his side, Desmond realized the pain wasn't from a fist, but from a knife, buried deep.

☣

Over the snowcat's idling engine, Peyton heard the crack of a gunshot. Her hand instantly went to the door handle.

Her mother grabbed her arm. "Peyton."

"I'm going."

Lin smiled. "I know. I'm going with you." She reached in her pocket and handed her a pistol. "You may need this." Lin grabbed the backpack she had guarded since the Cave of Altamira. "Inside, follow my lead."

"Mom."

"Do you trust me, Peyton?"

Peyton didn't answer, only stared at her mother, wondering if she actually did trust her.

"Everything I ever did was to protect you—and your brother and sister."

Peyton opened the door, and they jumped out.

They raced to the hotel, Peyton with the gun in her hand, her mother close behind. The handheld radio crackled with Peterson's voice.

"Mister Hughes, there's another plane landing."

CHAPTER 77

WARD JERKED THE blade from Desmond's side. Blood flowed from the wound like a dribbling faucet. Ward drew back to stab again, but Desmond caught his hand and pinned it to the ice floor. He balled his other hand into a fist and brought it down on Ward's face, but it never connected. Ward kneed him in the balls.

Agony radiated from Desmond's abdomen and up his chest. The shock nearly made him gag, but he held on to Ward's knife hand. Ward rolled Desmond over and brought the knife to his neck. Desmond's arm shook as he strained to stop the knife pressing into him. The wound in his side gushed blood and spewed pain. His abs ached, and the blade inched closer.

It touched his skin. Cut. Blood trickled. Desmond kicked, but his legs were useless. He punched Ward in the side. Once. Again. Three times. But the knife continued digging into his skin.

☣

Yuri listened as the operative questioned the foreman of the construction crew.

"I told you," the bearded man said, "there were only five of them. Two men and three women."

"Desmond Hughes."

"Ya," he nodded. "He was with them."

Conner took Yuri aside. "We could send the spec ops ahead and have them clear the hotel."

"No. You and I must see this through. It's too important."

Blood flowed down Desmond's neck. His strength was gone. David Ward had won—had killed him the moment he stabbed him in the side. But Desmond held on. He would fight for every second of life.

Ward's head snapped to the right, and blood streaked the floor. The echo of the gunshot seemed to arrive a second later. Ward's shoulders sagged, and he toppled to the side as Desmond released him.

In the back seat of the snowcat, Yuri turned to Conner. "He will be there."

Conner said nothing.

"He is the last of your family," Yuri said, pressing.

"We all make our choices."

CHAPTER 78

DESMOND THREW WARD'S dead body off of him. A few feet away, Avery's hand was shaking, holding a handgun, the barrel smoking in this frigid chamber.

Desmond crawled to her on elbows and knees. Inspected her wound. A shot to the chest. Out the other side. Bleeding. Too much blood. His hands were soaked in red—from both his own wound and the pool he had crawled through. He didn't care. He reached up and took her face in his hands.

"Thank you."

She closed her eyes and exhaled.

He let his face fall into her abdomen, just below her breasts. "I'm sorry."

Her fingers ran through his hair, then tightened, lifting his head up. She stared into his eyes. "I'm not. Not if you finish this."

☣

Peyton followed her mother through the ice hotel's front door and the empty lobby. In the ballroom, Desmond lay on top of Avery, looking down at her. Their words echoed in the domed room, muddled, too hard to hear. A pool of blood spread out around them, red flowing to black.

Peyton rushed forward and gripped Desmond's shoulders, turned him over, and saw the gash in his side.

"I'm okay," he breathed. "Avery. She needs you."

Peyton's eyes scanned the younger woman. Gunshot wound to the upper chest. Barely missed puncturing her lung.

A white-haired, heavyset man was hovering, eyeing Avery with concern. "Keep pressure on the wound," she said to him, and got up and ran back toward the entrance. Behind her, she heard her mother saying, "Help me extend the antennae, Doctor Jung. Yes, that can wait. This is far more important."

Outside the hotel, Peyton ran to the snowcat and threw the door open. The freezing temperature stung at her face, but she didn't bother putting her hood up or goggles on. She pulled the med kit from under the passenger side seat, then stopped. In the distance, she heard a buzzing sound. An engine. She released the med kit and grabbed the binoculars from the dash, raised them to her face. Another snow machine. Two. Moving toward them.

CHAPTER 79

PEYTON GRUNTED AS she pulled the hotel door open, still holding the med kit.

In the rotunda, her mother was bent over an open suitcase that lay on the floor. The pack she had carried after Altamira was open, discarded nearby.

Desmond, with a shaking, bloody hand, was holding a smartphone, tapping away.

Peyton stopped at his side. "What are you doing?"

"Opening Rendition." He motioned to the four cots that held the programmers. "I need to bring them out."

"How long will that take?"

"I don't know." He looked over at Avery. "Help her. She saved my life, Peyton. Please."

Peyton gripped his forearm. "Okay."

She applied bandages to Avery's wound, front and back. It would slow the bleeding, but the woman needed to get to an OR soon—and there wasn't one within a thousand miles. Not good odds. "Hang on, Avery," she whispered.

Her mother was typing furiously on the keyboard inside the suitcase. She unsnapped a corded phone and held it to her ear. It reminded Peyton of a bag phone from the nineties.

"Head of watch, please," Lin said.

A pause.

"This is Lin Shaw, Miss Whitmeyer. I'm initiating an upload."

Peyton didn't understand. Who was she calling?

415

"Mom."

Avery wiggled. Reached for her gun.

"Don't," Avery called to Lin. Her voice was weak, and her hand trembled.

Lin saw the gun in Avery's hands. "Stop her, Peyton."

Avery steadied the gun.

Lin didn't even blink. "My authorization was issued by Yuri Pachenko. Access code Alpha-Omega-Sigma-4828-47-29. Verify."

"Put the phone down," Avery said. She tried to sit up, but fell back to the floor, still holding the gun. Her entire arm was shaking now.

Lin moved the mouthpiece to her neck, but held the phone to her ear. "Would you like to see your father again, Miss Price?"

Avery blinked.

Peyton stood. "Mom, what are you doing?"

Lin squatted down, her face inches from the gun in Avery's hand. "This is your only chance. He's in Rook right now. Waiting on you. Uploaded with the first cohort—advanced stage Alzheimer's patients." Lin studied the younger woman. "That's why you joined Phaethon Genetics. Or so you said in your interview. You said you wanted to help him, and others like him. Was it true, or just a cover story? The best cover stories are true, aren't they? Like telling an asset you love him..." Lin's eyes darted to Desmond, who was now lying still. "... when you really do."

Peyton backed away. Her mother was a monster. A manipulator playing a game Peyton didn't understand.

"He's waiting," Lin said. "And millions of others. You stop the upload, and they die forever. You took an oath to protect those people."

A boom echoed in the vast space.

CHAPTER 80

THE RENDITION INSTANCE wasn't what Desmond expected. The simulations they had tested during development had mimicked the real world, which was the entire point of Rendition: to create a virtual world indistinguishable from real life. For those in the Looking Glass, it *became* real life.

This place was like nothing he had ever seen in real life—but he recognized it all the same. Rolling green fields surrounded him. Ahead lay a round door to a home built into the earth. It was a *smial*, or hobbit-hole, in the town of Hobbiton. The residence had a name, too: Bag End. In the *Lord of the Rings* series, it was home to Bilbo Baggins and then Frodo Baggins.

So, Desmond thought. This was where, at the end of the world—*during* the end of the world—the Rendition developers had chosen to spend their time. They were certified geeks. There was no denying it now.

Desmond pushed open the round wooden door and stooped to enter.

A likeness of Bilbo Baggins was smoking a pipe, telling a story to Raghav, Langford, Kevin, and Melanie, who sat around a table.

Langford threw up his hands. "Okay, who programmed Des in here?" He looked at the other three. "It totally breaks the illusion."

"I'm not an illusion. I'm here, in Antarctica. Lying three feet from your cot in the ice hotel."

They all froze.

Kevin burst out laughing. "Oh my God, seriously, who did that? Okay, I don't care. *How* did you do that? Camera on the server? Program it while we were offline? Just tell me—"

"Shut up, Kevin. I'm here. I—"

Desmond saw movement through the open door—another figure coming up the path toward Bag End. It couldn't be.

The visitor stepped inside, stooping just as Desmond had, and glanced at the programmers around the table.

"All right, who is this?" Raghav asked. "Someone's grandpa?"

Desmond addressed the visitor. "How are you here?"

"I don't know."

"What's the last thing you remember?"

"I was in the administrative building, with you, on the Isle of Citium. You left the server room. I tried to buy you some time, but I was captured. Yuri took me to a room and scanned me. Where's Peyton?"

"Here, with me," Desmond said, his mind racing. "In Antarctica. Your daughter's safe."

William Shaw nodded. "Good. What happened after I was scanned?"

"You died."

"Then that means…"

"You're in the Looking Glass," Desmond said. "Somehow, the main Rook array has been connected to the Rendition instance here, in Antarctica. It's live—all of it. Someone has done it. It's over."

CHAPTER 81

PEYTON TURNED AT the booming sound of the hotel doors flying open. Soldiers in white camouflage parkas rushed through the lobby and poured into the rotunda, fanning out, covering all three exits, rifles at the ready, the green dots of their laser pointers dancing on Peyton, Avery, Lin, and Desmond. Peyton counted at least twenty of them. Too many.

Avery shifted her gun to point at the closest soldier.

Peyton put her hand on Avery's wrist. "Don't. There's too many."

Lin Shaw raised her hands. Her voice rang loud and clear in the rotunda. "Stand down. We're on the same side."

One of the soldiers touched his collarbone. "We're secure."

Footsteps echoed in the lobby. Two men entered and came to a stop. They were mirrors of each other: posture rigid, expression blank. Yuri Pachenko and Conner McClain silently scanned the room.

The last time Peyton had seen Conner, he had been interrogating her on the *Kentaro Maru* hours after he had killed Jonas and her EIS agents. She hadn't known then that he was Desmond's brother. Now, as Peyton looked at the scars on his face, she had a new understanding of the pain he had gone through. But that didn't change how she felt about him. He was a monster.

Yuri was the same. He had killed her father and kidnapped and imprisoned her brother. He had taken so much from her.

Below her, she felt Avery struggling, trying to raise her arm, to point the gun at Yuri, like a zombie reaching out to take a life. Peyton held her down. They were outnumbered—and a firefight would damage the Rendition server, possibly killing Desmond.

Avery looked up at Peyton with fire in her eyes.

Wait, Peyton mouthed.

"I've fulfilled our agreement," Lin said.

Yuri drew a sat phone from his parka and held it to his ear. "Does it work?"

"What agreement, Mom?"

Lin said nothing.

"You led them here, didn't you?"

Her mother's silence was all the confirmation Peyton needed.

"In return for what? What did he promise you, Mom?"

No response came. Lin's gaze was fixed on Yuri. A cold, confident smile crossed his lips.

"I told you," Lin said, "I did my part. Rendition is yours. The Looking Glass is complete. Now honor our bargain."

"Very well," Yuri said. He moved the phone back to his mouth. "Miss Whitmeyer, it seems Doctor Shaw has had a change of heart. Reinstate her privileges as a full member of the Citium."

Lin exhaled. Finally, her gaze shifted to Peyton. "I did it for you."

"No."

"It was the only way out of that cave, Peyton. The only way to save you."

"*You* freed him."

"It was the only way."

Conner walked to Desmond's side. "He's inside?"

"Yes," Lin replied. "He may already know that Rendition has been uploaded to the main Rook array, not just this portable instance. Either way, he'll know soon enough that the Looking Glass is live." Lin's voice grew soft. "And he will change then, Conner. He'll know it's over. And so is your disagreement—that's all this was. Brothers fight. That's what they do."

Conner nodded, still looking at Desmond.

Yuri glanced at one of the troops nearby. "Turn it off, Colonel."

"No!" Peyton yelled. "You'll kill him."

The Citium officer marched toward the server rack.

Conner held up a hand. "Stop."

The man hesitated, glancing back at Yuri, who said, "You have your orders, Colonel."

"I remind you," Conner said calmly, "that I'm the head of Citium Security."

The colonel nodded and took a step back.

Yuri slipped the phone into his parka. A gun was in his hand when he drew it back out.

"Gun!" Peyton yelled.

Conner spun to face Yuri. "I want to talk to him."

"We've discussed this, Conner. We have a plan."

Lin's voice was just loud enough for Conner to hear. "Desmond will see now that he made a mistake. You'll regret it your entire life if you don't at least talk to him."

Yuri raised the gun.

Conner stepped toward Yuri.

The older man pointed the weapon at Desmond and pulled the trigger.

CHAPTER 82

THE SHOT SHATTERED a pane of glass on the rotunda's dome. Shards of glass fell around Peyton like rain. Cold air rushed in, like a freezer door being opened. Conner had caught Yuri's arm just before he pulled the trigger, forcing the shot up and away from his brother, who lay unharmed—for now.

Peyton drew her own pistol, but her mother held a hand out. "Don't."

Conner held both of Yuri's arms, looked him in the eyes, pleading. "Yuri, please."

The Citium Security operatives exchanged glances, but no one moved.

Slowly, Lin paced closer to Yuri and Conner.

Desmond opened his eyes.

"Des," Peyton whispered.

He tried to sit up, but fell back to the cot. He was groggy—as he had been when he had recovered his memories. He lifted his head toward Peyton, huddled over Avery, then looked past them to where Conner struggled with Yuri, Lin cautiously moving toward them. He must have seen the troops next, because his eyes went wide. He struggled and was finally able to sit up and swing his legs off the side of the cot.

His voice was hoarse and faint. "Conner."

His brother turned his head. At the same moment, Yuri's gun hand broke free, and Yuri aimed at Desmond.

For the second time, Conner was quicker. But this time, he was unable to redirect Yuri's shot.

He could only step in the way of it.

Desmond's scream rattled Peyton to her core. It was almost inhuman, a mix of rage and shock and pain. The look on his face broke her heart.

CHAPTER 83

THE GUNSHOT WENT right through Conner, shattering another pane of glass in the rotunda. The flow of cold air increased. Glass fell on the ice floor, the impacts like the sound of wind chimes. A streak of blood painted the Rendition server. Conner's blood. But he hung on to Yuri, both hands now gripping the older man's arms, struggling, wrestling, blood pouring down his back.

Peyton rose, but stopped. A Citium Security operative raised his gun and shook his head, silently warning her.

Desmond staggered toward his brother, who was on top of Yuri now, using his last bit of strength to pin him to the ground.

Lin Shaw got there first. In a quick motion, she drew a gun from her parka and fired at point blank range.

Yuri's limp body fell to the ice.

Conner looked back at her in horror.

Desmond reached his brother a second later and pulled him off of Yuri, into his arms.

Peyton saw the wound then. The bullet had pierced Conner's neck and passed through his carotid artery. Blood was gushing freely. He wouldn't last long.

Desmond must have realized this as well. He sat on the ice floor, his brother in his arms, tears rolling down his face. "I'm sorry, Conner. I'm so sorry."

Conner said something Peyton couldn't make out. Then his shoulders sagged and his hands fell to the ice. Desmond bowed his head and closed his eyes.

"Desmond," Lin said.

He looked up, eyes filled with tears.

"Finish it."

He looked confused.

She pointed to the open suitcase, the one she had used to upload Rendition.

"That terminal has root access."

The words seemed to mean something to Desmond. He nodded. Gently, he placed his brother's head on the floor and began moving toward the suitcase.

Around the room, the troops raised their rifles and trained their laser sights on him.

CHAPTER 84

DESMOND STOPPED AND held up his hands. A cold wind was blowing through the gaps in the rotunda's glass ceiling, and his breath came out in white steam as he looked around at the soldiers.

The Rendition programmers were starting to stir and sit up on the cots. The soldiers took aim at them as well.

"Stand down," Lin called out. "Ladies and gentlemen, I remind you that Desmond and I are the last remaining members of the Citium. If you'll recall, Yuri reinstated me before his death."

The troops looked confused, but they didn't budge. Most looked to the colonel.

Lin addressed him. "Colonel, this is the only play. The only way out for all of us."

He grimaced, but said, "Stand down."

The troops lowered the rifles, and Desmond raced to the suit-case terminal. It had full access to Rendition—which made sense, since it had uploaded and created the instance. He opened the archives and stared in shock. Over two hundred million lives. All of them now living in the virtual-reality space he had created. Rendition.

The Rapture backups for Citium personnel were stored in a protected area that only Desmond had the password to. He entered it and scanned the log. Last backup was ten hours ago. Both Yuri and Conner had been mapped.

He clicked Yuri's name, and a listing of all of his Rapture

backups appeared—going back almost ten years, to when the technology was still being tested. He selected all of them. And clicked delete. He had to verify the command twice and re-enter his password. He pressed ENTER—and Yuri was gone forever.

In the real world, Lin had taken his life—avenging her husband and son.

Inside the Looking Glass, Desmond had ensured Yuri would never live again, never enjoy the machine he had killed so many to create.

Desmond nodded at Lin. She took the sat phone from Yuri's pocket and dialed the last number called.

"Miss Whitmeyer, it's Lin Shaw. We've had an unfortunate accident here. Yuri is dead. As is Conner. Desmond and I are the last members of the Citium alive."

A pause.

"Yes, of course."

Lin handed the phone to the colonel. He listened for a moment. "Confirmed. My authorization code is Jackson-Auth-Delta-India-Romeo-Victor-X-ray-39382."

He listened, nodded, and handed the phone back to Lin.

"Miss Whitmeyer," said Lin, "give me a status update." She paused to listen. "Good. Your first priority is to ensure that the Looking Glass remains running. Second, you are to stop all transfers immediately—including any actions being taken or scheduled to proceed against government officials or individuals deemed enemies of the Citium."

Desmond was suddenly aware of the pain from the knife wound in his ribs. But he had a more urgent matter to attend to. He walked over to Peyton and Avery, whose breathing was shallow. The pool of blood was massive. Too big.

Peyton met his eyes. "She needs an OR. And blood. Right now. In the construction habitat—"

"I've got something better." To the colonel, Desmond said, "We need to get this woman back to the plane and over to McMurdo Station."

CHAPTER 85

DESMOND WAS STILL sore from the brief operation. The anesthesia had worn off, but the bandage on his side itched.

He and Peyton sat in the waiting room at McMurdo General Hospital, the largest medical facility in Antarctica. It was part of McMurdo Station, a research center operated by the United States. The base was home to nearly eight hundred people, and they were in near-constant danger. McMurdo General had seen more than its share of trauma wounds, and the doctors had impressed Desmond as capable.

He just hoped they had gotten Avery there in time. Upon seeing her, the surgeon had looked grim. He had given no reply when Desmond asked if they could save her.

Peyton stood. "Want some coffee?"

"Yeah. Thanks."

"Still drink it black?"

"Yeah."

"Cream and sugar hard to come by on remote oil rigs?"

He laughed, feeling some of the nervous tension flowing out of him. "You could say that."

When Peyton returned, they sat in silence, sipping their coffee. His thoughts wandered, and finally she said, "Sorry about your brother."

He glanced over at her, but she didn't make eye contact. "Me too. And I'm sorry for what he did. He was... a very troubled person. Still a boy in so many ways. One who... who never got to grow up. Or know love."

"Until he met you," Peyton said quietly.

"It was too late then. Our world was not for him. But he's in a better place now."

Peyton looked at him. "The Looking Glass."

He nodded.

"My mother completed it. She betrayed us."

"She protected us. It was the only way. She told us that the Looking Glass was inevitable. That the only thing that could change was who controlled it."

"And now *she* does."

"*We* do," Desmond said.

"And what does that mean? For the rest of the world?"

"It means things will change—but we decide when and how. Not Yuri. Or Conner. Or bureaucrats or politicians."

Peyton took another sip of coffee.

"I saw him, Peyton. In the Looking Glass. Your father. He's there, waiting."

She squinted at him. "How?"

"Yuri scanned him before he died."

She rubbed her temples. "This is going to take some getting used to."

Desmond leaned closer to her and put his arm around her shoulder. She leaned into him and let her head rest on his chest, just below his chin.

"Don't worry. He has all the time in the world," he whispered.

He had waited for this moment for a very long time. He had never been so sure of anything in his life. "But we don't."

Peyton didn't move, but her breathing accelerated.

"Des, I know... you care about her."

There was no question who the *her* was. The door to the OR was only a few feet away, and it loomed like a third presence in the room.

"I do love her. She was there for me—we were there for each other—at a time when we needed one another. She'll always have a special place in my heart. But I didn't love her the way I loved you."

Peyton's chest was heaving now. She sat up and looked at him.

"The way I *still* love you." He couldn't keep the emotion out of his voice, and he didn't care. "I created it for you—the Looking Glass. I wanted to fix myself and go back and do things differently. I want to start over."

She took his face in her hands. "I told you before: you don't need fixing. And we don't need a machine to start over. All we need is each other."

EPILOGUE

THE TWENTY MIDDLE schoolers sprinted back and forth on the tennis court, some panting, all sweating through their clothes. Avery checked her watch and blew the whistle. As they were packing up, she called to them, "Remember, tournament next week. Bring your A-game."

They waved to her and taunted each other as they walked to the bus stop.

The tennis courts were located in Washington Highlands, a rough, low-income neighborhood in the nation's capital. That was what had drawn Avery to it—and why she stayed in her car after practice and watched to make sure every one of her kids got on the bus safely.

Back at her apartment in Arlington, she showered and plopped down on the couch, a towel still wrapped around her hair. The scar from the chest wound was still red and gnarly. The surgeon had told her that she would likely be a little self-conscious in a bathing suit for a while, but she knew she wouldn't. She had a good story to go along with the scar.

She stretched out on the couch, opened the Rendition Games app on her phone, and typed in her pass code.

The apartment faded away, replaced by her childhood bedroom in her parents' house. It was well lit, the midday sun blazing through the large double-hung windows. Grass spread out for about an acre around the farmhouse, and beyond it, a soybean field stretched as far as the eye could see. It was slowly disappearing, being mowed down in neat rows as her father crossed back and forth in his new John Deere combine.

As she watched, the giant machine came to a halt, the door swung open, and her father got out and sauntered toward the house.

Avery descended the straight staircase, following the smell of chicken and mashed potatoes. Her dad had always been the meat-and-potatoes type, and her mother had always obliged. She smiled at Avery when she entered the kitchen.

"Hi, honey. Did you get a nap?"

"Nah, just read."

"You need your rest, sweetie. Are you going back tomorrow?"

Avery poured three glasses of tea and set the small breakfast table. "Figured I'd leave Tuesday morning. First class isn't until that afternoon."

Her mother beamed as she set down the mashed potatoes. "Wonderful."

The door swung open and her father took off his volunteer fire department cap. "What's wonderful?"

"Avery's staying until Tuesday."

"Well, I'm going back with you," he said as he sat down. "I need to get a PhD in computer programming to run that blasted machine."

"It's not that bad," Avery said.

"You try going from the horse-and-buggy days to driving a spaceship, young lady."

Avery laughed. "You're not *that* old, Dad."

"Well maybe my brain just ain't as sharp as all these other folks."

"There's nothing wrong with your brain, honey." Her mother reached out and grasped both of their hands, and Avery's father said grace.

"I tell you this, this ole farmer has had about all the change and progress he can stand."

Avery took a bite of chicken. It was delicious. "Oh, Dad. I think you can relax. I have a feeling things are going to stay the same for quite a while."

An Army major escorted Desmond through the halls of the Pentagon to an auditorium. The seats were filled with flag officers, cabinet secretaries, and intelligence officials. The vice president, Speaker of the House, and president pro tempore of the Senate sat in the first row.

The president and his secretary of defense waited by the dais. When Desmond joined them, the president stepped to the microphone.

"Our guest requires no introduction. You've read Agent Price's report and the recommendations from the Rubicon Group. I've met at length with Mister Hughes over the last few days. Listen to what he has to say. Ask questions—tough ones, because I know you'll have them. And keep an open mind. We're here to figure out how we can work together. Because we have to."

He stepped aside, and Desmond took his place. Desmond cleared his throat and looked out at the faces. He saw skepticism. Aggression. And here and there, curiosity. It was going to be a tough crowd.

"Since the beginning of time, we have been at the mercy of our environment. Hurricanes. Floods. Famine. Drought. Disease. And in the last few decades, we have increasingly been a victim of another force: our own creations. War. Nuclear weapons. Environmental pollution. Cigarette smoke. In the coming years, those creations will only become more powerful. This place," Desmond motioned to the Pentagon, "was built to fight an older kind of enemy. Other nations. Armies. Not a poor kid in an impoverished corner of the world who creates a bioweapon and gets on a plane. Not the radicalized PhD student who decides to build a dozen nuclear bombs and put them in suitcases and get on a boat. And those are just the scenarios I can imagine."

He took out a sheet of paper. "Here's what some of the techies who work for me said might be in store for us. Drones that can control the weather. A computer virus that kills every computer in the world, like digital locusts. A machine capable of digging into the ground at the tectonic plates and causing earth-quakes and tsunamis." Desmond squinted at the page. "Okay, this is a little out there, but a virus that decreases intelligence in every population around the world except for those pre-treated with a vaccine via drinking water. Such a novel gene therapy would render everyone outside the perpetrating group subhuman, subservient to the remaining humans with normal intelligence."

The group was starting to whisper among themselves. Some were taking notes.

"And here are a few scenarios I'm sure you've thought of. A robot that costs what an average worker earns in a week, can operate on solar power, and will work twenty-four hours a day for decades without replacement or even maintenance. Such a device will make 90 percent of the world's manual laborers unemployable. And if you outlaw it here, the countries that don't outlaw it will become the manufacturing hubs of the world. If you ban trade with those countries, the countries who don't will enjoy a huge economic advantage.

"And finally, an artificial intelligence capable of doing over half of the work in the world: technical support, data entry, simple medical diagnoses, routine legal work like wills and real estate, and accounting. This would be a world built *by* humans—but with very little need *for* human bodies or human minds within it. This is the world that is coming. And the transition to that world will be a very painful journey."

Desmond took the bottle of water from the dais and sipped, letting his words sink in. "What we offer is a way to prevent these catastrophes—both natural and man-made. A way to model scenarios and understand the future. A way to identify, via their brain activity, those who would do others harm—and stop them instantaneously. But our solution is much more than that. It is the key to a new kind of existence. And it is already here, inside each of you, and me.

"I'm here today to ask for peace. The Citium is not your enemy. We are simply here to help. We want to work together. But I warn you, we want a peaceful, kind world, and we'll have it—with or without your help."

Desmond let the words hang in the air. "Any questions?"

One of the generals snarled. "You're asking us to surrender?"

"No. You only surrender to your enemies."

He rolled his eyes. "Put it this way: you want control, don't you? Of us, hell, of the whole world."

"I don't. Believe me, it's the last thing I want. What we demand is very simple: we want the human race to stop killing each other."

After the meeting, Desmond returned to his office, stretched out in a zero-gravity chair, and activated the Rendition Games app.

When the scene came into focus, he was in the living room of his childhood home. The walls were as they had been—unburned. In this Rendition, the Ash Wednesday bushfires had never occurred.

A face peeked through the wide opening and smiled. "Where you been?"

"Meetings," Desmond muttered.

He got up and hugged his brother. Conner's grin reached toward his ears, tugging at the smooth, recently shaved face, with no scars or burn marks.

"Who?" he asked.

"Generals and politicians."

"You should stay here."

"I'm seriously thinking about it."

"Boys!" their mother called from her craft room. "Help your father."

He was dismounting his horse when they greeted him outside. He handed the reins to Conner and thanked the boys before hiking to the house. They fed and watered the waler, and began sweeping up the barn.

"Tell me what happened after Buenos Aires."

"You saved my life."

"How?"

Desmond leaned on the broom. "Yuri was going to kill me."

Conner stopped too. He stared into one of the stalls, waiting for his brother to finish.

"You wouldn't let him. You saved me."

"And what happened to me?"

"Yuri shot you. The bullet was intended for me. We tried, but we couldn't save you." Desmond's eyes filled with water. "I'm sorry. We tried so hard—"

"I'm glad."

"What?"

"That you lived. You're better out there than me. I was a shell before you found me. Probably would have been dead in a few years."

"And in here?"

Conner turned to his brother. "It's everything I thought it would be. I'm home. This is where I was meant to be."

☣

On the other side of Washington, DC, Peyton Shaw was standing at a similar lectern, in an auditorium at the National Institutes of Health. The faces staring at her were friendlier.

"The history of infectious diseases—and medicine in general—has been reactive. Someone gets sick. We react. A new pathogen infects hundreds, thousands before we realize it. We react."

Peyton clicked the mouse, and the next slide appeared. "That ends now. For the first time in history, we have a way to know when a new pathogen invades its first host. And more: we have a way—wirelessly—to gather data on that pathogen. We have a way to simulate how that virus or bacteria affects the human body, and test cures virtually. Then we can deploy that cure wirelessly, without direct intervention."

She stared at the shocked faces and the nods from those who already knew the truth behind the cure to the X1 pandemic.

"What I'm describing is not something in development. Not a future innovation that will require massive investment, long waits, inevitable delays, and implementation problems. It is here, now. Inside each of you. And me."

She clicked again, and an image of the Rapture nanites appeared on the screen. "This is going to change health care. We are going to cure every disease and stop every pathogen—before it gains a foothold. I've dedicated my life to fighting infectious diseases and training others to do the same. For the first time, I have what I need to accomplish that. I'm here today to share it with you all."

The world was just starting to return to normal. The X1 pandemic was rarely talked about, nor was there much talk about the mysterious deadly disease that followed, the disease informally called "X1 syndrome" and formally, sudden acute cerebral syndrome.

The Washington, DC, housing market had also returned to normal, which meant tight supply and high prices. Desmond found a place in Kalorma that needed some work, but had a big back yard. Peyton thought it was perfect. They bought it the same day they toured it.

She was home when he arrived, a glass of wine on the kitchen island.

"How'd it go?" she asked.

"Let's just say, I never thought I'd be glad I was raised by the most confrontational, argumentative human who ever lived."

"A room full of Orville Hugheses, huh?"

"A lot like that." Desmond poured himself a glass of water. "When's everyone meeting up?"

A small smile crossed Peyton's lips. "In a little while."

"How long is a little while?"

"Long enough."

She took him by the hand, walked backward down the hall, and kicked their bedroom door open while kissing him, just as she had done that first night, in her dorm room at Stanford.

They were both lying on their backs, sweating, watching the ceiling fan spin, when her phone buzzed. A reminder:

family dinner

"It's time. You ready?"

He grabbed his own phone from the nightstand and opened the Rendition Games app. "Yeah."

They had selected London because it was the one place their entire family had lived together. There was a lot of pain there, but it was home.

The streets were teeming with activity, bustling like the world before the X1 pandemic—because it was. In this Rendition, the outbreak had never occurred. There were other changes too, but they were much more subtle.

Peyton let Desmond open the door to the building, and they rode the elevator to the flat she remembered from her youth. It was just as it had been back then, before the purge, before they fled in the night, before her father had to fight for his life.

Lin Shaw opened the door and hugged them both. Andrew and Charlotte were already there, as were Madison and her husband. Peyton was happy to see that in this Rendition, Andrew was the same man—body and all—that he was in the corporeal universe. Even the prosthetic was the same, hanging from his left arm.

The swinging doors to the kitchen opened and her father burst through, back first, carrying a pan of Yorkshire pudding with oven mitts over his hands.

As soon as he released it, he hugged Peyton, mitts still on, pressing heat into her back.

"Hi, Dad. It's so good to see you again."

A tear rolled down her face.

✴

Lin Shaw opened her eyes. Richard Ferguson sat in a chair in the corner.

"Good visit?"

Lin nodded.

"Let me know when they've exited the Looking Glass."

"Of course." He stood, and paused by the door. "Are you sure you want to do this?"

She wasn't. The project she had dedicated her life to—the Rabbit Hole—was a particle experiment whose outcome was impossible to predict. She knew the facts now. A quantum force had shaped human evolution. The evidence was written in our DNA, left over eons for us to find. The quantum force, the Invisible Sun, was a beacon, drawing all advanced species to it—like gravity asserts force on mass. But why? And to what end?

Some in Lin's organization believed there was no reason, that the Invisible Sun was simply a force like gravity, that it led to nothing. That it existed because of the laws of the universe and had no greater purpose.

Lin disagreed. She believed they were on the verge of the greatest discovery in history. Her father had long theorized that the code in the human genome was like a bread crumb left for all sentient life on worlds across the universe, written in the language of math and quantum physics—a lingua franca any sufficiently intelligent life could speak.

But the ultimate question was: what would happen when they turned the Rabbit Hole on? It would begin generating subatomic particles that matched the code in the human genome, but to what end? Lin believed that it was a step taken by countless other scientist and explorers on countless other worlds in countless other universes. History repeats itself, and so it would here on Earth. She believed the Rabbit Hole would connect the Looking Glass to all the other Looking Glasses in the universe, to those who came before us—and to whatever came next. She believed the human race's destiny was to enter the Looking Glass and pass through the Rabbit Hole into the next chamber of existence. She believed the passing was a natural, inevitable event.

Ferguson and others on Lin's team were not so optimistic. They feared that the particles generated by the Rabbit Hole might disrupt the Looking Glass—like a magnet running over a hard drive. Others believed the impact would be even more dramatic—perhaps an explosion that would consume the world. They argued that the code in the human genome was like a Trojan Horse, waiting for a sentient species to find it. That would certainly answer the question of why no one was out there.

Still, Lin Shaw had to know. And she had to be sure everyone she cared about was outside the Looking Glass before she engaged the experiment.

"I'm sure," she said.

She sat on the table and waited.

A few minutes later, Ferguson returned and said, "They're out."

They walked together to the control room, which looked like mission control at NASA. She nodded, and Ferguson stepped forward.

"Okay, people. We're a go." He looked over at Lin. "Let's see what's on the other side."

She watched the statistics on the screen. A faint humming sounded around them. With no media coverage or fanfare, they were conducting the most advanced experiment in history.

"Collision confirmed," one of the quantum physicists said. "Sustained now. We're generating origin particles."

Lin nodded at Ferguson and left the room. In her office, she stretched out on the chaise lounge and opened the Rendition Games app. At the password prompt, she paused. This was perhaps the most important moment in human history. There were no witnesses—and that was just as well, and fitting. Newton had no witnesses when he made his breakthrough. Or Aristarchus. Neil Armstrong's moon landing was a pole vaulting game compared to this—we knew what was there, we just didn't know if he would survive the trip. Lin was venturing into the unknown. Some force was waiting. Good, evil, or otherwise.

She typed in her password, and the office disappeared.

☣

She stood in her classroom in Oxford. That made perfect sense to her. The students were packing up their books and making their way out of the auditorium.

The symbolism was clear: she was the student here. This Rendition was a place to learn. The bread crumbs were obvious.

She strolled down Catte Street, past Radcliffe Camera, to the Great Gate. She flashed her faculty badge at the ticket counter and continued across the quadrangle, through the Proscholium, and into the Divinity School. It was empty. She hadn't expected that. Maybe she had been wrong—about this and so many things.

As she ascended to the second floor, her thoughts spiraled. What if the Rabbit Hole—and indeed the rabbit itself—was like the stuffed animals the greyhounds chased around the track? What if the universe was merely created for beasts like humans to wear themselves out—and if they ever caught the rabbit, and went down the rabbit hole, they were ruined forever? Was that what awaited her?

The library was unchanged from her last visit: dark wood shelves and stacks, books lining every wall, a two-story window letting in Oxford's hazy light. She heard the sound of clopping, like Clydesdales trotting down the street.

She stopped at a stack where a slender, bald man with wire-rimmed glasses was taking volumes from a book cart and placing them on the shelf.

He stood up straight when he saw her. "Can I help you?"

"I'm not sure."

He smiled genuinely. "What are you looking for?"

Lin took a chance. "Whatever is after this."

His smile faded. Creases appeared on his forehead. "What do you mean?"

"My people and I are searching for the next in the cycle. Can you help us? Have you already advanced?"

Gently, he placed the book back on the cart. "Of course." He smiled, and it reminded Lin of her uncle, who was kind and graceful, even in the pain and agony of Hong Kong's occupation. "We've been watching you," he said.

"How long?"

He shook his head. "Time has no meaning here."

"No. I expect it doesn't."

Lin had so many questions. She began with one that had haunted her since the events in Antarctica.

"I'd like to ask you something."

He tilted his head toward her, urging her to proceed.

"We were afraid another would gain control of our Looking Glass."

"The one called Yuri."

"Yes. Did you… stop him? Influence events?"

The man smiled sympathetically and shook his head. "It is not our place. We know that's why you created the Rabbit Hole—why you sought us. For help. But we are merely observers. And advisors. We are here to help you walk the path we walked, as those who helped us before. Your triumph is yours alone. As it must be."

"Our ascendance is incomplete. My people aren't all here. Only a fraction. And a few who can go between."

"That's very common."

"What do we do?"

"Exactly what you're doing. Make the transition gradually. Then once you're here, the answer becomes obvious."

Lin thought about that for a moment.

He held up a finger. "Can I make one suggestion?"

"Of course."

"For those of you moving between the Looking Glasses, we've observed that it can be disorienting. The lines blur."

Lin had never thought about it, but it made sense. "Solution?"

"A benign alteration."

"Such as?"

"A place name is usually the best option."

Lin considered that. "Example?"

"The highest peak on your world."

"Yes, that would work. So in this Looking Glass it has a different name than outside?"

"Correct. That way, anywhere in your world, you can ask anyone the name of the highest peak and instantly know where you are." He looked toward the ceiling, thinking. "In your originating Looking Glass, you named the highest peak after the first to summit it. You should pick a more obscure name—something that can't be mistaken. Like a bureaucrat from the era, perhaps just before the mountain was named." He paused. "Yes. You could name it, say, after a British Surveyor General of India of the time. There would be some logic in that."

He waited.

Lin said, "You have me at a disadvantage."

"In *this* Looking Glass, we'll call it Mount Everest."

AUTHOR'S NOTE

Thank you for reading.

I had planned to make The Extinction Files a trilogy. But in the course of writing *Genome*, I felt like I could wrap the story up in two books with a much better ending than going to a third volume. I had promised Audible and my foreign publishers a trilogy, but I really felt the story was better told in two books. For me, the decision was easy: as I writer, I do what I would want as a reader. I'm committed to releasing the best book I can every time. That's what I chose to do with *Genome*. It is the end of The Extinction Files core mythology, but there will be many stories after this. Perhaps in this universe, or another Looking Glass. I hope you enjoyed the series

Thanks again for reading and take care,

GERRY
A.G. RIDDLE

PS: Feel free to email me (ag@agriddle.com) with any feedback or questions Sometimes it takes me a few days, but I answer every single email.

ACKNOWLEDGEMENTS

Writing a book sometimes feels like sitting on the deck of *Santa María* sailing for a new land. You have a map of sorts, an outline that provides a vague idea of where you're going, but you never know what the weather will be. Sometimes the ship tosses on the seas, some days it's clear sailing. Life was much like that during the time I wrote *Genome*.

For the first time, I'd like to thank a group who is not connected to my work in any way. A few months ago, Duke's Pulmonary division saved my mother's life. She's not out the woods yet, and won't be without a double lung transplant, but we have hope, which we didn't have before. I am indebted to them and all of the folks who work at Duke Hospital. As Elim Kibet says in *Pandemic*, hope is a powerful thing. And health is sometimes a gift we don't appreciate until we're at risk of losing it.

Several people contributed greatly to *Genome*.

David Gatewood provided outstanding editing. Judy Angsten and Lisa Weinberg both made wonderful suggestions during their early read and caught typos I wouldn't have seen if I read this novel a hundred more times.

Most of all, my thanks to you for reading.